DIAMOND
REVELATION

Also by Sheila Copeland

Saved and Single

Published by Kensington Publishing Corporation

DIAMOND
REVELATION

SHEILA COPELAND

Dafina
Books

KENSINGTON PUBLISHING CORP.
www.kensingtonbooks.com

DAFINA BOOKS are published by

Kensington Publishing Corp.
119 West 40th Street
New York, NY 10018

All Kensington Titles, Imprints, and Distributed Lines are available at special quantity discounts for bulk purchases for sales promotions, premiums, fund-raising, and educational or institutional use. Special book excerpts or customized printings can also be created to fit specific needs. For details, write or phone the office of the Kensington special sales manager: Kensington Publishing Corp., 119 West 40th Street, New York, NY 10018, attn: Special Sales Department, Phone: 1-800-221-2647.

Dafina Books and the Dafina logo Reg. U.S. Pat. & TM Off.

ISBN-13: 978-0-7582-1705-9
ISBN-10: 0-7582-1705-6

First trade paperback printing: November 2007
First mass market printing: October 2010

10 9 8 7 6 5 4 3 2 1

Printed in the United States of America

For the Diamonds in my life:

Ciara, Christopher, Colin,
Mia, Nyra Deja,
Amber, Grant, Sonny
Endiga, Taylor, Meshelle
Araina
You are all shining stars

And in memory of
La Shawn Johnson.
You fought a good fight. RIP.

Acknowledgments

Thank you, Heavenly Father, always, for the gift to touch, enlighten, entertain and inspire. This was a hard book with hard circumstances, but as always You are faithful in healing and seeing me through.

And to Michele Adams; Bible Enrichment Fellowship International Church; the Bowens Family—James, Betty, Tyrone and Mark; Greg Breda; Erma Byrd; Apostle Beverly "Bam" Crawford; Gabrianna Crawford; Coco—for your constant encouragement and friendship; Janine Haydel; the Holdness Family; Glenda Howard; Fran Hunter; the Johnson Family, here's your shout-out, "TT"; Lawrence—my true and faithful friend and partner—the best is yet to come; the Lee Family—Gerald, Rosiland, Christopher and Meshelle; Dr. Raul Mena; Dr. Maurice Berkowitz; Mom—for your love and support all the days of my life; Rosiland—girlfriend, you're the best! You definitely helped me get this child out of the womb. DR tried so hard not to come out; Dr. Raymond Scharf; Yvonne Simms—for California dreaming with me when we were kids sitting on the front porch in Cleveland; June McCrae Blanchard, Michele McCoy, La Ronda Sutton—for your encouragement and support. We became friends because of the "Chocolate"; the law firm of Miller and Pilikas—Darrell Miller, Jesse Connors for keeping the biz tight; my readers—for your support throughout the years and for waiting so patiently for this next installment. Can't believe it's been four years since the last book. I'll do my best to keep them coming. And to all the great artists whose music and lyrics were such an inspiration.

Vonnie Greenwade, Solombra Ingraham, Jan Petersen and your book clubs.

My heartfelt thanks to all of you.
Jeremiah 33:11

Sheila
www.sheilacopeland.com

I have a fear and it comes on me, and
my heart is greatly troubled.
—Job 3:25

DIAMOND
REVELATION

Prelude

It was so dark she could barely see as she maneuvered the Bentley convertible along Mulholland Drive. There was no other automobile like it in the world. 310 Motoring had designed it especially for her . . . from the glistening chestnut paint flecked with 24-karat gold to the twenty-inch custom alloy rims adorned with a pattern of rhinestones that everyone swore looked like real diamonds. The seats were covered with the softest butter leather, which offset the blond wood veneer on the dashboard.

It was eerily silent that night. The stars were barely visible. There were no cars on this stretch of the road until a set of headlights loomed out of nowhere, blinding her. The car honked as the Bentley swerved across the dividing line and back into the narrow single lane on the winding road.

A tear pushed its way out of her eye and rolled down her cheek. She was finally able to cry. Suddenly the tears poured like a deluge of rain, but they did nothing to ease her pain.

Sniffing, she took a healthy swig from an open bot-

tle of tequila in her lap and grimaced from the taste of
the alcohol. It burned like fire in her throat as the liquid
anesthesia served its purpose. Inside her Louis Vuitton
bag, her fingers grasped the smooth, cold barrel of the
gun. It wouldn't be long before the peace she so desperately sought would be found.

She knew exactly what she was looking for. Spot-
ting it, she drove up to the safety barricade and turned
off the motor. There was a spectacular view of the San
Fernando Valley. Lights sparkled and twinkled for
miles in the basin beneath. She sat there, taking it all in
one last time, and for a moment forgot why she had
come.

Her BlackBerry vibrated and played a series of
tones. She threw it out the window and quickly gulped
down more tequila, then tossed the bottle aside. Alcohol
spilled all over the seats and seeped into the golden, plush
floor mats that bore her name. The entire car smelled like
liquor, but she didn't care. There was nothing and no
one to care about now.

A huge, black diamond surrounded by a cluster of
white diamonds sparkled on her ring finger. She was so
faded that she was barely able to open the car door as
she staggered out of the automobile with the gun in
her hand.

A simple black dress adorned her goddess-like
physique. The moon pushed its way through the clouds,
illuminating her beautiful, tear-streaked face like a spotlight as a slight breeze gently tossed her hair.

She tried to walk in her Jimmy Choo shoes but tripped
and fell, sobbing and wallowing in the damp earth until
her hand touched the gun. It had landed only inches
from her body. She picked it up, held it to her head,
closed her eyes, and pulled the trigger.

Chapter 1

Sabre stared at the handsome young Korean like he was crazy. She was a fiery little thing—petite and curvy with deep olive skin and thick black hair that looked like silk after she applied the Dark and Lovely perm that no one knew she used. Her jet black almond eyes were piercing. They sparkled like cat's-eye marbles whenever she was angry. The combination of her hair and skin color made Sabre striking. No one was ever quite sure of her nationality—she was just beautiful, there was no question about that.

"What the hell do you mean you can't get everybody in the party?"

"Me and you are on the list. I wasn't able to get Sky in," the young man replied quietly.

They were in Marina del Rey for the Baby Phat party. Sabre was ready to be seen. Her Apple Bottoms jeans looked as if they had been made just for her even before her stylist had done a few alterations. A split on one leg revealed her hard-toned calf in a pair of rhinestone Manolo Blahniks.

"I had to call in a lot of favors to even get us on the

list." Victor Tung had flavor. He was a brilliant music journalist and gorgeous. Sabre had met him at the Vibe Awards before her CD dropped.

That boy is too fine, she had thought the moment she laid eyes on him. She was determined to have him. He was her boy toy. She was his famous honey. They used to have a lot of fun together attending all the A-list parties and functions. Now, she was beginning to wonder if he was still useful. Victor looked at her through a set of dark-slanted eyes with lashes so thick they looked as though they had been curled with mascara.

"What the hell is he talkin' about a favor? I got the number one record in the country. This shit ain't goin' down without me and my girl."

"You got that right," agreed Sky, her best friend since childhood. She sang with a deliberate twang. "Meet me at the maaaaall . . ."

"It's goin' down," Sabre sang back.

Both ladies laughed as they did the motorcycle dance to their own rendition of Yung Joc's club anthem.

Sabre took out a package of Newports and lit one. "I know somebody betta get my girl up in this party." She sucked her teeth and looked at Victor.

"You got that right." Sky, equally attractive but not at all concerned about her looks, rolled her eyes at Victor, too.

Sabre blew smoke rings into the chilly night air. Once the sun went down, the temperature always dropped by ten degrees in southern Cali. She took one last puff off the cigarette and threw it on the ground. "Fuck his stupid ass. He can go to the party by himself. I'll get us in." She strutted toward the entrance of the Marina Yacht Club, and Sky followed.

"Good evening, gentlemen." Sabre was suddenly

poised and controlled. Before she could say a word, a blond woman with a clipboard smiled at her.

"Now what the hell does this bitch want?" Sabre said to Sky, not caring at all if the woman heard.

"Sabre Cruz and guest. Welcome." The woman worked for the public relations firm handling the party. It was her job to spot celebrities and get them into the event with no hassle. She gave them Baby Phat wristbands for VIP. "Enjoy yourselves, ladies."

"Now that's what I'm talking 'bout." Sabre fastened the fluorescent band around her slender wrist.

"Hey, Miss Sabre." Some nameless guy flirted with her. This always happened.

"That's right, Sabre Cruz, baby," she yelled back.

Security guards parted like the Red Sea, allowing Sabre and Sky entrance to the party. The ladies strolled toward the yacht. The *Icon* was the sleekest thing in the water. The 120-foot yacht was parked in the harbor, while a Who's Who of Hollywood strolled its decks with flutes of champagne.

"I'm gonna cut Victor's silly ass loose." Sabre looked around for him. He wasn't far behind, following them up the walkway to the boat. "I don't know why I mess around with his ass."

"Because he's fine." Sky laughed. "And he gets you into all the parties."

"He used to get me in parties. I can get in by myself now. I don't need him."

"I thought he was your man."

"My man?" Sabre laughed. "Please. I can't have a nobody like him for my man. He ain't got no money. I want a man with some real paper."

"You got your own money, Sabre."

"And I'm gonna keep my money."

"I ain't sayin' she's a gold digga . . ." Sky chanted.

"But Sabre ain't messin' around with no broke niggas." She plucked a glass of champagne from a silver tray as they stepped onto the upper deck of the yacht. "I wonder where VIP at?"

A security guard wearing a headset stepped in front of them with his hands outstretched. "Excuse me, ladies, you'll have to wait here."

"*I* have to wait . . ." Sabre began with too much attitude. "Do you know who the fuck I am?"

"You certainly have a foul mouth, whoever you are, and you will have to wait," the man replied.

Sabre sucked her teeth and rolled her eyes as she watched several other guards with headsets escort a small throng of people in their direction. The girls could see Topaz glittering in diamonds. She was wearing a pair of white satin skinny jeans with a gold beaded halter. Her famous tresses were tied up into a ponytail. She seemed to glow from within. For a split second, Topaz's eyes fell on Sabre as she and Germain were quickly ushered by. Nina and Kyle, Keisha, and Eric, and Sean and Jade were also with them. All of the couples seemed to be having individual conversations as they were led down the passageway of the *Icon*.

"What the fuck is this shit?" Sabre was too put out. She turned and looked at Sky, who was practically staring. "I can't believe they had to hold me back so *her* has-been ass could go by. What's up with that shit?" Sabre pushed her way past the guard, who stopped them.

"What do you mean what's up with that? Sweet thang, she's a beautiful, classy star. Something you will never be." He smirked at Sabre.

"Fuck you, you fake-ass, wannabe, flashlight cop."

Sabre stared in the direction that Topaz and her entourage had gone. "And fuck their asses too. Fuckin' wannabe Black Friends."

"Black Friends?" Sky repeated, and laughed. "Girl, you crazy. We'd be hanging out with the black friends if yo ass hadn't ripped off ole girl's stuff. What the fuck were you thinkin'?"

"I wasn't thinkin' about Topaz's black ass. That's for damn sure." Sabre looked thoughtful all of a sudden. "I was thinkin' how good I was gonna look on TV in that red dress. I was tired of all that bubblegum shit Nina was giving us to wear."

"You were wrong, Sabre. Topaz was helping us and you stole that dress out of her closet."

"So . . . her fat ass couldn't wear it no more." Sabre would never forget the night of the VH1 Divas concert. Jamil had managed to get Sabre and Sky's group, So Fine, on the show performing with Topaz on "For the Love of Money." Topaz and So Fine delivered a show-stopping performance, and the ladies received a standing ovation. Everything was wonderful until Topaz realized Sabre was wearing a dress and jewelry that she had stolen from Topaz during a visit to her home. Topaz threatened to whip Sabre's ass and made her take off everything as soon as they were backstage. Even though her cousin, Nina, was managing So Fine, Topaz refused to have anything more to do with the group. Sabre's name was mud with Topaz from then on.

"Who wants to hang out with their fake asses anyway?" Sabre asked.

"You do." Sky snickered as they walked into the party.

Kimora Lee Simmons was known for giving the most fantastic parties. Draped in colorful Japanese silk and diamonds, Kimora was dazzling and too fabulous. She flitted around like a butterfly greeting her guests. She seemed happy that so many people had come to celebrate her Baby Phat cosmetics line, as she was introducing new shades of lipstick.

"She is so beautiful," Sky said as she and Sabre watched Kimora's every move.

"She a'ight. She wouldn't have none of that shit if it wasn't for Russell Simmons." Sabre turned up her nose at a tray of seafood appetizers.

"Girl, stop hatin'."

"Now that's what I call a man . . . a real man. And he's got plenty of paper." Sabre pulled Sky close and for once spoke loudly enough so only Sky could hear.

"Who are you talkin' about now?"

"Him," Sabre whispered through gritted teeth.

Germain Gradney and Kyle Ross walked by, and Kyle glanced in Sabre's direction and stopped.

"Sabre, Sky." Kyle kissed both of them on the cheek. "How are you guys?"

Both ladies smiled at Kyle, who was often described as a tall, cool drink of water.

"Hey, Kyle." Sabre looked at Germain and smiled.

"Y'all remember the doc, right?" Kyle asked Sabre and Sky, then grinned at his boy.

"We most certainly do," Sabre replied, turning up her wattage for Germain.

Kyle turned to Germain. "You know So Fine. Nina used to manage them."

Germain looked pensive for a moment, and then a smile came into his eyes. "Yes, I remember. How are you ladies doing?"

"I'm doin' fine. Dr. Gradney, do you have a card? I was thinking about having some work done." Sabre licked her lips and fixed her eyes on Germain. She watched as he produced a business card from his wallet and handed it to her. "Thank you." She looked at the card, then feasted her eyes over Germain again.

"You ladies have a great evening," Kyle said as he and Germain headed toward the bar.

"That has got to be the finest man on the planet." Sabre watched them order drinks.

"What kind of work are you having done?" Sky asked.

"Anything I want. And I'm not just talkin' 'bout cosmetic surgery."

Sky laughed, and Sabre looked down at her breasts that made very little of an impression under the halter top.

"I'm gettin' me some implants . . . so I can get my Pamela Anderson on."

"I heard that, cause you know you belong to the itty bitty titty committee."

"Bitch!" Sabre laughed.

"Ho!" Sky looked at her ample perky bosom and then at her friend. "Stop hatin', Sabre."

The girls finally made it to VIP where the "Black Friends" had the best table in the house. Nina spotted them and waved the girls over to the table.

Nina Ross was responsible for So Fine coming to Cali. She signed the group to Jamil's label and made their single, "First Kiss," a smash and the group a hit along with it. They made their way over to her. Nina, always dressed to the nines, was wearing the perfect black beaded cocktail dress.

"Hey you guys." She greeted them warmly and invited them to sit down. "Congratulations on having the number one record in the country, Sabre."

"Thanks, Nina." Sabre took a big sip out of a flute of Cristal.

"You know you should be with Revelation Music. Jamil would have wanted it that way."

Sabre said nothing as Nina continued speaking.

"Why haven't I seen you?" Nina asked. "You should have called so we could do lunch."

Sabre finished her flute of champagne. "I've been busy promoting my CD."

"You certainly have." Nina focused on Sky. "When did you get back to Cali? I saw your name listed in the credits on Sabre's CD. You did background vocals. You didn't call me either," Nina scolded playfully. "I'm not tryin' to sound like Momma. I miss you guys."

"I miss you too, Nina." Sky planted a kiss on Nina's cheek while Sabre sat frozen in her seat.

Nina fished two business cards out of her evening bag and handed them to the girls. "Sky, I'm CEO of Revelation now. Call me so we can catch up and have lunch."

"For real?" Sky was too excited.

"Yes, sweetie. We'll do lunch at The Ivy." Nina smiled warmly. "You come too, Sabre."

"Okay." Sabre finally smiled.

Sky looked at the card and grinned. "I'll call you to-morrow, Nina."

"Great." Nina fixed her attention back on her husband, Kyle, who was just returning to the table. Several security guards ushered Topaz away from the table. She paused to speak with Nina. "Come to the powder room with me."

"Okay." Nina picked up her handbag and smiled at the ladies again. "It was great seeing you guys." She made her way around the table to Topaz. "Did you see Sabre and Sky?"

"Come on, girl, before I wet myself." Topaz grinned impishly at Nina without acknowledging the girls.

"I know her ass heard Nina," Sabre said to Sky.

"I told you why ole girl ain't feelin' you. You stole her stuff."

"She's hatin' cause it looked better on me than it did on her."

Sky looked at her friend like she was crazy. "Girl, you are straight trippin'. Topaz is beautiful."

"Remember when we used to pretend to be her when we were little?" Sabre's question was sincere.

"I remember when *you* used to pretend to be her," Sky declared. "You even wanted us to call you Topaz when you had on that blond wig you stole out of the wig store downtown."

"Whatever." Sabre tossed her hair, as coarse and as shiny as a horse's tail. "That was then and this is now. I have the number one record. Not her."

Chapter 2

"Work that thang, baby, cause you got me so in love when you make it sang."

Nina turned around to glance at Niki, who was sitting behind her in a car seat. She shook her head and smiled. Her six-year-old daughter started singing before she learned to talk. They were on the way to Niki's school in Sherman Oaks. Her cousins Baby Doll and Chris also attended. Kyle usually dropped her off, but he was away on business.

"What are you singing, little girl?" Nina smiled at her daughter through the rearview mirror.

"It's Sabre, Mommy."

"Sabre?" Nina was shocked. Niki's favorite singer was Donnie McClurkin, but she also enjoyed CeCe Winans and Mary Mary.

"Where did you get that CD?"

"Daddy bought it for me," Niki replied, and continued singing. Nina was not surprised that the child knew every word, but she was used to hearing Niki serenade her with gospel music . . . not this.

"Mommy."

"Yes, baby." Nina met her daughter's eye again.

"Is Daddy in trouble?"

"No, baby." Nina tried not to smile. "Daddy knows I used to be Sabre's manager when she was in the singing group with Sky and Shawntay. He also knows how much you like her."

"What's a manager, Mommy?"

"It's the person who's in charge of a singer's career."

"Are you Aunty T's manager?"

"No, baby. Aunty T doesn't have a manager right now."

"Are you a manager on your new job?"

"I'm the CEO. It's kind of like a manager, but I work with the managers of all my artists. I'm in charge of making their CDs, getting the CDs played on the radio, and getting them into the stores."

"Oh."

Nina pulled into the schoolyard, and an attendant met them at the car.

"Mommy, can I go home with Baby Doll and Chris after school today?" Niki had already unfastened her seat belt. She hung over the front seat so she could look into her mother's face.

"I thought you were going to spend time with Nana today." Nina brushed a curly lock of hair out of Niki's face that had worked its way out of her ponytail.

"Nana doesn't have any children at her house." Niki stared at her through amber eyes and gave Nina a look that made it impossible for Nina to say no.

"Don't look at me like that." Nina pulled Niki into the front seat and tickled her. "I bet you gave your Daddy that look so he would buy you that CD."

Niki giggled as Nina covered her face with kisses. "I'll call Aunty T. If it's okay with her, you may go home with your cousins after school."

"It's always okay with Aunty T." Niki smiled, and Nina's heart melted.

Nina smiled too and hugged her daughter one last time. "I'll see you at home tonight. I love you, baby."

"I love you too, Mommy."

Nina watched the teacher's assistant lead Niki into the school before she drove off. Niki looked so adorable in her uniform with her hair in ponytails. *My baby is growing up too fast.* Niki was finishing her first year of kindergarten. She would be graduating in a few weeks. Nina had a celebration party to plan, and she quickly typed a few reminders in her BlackBerry while she was paused in traffic.

Thoughts of Niki flooded her mind until she pulled the Bentley into a reserved parking space that said "CEO Revelation" at the Music Group building in Burbank. Nina smiled every time she arrived because she still couldn't believe it was really true. She, Nina Beaubien Ross, was actually the head of one of the hottest hip-hop labels in the business.

"I am so fly. I'm going to be the next Sylvia Rhone," she announced the day she and Kyle signed the contract. They were co-heads of the label formerly known as Suicide Records, the brainchild of her late ex-fiancé, Jamil Winters, and his partner, India.

When Nina introduced a former high school classmate, Char Jackson, into the equation, a lot of drama and negativity resulted. Jamil, India, and Char all died very mysteriously. Nina was asked to take over the company by Jamil's mother. Nina, still feeling some-

what responsible for their deaths, vowed that Jamil's
musical legacy would continue.

Nina had big plans. Since she had all the experience
in the music business and her husband had none, she
appointed herself as the front person for the team. Her
first move was changing the name Suicide Records to
Revelation Music.

She strolled into the sixth-floor offices looking like
a sophisticated socialite in a white Armani pantsuit and
gold Manolo Blahniks rather than wearing clothing
stereotypical for the head of a hip-hop label. Her black
hair was brushed into an updo. With oversized black
Chanel shades and gold Chanel earrings, she looked
like a chocolate Audrey Hepburn.

"Good morning, Mrs. Ross." A receptionist greeted
her with the utmost respect as she breezed by, heading
toward the suite of offices that once belonged to Jamil.

"Mr. Katz is waiting in the conference room for you."
Her assistant, Anita, spoke in a serious tone as she
reached for Nina's Louis Vuitton briefcase and bag.

"I wasn't aware that I had a meeting with him." Nina
took off her shades and looked at Anita. Sherwin Katz
was the president of VMG, the distributor and financial
backer of Revelation Music. So technically, he was
Nina's boss.

"There was no meeting scheduled." Anita took several sips from a bottle of Fiji water. "He showed up ten
minutes ago asking for you."

"Thanks, Anita. I'll be right back." Nina walked the
few steps to the conference room and took a deep breath
as she pushed the door open. Sherwin Katz, an okay-
looking, middle-aged Jewish man with salt and pepper
hair, was reading *Billboard*.

"Sherwin, good morning." Nina gave him a warm smile. "How can I help you?"

"Sit down, Nina." Sherwin closed the magazine and focused on her as she pulled out a chair and slid into it. "We just went over the last quarter's profits. I know you're doing the best you can around here. We want to honor Jamil's wishes, but we really think we need to get a more experienced music exec in here to run things."

Nina crossed her legs. Trying really hard not to twitch, she focused on Sherwin's nose. She had to remain calm and collected. This was definitely not the time to get emotional.

"All of the income being generated is from previous projects. If you don't sign some talent and generate new income, we'll have to discontinue our relationship with Suicide."

"Revelation Music," Nina corrected Sherwin. "With all due respect, Sherwin, I discovered VMG's number one artist and moneymaker, Sabre Cruz, when she was a member of So Fine. I managed the group. I signed them to Suicide. If Sabre were still a Revelation artist, we wouldn't be having this conversation."

"We understand that, which is why I am having this conversation with you. We want this to work." Sherwin shifted out of attack mode. "Janice Winters insists you're the woman for the job, even with your limited experience. Maybe we should get you some help?" Sherwin looked hopeful.

"I can handle this. I know what needs to happen. I have a very competent staff. I'd like to give them a chance to prove themselves. We're looking for talent, but we won't just sign anyone. We're looking for a real superstar," Nina declared, fully confident.

"Wonderful, Nina, but it's the B and C talent that pay

the bills while you're looking for that superstar." Sherwin stood up and tossed the *Billboard* on the table. Nina hadn't noticed that Sabre was on the cover. "We'll review the sales figures again at the beginning of the next quarter. If things haven't started to turn, I'm definitely making changes." He left the conference room, and Nina collapsed on the long mahogany table.

How dare he threaten me! How dare he? And with my artist . . . "Ooh." Nina was seething. She grabbed the *Billboard* and studied the cover. Sabre was the industry's hottest young diva, and her second single was blazing up the charts. Her debut CD, *This is Sabre*, was steadily climbing *Billboard*'s Hot 100. Jamil planned for Sabre's solo career right from the start. He knew a diamond when he saw one. Just like he knew Topaz was a star and signed her to his first production deal.

Nina took one last look at the cover. Something about Sabre's piercing black eyes made her shiver. She took the magazine with her when she left the room.

"Everything okay, boss?" Anita gave Nina a tentative look.

"Nothing I can't handle." Nina smiled, hoping she sounded more confident than she felt. It was then that she noticed the company was unusually quiet. She couldn't remember when she had ever been in a record company and not heard music pouring out of the offices and into the halls. The building would be charged with energy and creativity so thick, you felt like you could touch it. There was nothing around her at Revelation but silence . . . even the phones were quiet.

Nina went into her office and closed the door. The walls were lined with platinum and gold discs heralding Jamil's numerous accomplishments as a producer and songwriter for a myriad of number one artists. She sat down behind her desk, covered her eyes with her hands, and slowly massaged her temples. All of a sudden she had an awful headache. "I won't let you down, Jamil. I promise," she whispered as she buzzed her executive assistant over the intercom. "Come on in, Anita. We've got a ton of work to do."

Chapter 3

Topaz woke up screaming.

"What is it, baby? What is it?" Germain's strong hands pulled her into his arms. She could feel his heart beating against hers. She looked into his eyes and knew immediately that everything was right in her world. Her breathing and racing heart regulated as soon as she snuggled up next to him. She inhaled his scent . . . a mixture of shaving gel, rubbing alcohol, and the soap he always scrubbed with before surgery.

"Bad dream again?" He looked concerned as he ran a thumb across her forehead.

It was more like a nightmare. She wanted to tell him so badly, but she couldn't. He might ask questions she was unable to answer.

"It's nothing," Topaz lied. In her dream, Topaz turned on the television and saw Niki floating underwater. She was screaming. "Mommy, help me. Help!" A trail of bubbles escaped out of the little girl's mouth with each plea for assistance until she slowly sank and disappeared from Topaz's sight. Topaz kept waiting for her cousin, Nina, to appear and rescue her child. But Nina never did.

The dream was recurring, and it was really starting to get under her skin. Was something wrong with Niki? Did the child really need her help? Nina was an excellent mother, so Topaz couldn't understand why Niki would want *her* help . . . unless something deeper was going on. *Maybe God is trying to tell me something,* Topaz thought.

For the moment, she pushed the dream out of her mind and kissed Germain gently on the cheek, then tossed back the covers and jumped out of bed. Duty called . . . she had a household to run. She stretched her arms over her head as she walked over to the huge window and admired the amazing view of the Pacific Ocean.

"Are you sure?" Germain got out of bed and stood behind her, wrapping his arms around her as he kissed her on one of her favorite spots behind her ear.

"Sure about what, baby?" She was hoping he had forgotten the dream.

"You had another bad dream. Are you okay?"

"Oh, that . . . Yes, I'm sure."

"I was just checking in case I needed to give you a prescription."

I have got to get him off of this. "I've got your prescription." Topaz's eyes still registered concern as her mood suddenly changed and laughter bubbled out of her. She pulled Germain into her arms and gave him a proper good morning kiss. "You'd better get out of here before I make you late for work again."

"That's one of the perks of being the boss. I can be late anytime I want." Dr. Germain Gradney was the most sought-after plastic surgeon in Hollywood. He had a thriving practice booked solid for months and was known as the plastic surgeon to the stars. The kiss definitely succeeded in taking his mind off the dream. He pulled her into the mint marble bath that resembled a lush tropical lagoon, and they both jumped in the huge steam shower. He loved her from the moment he first laid eyes on her, over twelve years ago, and he still couldn't get enough.

"So what's on your agenda today, pretty lady?" Germain handed her a white fluffy towel. "Anything special?"

"I have a couple of ideas for a song."

"You're going to write. That's wonderful, baby!" He watched her rub body oil into her flawless butterscotch skin. Taking the container, he squeezed oil onto his palms and massaged it into her shoulders and back.

"Mmmm. That feels so good, Dr. Gradney." She closed her eyes and relaxed as he continued the massage. "Your hands are so soothing."

"We aim to please," he said with smiling eyes.

"You always please me, Doctor," Topaz purred in her sexiest voice. She wanted him more than anything. She stood in the mirror over his-and-hers sinks and applied moisturizer to her face. Full pouty lips and deeply set topaz eyes stared back at her. She was named Topaz because of her golden skin tone, eyes, and hair.

Germain and Topaz met eyes and kissed again.

"Don't start what you can't finish." Germain rinsed the last bit of shaving gel from his face, exposing smooth skin. He was only a shade or two darker than his wife, and at times people mistook them for brother and sister.

"I can always finish what I start. But right now, I have to drive your children to school." She kissed him on the lips and took one last look in the mirror. "Call me later, sweetie."

In the kitchen, the children were finishing up breakfast with their nanny. Topaz smiled at her daughter. The resemblance between the two was uncanny. As some people would say, "Topaz spit the child out."

"Morning, Mommy." Turquoise refused to be called anything but Baby Doll. She puckered up a smaller version of her mother's lips in Topaz's direction.

"Good morning, sweetie." Topaz planted a kiss on her lips.

"I'll be waitin' up until you get home cause I can't sleep without you." Baby Doll, off-key as usual, was wearing the headphones to her iPod and singing along with Mary J. Blige.

Topaz lifted the headphones. "What did your daddy tell you about singing and listening to music while you're eating?"

"He said 'Work it, gurl'." Baby Doll laughed as she did the 1–2 step.

Topaz laughed along with her. "You are so silly. Finish your breakfast so we can get out of here, Miss Thing."

She focused next on twelve-year-old Chris, who was watching the Discovery Channel. Regular TV programming couldn't hold his interest. "How's my little genius?"

Chris laughed as Topaz rubbed her hand over her son's tawny short hair. She playfully pulled him into a headlock, and he looked at her through an identical set of topaz eyes and smiled.

"I'm cool, Mom. Just watching some TV." Chris kissed his mother on the cheek. He was almost as tall as Topaz.

Chris shared his father's thirst for knowledge. He was an excellent middle school student who made straight As at the Buckley School in Sherman Oaks. Baby Doll loved music, dance class, and her friends, but she wasn't interested in academics. She did love to read, because her father and Chris always had their noses in a book. Baby Doll had to do whatever they did. Germain breezed into the kitchen, and Baby Doll lit up like a Christmas tree. "Daddy, Daddy." The same little girl who had been so nonchalant with Topaz clamored for her father's attention. "Good morning, darlin'." He grabbed her up in a big bear hug and Baby Doll squealed with laughter. Topaz smiled as she watched them. They were wonderful children, and Germain was a great father. He hugged Chris, kissed him on the head, and left.

She silently thanked God for her wonderful family as she watched Germain drive away in his convertible Porsche. She was so blessed to have them. It still pained her to think of a time when she was not so grateful—Germain was in medical school and Chris was barely a year old. She left them in Maryland to go to Los Angeles to pursue a singing career. *I was such a fool,* she thought for the thousandth time.

Germain, always supportive of her, had allowed her to go to California for a semester. Caught up in the lure of the limelight, she refused to return home to her husband and son. Like a fool, she divorced him and married Baby Doll's father, the late Gunther Lawrence, a brilliant film director. Gunther's personal issues, a bad heart, and a heavy cocaine habit sent him to an early grave.

It had been a long, hard journey, but eventually she and Germain reconciled and remarried. Topaz had promised herself that nothing was ever going to come between them again.

"Come on, Mommy. Let's go." Baby Doll tugged on Topaz's hand, bringing her back into the present. Although she employed a nanny, several housekeepers, and a personal chef, there were certain duties she insisted on doing for the family herself. Driving the children to school was one of them.

Topaz picked up Baby Doll's pink Princess backpack, loaded the children into her black Range Rover, and headed to the Valley.

Chapter 4

The building was tucked away in the Marina on Palawan Way. Crisp, blue water dotted with white sailboats provided a breathtakingly beautiful view. It was an absolutely perfect day in southern California. The best things in life really are free.

Topaz and Nina closed the doors of the Bentley and stared at the building and then each other. It was obviously vacant, and there wasn't a sign of activity anywhere.

"Are you sure this is the right place?" Topaz looked at Nina, who was already scrolling through her Black-Berry to make a phone call. Before Nina made the call Jade appeared in the doorway with a bottle of Cristal and champagne flutes. "Welcome to The Diamond, ladies."

"The Diamond?" Topaz questioned. "I thought we were meeting y'all for lunch and Girlfriend Day. What are y'all up to?"

Nina stuffed the car keys inside her bag as she reached to hug Jade, a stunning biracial woman who was both Jamaican and Japanese. "I demand an explanation."

"I demand to know why your skirt is so dang short." Jade twirled Nina around. "Girl, if you even try to bend over you're going to show everything the good Lord gave you."

"That skirt is pretty short, Ma," Topaz agreed.

Everyone focused on Nina, whose lean, long legs seemed endless underneath the pink mini she wore all too well. Her black hair was pulled up into a ponytail, and she did a little dance in the pink rhinestone Jimmy Choos that set off the outfit perfectly.

"Paris Hilton ain't got nothin' on me." Nina struck a pose and stared at the women through a pair of Louis Vuitton shades.

"Nothin' but her daddy's money. My brother-in-law must have been asleep when you left the house wearing that." Jade and Nina were married to the extremely handsome Ross brothers, Sean and Kyle.

"My husband saw me when I departed the premises. You guys just need to stop hatin'," Nina said defensively.

"You know we love you Ni-Ni," said Keisha, who was a naturally beautiful sista. Full lips and hips— there was no question she was a black girl, and proud of it. She was always trying something new with her thick, coarse hair that grew like wildfire.

Keisha gave Nina a hug as she led her inside the building. Jade and Topaz followed.

Windows everywhere offered a view of the water. Walnut-colored peg and groove hardwood floors ran throughout the building. A deep rose paint covered the walls to create a peaceful, elegant atmosphere.

"This place is beautiful," Topaz noted.

"Are you guys opening a restaurant?" Nina asked eagerly.

"Yes," Keisha squealed. "Isn't it fabulous? And the food is gonna be off da hook. There's nothing like it anywhere in the Marina or Los Angeles."

"Great." Topaz smiled. "So where is the food? I'm hungry."

"Girl . . ." Keisha could only laugh. Everyone knew how much Topaz loved to eat. It was amazing how her figure always looked so good. She maintained a size 6, even after the birth of her children. Some people were just blessed with great genes, and Topaz was one of them. All of the ladies maintained their physiques by watching their diets and working out. It was a must for Hollywood wives and divas.

"What's up with that Cris, darlin'?" Topaz was coy as Jade poured flutes of champagne and handed glasses to them.

"Time to get this party started." Jade lifted her champagne proudly. "Here's to Diamonds."

"Diamonds," the women chorused, and clinked glasses.

Topaz finished her glass and gave them a wicked grin. "Most definitely a girl's best friend."

"What? Diamonds or champagne?" Keisha demanded.

The women paused momentarily, giving Keisha's question full consideration.

"Both," the ladies all agreed, and laughed.

Jade refilled their flutes and led the girlfriends on a tour of the building. There was a time when insecurity and jealousy threatened to keep the women at odds. Time, patience, and a lot of love and forgiveness helped them to overcome their issues. Now the ladies were a tightly knit group.

Jade led them into a room with a stage and bar. "This is the club. We want to have live performances several times a week, like the House of Blues."

"This is so fly," Nina said, then smiled at Jade and Keisha with appreciation.

"We're going to use my artwork for the walls," Jade explained with sweeping gestures.

"But of course," Nina teased, mimicking her.

Jade, once a struggling painter, was now internationally known for her Caribbean- and Japanese-influenced paintings. Her marriage to Sean, a retired NBA superstar, had catapulted her into the spotlight and her art into the homes of Hollywood's rich and famous, the lobbies of Ritz Carltons worldwide, and countless office buildings. She was also the owner of the Jade Kimura Gallery in Beverly Hills, a birthday gift from Sean the first year they married.

Jade made a face at Nina. "I've been working on a special collection for The Diamond."

"She won't let anyone see it," Keisha protested.

"Sean hasn't even seen anything, so don't think you're not special. You can see everything when I'm done," Jade declared.

"We're also going to have a separate shop where you'll be able to purchase the fellas' basketball gear." Keisha was too pleased.

"We know you want everyone to come here to buy Eric Johnson basketball gear. That's what all of this is really about," Nina teased with a twinkle in her eye.

"That is so not true." Keisha tried to look surprised.

"Oh please." Topaz waved a perfectly manicured

hand in the air. "Everybody knows how much you love you some Er-wick."

If anyone did know, it was certainly Topaz. She was there from the beginning. During a trip to New York for a photo shoot, Topaz met Sean, who was celebrating his birthday with Eric. Best friends and teammates, both of the guys were single then. When Eric laid eyes on Keisha, it was love at first sight.

"Miss T can't leave home without Germain. I'm surprised to see you here," Keisha fired back. "Did the good doctor have to work today?"

Now it was Topaz's turn to play confused.

Jade laughed. "You guys are both stuck on stupid when it comes to your men."

Nina looked at Topaz. "I know you don't want me to start talking about you."

"I don't know what you're talkin' about. I'd never miss Girlfriend Day," Topaz countered.

"Please . . ." Nina folded her arms and looked at Jade and Keisha. "Did I tell you guys about the time Topaz . . ."

"I hope The Diamond is a big success, y'all," Topaz cut in. "Isn't that food ready yet?"

There was more laughter as Jade led them to a table set with the most exquisite hand-painted china. The brushstrokes, in rose, black, and just a hint of gold, were obviously Japanese.

"Jade, this china is exquisite." Topaz picked up the plate to further admire it.

"Thank you." Jade poured sparkling ice water into glasses.

"These are beautiful, J. Did you get them at Neiman's?" Nina ran her finger around the golden rim of her dinner plate.

"I made those," Jade said, and spread a crisp white napkin in her lap.

Keisha closely inspected the pieces in her place setting.

"Get outta here! You really made these?"

"Un-huh," Jade said nonchalantly. "For my ceramics class at Spelman."

"You're kidding." Topaz's face registered her shock. "Girl, you are the most creative person on the planet."

"These dishes should be in Neiman's." Nina poured more champagne.

Topaz looked at Jade and couldn't help thinking about the insecure girl Sean married and the sophisticated, confident woman she was now. Sean was once madly in love with Topaz, who was very attracted to Sean's celebrity, not Sean.

"You guys. Thank you, but forget the plates. Focus on what's about to be served on the plates." Jade was always the epitome of elegance, even in a pair of jeans. Her hair was pulled back into a single braid with bangs cut bluntly across her forehead that accentuated her Japanese eyes. She struck a small gong, and the ladies sat back in anticipation.

A Japanese man appeared with a tray of appetizers. "This is Takashi. He's one of our sushi chefs." Jade conversed with him in Japanese as he placed a wooden chop block in front of them with an assortment of spicy tuna, California, and shrimp tempura rolls. A waiter also brought out crispy wontons, vegetable spring rolls, and tangy sweet dipping sauces.

"Mmmh." Topaz had already mixed a bit of wasabi into her dish of soy sauce. She picked up a pair of chopsticks and quickly popped a tuna roll in her mouth.

"We didn't bless the food yet, Miss Piggy," Keisha teased as the ladies held hands and prayed.

"I blessed my food long time ago." Topaz was chewing and talking at the same time. For such a celebrated pop singer, Topaz was really just a gorgeous homegirl.

Next, a waiter served stir-fried collard greens, saffron rice, curried goat, grilled Chilean sea bass, fried plantain, and jalapeno and cheese cornbread.

"These are just a few of the dishes we'll serve. The menu is comprised of soul food from different countries." Those were the last words Jade spoke as the women dug in.

"This food is incredible." Nina dropped her fork and groaned. "It's so good, I'm about to hurt myself."

Topaz took one last bite and laid her chopsticks down. "That was too fabulous. Germain would love this. When do y'all open for business?"

"Soon." Keisha looked at the remains on her plate and sighed. "We've got a few loose ends to tie up before the grand opening."

"I can't believe y'all kept this a secret from us. You've been working on this for a while," Topaz said.

"Like you guys don't have secrets we don't know about," Jade taunted while Topaz and Nina exchanged glances.

"We've been working on The Diamond about a year now," Keisha explained.

"Nina, after all the drama you went through managing that girl group with Jamil and his label, we didn't want to bother you with our little restaurant drama," Jade explained.

"Jade saw the building one morning when she was out jogging. She always wanted to do a celebrity-owned restaurant with Sean, so we came on board too. And now we have The Diamond," Keisha added proudly.

Nina was up and walking around. "I could showcase my artists here."

"That would be fantastic, Miss Revelation Music." Jade smiled at her sister-in-law.

"Maybe Topaz will even come through and bless the mike." Keisha smiled at her best friend. "Couldn't you see her with no makeup, hair all curly, strumming an acoustic guitar, singing ballads?"

"Standing room only," Jade agreed.

"Topaz? No makeup? With a guitar? Never." Nina keeled over in a fit of laughter. "That's not her image."

Topaz pushed grains of rice around her plate with a chopstick. "I do play the guitar, Nina."

"You're kidding?" Nina was shocked. "I never knew that and I know everything about you."

"There are a lot of things you *don't* know about me." Topaz wasn't smiling.

"Hey . . ." Keisha cut in before things escalated further. "What do I know? I'm not a music exec. I can't remember the last CD I bought. New Edition's *Candy Girl*?"

"*Candy Girl?*" Nina laughed. Jade joined in and finally Topaz did too. "You'd better stay in the restaurant business, Keisha, and leave the music biz to me."

The waiter returned with another magnum of Cristal and four small beautifully wrapped gift boxes.

"Jade, what did you do now?" Keisha asked.

"Happy Girlfriend Day!" Jade smiled happily while the ladies inspected the packages.

"This is too beautiful to open." Nina examined her gift carefully.

"Oh my." Topaz held up a pair of black crystal earrings. "I will be too fabulous in these, y'all." She immediately took off the ones she was wearing.

"Not as fabulous as I will be in these." Nina held up a duplicate pair. "They're pink, my favorite color."

"What else would a princess wear?" Jade smiled.

"Chocolate! Now these are too fine." Keisha looked at her business partner and held up her pair. "Jade, are these real diamonds?"

"They sure are." Jade exposed a pair of white diamonds identical to the others. "I just wanted to give my girls a little bling for Girlfriend Day to celebrate The Diamond."

"I didn't know about these." Keisha clipped the earrings onto her earlobes. "Miss Jade certainly kept this from me."

"Everyone's got secrets." Jade laughed. "I only wanted you to be surprised, too."

Topaz refilled her glass with champagne. She was silent as she watched the golden liquid sparkle and pop as it rose to the top of her glass.

"Y'all are too fabulous here at The Diamond. Too fabulous." Topaz drawled like the southern belle she was and planted a kiss on Jade's cheek.

Chapter 5

Topaz noticed the outside of The Diamond had been given an extreme makeover when she arrived. The building was painted gray and trimmed in black and cranberry. There was a deck overlooking the water; absolutely perfect for al fresco dining in southern Cali. It offered a magnificent view of the boats in the harbor. A set of stairs led right down to the beach. Bougainvillea spilled out of flower boxes, adding splashes of color. She sat in her Range Rover, admiring the upgrades.

A Pepsi truck was parked by the delivery entrance. Topaz followed cases of ginger ale past the kitchen to the office where Keisha was listening to Donald Lawrence and typing on the computer.

"Hey, gurl. Come on in. I was working on bookings for the club and restaurant. We've got quite a few, thanks to Nina, and we haven't officially opened."

"Leave it to Miss Nina." There was a box of menus, and Topaz picked one up. "The Diamond" was written in platinum across a huge solitaire stone. She flipped it open to the entrees.

"The Ruby . . . prime filet mignon, jumbo lobster tail,

Madeira sauce, drawn butter. The Sapphire . . . grilled mahi mahi, stir-fried rice, vegetables, Mediterranean tropical fruit salsa. The Pearl. . . ."

"Stop it," Keisha interrupted. "I was already hungry. Now I'm starving."

"Anybody around to whip up something to eat?" Topaz looked hopeful.

"No. But I've been thinking about an In-N-Out burger all morning." Keisha pulled her bag out of the desk.

"That'll work for me." Humming softly, Topaz disengaged the alarm on the Range Rover and drove away from the Marina.

"So much for five-star dining." Keisha laughed as they sat down with bags of burgers, fries, and chocolate shakes out on the patio of The Diamond.

"Junk food rules." Topaz swirled fries through ketchup and stuffed them in her mouth.

"It sure does." Keisha took another bite of her burger and swallowed. "We were trying to name a dish after you for the menu. I finally figured it out. The Topaz . . . grilled, chopped sirloin, steak cut fries, Boston Bibb lettuce, and sliced hothouse tomatoes. We'll charge twenty bucks for it like they do at The Ivy."

Topaz nodded her approval as she put more ketchup on the rest of her fries.

"Jade created her own dish, too. Garlic roasted jumbo prawns, light tomato cream, angel hair pasta, and grilled asparagus," Keisha said.

"That sounds delicious. I thought you guys were only doing soul food." Topaz finished the last bite of her double cheeseburger.

"That's the specialty of the house, but we have to include a few American and seafood entrees to make sure we have something for everyone. Everybody can't handle the exotic stuff, so we're naming the common dishes after jewels," Keisha explained and laughed. "Gurl, did you realize that you and Jade are both named after jewels?"

"So . . . what are you trying to say? We're not spicy or something, cause I got plenty of spice, baby."

"No." Keisha laughed. "I just wonder what Sean was thinking . . . dating two women named after jewels. That is so crazy."

Topaz smiled. "Why? Because he likes the finer things in life? Nina always said Sean sure knew how to pick his women . . . that we were both divas."

"Nina sure called that one because y'all do have a lot in common."

"Like what?" Topaz stopped chewing and fixed her eyes on Keisha.

"Both of you are extremely talented artists who tend to operate in high drama mode."

"Excuse you?" There wasn't a hint of a smile on Topaz's face.

"You know y'all are a couple of drama queens."

Topaz smiled at the thought. "It's still hard to believe she's one of my best friends now. I remember when I couldn't stand being in the same room with her."

"Me neither. And now she's one of my best friends, too, and my business partner." Keisha set chilled bottles of water in front of them. "But I really had my doubts about the two of you becoming friends. She was so insecure over your friendship with Sean. I always wondered what that was about."

Keisha's cell phone rang, interrupting the conversation.

Topaz felt her blood pressure rise as her heartbeat escalated. Her friendship with Sean during his and Jade's first year of marriage was something Topaz never thought about. She sipped the water to calm her nerves.

Keisha finished the call and looked at Topaz. "I'm sorry. What were we talking about?"

"Jade. That girl is mad talented. I still can't believe those dishes she made. Weren't they the most beautiful things you ever saw?"

"They were too fabulous. Jade is really at a great place in her life. She's matured enough to be a good wife and mother but still be Jade."

"I know what that feels like." Topaz spoke slowly. "I love being a wife and a mother now . . . even more than singing . . ." Her voice trailed off as she waited for Keisha's response.

"Really, T?" A huge smile lit up Keisha's face.

Topaz nodded.

"Wow! I never thought I'd hear you say that." Keisha looked at Topaz as though she were seeing her for the first time.

"I'm surprised at myself, too. I really don't miss the music biz. I love everything about my life now . . . my beautiful babies and my beautiful man." Topaz was beaming.

"Don't tell me prayer doesn't work. You finally grew up. Girl, I am so happy for you." Keisha smiled and hugged her friend. "Do you know some people leave the planet without learning that lesson?"

"That would be a tragedy." Topaz's face clouded over at the thought of such loss. "I thank God every day for my wonderful family and friends." She squeezed Keisha's hand.

"And no matter what mistakes I made in the past, I always loved my little boy and I always loved Germain." Topaz wiped a tear from her eye.

"I know, sweetie. Now the past is where it should be . . . in the past," Keisha declared firmly as her cell rang again.

Topaz's thoughts drifted to Niki. She dreamed about Niki again and woke up screaming. She was taking a nap on the sofa in the family room, and when she opened her eyes, Chris was standing in front of her looking very frightened.

Keisha hung up the telephone. "I'm sorry, girl. I should turn that thing off, but I might miss an important call."

"It's okay, Keisha. Really. Handle your business," Topaz reassured her.

Keisha made some notes in a file. "Have you had any more of those dreams about Niki lately?"

Damn, Topaz thought. *Is the girl some kind of mind reader or what? I know she's always talking about how God shows her things, but this is kinda scary.*

"No," Topaz answered quietly. "I haven't had that dream again since I told you about it."

"Good." Keisha closed the file and focused her attention back on Topaz. "Cause that was pretty weird. If you were still having them, I was going to suggest you see a therapist."

"A therapist?" Topaz spat the word out like poison. "I'm not crazy."

"No one is saying you're crazy. But something's going on. No one has dreams like that for no reason. A therapist could help you sort things out."

"I don't need a therapist to help me sort anything out. I only had one bad dream," Topaz lied.

"And you haven't had any more. That's what's important. You're probably just pregnant."

"Pregnant?" Topaz looked at Keisha like she was crazy.

Keisha laughed heartily. "I was just trying to lighten things up."

"Not like that." Topaz opened a fresh bottle of water. She took a few sips, readying herself for anything Keisha might throw her way.

"So, were you feeling what I said about performing here at The Diamond with your guitar and no bling . . . just Topaz?"

"You were serious about that?"

"Of course I was."

Topaz was silent for several moments before she spoke. "I was about to tell you I'd love to do it when Nina said that wasn't my image."

"Nina did go there, didn't she?" Keisha recalled.

"I've been writing songs for the last year. All types of songs about a lot of different things, but mostly about love, relationships, life."

"Has Nina heard any of them?"

"No."

"Why not?"

"I don't know. I didn't even tell her that I've been writing."

Keisha was shocked. "Why not? Nina's always had a lot of smarts about the business."

"Probably because I thought she wouldn't like them. This music is totally different from the stuff on my first two CDs."

"You should let her hear them. She *is* the head of Revelation Music now."

"Don't you want to hear them?" Topaz fixed her amber eyes on Keisha.

"Of course I do. You know I'm always your number one fan," Keisha replied. "I can't wait to hear what you've got."

"Wonderful." Topaz took a CD out of her bag and handed it to Keisha. "I brought a few songs with me just in case I needed to leave my material with The Diamond's owner."

"I can't wait to hear this." Keisha headed toward the club, and Topaz stopped her. "Why don't we listen to them in the Rover. I've got a bumpin' audio system. Somehow the club just seems so big and impersonal."

"Whatever, gurl. I just want to hear your music."

Keisha and Topaz went outside to the parking lot and got in the car. Topaz placed a CD in the player and tried not to look at Keisha for a reaction. When the three songs completed, Keisha was practically whispering.

"That was amazing. Topaz . . ." Keisha shook her head. "I can't believe that was really you. I didn't know you could bring it like that."

Topaz squealed with excitement. "You really like it, Key?"

"Like it? I loved it. Gurl . . . you came neo soul, gospel, jazz, R and B. It was . . ."

"Me," Topaz quietly interjected.

"I honestly didn't know you could sound like that."

"I realized I've been a little too flossed and polished," Topaz explained. "People want the real thing. I'm just not sure if they want it from me."

"Has Germain heard this?" Keisha inquired.

"Of course." Topaz was full of smiles. "Germain

loves my music. He said this was the best he's ever heard me sound."

"He's right. How many songs have you written?"

"More than enough for a couple of CDs." Topaz was excited.

"Can I keep these songs to play for Eric?" Keisha picked up the CD case.

"Sure." Topaz smiled as she watched Keisha typing on her BlackBerry.

"I can access the club's schedule from my Berry. I just slotted you in. Is three months enough time for you to get a show together? Remember, you're not wearing any makeup." Keisha laughed.

"You were serious about that too?" Topaz giggled nervously.

"As a heart attack. I can just see you in a pair of faded jeans and some cute little sexy top with your guitar . . ."

"My guitar? Do you realize that I haven't played in years? And you want me to perform with it?" A million thoughts were exploding in Topaz's mind as they talked.

"That's why this is so perfect. You know how artists are always reinventing themselves."

"But I'm in between deals and I don't have a manager or a label," Topaz protested.

"We're talking about one night and one show. It'll be your Unplugged. . . . Hey . . . you know we should get MTV to come and make it a special."

"MTV?"

"Yes, girlfriend. That would be so hot. And then you put out an album."

"I don't know, Keisha. What if my fans hate it?" Topaz was still skeptical.

"Just get out the guitar and start practicing. The club will take care of everything else."

"Keisha . . ."

"Just trust me, girl. It'll be a night to remember," Keisha promised.

Chapter 6

It was hotter than July in Burbank and it was only mid-June. It was almost ten-thirty in the morning and the streets were eerily quiet. Everyone was inside cooling themselves in some form of air conditioning. Topaz pressed the number six once she was inside the elevator at the Burbank Music building. Despite the coolness inside, she could feel beads of perspiration forming around her hairline and over her full top lip. As the elevator began its ascent, she didn't know why she felt so nervous. Nina had been more than willing to take the meeting and hear her ideas. During Topaz's career, she had sold millions of CDs, which had been certified platinum several times over.

"There is no reason why Nina wouldn't want the Grammy-award-winning, beautiful wife of Dr. Gradney," Germain reminded her. "Every record label on the planet would sign you to a deal. And don't forget Nina is your best friend and cousin."

"Isn't that called nepotism?" Topaz, never big on words, learned its meaning just the other night while looking over her son's spelling homework.

"No, baby. Nina signing you to a deal would not be nepotism. If you hadn't already proven yourself, that would be different. If anyone could be accused of nepotism, it would be Nina because she never ran a label."

Topaz sighed with relief. Germain even offered to attend the meeting with her, but Topaz told him that wasn't necessary. But they were going to have dinner at G. Garvin's later that evening to celebrate the new music deal she would certainly be offered.

So why the hell am I so nervous then? Topaz asked herself, but she already knew the answer. She couldn't fight off the insecurity about her age. It was a fact she constantly dealt with despite her countless accolades and accomplishments. She knew she was older than most of the artists she deemed worthy competitors. Pop divas were superstars and millionaires at seventeen now, and even though she was still beautiful, Topaz couldn't help feeling that she was as old as dirt.

Jamil's comments about her and Sabre the night of the Divas concert had only helped to fuel her growing fears. His words constantly played over and over in her mind. "If you're gonna lose sleep over any female in the room, this is the one," Jamil had said, referring to Sabre, whom he called gorgeous. Topaz could see Sabre now all snuggled up under Jamil like she was his woman.

I wonder if they were sleeping together, Topaz wondered for the first time as she recalled the scene in her mind. *That ho probably was having sex with him,* Topaz concluded. It had only been a few weeks since his fiancée, India, had been murdered. But Jamil was still a man, and Sabre was a pretty young thing. "I'm gonna sign her to a solo deal in a few years and she's gonna blow up. Sabre is a diamond," Topaz remembered Jamil saying. And it was no secret that Jamil had purchased the five-carat diamond she wore around her neck from Jacob the Jeweler the day after the concert.

That was less than two years ago, and now Sabre was signed to a solo deal. She had indeed blown up. Sabre had the number one song on the radio. Her ever-growing popularity seemed endless. People loved Sabre. She was in demand. Topaz and Baby Doll watched her on *TRL* just yesterday.

After I was finally able to get Jamil's words out of my head before my solo performance on VH1, that little bitch had the audacity to walk on stage while I was singing, wearing my dress that she stole from my house, Topaz remembered angrily.

It had taken every ounce of willpower Topaz had to not go off on Sabre during the song. Topaz still wanted to kill Sabre every time she laid eyes on her, which was all the time now that the young diva was really headed for superstar status.

"Hell no," Topaz said out loud. *This is an important meeting,* she reminded herself. *This is not the time to trip about Sabre.*

She looked down at the new pair of Apple Bottoms that she purchased especially for her meeting with Nina. She shampooed and conditioned her hair before she left the house, and it had dried into lots of curly ringlets with gold, blond, and copper highlights. Her lips sparkled with her favorite shade of MAC lip gloss and she had only applied mascara.

After what seemed like forever, the elevator doors

opened and Topaz stepped into Revelation Music offices where the receptionist led her to the conference room. Her eyes fell on a framed poster of So Fine's CD cover on a wall. When she saw Sabre, her anger was as fresh as ever. Hood rat, bitch, and a couple of other expletives passed quickly through her mind. Then she saw the plaque from the National Academy of Recording Arts and Sciences for her last CD that sold over five million copies. Before she could look any further, Nina appeared dressed in the cutest pink sundress and her pink diamond earrings.

"Hey cuz." Nina kissed Topaz on the cheek before she arranged her BlackBerry, a tablet of yellow legal paper, and pen in front of her on the conference table.

"That's a very pretty dress," Topaz remarked. "It goes perfectly with your pink diamonds."

"Thanks. I got it in a boutique at the Lennox Mall in Buckhead while I was in the ATL." Nina smiled at Topaz as a few additional people joined them at the table. "I hope you don't mind, but I asked Danny, my A&R executive, and a few other staff members to join us."

Topaz smiled at them and whispered so only Nina could hear. "I wanted to talk to you, not them."

"I already know where this is going, girlfriend. We don't have a lot of time. This way we can accomplish everything in one meeting." Nina folded her arms and reclined in her chair and began making introductions. "So let's do this. Meet Danny, the best A and R man in the business; Cookie, the head of video; and Anita, my executive assistant."

Topaz gave everyone her best smile.

"I just want to welcome you to Revelation in advance." Danny was almost blushing. "I've been a fan since your first CD. This is truly an honor."

Topaz smiled warmly at Danny. She felt herself begin to relax in the chilly conference room.

"That goes double for me." Cookie smiled at Topaz. "I look forward to working with you to capture your music visually."

"A'ight, girl. What's up? You said you have something for us to listen to?" Nina demanded excitedly.

"I sure do." Topaz took out the CD of her songs and placed it on the table. Nina snatched it up and handed it to Danny. "Music maestro."

Topaz watched as he walked over to the audio equipment and placed the disc in the player. "I've been writing and recording my own material for the last year or so. I've been thinking it's time to do something with it, so here we are."

Danny cranked the volume as Topaz's voice flowed through the speakers.

Her vocals were strong and clear. The melody was hypnotic and the acoustic guitars soothing. The track was clean except for light percussion that she had programmed. After the third song Danny clicked off the CD.

"I'm speechless." Danny looked around searching the others' faces. "That was phenomenal, incredible." He took Topaz's hand and kissed it. "Mesmerizing."

Topaz was too pleased. She looked at Nina, who was busily writing notes.

"It's a different sound for you," Cookie began, carefully choosing her words. "Definitely not what I was expecting, but I like it. I like it a lot."

"It's nice, T. Real nice. Do you have a publishing deal?" Nina inquired.

"No," Topaz replied, quietly wondering where Nina was going with this particular question.

"We'll have to hook something up for you because the material is absolutely wonderful."

Topaz finally relaxed now that Nina had given it her stamp of approval. "I'm so glad you like it."

"However . . ." Nina cut in. "I don't feel it's right for you."

"What?" Topaz's mouth dropped open in surprise.

"I agree," Cookie added quickly. "You're this gorgeous, glamorous pop diva. That's your image. It is so not you."

"My sentiments, exactly." Nina tossed her pen on the table. "If you recorded that material, it would prove disastrous to your career."

"I disagree." Danny was on his feet. "Young people are looking for the real deal. This is as real as you can get."

"Young people want to go clubbing. They want music you can dance to," Nina countered.

"So let her write a couple of dance tunes. If they don't work, we've got plenty of material in Jamil's catalogue to choose from." Danny winked at Topaz.

"Do you think Jamil would record this material?" It was the first time Anita had spoken during the entire meeting.

Everyone was quiet as they pondered Anita's words.

"No." Cookie shook her head emphatically. "Jamil was about hip-hop and club tunes."

"Jamil was also about real raw talent," Danny cut in. "And that's what this is. We add some instrumentation, poof . . . we've got some great R&B here. It's neo soul . . . it's fresh and it's hot."

"Neo soul artists don't sell as well as pop artists. Topaz is pop," Nina pointed out.

"This is pop," Danny countered. "It will sell, because Topaz is singing it."

"I think Jamil would have loved it, just like I do." Anita obviously only spoke when she had something to say.

Topaz looked at Nina, who was seated at the head of the table doodling on the pad. She felt a knot forming in her stomach, and she was beginning to sweat profusely.

"Jamil loved Topaz," Nina began quietly. "He signed her to her first deal. He produced her second album and wanted to sign her to this label to produce her third. He'd be on the phone with legal right now nailing out the details of the contract. But would he sign her to do this material? I worked very closely with Jamil over the years . . . I was almost his wife, so I think I know him and his music pretty well, which is why I've been given the task of running Revelation Music. Based on that . . . I have to say no. It's too risky, and the label can't afford to take any chances right now."

No? Topaz couldn't believe what she was hearing . . . and from Nina, who had been a part of her career from the beginning and by her side ever since. *No from my blood?* Although Nina had a sister, she and Topaz were closer than close. Topaz still couldn't believe what she was hearing. Danny handed Topaz the CD with an apologetic glance as the others left the conference room.

"No hard feelings, right cuz?" Nina held out her arms to give Topaz a hug. "It's only business."

"It's only business," Topaz agreed. She kissed Nina on the cheek, dropped her CD in her bag, and left the building as quickly as she could.

Chapter 7

Traffic on Robertson Boulevard between Third Street and Beverly Boulevard, the heart of the interior design district, was always congested. Probably because of the paparazzi and other stargazers trying to catch celebrities at The Ivy or some fancy boutique like Kitson that the younger celebs were known to frequent.

Nina was seated on the sunny patio of The Ivy at her favorite table where she could people watch. She ordered an apple martini while she waited for Sky and Sabre, who were running late. A waiter seated Demi Moore and Ashton Kutcher at a nearby table. She popped out of her seat to greet the host of *Punk'd* and his wife. Nina had been Ashton's contact when the show wanted to punk Topaz.

Back at her table, Nina made note of information Ashton had given her about an upcoming event he wanted Topaz to attend. She sat there staring at the slice of apple in her drink. *It seems like no matter what I do in this business, my connections to the real players in Hollywood are always because of Topaz.*

Nina constantly tried to create a distinct separation

in her life between her and Topaz, but things always seemed to begin and end with her famous cousin. Even though she had written an intriguing *New York Times* best-selling novel about her adventures in Hollywood, they had come from her life as Topaz's personal assistant and cousin. It didn't help Nina's ego when her editor insisted that she mention her relationship to Topaz in Nina's brief biography on the back of the book. Nina's first real high-paying job had been as Topaz's assistant. She met Jamil, her best friends, and even her husband either through or with Topaz. But this new position at Revelation Music was an opportunity for Nina to leave her own personal mark in the industry.

Her BlackBerry vibrated. She read the message and quickly typed a response and looked up to see Sky speaking with the maitre d'. She studied Sabre as the ladies approached her table. *As gorgeous as Sabre is, she has no real star power*, Nina realized. That je ne sais quois—the "it" factor—that special something that made her stand out in a crowded room, unlike Topaz who stopped traffic everywhere she went.

Nina thought about the meeting with her cousin for the thousandth time and wondered yet again if she made the right decision. *Did my desire to separate my life from my cousin's subconsciously factor into my decision to pass on her music? The songs were exceptionally good. I didn't know Topaz could write like that.*

"Always go with your first inclination," Kyle always told her.

No one wants to see Topaz trying to be India.Arie . . . just like no one would want to see India.Arie trying to be Topaz, Nina reassured herself.

Sabre and Sky walked over to the table as Nina

wrestled with her thoughts. "Ladies." Nina stood and greeted them warmly. "I'm so glad you could make it."

"Sorry we're late, Nina, but the traffic was terrible." Sky had on a banana-colored sundress with sandals. She had pinned her hair up, and the gold chandelier earrings were the perfect accessory for bare shoulders and marvelous skin. Sabre had on faded jeans and a "Baby Girl" T-shirt. She could have been some cute teenager at the mall rather than the hottest thing in music. *Someone really needs to groom her,* Nina couldn't help thinking. After they ordered lunch and drinks, Nina went right to work.

"Sky, how would you like to be a Revelation artist?"

Sky's eyes widened with surprise. Sabre was equally shocked.

"Me?" Sky finally blurted out.

"Her?" Sabre sputtered without thinking.

"Yes, of course you. Why not you?" Nina sipped a fresh martini. "You were a member of So Fine. You should have your own deal just like Sabre."

"Wow. I never thought about being a solo artist." Sky's humility was refreshing.

A waiter served them lunch.

"Did you think about being a solo artist when you were in the group, Sabre?" Nina poured dressing on her salad.

Sabre nodded her head up and down as she swallowed a bite of her burger. "I always wanted to be a solo artist. The group helped get me there." Sabre reached for the ketchup.

"I never knew that." Sky looked at Sabre.

"Yes, you did. The other day you said that I was the

one who always wanted to be Topaz when we were little," Sabre defended.

"But we were just kids and we were pretending,"
Sky fired back.

"You used to pretend to be her too," Sabre countered.

"Maybe you were pretending, Sky, but Sabre was
obviously very serious. That's why she's a solo artist
now." Nina buttered a hard roll while Sky sat back in
her chair and reflected on Nina's words.

"So what do you want to do, Sky?" Nina asked.

"I love singing. I did background vocals on Sabre's
CD. We wrote a couple of songs together. I love being
in the studio, but I love performing the most."

Nina laughed. "All of this passion from someone
who was only pretending to be a singer. Have you been
working on your rhymes?"

"Not as much as I should," Sky confessed.

"You were so great on 'First Kiss'. I'm surprised
Sabre didn't ask you to rap on a cut." Nina smiled at
Sabre.

"Yeah, why didn't you ask me to rap on a cut?" Sky
looked at Sabre.

"I didn't think about it and neither did any of my
producers." Sabre crunched on a dill pickle spear.

"Sky." Nina was back in control. "Jamil has a great
catalogue of unrecorded material and I'd like to get you
in the studio with several producers. I think JD would
be the absolute perfect producer to team you up with.
I'd like to get Jermaine to do a couple of tracks. Let's
get you in the studio and see what kind of magic we
can create." Nina took out her BlackBerry and quickly
made a call.

"Hey, Nita. Can you hook me up with JD? I want to

get Sky in the studio ASAP." Nina looked up and smiled at Sky, who was ready to explode from excitement.

"Sabre, I'm going in the studio with Jermaine Dupree. I can't believe it." Sky's voice was two octaves higher than normal.

Sabre carefully chewed on a carrot.

Nina was still on the phone. "Yes, I'm with Sky at The Ivy right now. We were just finishing lunch. Can we be there in forty-five minutes?" Nina looked at Sky, who eagerly bobbed her head up and down. "Cool beans." Nina clicked off her cell.

"You can ride to the studio with me, Sky." Nina gave both girls a plastic smile.

"Sabre, you should come, too," Sky suggested.

Nina opened her mouth to speak, but before she could say anything, Sabre spoke up.

"I have to meet Victor. I'm doing Nick Cannon's show this evening." Sabre took out her Sidekick. "I gotta go now."

"We need to leave now, too. We don't want to keep Jermaine waiting." Nina paid the bill with a black American Express card.

The three of them stood curbside waiting for the valet with the cars.

Sky was elated. "Sabre, this is too cool. Now we can be superstars together. I'll tell you everything . . ."

"You a star?" Sabre laughed nastily as she cut Sky off. "You definitely got jokes. Me and you will never be superstars together. I'm the only star up in this piece, babe." She put on a pair of sunglasses and placed a hand on her hip. "You can be all up in the studio with JD, Jay-Z, and Diddy, but it ain't gonna help your nonsinging ass."

Sky stared at Sabre, speechless and amazed.

Nina, who had been on the phone, missed the exchange between the former group members and best friends. She clicked off her cell and smiled at the girls. "I can't get over the two of you pretending to be Topaz when you were younger. That is so cute. I can't wait to tell T," Nina commented.

VMG had upgraded Sabre's PT Cruiser to a C class Mercedes. A couple of photographers snapped away as she got into it.

Hollywood's It girl. "Humph," Nina grunted out loud. *The media is too powerful. It can make you anything it wants you to be.*

The attendant parked the Bentley in front of Nina. She carefully scrutinized Sky as she walked around to get inside. She was a very pretty girl with an excellent figure. It wouldn't take much grooming to mold her into a great solo artist. The time she spent as a member of So Fine had adequately prepared her. Nina was more than willing to navigate Sky into the major leagues.

Yep . . . I know Sky can do this. She has everything Sabre has, plus she can rap. If Topaz no longer wants to be a pop superstar, then I'll just have to create another one.

As Sky got into the car, Nina relaxed for the first time in weeks. *Finally . . . I'm going to make a name for myself in this business.*

Chapter 8

Sabre, lying on her back in the full-sized bed, stared at the ceiling fan as it spun around. It was the first time in months that her schedule had permitted her to relax. She had been reading, but now Eric Jerome Dickey's latest book rested on her stomach. She had always loved to read because she could escape into the lives of the characters. It was also something she could do alone, and Sabre had spent lots of time alone.

Victor talked in his sleep. He coiled around her like a snake warming itself in the sun, wearing only a pair of blue boxers. Sabre focused on his muscles rippling underneath his smooth skin toasted golden brown by the California sun. She ran her index finger across his forearm and instantly regretted touching him the moment he rolled over and opened his eyes.

"Hey, baby." Victor gave her a little smile as he massaged Sabre's knee and began working his way up her inner thigh.

"Stop it." Sabre slapped his hand off her and reached for the book she had been reading.

Victor laughed and continued the game, paying her

mood little attention because Sabre was always a bitch. He kissed her gently on the lips until he felt her kissing him back.

"Why did you stop?" Sabre tossed the book on the floor and climbed on top of Victor until she straddled him. She kissed him slow and hard until neither of them could stand it and then she stopped.

"Sabre . . ." Victor hoped he wasn't begging. He hated the way she made him feel so out of control.

"Say, please." Sabre tried not to giggle, but she loved being in control. Men could be such pushovers when it came to sex. Before she knew what was happening, Victor flipped her off him. He climbed on top of her and slowly traced her full lips with a finger.

"Stop it, Victor." Sabre lay writhing beneath him. "Get the fuck off me."

He laughed and covered her hands with his, causing her to twist and turn even more. "I love it when you play hard to get. You are so damn sexy and hot." He watched her squirming beneath him and tried to kiss her.

"I told you to get the fuck off me, you stupid-ass son of a bitch. Get off me." Her scream was bloodcurdling. There was a crazed look in her eyes that frightened him. She pushed him off her and he fell on the floor. Sabre ran into the kitchen and returned with a huge butcher knife and charged toward Victor. His eyes grew wide with horror as she brandished her weapon, and he frantically tried to get out of her way.

"I'll kill your fucking ass if you ever touch me again." Sabre pointed the knife at him.

Victor rolled across the bed as she plunged the knife into the mattress with every ounce of strength she had.

"I swear I'll kill your motherfuckin' ass."

Sky came in from shopping while Sabre was scream-ing. "What's going on in here? I could hear you screaming downstairs, Sabre." She looked at Victor and then Sabre for some sort of explanation. "Did you guys have another fight?"

Victor was never so glad to see anyone in his life. He slipped into the bathroom and returned wearing sweats. "You guys need to find another place to live be-cause you can't stay here anymore. I don't trust her crazy ass. She tried to kill me," Victor said and bolted out of the apartment.

"Sabre?" Sky looked at her friend and was surprised when she broke into tears.

"Him touched me." Sabre cried tears from deep within. Sky had never seen her like this . . . except when her grandmother died a few years ago.

Sky held her friend, watching her cry crocodile tears, and tried to think of something to say to calm Sabre down. It was then that Sky saw the huge knife stuck in the mattress. Sky pulled it out and stashed it under the bed. "Sabre, what happened?"

"I told you, him touched me." Sabre was talking and sounding just like a three-year-old.

"Who touched you? Victor?"

"Un-huh." Sabre sniffed and appeared to be slightly calmer.

"What are you talking about? Victor's your boyfriend. He's always touching you and you've never tried to stab him with a butcher knife before, have you?"

"No. But I told him to stop." Sabre dried the last of her tears.

"Stop what? You're not making sense, girl."

"I don't want to talk about it." Sabre went into the bathroom and turned on the shower.

Sky looked at her like she was crazy. "Girl, you are scarin' me. Sometimes I think you're crazy."

"Whatever." Sabre slammed the bathroom door closed, and Sky shook her head. Sky thought about taking the knife back into the kitchen but decided against it. Sabre was acting very strangely.

Sabre looked at her reflection in the mirror. She wasn't ready to move. Victor lived in Hollywood and the location was great. She was saving for a condo in Malibu. She was going to have to think of something to keep her and Sky from being evicted. But what? Victor did all the cooking. He would whip up the healthiest dishes with vegetables, shrimp, or chicken. And she wasn't about to clean. That definitely wasn't an option. *Maybe I could get Sky to do a threesome.* Victor had suggested it when Sky first arrived and Sabre moved her into his apartment. Victor could get pretty freaky, but nothing he ever did in bed surprised Sabre, who was even freakier . . . until that morning.

Sabre cried a fresh batch of tears. Would the awful memories ever go away? "Maybe I should tell Sky," she thought out loud. "I can't," she cried. "I can't," she told her reflection. Sabre jumped in the shower and scrubbed her body until her skin was sore. She had kept her secrets too long.

Martina Cruz, Sabre's mother, was only seventeen when Sabre was born. Tina, a straight A student, had the world in her hands. She graduated early and was accepted to every college she applied to from New York University to Stanford. Tina had the lofty ambition of becoming a pediatrician, and the Puerto Rican teen was on her way.

A pretty, dark-skinned Latina, she was sheltered from life in her Bedford-Stuyvesant neighborhood of Brooklyn. Marisol, her single mother, worked three jobs to ensure that her daughters had the best. Tina's older sisters attended Catholic school, college, then married well. She was expected to follow in their steps.

Tina had decided to attend Stanford when she went to a school party with a friend. There she met Darren, who was articulate, intelligent, and well read. She had never known anyone like him, and he felt the same way about her. She was his delicate, sweet flower. They were inseparable. Several months later, right before Tina was scheduled to depart for Stanford, she discovered she was pregnant. When Marisol learned that her daughter was expecting and insisted on having the baby, Marisol withdrew all support and refused to have anything further to do with her.

Tina decided she would attend New York University, have the baby, put the baby up for adoption, complete her education at Stanford, and apply to medical school. The schoolwork was more difficult than she expected, and her pregnancy was complicated. It seemed like she was always sick. She was eventually fired from her part-time job. Darren got her evicted from her dorm because they were always fighting, so Tina dropped her classes, took a leave of absence from school, and moved in with Darren, who she thought attended a junior college in Queens. It was all too late when she realized that she had been conned by a smooth-talking drug dealer.

Tina had her baby, and like most pregnant teens she ended up on welfare. Although she loved her baby girl, she wasn't ready to be a mother. Marisol refused to speak to her, let alone offer assistance. Tina had brought shame on the family. Bored and depressed, she started smoking weed with Darren, but the high wasn't enough to make her forget her problems, so she decided to try some of the crack cocaine Darren had left in the apartment. It gave her a high that took away her pain. Tina refused to cook, clean, or take care of the baby. Her sole agenda was finding a way to support her new habit.

At first, Darren helped with the baby. He even cooked and cleaned, but constant fights with Tina over sex, drugs, and money drove him away from the apartment for days at a time. Tina fled to the streets to support her habit. She would leave the baby wet, hungry, and alone in the apartment. One of the neighbors finally called Children's Services. Sabre was placed in foster care, and Tina and Darren were evicted from the apartment.

Marisol still refused to care for her young granddaughter, and Tina turned to prostitution to support her habit while Sabre was moved from foster home to foster home until Tina entered rehab, got some career training, and took Sabre out of foster care five years later.

Tina received a placement in the accounting department at the county hospital in Brooklyn. Mother and daughter moved into a decent one-bedroom. She also received money and food stamps in addition to her part-time hours. Tina's social worker tried to simplify her life so Tina and Sabre could bond, making Sabre's transition back to her mother as smooth as possible. Sabre had already been placed too many times for her five years, and she hoped this would be the last.

Sabre was extremely bright, but she didn't get along well with the other children. She thrived in kindergarten and she seemed to be forming an attachment to her mother. Tina picked her up from school every day. Together they prepared dinner, read books, played music, and watched television.

When Sabre was promoted to first grade, Tina took on additional hours at the hospital. Over time, the job became boring and routine, so she lost interest. She was either late or called in sick, missing days at a time until she was fired. Once Darren resurfaced and moved back in, Tina was doing crack again—depressed with her course of life.

Darren hung around for several years, but Sabre had little to do with him. He was always yelling because Tina was drunk or high. Sabre entertained herself with books and music in the bedroom. When Darren was arrested and sent to prison for selling drugs, Tina, alone again, sought the company of an older neighbor. Mr. Rufus was a quiet man who drove a bus. Tina liked him because he had a weekly paycheck and purchased drugs for her and a bottle of Seagram's for himself. They would spend the night getting high while Sabre stayed in the bedroom.

Since Tina had followed the family tradition of Catholic school, Sabre knew how to dress herself in her uniform for school. She received breakfast and hot lunch at school, and hoped there would be dinner at home if Tina hadn't sold the food stamps for drug money.

Sabre would never forget her eighth birthday. Tina was sober when she arrived home from school. She had bought Kentucky Fried Chicken and strawberry soda and announced they were having a celebration. No one had ever given Sabre a birthday party. It was the best night of her life. She and her mother were playing music and doing the latest dances when Mr.

Rufus knocked at their door. When Tina let him in,
Sabre immediately went in the bedroom. She was
angry with Tina for allowing him to come over and
spoil her party. She turned on the radio, but she could
still hear Mr. Rufus's irritating, drunken laughter. She
would know it anywhere.

It was several hours before things were quiet in the
living room, and Sabre knew they had both passed out.
She was asleep when she heard someone enter her
room.

"Tina?" Sabre called out. "Is that you?" She felt
someone get into her bed and fear raced through her
young body. She couldn't stand being touched, not even
by Tina.

"Your junkie mama passed out so I came in here to
spend a little time with you," Sabre heard Mr. Rufus
say.

"What do you want?" Sabre moved over as far as
she could in the bed. She didn't like sleeping in the bed
with anyone, especially after living in a home where all
the children were forced to sleep in the same bed. If
she didn't get pissed on, one of her foster brothers was
always pulling down her panties throughout the night.
She tried to tell her foster mother, but no one ever did
anything about it. She did tell her social worker and
she was removed from the home. It was the last home
she was placed in before she came to live with Tina.

"I came in here to spend a little time with you." Mr.
Rufus slurred his words and his breath smelled like alcohol and cigarettes.

"I don't want company." Sabre scooted over until
she almost fell out on the floor.

Mr. Rufus laughed as he grabbed her by the ankle
and pulled her back across the bed to him.

"Tina!" Sabre screamed as loud as she could.

Mr. Rufus put his hand over her mouth, and she bit down hard on one of his fingers and he slapped her.

"Shut up, you little bitch." He pulled her pajama pants down and she screamed out again for Tina. He raised his hand to slap her again and she whimpered. He traced her lips with his finger as he pulled off her pajama pants. "You're a pretty little thing. I've been waiting to get to you for a long time. It was definitely worth the wait."

He pinned her hands down under his. Sabre twisted and turned beneath him while he touched, fondled, and licked her in places where no eight-year-old should have ever been touched. It was an abomination. Shortly afterward, Sabre went to live with her grandmother, Marisol. She never saw or heard from Tina again.

Sabre stood under the running water of the shower still scrubbing her skin. She had managed to push that night and Mr. Rufus out of mind until Victor made her remember. She knew if things had gone any further, she would have killed Victor when it was really Mr. Rufus she wanted dead.

Chapter 9

The grand opening of The Diamond was a festive occasion. It began Saturday morning with a blood drive for Chocolate Affair, the foundation established by Nina and Keisha to raise funds and awareness for sickle cell disease research after Niki was diagnosed with the blood disorder.

"Can you believe all the people?" Nina, Kyle, and Niki were the first to arrive. Nina was wearing her pink, her favorite color. She had also dressed Niki in the same. Kyle was too handsome in a pink Nike sweatshirt. Nina had found it in Atlanta. Despite everyone warning her that Kyle would never wear the shirt, he had loved it.

He looked at the line of people wrapped around the building. "I'm impressed. All of these people up and out on a Saturday morning to give blood. Keisha really hooked this up."

"You should see the spread Jade set up outside." Sean placed a tub filled with an assortment of juices and ice on the floor. He hugged his brother and kissed

Nina. "Everyone who donates blood gets free breakfast. It's been on Power 106 all week. They're gonna be here all day broadcasting live."

"Great marketing." Kyle opened a Snapple and drank it in a few seconds. "I knew there had to be a catch."

"Uncle Sean, Uncle Sean." Niki was too excited as she extended her arms to her uncle, and Sean plucked the little girl out of his brother's arms.

"How's my beautiful niece today?" Sean smiled and Niki melted.

"Can you believe this?" Kyle looked at Nina and pretended to be mad. "Now I know how Kirk felt when his daughter, Kyrie, was a baby."

"Some of us just got it like that," Sean said, and smirked.

"They just love your behind because you're a big old kid," Kyle teased. "They think you're the same age as them."

"Good morning, everyone." Jade came out of the kitchen with a huge tray of scrambled eggs with cheese.

"Dang, girl." Kyle was practically drooling. "Where are you going with those eggs?"

"Out on the deck with the rest of the food." Jade laughed as she led the procession through the restaurant and outside. "You guys have me feeling like the Pied Piper up in here."

Topaz and Germain looked up from making plates for themselves when the others arrived. Topaz flashed a dazzling smile and added a few slices of bacon to her plate.

"Hey y'all, good morning," Germain greeted them cheerfully.

"I was wondering if y'all had scrambled eggs." Topaz helped herself as Jade inserted the tray into the chafing dish.

"Can you believe these two? Out here feeding their faces as usual." Kyle shook his head and laughed. "You're supposed to give blood first, then eat."

"Okay, Kyle," Germain replied a little too softly. "Aren't we looking too pretty in pink today."

Sean, who was helping himself from Jade's mouth-watering buffet, paused to laugh at his brother.

"The doc is just hating. He knows I look good," Kyle declared, and everyone laughed.

"Hey. . . . What's goin' on out here? I was wondering where all of you were." Keisha put the covers on all of the chafing dishes. "You're not supposed to eat until you give blood. Now get in there, all of you. You're supposed to be setting an example."

"I tried to tell them that," Sean said as he shoveled more eggs into his mouth.

"Sure you did. That's why you got egg all over your face?" Keisha forced herself not to smile as the others howled with laughter.

Eric lifted a lid off the chafing dish. "What's happenin', people?"

"Man, your woman is tough." Kyle was all set to spear a couple of slices of French toast when Keisha shut down the food. He took Nina by the arm and picked up Niki, who was playing with Baby Doll and Chris. "Come on, baby. Let's do this so I can come back and finish eating."

"Baby, why don't you go first?" Nina suggested ever so sweetly. She glanced inside the club where tables and cots were set up.

"You're scared," Kyle realized.

"I am not."

"Are too."

"Whatever."

Kyle laughed as he watched his wife march up to the table, close her eyes, and stick out her arm. She screwed up her face expecting to feel the prick of the needle.

"Have a seat, Nina," a female voice politely requested. "I need you to fill out these forms first and then the nurse needs to check your blood pressure."

Nina's eyes popped open and locked on the face in front of her. "I know you," Nina said out loud as she tried to recall how she knew the woman.

"Dr. Rosalyn Lawrence." She held out a hand to Nina. "I'm Dr. Nichols's research assistant. We worked with you guys on the very first Chocolate Affair."

Keisha's father, Melvyn Nichols, a renowned hematologist, operated the largest research center in the country for sickle cell disease.

"That's right." Nina smiled, still thinking that wasn't how she knew the woman. "Thank you so much for traveling all the way from Atlanta. We really appreciate your running the blood drive for us."

"No, we appreciate you. Do you know how many lives you'll save?" Dr. Lawrence stuck a needle into Nina's vein and began withdrawing the unit of blood.

"I know how important your work is. I thank God because my little girl hasn't been sick since she was diagnosed. You will always have my support until you find a cure."

"If more people thought like you, we'd have a cure. Now that wasn't so bad, was it?"

"No, it wasn't." Nina's BlackBerry vibrated. She checked it and smiled at the doctor. "One of my artists."

"Are you working in music again? If I remember correctly, the last time we were together you were working on your first novel?"

"Yes, I am back in music. I'm running Revelation Music." Nina was surprised by how much the woman knew about her. She did work with Dr. Nichols, who was one of her foundation's board members.

"That's impressive and a lot of hard work, I'm sure. You must be extremely busy." Dr. Lawrence quickly shuffled through a stack of paperwork.

"I am, but I have an understanding husband and a lot of help."

"Isn't Revelation Music Jamil's old label?"

"Yes. A lot of people in the business can't even remember that Revelation used to be called Suicide or either they still call it Suicide."

Dr. Lawrence laughed. "I read a lot when I'm not working. I've always been fascinated by the music business."

Nina took a business card out of her purse and handed it to Dr. Lawrence. "One of my artists will be showcasing here next week. I don't know how long you'll be in town, but give my office a call if you'd like to come."

"I will be in town for a few days visiting family. If Dr. Nichols can spare me out of the lab a few more days, I'd love to come."

"Great." Nina smiled warmly. Dr. Lawrence put a Band-Aid on her arm. Baby Doll and Niki ran over and climbed into her lap, and Nina laughed. "Say hello to Dr. Lawrence, you guys."

Nina smoothed Niki's hair as both little girls spoke.

"This is my daughter, Kendall Nicole, but we just call her Niki," Nina offered proudly.

"And I'm Baby Doll."

"She insists that everyone call her that." Nina tried not to laugh as she spoke. "Her real name is Turquoise. She's my cousin's daughter."

"So you two are cousins?" The doctor smiled at both of the girls.

"Yes," Baby Doll answered for them.

"Where'd you get a name like Baby Doll?" Dr. Lawrence was terribly interested in her.

"From my brother and my daddy."

"Your daddy?"

"Yes." Baby Doll looked directly into Dr. Lawrence's eyes.

"Humph. Well, it's a beautiful name for a beautiful little girl."

"Come on, Niki, let's go see Daddy." Baby Doll was bored with the doctor, so she grabbed Niki and they raced away.

"They are so beautiful with those golden eyes. They could almost be sisters." Dr. Lawrence focused on Nina.

"They get that all the time. They're cousins who fight and play like sisters."

Nina found Kyle outside with a stack of French toast and bacon. "I knew you'd be out here. Give me a bite of that."

Kyle cut a square of toast and Nina opened her mouth. He grinned like a little boy as he pretended to feed her. He could barely contain himself when Nina chomped down on nothing when he quickly pulled the fork out of her mouth.

She hit him with her napkin. "You are so wrong."

"Okay, here." Kyle held the French toast for her again.

"I don't trust you." Nina saw Sabre strut across the room out of the corner of her eye and focused on her. She had arrived alone and was working the party. She was terribly overdressed but looked fabulous in a Dolce & Gabbana dress that would have been marvelous for the party later that evening.

"What are you doing?" Kyle was disappointed that his wife had lost interest in him already.

Nina signaled with her eyes for him to watch Sabre, who was drooling all over Dwyane Wade. There were quite a few ballplayers in the room now who had come to the event at Sean and Eric's request.

"Isn't that your girl?" Kyle was also interested in Sabre's charade.

"Humph." Nina rolled her eyes. "She's not my girl."

"Did I tell you she hit on the doc the night of the Baby Phat party?"

"Sabre hit on Germain?" Nina was in shock. "You never told me that."

"It must have slipped my mind." Kyle watched Sabre with renewed interest as she struck up a conversation with LeBron James.

"She must have a death wish." Nina laughed.

"The doc was clueless and she was throwing him major action."

"It would take an army to keep Topaz off Sabre if she ever tried to hit on Germain in front of Topaz."

Topaz walked through the restaurant. LeBron stopped talking the moment he laid eyes on her, and the smile faded from Sabre's face.

Topaz paused to speak and the cameras flashed like crazy as the NBA superstar posed with both of the

ladies. Sabre had more moves than one of America's
Next Top Models. Nina and Kyle were all over themselves with laughter.

"Your girl Sabre is hilarious." Kyle shook his head.

Photographers gathered to take advantage of the
photo op, and more celebrities were added to the
group; Sean, Eric, Magic Johnson, and Baron Davis
posed while the ladies remained front and center.
Tyrese also joined Topaz and Sabre for photos. Sabre
was all over herself when the handsome actor gave her
his brilliant, trademark smile and said he liked her
music. Topaz was about to walk away when he pulled
Topaz to the side, much to Sabre's dismay.

*She needs to take her old ass somewhere else. This is
my time to shine and I just know that sexy ass Tyrese was
feelin' me. That damn Topaz is seriously blockin' my action,* Sabre thought as she watched Topaz laugh and
converse with Tyrese, who was telling her about his latest film project. He thought she would be perfect as the
female lead in the movie. Topaz looked at Germain
standing on the side, waiting patiently, and wished she
had never agreed to take the first photograph, but she
wanted to help with the blood drive any way she could.
She could see Sabre through her peripheral vision trying to steal the show. It was the first time Topaz was
that close to her for a long time.

*That dress is totally inappropriate, but it really looks
good on her,* Topaz thought. She was very familiar with
the garment because it was by one of her favorite designers. She had even tried the dress on, but it did nothing for her figure. Sabre was tiny but curvaceous, and it
looked absolutely perfect on her. Topaz could tell she
had been working out and surmised that she probably

was a size 2. *Possibly even a zero.* Topaz sucked in her stomach and stood up straight as she cast Sabre a sideways glance. *I remember when I used to be her size.*

When the last photo was taken, Topaz approached Sabre. "Nice dress."

"Thank you." Sabre smiled warmly at Topaz, thinking the two of them might become friends yet.

"Who'd you steal that from?" Topaz flipped her hair over one shoulder and sauntered over to Germain and kissed him.

Sabre stood there with her mouth hanging open, still trying to think of a comeback line. She watched Topaz and Germain kissing until Baby Doll, Chris, and Niki interrupted them. Germain picked up both of the little girls. A photographer took several pictures of them. Keisha and Eric joined them for more photos with their daughter, Kendra, and their son, Eric Jr.

"Look at you, Kendra. You are growing up too fast. You look just like your mom when she was your age." Topaz pulled the ten-year-old into her arms. "Doesn't she look just like Keisha, Germain?"

Sabre tried to be inconspicuous as she watched the "Black Friends." Jade and Sean joined the group with their six-year-old, Kobe, and finally Nina and Kyle. The friends seemed oblivious to the paparazzi, choosing instead to enjoy one another.

"Are you not talking to Nina?" Keisha whispered to Topaz. "That is so unlike you two."

Topaz looked at Nina, who was posing in photos with Jade. "She seems to be a little full of herself ever since she became Miss Revelation Music."

"You know how Nina throws herself into her work." Keisha smoothed Baby Doll's hair. "She's probably just very nervous about taking over for Jamil and wants to do a good job."

"Humph," Topaz grunted.

"You know that's the little sister you never had."

"You're right." Topaz sighed. "Gurl, where is my mind? I didn't give blood yet."

Keisha laughed. "You'd better get in there."

Topaz passed Sabre sitting at a table alone when she headed into the club, where people were still giving blood. A nurse handed her a form to fill out and told her the doctor would be right with her. She was looking around for Germain when she heard "How's my beautiful niece, Turquoise, Topaz Lawrence?"

Lawrence? Topaz spun around and looked up at Dr. Rosalyn Lawrence. "Oh my God. What the hell are *you* doing here?"

"Working." Dr. Lawrence placed a blood pressure cuff on Topaz's arm and pumped it up. "Did you forget that I work with Dr. Nichols in Atlanta?"

"I'll have to talk to Dr. Nichols about who he hires."

"What makes you think he'll listen to you? Because you're famous? Dr. Nichols is concerned with important things like finding a cure for these babies. Not the whims of a self-centered, spoiled singer." Dr. Lawrence wrote down some information on Topaz's form.

"Don't get mad at me because you're an ugly-ass bitch. That's your fault, not mine."

"If I was upset at you, it would be because you refuse to let my brother's daughter have a relationship with his family. But if you're angry because you're a has-been, that's your fault, not mine."

"Has-been?" Topaz laughed out loud. "I could never

be a has-been, sweetheart. And because you and your family are a bunch of gangbangin', greedy, money hungry, South Central lowlifes is why you don't have a relationship with my daughter. Don't forget you signed that agreement. You chose money over my daughter and that's the smartest thing you ever did."

Sabre moved closer to Topaz, who was so angry she didn't even notice.

"I don't know what my brother saw in you."

"I don't know what I saw in your brother."

"If he hadn't married you, he would still be alive."

"Oh please." Topaz paused to laugh. "Your family is the reason Gunther isn't alive. He had a bad heart and took drugs before I met him. Gunther never talked about any of you. He never introduced me to any of you and he didn't leave anything to any of you. I never knew you existed until the funeral, so you've got to come up with something better than that, sweetheart."

The nurse came over and informed Topaz she was done giving blood.

"That wasn't as bad as I thought it would be except I had to see you. And don't forget about that restraining order. If I ever told Dr. Nichols about that, you wouldn't have a job so I suggest you take your ass back to Atlanta and leave me alone."

Topaz rejoined her family and friends, as Rosalyn began packing up supplies.

The doctor was flipping through a stack of paperwork from the blood donors when she came across Nina's. "Humph," she said as she quickly read over the form, noting pertinent information. "That can't be right." She found Kyle's paperwork, and after reading through it, she frowned. "Something's terribly wrong." She pulled their information out, wrote something on a Post-It, and paper-clipped everything together.

"Is this where you give blood?" Sabre interrupted. She smiled warmly as she stared Dr. Lawrence up and down.

Chapter 10

"Baby, please?"

Topaz and Germain were having breakfast on the patio of their Pacific Palisades estate, and the view of the Pacific Ocean was placid and vibrantly blue. Germain folded the newspaper he had been trying to read and looked across the table at his wife.

"Have you been watching *Nip/Tuck* again?"

"Germain." She tossed the crisp linen napkin lying in her lap at her husband. "Please?"

"No."

"Germain."

"For the thousandth time, you don't need any cosmetic surgery. You look fine."

Topaz tossed her spoon into the dish of assorted fruits and pouted. "You're my husband. Of course you're going to say that." She stood up from her chair, walked around the table, stood next to him, lifted up her shirt, and pinched over an inch of flesh from her midsection. "I just want you to get rid of this and give my boobies a lift. Maybe even some implants, huh?" She looked at her cleavage and then her husband. "What do you think?"

"Now you're being ridiculous."

"You don't understand the music industry," Topaz whined. "I'm thirty now and these girls are coming into the business younger and younger with perfect bodies. If I'm going to compete I have to tighten up my game."

"You just need to spend a little extra time in the gym," Germain suggested.

"Exercise won't do it. I need a little extra help with this one. I'm not eighteen anymore, and you know even eighteen-year-olds are having procedures these days."

Germain let out a deep long sigh. "Baby, does this have anything to do with Nina not liking your music? You know she's not the only label in town."

"No, baby." Topaz knew she was telling a half truth. Nina's passing on her music had only heightened her insecurities. "I just want to be the best I can be. I can't help it if my husband happens to be the best cosmetic surgeon in the business."

"I know how you are once you've made up your mind about something. If I don't do the surgery, you'll just find someone who will. I'm not having the quacks in this city touch my wife. If I do your procedure, I know it'll be done right."

"Oh, thank you, baby." Topaz sat in his lap and kissed him. "You don't know what this means to me."

It was still dark and Topaz was still half-asleep when the limousine picked up Keisha so she could accompany Topaz to the hospital for surgery.

"You know Germain wants me to talk you out of this," Keisha said with a yawn.

"You're not going to waste time trying to do that, are you?" Topaz tried to smile despite the earliness of the hour.

"Nope. I know which battles to pick. Talking the diva out of liposuction and a boob job isn't worth the energy. I've been thinking about getting a little lipo myself."

"Not you, too?" Topaz was wide awake now.

"You're right." Keisha smiled. "But that's what I told Germain. I had to tell him something to get him off your case."

"Thanks, Key. I don't think Germain really understands how competitive the music business is. These girls are signing deals younger and younger. By thirty, you're old and a has-been."

Rosalyn Lawrence's bitter words still hurt. Topaz had done a good job of putting the young doctor in her place, but whoever said "sticks and stones may break my bones but words will never hurt me" never worked in the entertainment industry.

"You're not worried about being a has-been, are you?"

"No," Topaz lied again. It seemed as though she wasn't being honest about her real feelings with anyone these days. *Some things are just better left unsaid,* she decided.

The limo stopped in front of Cedars-Sinai and the ladies went inside to check in Topaz. She was in bed and very relaxed after the nurse gave her a shot of Valium.

"Did I tell you about my encounter with Dr. Lawrence at the grand opening?" Topaz's golden eyes looked like huge glass marbles as she stared at Keisha.

"No, honey."

"She is such a bitch. I don't know why your father has her working for him."

"She's the best in the business. She's good at what she does and the pediatric patients love her. Daddy wants her to continue her research, but he's torn because the children love her too."

"Humph." Topaz twisted on the gurney. "I don't see how anyone could love that bitch."

"Topaz." Keisha couldn't remember when she had heard her friend speak about someone so harshly.

"You know she tried to blame me for Gunther's death?"

Keisha's mouth dropped open in surprise. "No, she didn't."

"She wanted me to let Baby Doll spend time with the family."

Keisha shook her head.

"I'd like to take her and that bitch Sabre and throw them off the damn planet." Topaz was definitely relaxed.

"It must be the Valium," Keisha whispered to herself as Germain walked up dressed in hospital greens.

"Hi, baby," he whispered in Topaz's ear, and her eyes popped open.

"Germain." She smiled up at her husband. "I thought I was dreaming."

"You know it's not too late. You can still change your mind." Germain looked at her chart and made a few notes.

"No way, baby." Topaz smiled. "I can't wait to have your hands all over this body, doctor."

Germain blushed and Keisha giggled.

"It's the drugs," Keisha whispered in Germain's ear.

"Thanks for being here with her, Key. It's an easy procedure."

"Are the kids gonna be okay?"

"Kyle's taking them home after school."

Topaz sat up in bed with the weirdest look on her face. "You mean Nina's going to have all my children?"

"Just for a couple of nights, baby. When you're up and about again, they'll come back home." Germain kissed Topaz again and left her room.

"She already has everything." Topaz looked like a madwoman. "She can't have all my children, Keisha."

"They'll be fine, T. I'll even go by and check on them if you want." Keisha was very reassuring.

"Okay. Keisha, I have a secret I need to tell you."

"What secret?"

"It's a big secret and you have to promise not to tell anyone." Topaz sounded like she was five years old.

"I promise," Keisha said softly.

"I have . . ." Topaz began.

"Ready to go see that fabulous man of yours?" A nurse entered the room with an orderly.

"Okay." Topaz relaxed, and the orderly wheeled her out of the room. "Time to go see my man now so he can make me beautiful again." Topaz gave them a Miss America wave, and Keisha finally laughed.

How could the most beautiful girl in the world not think she was beautiful anymore? Keisha went outside to make a few calls while she waited for Topaz to complete her procedure. She took out her BlackBerry and speed dialed.

"Hey, gurl. Are you still in the studio?"

"All night, every night. Just trying to get everything

ready for Sky's showcase next week," Nina yelled into the phone.

"Your cousin's having surgery."

"Who? Topaz?"

"That's the only cousin I know of yours." Keisha took out a bottle of water. She heard the music fade as Nina apparently left the studio.

"Wow. Is she okay?"

"She'll be fine. Germain's doing a procedure. Didn't you know?"

"I've been so crazy between trying to get these songs done and tightening up Sky's image for the showcase, I don't know much of anything these days," Nina confessed.

"Kyle's bringing Baby Doll and Chris to your house for a few days."

"That's fine. I know he and Niki will enjoy having them."

"Is everything okay between you and Topaz?" Keisha was never one to hold back when she wanted to know something.

"What made you ask that? Did Topaz say something to you?" Nina demanded.

"Just a vibe I've picked up, that's all."

"Oh. I've just been really busy with the label. I haven't seen much of anyone except Sky, my staff, and her producers."

"How's everything going?" Keisha doodled across the top of her page.

"Wonderful. Sky's gonna be a force to reckon with in this business."

"That's great, Nina. Call me if you foresee any changes for the showcase."

Keisha hung up and made the rest of her calls, but

she couldn't get her conversation with Topaz off her mind. *I wonder what secret she has that she was going to tell me. I knew she'd been keeping something from me. And why would she trip over the kids going to Nina and Kyle's? Was she talking crazy because she was medicated or was the medication causing her to speak what was really on her mind?*

Keisha had lunch and made more phone calls before she returned to Topaz's room. Less than half an hour later, an orderly wheeled Topaz back into the room. She was sleeping peacefully when Germain entered moments later.

"Hey, pretty girl. You're back in your room with Key. You can wake up, sleepyhead." Germain kissed her and she opened her eyes.

"Hi, baby." Topaz smiled at Germain, and Keisha tiptoed out of the room to give them privacy.

Keisha always told Topaz she was blessed to have a man love her the way Germain did. Life and love were precious, and she believed her friend finally realized it. Germain found her waiting outside Topaz's room.

"Thanks, Key. I'm going to let her stay overnight. The nurses will have to deal with the diva when the pain hits and not me. Are you gonna hang around?"

"Sure. Eric's on a road trip so I can hang out."

"Good. I'll bring y'all some dinner from P.F. Chang's. It's right around the corner at the Beverly Center. You know the diva loves Chinese." Germain kissed her on the cheek and left the floor.

Topaz was awake when Keisha entered the room. "Hey, diva."

"Game recognizes game," Topaz replied softly.

"How do you feel?"

"Like I need a pain shot."

Keisha rang for the nurse. "I can't believe you put yourself through all this pain."

"Beauty takes pain. It'll go away and then it'll all be worth it."

The nurse entered the room and gave Topaz some medication.

"Hey, party over here."

"You are so silly." Keisha laughed.

Topaz smiled as she drifted off to sleep. "Key, promise you'll take care of my pretty little babies if something ever happens to me?"

"Topaz . . . nothing's going to happen to you."

"Promise me, Key, promise."

Keisha was surprised that Topaz was so serious. Even though she and Eric had purchased life insurance policies, they never thought for one minute they wouldn't be around to take care of their children. Topaz had just undergone surgery, but if she was so concerned about something happening to her, why would she even go through with such a risky, unnecessary procedure? *It has to be the drugs that are making her act so crazy,* Keisha deduced.

"You didn't promise, Key," Topaz warbled, speaking with her eyes closed.

"I promise, T."

"Good," Topaz mumbled as she drifted off to sleep.

Chapter 11

Kyle rolled over and reached out for Nina, but she wasn't in her spot next to him in their California king-sized bed. He groaned and dragged himself into the Italian marble bath, but she wasn't there, nor was she downstairs in their office on the computer. "Where the hell is my woman?" he grumbled out loud. "A brother is in need of some loving."

Niki's room was also on the second floor of the Malibu tri-level oceanfront estate. He peeked inside and smiled when he saw that she was still asleep. He looked at the digital clock on her wall and was shocked when it displayed that it was almost noon.

"What the hell?" Kyle went down another level to the family room, expecting to see his wife stretched out on one of the sofas in front of the big-screen TV, but again he was disappointed because there were no traces of Nina anywhere. As a last resort, he checked the five-car garage for her Bentley. It was parked next to his, but when he saw her Range Rover was missing, Kyle realized that she never came home.

"She didn't call, send a text message . . . nothing."

He scrolled through his BlackBerry one more time before he angrily typed, "Where are you?" He pressed Send and tried to be patient while he waited for her response.

In the kitchen, he poured the last drops of his favorite apple cranberry juice into a glass. He searched the fridge and the pantry for another container, but there was none. Now he was pissed . . . and there was still no response to his text message, so he typed another. Before he could put the phone down it vibrated, alerting him that there was a new message. "That better be her."

"In the studio, baby. Been here all nite."

"What?" Kyle yelled.

"Why are you yelling, Daddy?" Niki came into the kitchen wearing her school uniform.

"Good morning, baby." Kyle scooped the little girl up and gave her a big kiss until she giggled. "How's my favorite girl?"

"I'm fine, Daddy. Are you taking me to school today?"

Kyle glanced at the clock again. It was almost one. "No, baby, because by the time I get you to school, it'll be time for you to come home. So you and I are going to have a special day together. Let's get you out of this uniform and into something beautiful first."

"Okay, can I wear my pink dress, please? Please, Daddy?" When Niki fixed her huge golden eyes on her father and smiled, he felt his heart melt.

"Sure, Princess." Kyle took Niki up to her room, found her favorite dress, and ran her bathwater.

"I want bubbles, Daddy." She hummed as he poured in her favorite coconut lime fragrance. He set out pink fluffy towels and body butter, and he put toothpaste on her Barbie toothbrush. He came back into the bedroom and put the pink dress, underwear, a sweater, and sandals on her bed.

"Okay, Niki. I put everything out for you. I'm going upstairs to check Mom's fridge for juice. I'll be right back."

"Daddy, you forgot my music," Niki yelled as she splashed around in the bathtub.

"No, I didn't. I'm turning it on now."

Kyle shook his head as he pressed the power button on the player and Sabre's latest flooded his ears. "This is what I get for being such a womanizer," he mumbled to himself. "I'm surrounded in a house of divas."

"I'm so sexy." Kyle heard Niki singing along with Sabre.

"I know one thing we're going to do today is buy you some new gospel CDs. I can't take too much of that crap, and I definitely don't want you singing it." Kyle was talking to himself again.

He dashed up the stairs to the office that overlooked the Pacific Ocean. The swimming pool and Jacuzzi were sparkling. He could see the pool man loading his chemicals and equipment on the back of his pickup. The large cozy office had a fireplace, a big overstuffed sofa, a 27-inch flat screen, and his-and-her desks that faced each other. Special built-in bookshelves filled with all types of books lined the walls. He, Nina, and Niki frequented the Barnes & Noble in the Malibu Colony on a regular basis. He opened the mini refrigerator and spotted an unopened container of juice. "Thank God for small favors." He grabbed it and headed back downstairs to his daughter's room, where Niki was still singing in the tub.

"Okay, Niki. You need to come out and get dressed, so I can get dressed, and we'll go have lunch."

Niki climbed out of the bathtub and wrapped herself in the towel. "You didn't heat my towel, Daddy."

"I know, baby. It's warm outside. I heat your bath towel when it's chilly so my little princess can stay warm." He cuddled her in the towel and dried her off. "You smell like coconut."

Niki giggled and began rubbing the body butter into her skin. "Go get dressed, Daddy, so we can go eat. I'm hungry."

"She's getting to be a bossy little thing, just like her mother. The Lord knows He's paying me back for being a ladies' man." Normally, he would have shared his thoughts with Nina, so he had no choice but to talk to himself.

Father and daughter were finally dressed and on their way in Kyle's Bentley. It was time for a late lunch when they arrived at the Chart House. Kyle ordered grilled fish for himself and shrimp scampi for Niki.

"Daddy, I miss Mommy. Can we go see her at her job?" Niki finished the last of her seafood.

"That's a great idea, Princess." He took out his BlackBerry and sent Nina a message before he cut into a huge slice of strawberry shortcake. "I have to find out where Mommy is working," he explained. Moments later, the phone beeped.

"Can I check it, please?"

Kyle pushed the BlackBerry across the table to Niki.

"Come on by. We're at . . ." Niki gave the phone to Kyle. "What's that word, Daddy?"

"Larrabee Sound." Kyle signed the credit card slip and scooped up Niki. "Let's roll, Baby Girl."

They arrived at the studio about forty-five minutes later. Nina was sitting behind the mixing board between the engineer and a young hip-hop producer, who was in his mid to late twenties. Her face lit up like a Christmas tree when she saw Kyle and Niki.

"Hi, honey." Nina grabbed her husband and daughter and kissed them both. "Come on in, you guys." She picked up Niki and carried her back to her chair. It was then that Kyle noticed his wife was wearing low-riding jeans with a red halter top and stilettos. He couldn't help focusing on her tight little butt and slim hips. There was a tattoo of Minnie Mouse at the base of her spine.

"Nina," Kyle whispered angrily.

She whirled around, completely surprised, because he rarely if ever called her by her first name or spoke to her with that tone.

"I'd like to speak to you privately, please."

"I can't talk right now. You'll have to wait until we take a break." She sat down in her chair, pulled up another chair for Kyle, and sat Niki in her lap. She patted the chair seat and looked up hopefully at her husband. He sat down, but she knew he wasn't pleased. Nina did her best to refocus on Sky, who was in the recording booth.

"Sky's showcase is in a few days. We've got to nail these tracks ASAP so she can begin rehearsal," Nina explained to Kyle.

"I'm the co-chief executive officer of this label and I don't know anything," Kyle practically yelled. He was angry with Nina for a slew of reasons.

"I'll be back in a few," Nina whispered to the producer. She sat Niki in her chair. "You sit in Mommy's chair and watch Sky sing while I go outside and talk to Daddy."

Nina took Kyle by the hand and led him out of the studio into the break room.

"You passed on your cousin's project to sign Sky?" Kyle fired at her.

Nina opened her mouth and closed it. "How did you know about that?" she finally said.

"Germain told me. You know he is my best friend."

"Things have been absolutely crazy ever since I heard Topaz's music. I didn't think it was right for her image. Sherwin has been on me to sign new talent and generate income. Sky fell into my lap. I was able to get her in with Jermaine Dupree, but I had to move fast. Producers like these are booked months in advance, so when I had the opportunity to get Sky's project going so quickly, I had to take advantage of it. Didn't Sky sound great?"

"Not really."

"I think she has everything these kids want. Sky's the total package. She's gorgeous, she can rap, and she has a great body. Plus she can sing. And with the right music, that means lots of radio play and sales," Nina defended.

"What the hell are you wearing?" Her outfit was probably bothering Kyle more than anything.

"Jeans and a halter. What's the big deal?" Nina looked down at her pants expecting to find a rip or a soiled spot.

"The problem is you're practically naked in a room full of men."

"Naked?" Nina looked at her outfit and laughed. "No, I'm not."

"I've never even seen you in those jeans or that top."

"But they look good on me, don't they, baby?" Nina

stroked his face and laughed, doing her best to lighten the moment. "I had Anita pick up a few things for me from Fred Segal. My wardrobe has become really conservative. I wanted the guys to be comfortable with me while we're in the studio."

"They might get a little too comfortable if you're wearing that."

"What are you trying to say, Kyle?"

"You look like a hoochie. I don't want my wife going around looking like a hoochie."

"A hoochie?"

"You heard me."

"I dressed this way when you met me."

"No, you didn't, because women weren't wearing jeans with their thongs hanging out."

"My thong isn't hanging out." Nina felt the back of her pants just to be sure. "I would never wear anything that exposes my underwear. I'm nobody's skank. You know me better than that." Nina looked like she wanted to cry.

"You certainly don't look much like a wife and mother either."

"Did you come down here to fight with me? Because I don't have time for this now. We can fight when I get home."

"You plan on coming home tonight?"

"Yes."

"Niki didn't get to school this morning because I overslept."

"Where was Rosa? She should have gotten Niki up and off to school."

"She's off on Wednesday. I reached out for you this morning and you weren't home. Never came home and you didn't even bother to call." He had finally said it.

"I'm sorry, baby." Nina pulled Kyle into her arms, but she could feel the resistance in his body.

"If I had known running Jamil's label would be like this, I would never have agreed."

"You don't tell me anything. You don't ask my opinion. You rarely see me or Niki. What am I in this partnership? Your live-in babysitter?"

"You know I don't feel that way," Nina replied quietly. "I just know more about the music industry than you."

"You couldn't take the time to teach me?"

"No. I had to get things rolling. Sherwin wanted to replace me."

"You never told me that."

"I was too embarrassed to tell anyone."

"I'm your husband." Kyle looked at Nina as though he were seeing her for the first time. "We should be able to tell one another anything."

There was an uncomfortable silence between them as Nina stood there staring at the floor and Kyle stared at Nina. She knew he was looking at her, but she couldn't meet his eye. This was something she had to do alone. He would never understand her reasoning.

"Could you go get my daughter, please? There's nothing here for us."

Nina turned and walked out of the break room without another word. When she returned to the studio, Sky was sitting in her chair playing with Niki. The producer and the engineer were reviewing a portion of the track.

"Hi, Mommy." Niki looked up and smiled. She was delighted to be with her mother and to be around the music.

Nina sat in Kyle's vacant chair and lifted Niki into her lap. "Baby, Daddy's waiting for you by the door."

"Mommy, is Daddy in trouble?"

"No, baby. Daddy's just ready to go now and you have to go with him."

"Are you coming with us?"

"I have to work, Niki."

"Are you coming home tonight?"

"Yes."

"Can I stay with you?" Niki fixed her golden eyes on her mother.

"No, sweetie. It will probably be very late by the time we're done. Sky has to finish this song and then she's going to start another one. We have to work really hard while the guys are here to work with us."

"But I want to stay, Mommy. I'll be a good girl." Niki started to cry.

"I know, baby." Nina rocked her daughter in her arms and kissed her. "Niki, if you don't stop crying, I'm going to cry too."

"But I want to stay," she wailed.

"I know, baby, but if you stay with me, then Daddy's going to be all alone. You don't want that, do you?"

Niki buried her face in her mother's red top. "No."

"Good. That's Mommy's sweet girl." She kissed her again and carried her to Kyle, who was waiting by the door. He looked at Niki's face and gave Nina a look-what-you've-done-now look.

Nina ignored it and tried to cheer up Niki. "You can sleep in my bed. When I come home, I'll put you in your bed. Okay?"

"Okay."

Nina handed the little girl to Kyle. "Why don't you guys go over to Aunty Jade and Uncle Sean's for dinner? Then you can make it back out to Malibu after the traffic dies down."

"We'll take that into consideration." Kyle shifted Niki in his arms. "Tell Mommy good-bye."

"Bye, Mommy." She allowed Nina to kiss her and then rested her head on Kyle's shoulder.

"See you later, okay?" Nina kissed Kyle on the cheek, but she knew he was even angrier with her now because Niki was upset. "I love you guys."

"Love you, too." Niki waved as Kyle carried her out of the studio.

Nina returned to her seat and collapsed in her chair. The producer was still reviewing the track and giving notes to Sky.

At this rate I'll never get out of here. Sky had a lot of work to do, and the visit from Niki and Kyle had totally interrupted her flow. She put her head in her hands and wondered for the thousandth time what she had gotten herself into, and then her mind went to Topaz. Kyle had told her in so many words that he felt she had made a mistake by passing on her project and signing Sky. She got up and whispered a request in the producer's ear.

"Sure." He grinned at Nina, exposing a platinum and diamond-encrusted grill and reached into his bag. "Anything for you, pretty lady."

Nina took what he gave her and headed outside. It had been a long time and she didn't feel comfortable doing it in front of strangers. She climbed into her Range Rover, her favorite vehicle. It always represented an accomplishment to her because she saved and purchased it with money she earned working for Topaz and Jamil. She took out the blunt, lit it with a match, and inhaled. It had been years since she had smoked, and now she felt the drug enter her body almost immediately. She took a second hit and felt the stress she had been carrying for months lift. After a few more hits, thoughts of Kyle, Niki, Topaz, Sky, and Revelation Music also vanished into the night air as she exhaled.

Chapter 12

Sabre and her publicist, Mimi, were in the greenroom at *The Tyra Banks Show.* Sabre walked around the room, nibbling on carrots from a vegetable tray. It was a very important interview and she wasn't about to admit to anyone how nervous she was. The label had also just released the second single from her CD, and it was the most requested song at radio stations everywhere.

Mimi was the typical southern California blonde who could have been a beach babe and married well by being some rich man's trophy wife. But while Mimi was obviously beautiful, she was also as smart as a whip. She chatted away on her BlackBerry as she flipped through the latest issue of *InStyle* magazine. Mimi, who only represented A-list hotties, promised VMG that she would take Sabre's career to the next level.

The Tyra Banks Show was just one of several major promotional efforts Mimi promised and delivered. Mimi also convinced the label to hire a new wardrobe stylist as well as a hairstylist and makeup artist to accompany

Sabre on all of her personal appearances. No more half-done make-up and hair. Sabre's glam squad had already done their thing, and she looked like a million dollars.

"You should get dressed now, Sabe. You're going on first." Mimi looked her up and down and went back to the magazine. "You look hot."

"Thanks, Mimi." *My name is Sabre,* she always wanted to remind Mimi. *I can't stand it when she calls me that.* But Mimi was pretty cool for a white girl and Sabre really liked her so she let her get away with it. Mimi was fun like a big sister. She was always telling Sabre funny little stories about other celebrities and giving her pointers and tips on the latest hot designers that anyone who was anyone had to wear. She also treated Sabre like a star and made sure everyone else did too.

For *The Tyra Banks Show* performance, Sabre was wearing an orange halter dress trimmed in gold with gold Jimmy Choos and orange and gold Swarovski crystal earrings that were designed to go with the dress. Ever since Topaz stepped up the game by performing in couture fashions, new young singers had to follow suit. Dawn, her new stylist, knew where to shop and she had great connections. She practically threw away all of Sabre's old clothing.

Sabre's hair was done on the set. Eduardo, her too-pretty-for-a-man stylist, claimed to be anything but black. Creole, Indian, Italian, or Puerto Rican, he was a different ethnicity for every day of the week. "Create the fantasy," he constantly told her, gesticulating with his hands and a crazed look in his eyes.

"Miss Thing," as he sometimes referred to himself,

added extensions to Sabre's hair and it had never looked better. It was super thick, super long, and flowing. Sabre was delighted because everyone thought it was really all her hair.

The stage manager came in and informed Sabre that it was time for her to go on. She took one last sip of tea and followed him out of the greenroom to the stage. Sabre stood there anticipating the first strains of the track. The curtain went up, and she transformed into an entirely different personality.

"I'm so in love with you. I'll do whatever you want me to because I want to be yours." She sang from deep down within her soul like she meant it. When she completed the song, her face was wet with tears. She crumpled into a ball and dropped to the floor. The audience gave her a standing ovation. Sabre couldn't speak or think. She had emptied herself completely. She felt reborn, brand new. The stage manager tapped her on the shoulder, and she rose to her feet. She was glad he was there to lead her back to the greenroom, so she didn't have to think.

Mimi grabbed Sabre and hugged her when she walked into the room. For the first time in her young life, she didn't feel repulsed because someone touched her. "You were fantabulous." When Mimi finally released her there were tears in her clear blue eyes.

"She created the fantasy," Sabre heard Eduardo say.

Sabre smiled as Dawn pushed her into the dressing room and handed her the cherry and black halter top she would wear over cropped jeans with black beaded stilettos. The top was really cute on Sabre, who made a mental once again to get herself some implants. Eduardo whisked her hair up into a ponytail with bangs across her face. Dawn handed her a large pair of gold hoop earrings that almost touched her shoulders. Lolita, her makeup artist, was a soft-spoken Filipino young lady who could beat a face. She touched up Sabre's lipstick and back onstage she went. When Tyra introduced her, she strutted down that runway like a model at the Collections.

Tyra greeted her warmly as the audience continued to cheer. *They really do love me,* Sabre thought as she looked out at the audience into a sea of faces.

"Thank you," Sabre said ever so sweetly. The applause finally subsided, and the interview began.

Tyra started her first question right away. "What was it like working with a fabulous producer like Jamil?"

"Jamil changed my life," Sabre solemnly said.

She thought about the diamond he had custom designed for her, and a lump came in her throat. She reached up to touch it, but Dawn made her take it off. She wasn't having that blingy shit interfere with her outfit. "Jamil taught So Fine the business of the business. He recorded our album that went platinum."

"Y'all remember 'First Kiss'?" Sabre grinned when the audience cheered. When she sang a bit of the hook, everyone joined in. "That was Jamil, y'all. May he rest in peace." It was actually Nina and Char, but nobody wanted to hear about them.

A clip of So Fine performing on the VH1 Divas special providing backup vocals for Topaz was shown next. Sabre felt her demons stirring within because she knew a question about Topaz would be asked. She fought the urge to yell "fuck that old bitch" as she smiled ever so sweetly.

"Meeting Topaz was awesome. Our manager went to high school with Topaz's cousin, Nina. When we auditioned, Topaz was there. She invited us to her house and gave us lots of advice. I'm even wearing her dress in that clip. It was So Fine's first television performance. When I had that dress on, I knew I was a diva too." Sabre grinned. She was really enjoying herself.

"I felt so fortunate to work with Jamil because I was always a huge fan of Topaz's. He produced her hits and then he produced our hits. When I was a little girl, I'd read the credits on her CD and dream about being a star with my own CD. My dream came true." Sabre looked into the camera and smiled as prettily as she could.

Let the bitch ever say I stole her fucking dress after this and she'll look like a damn fool, Sabre thought as she continued the interview.

Tyra chatted with Sabre like they were girlfriends hanging out on the sofa in front of the TV with a bowl of popcorn. Sabre was really comfortable.

Mimi also secured a layout in a holiday edition of *Seventeen.* With Tyra's connections in the fashion industry, the show's producers were able to get a photo from the shoot. There was a collective gasp throughout the audience when the photo appeared on the monitors. Sabre was breathtakingly gorgeous in a midnight blue party dress accented with bold silver jewelry. With silver lipstick and dark smoky eyes, she was almost unrecognizable and looked like another person . . . extremely sophisticated and very worldly.

"Sure, I have a couple of hidden talents," Sabre confessed to Tyra, and giggled. "Watch this." The camera went in for a close-up as Sabre stuck her tongue on her nose. Then she moved off the sofa and did a full split, which drew howls and cat whistles from the audience.

"You guys are funny," Sabre said, and laughed. "I had to do splits because I was a cheerleader." After she performed her smash hit single, Sabre's segment was over.

When Sabre arrived backstage, Eduardo ran up to her.

"You are such a star, Miss Thing. I bow humbly before you."

"Ahhhh," the rest of Sabre's glam squad chorused as Eduardo handed her a rose.

"Thank you, guys. You're the best team in the world." Sabre was sweeter than sugar.

"Girlfriend, when you did that split I said, oh no, she didn't. You're going to have every man on the planet groveling at your feet. I can't stand that much competition," Eduardo declared as he tried to focus the attention back on himself.

"She going to have the universe groveling at her feet. I hear Oprah calling, darling, because you just became an OPP." Mimi smiled proudly.

"What's an OPP?" Lolita asked quietly.

"Oh, chile, where were you?" Eduardo was in the middle of the group gyrating his hips. "Everybody knows OPP means other people's puss . . ."

"Don't say it," Dawn cut in. "Boy, you are so nasty. We can't take you nowhere. Cuttin' up like this at *The Tyra Banks Show*."

"Aw, hell. Let's call Miss Tyra in here and ask her because you know girlfriend knows what it means." Eduardo grinned.

"Well, it certainly doesn't mean other people's puss or whatever it was you were about to say," Mimi chided while the others burst into laughter. "What?" She stared at them with a blank expression on her face.

"It means other people's property. It's from an old song by Naughty by Nature," Dawn explained quietly. "Eduardo was just being his usual nasty self."

Mimi looked totally irritated with the glam squad. She turned to Sabre and focused her attention solely on her. "Well, in this case, it doesn't mean any of that. It means Oprah's personal friend, which Tyra definitely is and you will be too." She put her arm around Sabre and led her to the door. "Come on. Let's go have a drink and celebrate. Dawn can drop those things by your place."

Everyone had to hug and kiss Sabre before she could leave. Mimi stood by the door like a watchdog, waiting with a smile plastered on her face. After all, she would be leaving with the star, not them. Their work was done.

"Make sure you do something I would do." Eduardo laughed happily.

"Mimi, can you hook me up with an organization that does stuff for breast cancer? My grandmother died from breast cancer and I'd really like to do something to help them out in memory of my grandmother," Sabre asked as Mimi drove them down Melrose in her BMW to their next destination.

"Oh, sweetie. I'm so sorry." Mimi turned her big blue eyes on Sabre when they paused in traffic. "There are lots of things we can find for you to do like the Revlon walk that Halle does every year."

"That sounds interesting. I'd like to do something else, something different." Sabre thought about the

Chocolate Affair that the "Black Friends" recently held but decided against mentioning it.

"I'll do some research. We'll come up with something absolutely perfect." Mimi did a U-turn on Melrose and stopped the car in front of a nondescript building with a line of people waiting to go inside. A parking attendant opened the door.

"You've been to Dolce before, haven't you?" Mimi asked as they walked right inside. Sabre looked blank so Mimi kept talking. "Ashton Kutcher is one of the owners. You do know who he is, don't you?"

Sabre resisted the urge to kick Mimi's ass right there in the middle of Dolce. Instead she ignored her. *Do I know who Ashton Kutcher is? Stupid ass bitch.* But Mimi was much too valuable to her, so she focused on the black leather tablecloths covering the table in the booth.

The dimly lit restaurant was noisy, but Sabre immediately loved its clublike atmosphere. She eagerly opened the menu the waiter placed in front of her. Much to her chagrin, it was written in Italian, and what few words there were in English she couldn't understand. *Don't they have any cheeseburgers in this fucking place?* Sabre continued flipping through the menu, frustrated. She couldn't even buy a clue. She tossed her menu back on the table and looked up to see Jennifer Aniston and her date being seated at a nearby table.

"Is that the girl from *Friends* that was married to Brad Pitt?" Sabre tried her best not to yell.

"Yes." Mimi smiled and closed her menu. "What do you want to eat?"

"I'm not hungry," Sabre lied. She hadn't eaten all

day because she was nervous about doing Tyra's show and now her stomach was growling.

"Sure you are," Mimi replied, taking charge as usual. When the waiter came she ordered salmon for herself, spaghetti with seafood for Sabre, Caesar salad, and chocolate soufflé with vanilla bean ice cream for them to share. "Diddy's here with a bunch of friends. We'll have to go to the Hamptons to one of his parties," Mimi offered. "I want you to come here as often as you can so you can be photographed and written about in the tabloids. Bring your friends."

Maybe I can bring Victor here. Sabre tentatively cut into the pasta covered with white sauce. She had never eaten spaghetti that wasn't drenched in red tomato sauce. She was surprised when she actually liked it. She would have to get the name of the dish from Mimi before she came again.

Her mind drifted to Sky. *This would be the perfect spot for us to have drinks and talk to all the rich cuties.* But she hadn't spoken to Sky since they had lunch at The Ivy with Nina. She knew she had behaved like a real bitch, and now she was sorry. It would be a miracle if Sky even spoke to her. *Maybe we can be stars together. I can't always hang out with Mimi.*

A waiter brought the soufflé and served it. Sabre had never tasted anything as good as that soufflé in her life. She finished her portion before she realized it and caught herself eyeing Mimi's, who was sending text messages on her BlackBerry. She pushed the plate across the table to Sabre.

"Here sweetie, finish mine. You're the one with the trainer."

"No thanks, Mimi. I can't eat another bite." Sabre

wanted the rest of that soufflé badly, but she wasn't eating anyone's leftovers again, not even Mimi's. She did enough of that when she was in foster care. Now she was a bona fide A-list star and everyone knew it. She had fought all of her life and survived. *I made it.* The realization suddenly hit her. *Like Grandma always said, cream rises to the top.*

Chapter 13

Nina rolled up to The Diamond in her Range Rover, pulled into the lot, and parked as far away as she could from the building. She reached in her bag and pulled out the plastic baggie of chronic she just purchased and rolled herself a blunt. She looked around to be sure no one was watching when she lit it and took a big hit.

Her BlackBerry buzzed and vibrated, but she ignored it. "Can't a sista just get a few minutes to herself?" Nina yelled at the device. The day of Sky's showcase had finally arrived, and she wanted to be ready for anything. She inhaled one last time and carefully extinguished the marijuana cigarette. Waves of guilt flooded her heart and mind as she found a small container of air freshener and sprayed the car. She hadn't been high since the day she became a wife and mother. *No more after the showcase*, she had promised herself. *It'll all be over after tonight.* She rolled down the windows and sprayed Marc Jacobs in her hair and on her hands and clothing.

The BlackBerry vibrated again, and this time she answered.

"Nina." It was Kenjay, Sky's young manager, who was also a rapper. He came to the studio one night while Missy Elliott was laying down tracks, trying to talk Missy into listening to his CD and Nina into giving him a deal. Kenjay said he was the next Jay-Z, but his rhymes were tired and his beats and flow were terrible. So he called himself a manager, ordered business cards, and became a permanent fixture in Sky's life. He was also from Brooklyn and grew up in her hood. Sky had been lonely ever since Sabre dissed her, so Kenjay quickly became her new best friend.

"What is it now, Kenjay?" He'd called on Nina incessantly during the last few weeks. The jury was still out deciding if he was more of a hindrance than a help.

"I need to get ten more of my peeps in the showcase."

"Ten? Are you crazy? We're over capacity already."

"But I gotta get 'em in."

"Who are these people, Kenjay?"

"Some of my boys are flying in from New York. They've all got major connections in the biz."

"What kind of connections?"

"One of 'em did some work with Keyshia Cole. He said she's looking for an opening act for her tour."

"I haven't heard anything about Keyshia Cole going on tour, although it would be an excellent opportunity for Sky."

"That's why I gotta get my boy in tonight."

"A'ight, Kenjay, this better be legit. Call Anita and tell her I said to put them on the guest list."

"Cool. I'm out."

Nina clicked off and her phone rang again. "Talk," she answered dryly.

"It's Kyle, your husband. Remember me?"

"Hey, honey." Nina smiled into the phone. "You're coming tonight, right?"

"I might."

"Kyle, please come. Sky's gonna knock this one out of the ballpark, to use one of your sports analogies. You have to be here."

There was a long silence before he spoke. "I'll be there."

"Okay, baby. I'll see you later. I love you," Nina added sincerely, but he had already hung up the phone. She sat there thinking about her husband. Somehow things had really gone south in her marriage. Kyle would never hang up on her without saying good-bye or cracking one of his dumb jokes. *I'll take him away for some alone time as soon as all of this is over,* she promised, and typed a reminder to check into tickets for Hawaii and Jamaica.

Nina grabbed her briefcase and a few other bags and slid out of the truck. She thought she had lost her buzz until she felt a little off balance as she pulled open the door to the restaurant. Jade was in deep conversation with one of the finest black men Nina had ever seen. A smile lit up Jade's face as soon as she saw Nina.

"Here's Nina now. This is her event tonight, and I want everything a thousand percent right. It's a very important showcase for Revelation Music." Jade spoke with authority. "This is Greggo, Nina. He's The Diamond's new restaurant manager."

Greggo was a tall, handsome Jamaican man with smooth, dark chocolate skin and beautiful white teeth.

He shook Nina's hand. "Everything is under control and running right on schedule."

Nina watched him walk away. "Damn, girl. Where'd you find him? He is fine as shit."

Jade's eyes widened, surprised by Nina's language. "Greggo's my cousin. Why are you talking like that? I should wash your mouth out with soap."

"I'm sorry, girl. It's from being in the studio with those hip-hop producers."

"Just watch the expletives. Next thing I'll be using them, and you know how Sean is. Sometimes I think I'm living with my father."

"I hear you, girl, but that's just his way of loving you. And Kyle *is* his older brother." Nina laughed and Jade joined in.

"You're in an awfully good mood. You sounded so stressed when we spoke earlier." Jade led her to a table and placed a plate of assorted rolls in front of her.

"Just lettin' off a little steam. I had to chill before I blew a gasket. I've been stressed about this showcase for weeks."

"Well, you can relax now."

"I won't relax until Sky's CD is in the store and at number one on *Billboard*'s Hot 100."

Nina was just about to bite into a roll when her cell rang. She groaned and looked at the display. "It's Sky. I'd better take it." She spoke into the headpiece. "What's going on, Sky?"

"Nina, my clothes for the showcase don't fit," Sky yelled.

"What do you mean your clothes don't fit?" Nina yelled back. "I saw you in them the other day and you looked wonderful."

"I got my period today. I'm really bloated and I can't zip up my pants." Sky was crying hysterically.

"Calm down, Sky. Call Kenjay and have him take you shopping," Nina commanded.

"I don't want to go shopping with Kenjay. He doesn't know anything about fashion. Can't you take me?"

Nina let out a long sigh. "I have to arrange the seating for the show, Sky. Isn't there anyone else you can call?"

"I'll take her shopping," Jade offered.

Nina focused on Jade. "You have a restaurant to run. You can't go shopping."

"That's why I hired Greggo. It'll be fun."

"Okay." Nina resumed her conversation with Sky. "Jade's gonna help you pick out something."

Sky sniffed and blew her nose. "Is she the pretty black Chinese girl who handpainted our jeans for the So Fine showcase?"

"That's her, but Jade's not Chinese."

"I loved those jeans. I still have mine," Sky continued.

Nina clicked off her BlackBerry and looked at Jade. "I have been putting out fires all day long. I put one out and another is already blazing."

"How do you say it? I got this." Jade smiled again and Nina teared up. "Aw, honey. Everything's gonna be just fine."

"You don't know how hard things have been," Nina cried. "I've been in the studio for weeks. Kyle's mad at me. I haven't spent any time with Niki, and Mr. Katz is just waiting for me to fuck up so he can fire me."

Jade was silent as she rubbed Nina's back. Nina reached into her handbag and took a credit card out of her wallet.

"Girl, put that thing away. I told you, I got this."

"You're the best friend in the world. I could have never done this showcase without you." Tears streamed out of Nina's eyes.

"Just don't stay out all night again without telling Kyle."

"You know about that?"

"You know there are no secrets between the Ross brothers."

That's what you think, Nina almost said.

"Sit here, do your seating, and take your calls. I'll be back with your superstar artist." Jade grinned.

"Jade, don't let Sky talk you into any of that tacky hip-hop shit."

"I got this, girl." Jade was out the door.

Nina's focus had been solely on Sky, and now the significance of the event hit her like a ton of bricks as she looked over all the RSVPs—Big Boy at Power 106, the hottest hip-hop station on the planet. Everyone wanted to be on Big Boy's show. Dre and the Game, Lil Jon, E-40, and Eve were just a few of the celebrities attending. *Billboard, Vibe, The Source,* and *XXL* were also on the list.

Tonight isn't about Sky or me, but Jamil, Nina realized. People were coming to support Jamil and the new venture that would carry on his musical legacy. Sky and Nina had been given the opportunity of a lifetime.

Nina was shaking when she left Greggo to finish the seating arrangements. She snuck back out to her truck to finish off the blunt. Her nerves were fried and she needed to chill. Surprisingly her phone was quiet.

When she returned to the restaurant she was nicely buzzed. Jade and Sky walked in right behind her. Nina followed them into Sky's dressing room so the hairstylist could put a few curls in her hair.

"Where's my tea?" Sky demanded. It was more than obvious that she was nervous. "I need tea. I have to warm up my voice."

There were no beverages or food in the dressing room, only a huge bouquet of flowers.

"Sky needs tea. And there's no food in the dressing room," Nina barked at Greggo. "Where's the food for the dressing room?"

"There was no food or tea ordered for the dressing room," Greggo replied.

"Singers always need tea before a performance." Nina looked at Greggo like he was an idiot. "Even if they don't drink the damn tea, it's always there."

"Then that request should have been included in the artist's rider," Greggo fired back smoothly.

"Didn't you get a rider?"

"If we had, we wouldn't be having this conversation."

"What's going on?" Jade walked up as things continued to escalate between Nina and Greggo.

"There's no tea or food in Sky's dressing room," Nina repeated.

"We can fix that. Greggo, have one of the girls take a teapot of hot water, tea bags . . ."

"Honey," Nina cut in.

"And honey into the dressing room," Jade requested.

"Those things should have been there in the first place," Nina snapped.

"What about my sound check, Nina? I haven't had a sound check." Sky looked beautiful in the Versace dress and shoes that Jade had helped her pick out, but she still seemed to be coming unglued with every passing minute.

"I'm going to kill Kenjay's fucking inexperienced ass," Nina yelled. "He's supposed to be handling these things, not me." Nina took out her BlackBerry. "Kenjay, where the hell are you?"

"I'm just leaving the airport. I'll be there in a few."

"Get your ass over here now and take care of your artist," Nina ordered.

"I'm on it."

"What do you need to do a sound check, Nina?" Jade asked calmly.

"The sound engineer and Sky."

"He's here. Let's do it now."

Nina dug in her briefcase. "Thank God I brought copies of the tracks."

People were beginning to arrive when Sky did her sound check. Jamil's mom, Janice, arrived with friends and family members. "I am so excited about this evening, Nina." Janice kissed and hugged her. "People have been calling me all day."

Nina smiled warmly. "Tell me about it."

"Everything looks perfect. Jamil would be so proud."

Kyle came in with Germain, and Nina went to greet him. "Hi, honey. You came." She kissed and hugged her husband. "I'm so glad to see you, baby."

"What about me? You don't see me standing here?" Germain teased.

"Hey you." Nina hugged Germain. "Where's your wifey?"

"She's a little under the weather, but she sent me to represent." Germain's smile could melt ice.

Sure she's under the weather. Nina knew how Topaz

could be when she didn't want to do something, but Nina couldn't believe that Topaz didn't show up for the showcase. *She should be here to support Jamil. He signed her to her first deal.*

"You handsome gentlemen are sitting at my table." Nina pointed at a table in front, next to Janice Winters.

Sabre came in with Dr. Lawrence. Missy showed up unexpectedly with a small entourage. She was in town and wanted to see Sky perform live.

"Oh my God," Nina whispered to herself. *Celebrities are showing up that didn't RSVP.*

She found VIP seats for everyone, then 50 Cent rolled in with a large group. He had two reasons for coming. He was one of Jamil's friends and he had heard about the restaurant.

Nina went back into Sky's dressing room grinning ear to ear. "It's standing room only. You'll never believe who came."

"Who?" Sky demanded.

"50, Missy, Dre, The Game . . ."

"50 Cent is here?" Sky's mouth dropped open in surprise. "I love him. I can't believe he came to see me."

"He's here." Nina smiled.

"Nina, you'd better come out here." Jade was at the door again. "Kenjay is here with about twenty people and there's no more room anywhere."

"Leave his tired ass outside. I don't have any more time to waste on his incompetent ass. It's showtime, Sky." Nina was ordering people around like the commander and chief. She finally joined Kyle at their table. As the houselights dimmed, she could hear Kenjay outside yelling.

"I know somebody betta let me up in this piece or there won't be a show tonight. I'll blow the mother-fucker up."

Nina closed her eyes and prayed security would keep him outside as Sky walked onto the stage. Her background singers were in position and the track was bumpin'. Sky danced around and stepped up to the mike. She looked out into the crowd and saw Dre and The Game, then looked down at 50 and caught the worse case of stage fright. She began to sing and her voice screeched—like fingernails on a chalkboard.

"She sounds terrible. What's up with your artist?" Kyle whispered.

"I don't know." Nina felt herself shaking. "She must be nervous."

"Nervous? That girl can't sing. I tried to tell you that, but you weren't listening to me. I still can't be-lieve you passed on Topaz. You don't know what the hell you're doing, do you?"

Someone let Kenjay inside. He was at the bar yelling for a waitress.

"Can a real playa get a bottle of Cris up in this motherfucker?" Kenjay was obviously drunk. Nina was so embarrassed she wanted to hide under the table. He spotted Nina and headed in her direction. "What's up with you not lettin' me in, bitch?" Kenjay stood there glaring at her as Kyle stood up, towering over the diminutive wannabe rapper.

"Bitch? There are no bitches in here, son." Most people forgot about Sky and focused on the men. Their drama was way more exciting.

"You apologize to my wife right now before I wipe up the floor with your ass," Kyle continued.

"It's okay, Kyle. Really. Kenjay's drunk." Nina tried

to whisper. She knew most of the younger guys were
packing. They wouldn't think twice about pulling a
gun out and firing it.

"Shut up, Nina. I'm handling this. He's gonna be re-
spectful to you, and he's gonna respect my brother's
club." Kyle had never spoken to her in that tone.

Meanwhile, Sky sang every note but the right one.

"You betta listen to your wife, punk. Don't be tryin'
to be supaman and get yo ass smoked."

"Kyle," Nina whispered. "Let it go."

"I said apologize to my wife, man." Kyle had a wild,
crazed look in his eyes.

"I ain't apologizing to nobody, punk."

Without another word, Kyle grabbed Kenjay by the
collar and dragged him out of the club. Despite the
scuffle, Sky was the consummate professional and
continued singing. However, no one could see past her
horrible singing to admire her professionalism. Eve
was shaking her head.

"Damn, I thought baby girl could sing. Are you sure
this is one of Jamil's artists?" Big Boy asked Nina.

After Sky completely massacred the first song there
was a trickle of applause. Someone was being very polite. Sky took a drink of water and adjusted her microphone.

"As if that's going to help her nonsingin' ass sing
any better," Nina heard someone say that sounded like
Sabre.

Kyle returned to the table and looked at Nina.
"What kind of operation are you running?"

"I should have ordered additional security. I wasn't
thinking," Nina replied quietly.

"You've been doing a lot of that lately."

"What?"

"Not thinking."

Mr. Katz got up from the table. "I've seen enough of this."

A few other people also left, but most stayed until the end. Janice was the gracious hostess and thanked everyone for coming. It did turn into a party after the deejay played songs from the list Janice compiled of Jamil's greatest hits. Jade instructed the staff to serve the Cristal and food. Nobody was turning down free food and alcohol no matter how bad the entertainment. Kenjay, totally unconcerned that Sky was crying hysterically in the dressing room and refused to come out or that he had made a fool of himself, took advantage of the star-studded audience and ran around passing out his CDs to anyone who would take them, while making sure he stayed clear of Kyle.

"The night was a complete disaster," the review in the *Hollywood Reporter* began. "Superstar producer Jamil Winters would turn over in his grave at what neophyte CEO Nina Ross promised would be the continuation of Winters' legendary musical dynasty. Ross, however, did get one thing right; it truly was an evening of dynasty, because that's just what Sky Jackson, the label's launch artist, did on stage . . . die nastily. And it wasn't because of the old-fashioned barroom brawl that broke out during Jackson's lackluster performance when Ross's husband defended her honor. It was from the worst singing anyone ever heard. On the contrary, The Diamond did serve up some of the best gumbo and fried chicken I ever ate that was . . . definitely to die for."

Chapter 14

Topaz brushed Baby Doll's blond hair until it glistened, then pulled it into a ponytail and fastened it with her favorite rhinestone clip while Niki watched. Topaz scooped a dab of Brilliant on her fingers and rubbed it on her daughter's hair.

"There, don't you look beautiful for your Jack and Jill photographs." Topaz smiled. "Okay, your turn, Niki."

Baby Doll got off the stool in Topaz's dressing room and watched Niki climb up. Topaz ran a comb through Niki's dark brown hair with golden highlights. She couldn't help admiring the little girl's copper skin and hair, thinking it was the exact same color as her and Nina's Aunty Lynn, their mothers' eldest sister.

"I met Daddy at my Jack and Jill cotillion when I was eighteen." Topaz smiled as she reflected. She took a framed photo off the dressing table and handed it to Niki.

"Let me see." Baby Doll snatched the photograph from Niki. "He's my daddy, not yours."

"Turquoise Gradney. That wasn't nice. Give that back to your cousin and apologize at once."

"But he isn't her daddy, he's mine," Baby Doll protested as a scowl took over her pretty face.

"I don't care. Do what I said." Topaz continued combing Niki's hair.

"No."

"Do you want me to spank you?" Topaz combed Niki's hair into a ponytail identical to Baby Doll's.

"You never spank me, Mommy." Baby Doll laughed. "You always get Daddy to do it and he just taps me on the leg." Baby Doll smiled while she continued to look at the photograph. "You look real pretty, Mommy. See, Niki?"

Topaz smiled at the photograph Baby Doll held up in front of her and Niki. "I did look pretty, didn't I?"

"Yes, Aunty." Topaz finished Niki's hair and kissed her on the cheek. Baby Doll handed the photo to Niki and squeezed herself in between Niki and Topaz.

"I want a kiss, too, Mommy."

Topaz kissed Baby Doll and smiled at both girls. "Okay, we'd better get moving so we're not late for the tea." Topaz took a pink silk dress off of a hanger and helped Baby Doll into it. The dress was custom designed especially for the tea. She smiled at her thin, straight frame. She would be tall and leggy one day with the perfect body structure for strutting the catwalks of Paris and Milan; however, eight-year-old Baby Doll had her heart set on becoming a singer like Topaz, even though as old folks said, "She couldn't carry a tune in a bucket."

Niki also had a pink dress just like Baby Doll's. Topaz had the tailor duplicate Baby Doll's because it would be one less thing for the girls to fight over. Nina would have taken Niki to the tea, but ever since the showcase, she was holed up in her bedroom in Malibu and asked Topaz to take Niki for her. It was actually Kyle who called and made the request. Nina hadn't spoken to Topaz since their meeting.

Topaz smiled as she slid the dress on Niki because the child already had a booty and a waistline . . . and she could sing. Niki started singing before she could talk or walk. Topaz tried not to laugh as she thought about Niki onstage singing "My milkshake brings all the boys to the yard" and talking about being so "booty-licious." Kyle would have a stroke.

She helped the ladies into white patent leather Mary Janes and gave them each a pair of white gloves and summer white Louis Vuitton purses that Nina had sent over.

"Aunty Nina sent you guys those purses. I think she said there's some Hello Kitty stuff inside. You guys can play with it until I get dressed, and don't get anything on those dresses." Topaz tried to sound like she meant business although the girls knew she was a pushover. Germain and Nina were the disciplinarians. Kyle was also a softie, like her.

Topaz slipped into the pink and gold silk Roberto Cavalli suit she had purchased for the occasion. Her hair and makeup were done by her personal stylists at the house. The elegant updo was perfect. She carefully placed a pink hat on her head and slipped on a pair of pink and gold Jimmy Choos.

"I look good." She twirled in the mirror, admiring her new physique in the new outfit. Her hourglass figure curved perfectly in all the right places again. He had taken just enough off her waistline, and her breasts were firm and high, standing at attention. "My man does fabulous work." No wonder every woman in Holly-wood—red, black, brown, yellow, and white—was trying to get an appointment. His consults were booked at least six months in advance and he rarely, if ever, had a cancellation.

Topaz, feeling too beautiful, switched down the stairs to Baby Doll's Cheetah Girls bedroom where the little girls had managed to sit still and not get anything on their dresses. "Let's go, little beauties. Our public awaits us."

Topaz led them out to her Rolls Royce limo, trailing the scent of Escada wherever she went. Her driver, Marko, got out and opened the door and assisted each of them into the car.

"You ladies look mighty fine today. Mighty fine," Marko told them.

"Thank you," they all chorused. It was obvious the girls felt beautiful, too.

"Marko, stop by Dr. Gradney's office, please. I need to see my husband for a quick minute," Topaz requested.

Minutes later, the limo pulled up in front of Germain's office in the Cedars tower. "Come on, ladies. Let's go show Daddy how beautiful we all look." As Topaz led them into the building, everyone turned around to stare. She walked into Germain's office where his secretary informed her that he was in the middle of a consult. They were just about to go into his office when he came out of one of the examining rooms.

"Daddy." Baby Doll was the first one in his arms while Niki stood there shyly holding Topaz's hand.

"I know I am a blessed man. Look at all these beautiful angels God gave me." Germain couldn't stop grinning. "You come on over here and give me a hug, too, Miss Niki."

Niki went to Germain and couldn't stop giggling when he gave her a bear hug. "Hug Aunty, Uncle G."

"Come here, woman." He took Topaz into his arms and gave her a kiss that left her reeling. She was still in his arms when the door to one of the examination rooms opened and Sabre walked out.

"Dr. Gradney, I'd like to go ahead with the surgery as soon as I can," Sabre said, not realizing who Topaz was until Baby Doll recognized her.

"Hi, Sabre. I didn't know you knew my daddy. I love your new CD."

"Hi, Sabre." Niki let go of Topaz's hand and stood next to Baby Doll.

"Hi, Baby Doll. Hi, Niki." Sabre bent down and hugged each of the girls while Topaz stared at her with eyes as cold and hard as cat's-eye marbles.

"That's right, I forgot all of y'all know each other." Germain smiled warmly, always the charming southern gentleman.

"We've met," Topaz offered coolly while Sabre was at a total loss for words.

Sabre stood only inches away from Topaz, the closest she had been to her in months. She was still awed by the veteran singer's presence. Something way down deep inside of Sabre told her that no matter how many records she ever sold, she would never be as beautiful, talented, poised, or confident. Topaz exuded power from within that money couldn't buy.

All of a sudden, Sabre felt like the little girl who used to play with the blond wig, pretending to be a singer. She looked at the beautiful woman in the pink and gold designer suit and wanted her life more than anything. She was married to the finest man on the

planet who was also a famous plastic surgeon. She also
had a pretty little girl and a very handsome son. It was-
n't fair how some people just got everything. Sabre felt
her demons rising, but they were overcome by her awe
and admiration for Topaz, which rendered her speechless.

"The ladies are on their way to a Jack and Jill tea for
mothers and daughters," Germain said proudly.

What the fuck is a Jack and Jill tea? Sabre wondered,
angry because she hadn't been invited and also because there was no beautiful mother for her to go with
if she had received an invitation. She stood there with a
silly smile plastered on her face.

"What are *you* doing here?" Topaz asked coolly.

"Getting a consult." Sabre found her voice.

Topaz looked Sabre up and down and wondered
why she had felt so insecure. "Ladies, we'd better get
going. We don't want to be late." Topaz turned and
headed for the door until Germain's Afro-centric secretary begged them to take a picture.

"That's a great idea." Germain stood, flanked by his
favorite ladies. For one of the photos, he picked up
Niki and held her in his arms because she was so little.

"Okay, we have to go now," Topaz repeated. "Baby,
are you done for the day?" she asked as she kissed
Germain softly on the lips.

"If I can find one of my anesthesiologists, I'm going
to do Miss Cruz's procedure."

"Okay, baby. Don't forget we're going out to dinner. I love you."

"Bye, Sabre." Niki waved. "Bye, Uncle G."

"Bye, Daddy." Baby Doll blew a kiss at her father.
"Bye, Sabre."

Sabre felt some of the ice around her heart melt as

she waved at the girls. For the first time in her life, she wondered what it would be like to have a family.

Topaz and the girls stole the show at the annual mother–daughter tea the moment they walked into the Beverly Hills Hotel. Topaz received compliment after compliment about her beautiful daughters. Baby Doll eventually grew tired of telling everyone Niki was not her sister but her cousin.

"I'm bored, Mommy. This food is nasty." Baby Doll tossed a half-eaten watercress sandwich back onto her plate. "Can we leave now and go get something else to eat?"

"Aunty, can we get Chinese food?" Niki asked sweetly. "Please?"

"Yeah, Mommy. Chinese food," Baby Doll agreed.

"Okay, I'll ask Daddy and Chris to meet us at Mr. Chow's." Topaz took out her cell, made the call, and hung up smiling. "Daddy and Chris are coming."

"Yay," the girls chorused.

Topaz grabbed the photographs of her with Baby Doll and Niki taken by a professional photographer and left. Her limo was waiting, and they arrived at Mr. Chow's in no time, where the paparazzi were all over them once they were out of the car. Germain wasn't at the restaurant yet, so Marko whisked them safely inside where the romantic lighting set the mood for an intimate family dinner.

Topaz was excited. She couldn't remember the last time the family dressed up and went out to dinner. It was so nice to have Niki there too. She felt Niki's little hand slide into hers, and her heart melted. But Niki had that effect on everyone . . . she was Nina and Kyle's little sweetheart. Restaurant patrons couldn't help watching as Topaz was led to one of the best tables in the house. Topaz had been a regular at Mr. Chow's for years and the staff knew her well. She usually ordered the same thing: wonton soup, the Peking duck with crispy pancakes and plum sauce, black pepper lobster, fried rice, and veggies. They were munching on wontons and shrimp dumplings when the guys arrived looking very handsome in suits with ties.

"That was perfect timing." Topaz smiled at Germain and Chris, who kissed everyone, then sat down and dug in.

"You look so beautiful, Mother." Chris was already a charmer like his daddy. "I love that hairstyle. Is it new?"

"Sophia tried something new. I really like it." Topaz smiled at her firstborn. He was growing up so quickly. The girls in his class were already calling the house for him. She watched him serve Niki more rice and lobster. He was such a little gentleman—a kind, sensitive child.

Baby Doll, already done with her meal, was talking to Germain. A waiter brought Germain a bottle of Cristal, popped the cork, and poured him a glass. He approved the champagne and served Topaz a glass, which she lifted to make a toast.

"To my wonderful husband and beautiful family. I love you."

"I love you," everyone chorused.

"May I taste the champagne, Dad?" Chris focused his golden eyes on his father.

"Sure, son." Germain poured a small amount into his glass.

"Me too, Daddy." Baby Doll wasn't about to be left out.

"Me too, Daddy, I mean Uncle G," Niki said, and smiled.

"See what you started." Topaz smiled as she watched Germain pour the girls a spot of Cristal.

"They all have the same eyes and they ganged up on me." Germain laughed. "I'm always outnumbered."

"I know," Topaz agreed. "Those eyes are the weirdest thing."

"What's so weird about it? They got them from you." Germain was still eating Peking duck. He rolled some of it up into one of the thin pancakes and dabbed it with plum sauce. "Chinese tacos."

"I was just thinking how much Niki looks like my mom's oldest sister, Lynn. You know who I'm talking about. She lives in China. Her husband works at the American Embassy in intelligence."

"I remember her." Niki was sitting beside Germain, and he ran his hand across her hair. "But I've never seen anyone else in your family with those golden eyes but you, pretty girl."

"Uncle G." Niki rubbed his arm deeply tanned by the sun. "I don't feel well."

"What do you mean you don't feel well? Does something hurt?"

"Yes." Huge crocodile tears rolled out of Niki's eyes.

"What hurts, baby?" Germain rubbed her back.

Topaz felt a lump forming in her throat. *Not that . . . not again.*

"Everything hurts. My back, my arms, my legs . . . It hurts, Uncle G. It hurts. I want Mommy."

Topaz was already dialing Nina while Germain paid the check. It rang and rang, but there was no answer.

Everyone was silent as Chris took Baby Doll by the hand and Germain carried Niki out to the limo.

"Come on, Nina. Answer." Topaz tried Nina's cell phone several times, then called Kyle, who did answer. Topaz was doing her best to remain calm. "Niki isn't feeling well, Kyle. We're taking her to the ER at Cedars."

"I'm on my way."

Marko took everyone in the limo to Cedars, where the nurse took Niki into an examination room almost immediately.

"Her name is Kendall Nicole Ross and she has sickle cell disease," Germain informed the doctor. Germain held Niki the entire time the doctor examined her while Topaz just watched and wrung her hands. She felt so helpless.

They gave Niki an IV with medication for pain, and she fell asleep in Germain's arms. Topaz kissed Niki, and then Germain kissed her ever so gently.

"She looks like a little angel," Germain said.

She was still resting in his arms when Kyle, Sean, and Jade arrived.

"Where's Nina?" Topaz demanded.

"Your guess is as good as mine," Kyle replied. "Thanks for taking care of my baby girl, you guys. I'll take her now, Doc." Kyle took Niki from Germain, and she opened her eyes.

"Daddy. I missed you." Niki smiled at Kyle.

"I missed you, too, baby girl. You know you're my little road dog." Kyle put up a good fight against the tears while Germain was about to take Topaz and slip out of the door.

"Daddy, where's Uncle G?" Niki asked.

"I'm here, pretty girl. Right here." Germain fought against the tears that wanted to flow.

Topaz swallowed hard and quickly brushed away a tear when she heard him call Niki by the name that was exclusively for Topaz. She was such a precious, sweet little girl.

"Thank you for taking such good care of me, Uncle G." Niki reached out to hug him. "I love you."

"Me too," Germain mumbled, unable to talk, crying silently as he hugged the little girl who had quietly stolen his heart.

Chapter 15

Nina, alone in the dark, lay curled up in the middle of the California king-sized bed, listening to her BlackBerry ring. It rang until Nina finally answered. "Hello." She rolled on her back and removed the pink satin sleep mask covering her eyes.

"Nina, hi. It's Rosalyn Lawrence. How are you?"

Nina reached into her Louis Vuitton bag and pulled out a Tiffany cigarette case filled with perfectly rolled blunts. She lit one with the matching platinum lighter and inhaled.

"Nina, are you there?"

Nina held the smoke inside her lungs as long as she could and exhaled. "Yeah, I'm here. What do you want?"

"Nina, you don't sound like yourself. Are you okay?"

"I'm fine, Rosalyn. What do you want?" Nina didn't care if she sounded rude or irritated. She was in a foul mood and ready to inflict it on the first person who came her way.

"I was calling about Niki. I'm sorry to hear she wasn't feeling well. I could tell your husband was upset when he phoned Dr. Nichols, who is in Washington, DC, meeting with the Centers for Disease Control."

Nina had no idea that Niki had been sick or that Kyle tried to call Dr. Nichols. She hadn't returned anyone's calls for the last week. When Kyle refused to come to Maui with her after that embarrassing showcase, she came alone and spent the entire time in bed in an oceanfront suite at the Ritz Carlton.

"I've already spoken to my husband, and Niki's fine," Nina lied as she frantically scrolled through past calls. They were all there; numerous calls from Topaz and Kyle. She thought he was calling to make up with her, and he called to tell her that their daughter was sick. *Oh my God. I'm a terrible mother.*

"Nina, are you there?" Now Dr. Lawrence was irritated.

"I really appreciate you calling, Dr. Lawrence." Nina was just seconds away from disconnecting the call.

"Nina, you haven't heard one damn thing I said."

"Excuse you?" Nina began.

"Excuse you," Dr. Lawrence cut in. "I've been trying to tell you that according to the paperwork you and Kyle filled out when you gave blood, there is no way that you and Kyle can be Nicole's biological parents."

Nina was silent as she tried to collect her thoughts. She was too faded to think clearly, yet alone respond to the doctor's gross accusation.

"Then the paperwork must be wrong," Nina replied coolly.

"No, the paperwork is correct, because the blood types given on the paperwork match the blood that came out of you and your husband's veins."

Nina was silent as her brain raced, trying to figure out how an error of this magnitude had been made.

"There's only one thing that is incorrect. You and Kyle cannot be, nor will you ever be, Niki's biological parents. It is humanly impossible. Now you have a nice day, Mrs. Ross." Dr. Lawrence hung up before Nina could say another word.

Nina finished the blunt she was smoking, then got out of bed and pulled open the heavy drapes to reveal a magnificent day. The sky was bluer than usual, and there wasn't a cloud anywhere. The palm trees were vibrantly green; and the Pacific was a royal blue, swirling mass against the white powder sand beaches. Everything was kicked up a notch in Maui.

Nina thought about taking a book and spending the day at the beach in a cabana but decided instead to visit the spa for her favorite shea butter and warm honey wrap followed by a tropical body polish. She always made a trip to the spa whenever she was in Maui. She couldn't wait to get there because she was long overdue for a day of pampering.

Kyle bounced the basketball across the floor as he walked up to the door and knocked. He stuck his head inside the guest room located downstairs by the kitchen. Sky looked up and smiled. "Hey, Mr. Ross."

"Sky, Mr. Ross is my dad. You can call me Kyle." He smiled, and Sky couldn't help thinking how handsome he was.

"Okay, Kyle."

"Cool. I know I'm getting older, but I'm not that old yet."

Sky giggled and Kyle laughed.

"My baby girl's upstairs resting. Rosa, her nanny, is here, but I know Niki's going to want to hang out with you. Do you mind?"

"Mr. Ross, I'm sorry, Kyle. I don't mind watching Niki. I'm gonna be here anyway."

"You're here to regroup and get yourself together, not be a babysitter. Don't think you have to watch Niki."

"She's so sweet. I don't mind, really," Sky said, and smiled.

"Cool. I'm going into the city to shoot hoops with my brother and probably grab some dinner. I'll be back later on tonight. There's cash in the cookie jar and a ton of menus if you guys want to order some takeout. If you decide to use the pool or go to the beach, don't let Niki get in any water."

"Okay. Have you talked to Nina?" Sky closed her suitcase and stood up.

"Yeah. She's chilling for a few days in Maui." Kyle hated lying, but he was tired of the questions about his personal life. He hadn't spoken to Nina since she left for Hawaii. He was still angry because she chose to go to Maui without him. He had called the Ritz Carlton after she hadn't returned his calls when Niki was ill, just to be sure she was there, but hung up after the call rang through to her room.

"Oh, cool."

"Catch ya later, Miss Sky." Kyle was out the door in a flash and unlocking his Escalade parked in the driveway. Sky relaxed when she heard him drive away, happy to have the house all to herself.

Sky had been so busy preparing for the showcase, she didn't have time to look for a new place since Victor had kicked her and Sabre out. Victor had phoned

Sky on the down low and told her that she could hang out at his place as long as she needed, but Sky didn't trust Sabre or Victor after she found the knife stuck in the mattress. Who knew what type of kinky sex game the two of them had been playing, and she didn't want to get in the middle of their craziness.

Sky was surprised when her Sidekick rang, indicating she had a message. She was even more surprised when she checked it and saw the message was from Sabre.

"Long time no talk to," Sabre answered when Sky returned the call.

"I know you were at my showcase when I bombed, Sabre, so if you're calling to rub it in my face, don't bother. I know I sucked."

"I'm not calling you about the showcase. You're my girl. I just wanted us to hang out or go shopping."

"Really?"

"Really."

"Okay. I'm in Malibu. What do you want to do?"

"Malibu? What are *you* doing in Malibu?"

"I'm staying with Nina and Kyle. I'm supposed to be looking for an apartment, but I haven't had time."

"I've been busy too. I just got back from a promotional tour. It was bananas. I've got free time today. I could come to Malibu and we can look at places out there. You know we always said we were gonna buy a house in Malibu."

"We sure did, didn't we?" Sky smiled as she recalled the childhood dream. "Okay," she agreed excitedly. "See you when you get here."

Niki and Sky were eating a Thai barbecued chicken pizza from the California Pizza Kitchen when Sabre rang the doorbell. Sky went to answer it, and Niki followed her.

"Hey, Sky." Sabre walked in wearing the cutest pair of cargo pants with heels and a cowboy hat.

"Sabre." Niki ran toward her with her arms extended.

"Hi, Niki." Sabre bent down and hugged Niki. "How are you?"

Niki took Sabre by the hand. "Did you come to visit me and Sky?"

"I sure did." Strangely, Sabre was not uncomfortable holding Niki's hand. "What are you guys doing?"

"Eating pizza. You want some?" Niki offered politely.

"Girl, look at you." Sky stopped the procession back into the family room. "You got boobs."

"I sure did." Sabre grinned proudly and pulled up her top, revealing a perfect pair of C cups. "Wanna feel 'em?"

"Sabre," Sky whispered through gritted teeth, "not in front of Niki."

"Whatever." Sabre looked blank as she pulled down her top. "Dr. Gradney did them for me."

"We can talk about that later, Sabre." Sky watched Niki climb back on the sofa and continue eating pizza.

"Are you ready to go?" Sabre sat down and tapped her foot impatiently.

"I don't want to leave Niki by herself," Sky began.

"What, are you babysitting? You should have told me that before I drove all the way out here."

"Are you free tomorrow?" Sky pulled another slice of pizza out of the pie and bit into it.

"Yeah." Sabre grabbed the last slice of pizza.

"Spend the night and we can get started early. Kyle will be here, so Niki won't be alone." Sky cleaned up all of the dishes and carried them into the kitchen.

"So what are we going to do now? I didn't come out here to be bored." Sabre licked the last bit of cheese from her fingers. "You got any more pizza? I'm hungry."

"No. That was Niki's pizza. We can order some takeout. There's a bunch of menus."

"Whatever." Sabre flipped through the channels on the big screen. "I wanted to go look at houses."

"We can still look at houses. Let's go look on the Internet," Sky suggested.

"Okay." Sabre perked up immediately. "That's cool. Come on, Miss Niki."

Sky led them upstairs to Nina and Kyle's office where the computers were located.

"Look at all those books." Sabre walked over to bookcases lined with all types of books. "I love to read."

Sky watched as Niki signed onto Nina's computer while Sabre made herself comfortable on the overstuffed pillows in front of the bookcases. "You love to read?"

"Hell, yeah." Sky took a book on African art off the shelf and flipped through it. She felt like a kid in a candy store. "This is like being at the motherfuckin' library."

Sky flinched at Sabre's choice of words and looked at Niki, trying to determine if the little girl noticed Sabre's foul language. Sky looked at Sabre and immediately regretted that she invited her over. She closed her eyes, shook her head, and took a deep breath before she did a search on the Internet and found available houses and condominiums in the area. Sky pulled up house after house, most of which she knew were too expensive for Sabre to rent or buy. She glanced over at Sabre, who was still engrossed in a book. Niki went to her room to watch cartoons.

"We're in London working on T's CD. It's cold and it's been raining for days. I'm tired of hanging out in this townhouse with T and Jamil. He is such a pig. What did I ever see in him? I wish T would have this baby because she is getting on my last nerve. I miss Kyle and I want to go home."

Sabre flipped through the pages and paused to read another entry.

"T finally had the baby. I hired a midwife to help with the delivery. She had the most beautiful little girl. She popped out real quick and easy. T said she was easier than Chris and Turquoise. I was hoping T would keep the baby. But when she came out so dark, T knew she wasn't Germain's. She wanted me to put her up for adoption. At first, I thought T was playing, but she wouldn't touch the baby or even look at her. She wouldn't even feed her. So I got some formula and I'm the baby's mommy. But I can't put her up for adoption and leave her over here in this foreign country. Who knows what kind of people would adopt her? Black babies have it bad enough in America, God knows what would happen to one over here. So I made a decision. I'm going to keep the baby and raise her as my own."

"That fucking bitch," Sabre whispered, seething with anger. She flipped to yet another entry.

"The funniest thing just happened. Kyle just showed up. He said God told him I needed him. I sure did. I told him everything. He wants to marry me and we'll raise the baby as our own. We just filled out the birth certificate. Her name is Kendall Nicole Ross and Nina Beaubien Ross and Kyle Ross are her mother and father. We're going back to the States in a couple of weeks. I wonder if everyone's going to believe that I really had a baby. Now T can marry Germain and he never has to know she had a baby."

Sabre snapped the journal closed. She was still fuming. *Topaz is such a bitch. Just like my fuckin' mother and every other mother whose kids have been placed in foster care because the mommas are on drugs or running around after some stupid-ass man. Everybody thinks Topaz is so fucking sweet and so fucking perfect. I wonder what people would think if they knew she gave up her baby so she could keep her man . . . fucking bitch.*

Sabre glanced up at Sky, who was still working on the computer. With the journal in her hand, she crept downstairs and stashed it in her bag. After drinking a glass of water she went back upstairs where she paused in the doorway of Niki's room. The child was hugging her teddy bear and watching TV. *I knew there was some reason why I always loved this little girl. We're kindred spirits.*

Sabre picked Niki up, sat her in her lap, and kissed her on the cheek. "I love you, Niki."

"I love you, too, Sabre." Niki smiled at her with huge golden eyes.

Sabre felt her heart grow a little larger as she sat there holding Niki. She had never told anyone in her entire life except Grandma Marisol that she loved them. "Is this your baby?" Sabre held up a pink teddy bear that had seen better days.

"Un-huh," Niki nodded, and took the bear from Sabre.

"What's her name?"

"Teddy."

A genuine smile found its way onto Sabre's face. "My baby's name is Bear."

Sky found them watching DVDs. "Hey, girl. I found all these fabulous houses on the Internet." Sky held up a stack of paper with housing information.

"I won't be able to go house hunting tomorrow. Mimi, my publicist, called with an emergency appointment, so I'm going back to the city tonight." Sabre took the printouts from Sky and stuffed them in her bag on top of Nina's journal. "I'll look at these later."

Sky sighed with relief and climbed into bed with Niki to watch *Over the Hedge*. When Kyle returned from the city, they were both asleep.

Kyle went up to his bedroom to shower. He took off his watch and left his Nikes and socks in the middle of the floor, went into the bathroom, turned on the steam shower, and left his workout clothes in the middle of the bathroom floor. Nina wasn't around to make him pick them up so he was doing what he wanted, just like a bad little boy. He thought he heard his cell phone ring so he came out of the shower and ran smack into Nina.

"Aggggg," he yelled, standing in front of her completely nude. "You scared the mess out of me. I didn't hear you come in."

Nina just stood there staring at him with the strangest look on her face.

"Why didn't you tell me you were coming home, woman?"

"Sit down, Kyle, we need to talk. We've got a major situation on our hands."

Chapter 16

The Beverly Hills Hotel, often referred to as the Pink Palace, is located on Sunset Boulevard in the heart of Beverly Hills. Surrounded by twelve acres of lush tropical gardens and exotic flowers, it provides privacy and is one of the most beautiful hotels in the world. Also a local spot for Hollywood stargazing, it is definitely a place to be seen.

Sabre wasn't trying to be seen when she arrived at the hotel in a black stretch limo. She wore her hair pulled back in a ponytail under a white Von Dutch baseball cap, extremely dark oversized shades, very little makeup, and a pair of Guess jeans; her new boobs filled out the white Von Dutch tee very nicely. She tried to suppress a grin when she heard someone cat whistle. The valet parking attendants weren't really sure who she was, but they all agreed she had to be *somebody*.

The driver took an oversized Louis Vuitton bag out of the trunk and gave it to Sabre, who disappeared inside the hotel, then out again to a walkway that led to one of its infamous bungalows. There was no need to register at the front desk because the room key was messengered earlier that morning.

Once Sabre was safely inside the room, she slowly exhaled. There was a magnum of Cristal chilling in an ice bucket. She popped the cork, poured herself a glass, drank it quickly, and poured another. She took it with her into the marble bath, turned on the water in the tub, and splashed in some of the organic rose otto bath oil that her secret lover wanted her to use. It was sent from Neiman's for the first of their trysts. He explained that rose oil was very expensive because it was made from thousands of petals crushed at dawn. Sabre could have cared less, but the oil did leave her skin extremely soft.

She took out a black silk teddy and laid it out on the bed, undressed, and soaked her body in the rose-scented water. By the time she ordered lunch, put on makeup, and did her hair, he would be done with his eighteen holes of golf and ready for her.

Sabre enjoyed the privacy of the suite. She was totally at ease and free to be herself. No ordering or trying foods she didn't like or want to impress someone else. She unlocked the front door and went into the bathroom to blow-dry her hair. Room service would come inside, leave her tray, and take the crisp fifty-dollar bill that she tucked inside an envelope. There would be no signed room service ticket for people to gossip about. This liaison required the utmost discretion.

Sabre put one last curl in her hair and went back into the suite where her lunch from the Polo Lounge was sitting on a small linen-covered table. "Yes," she exclaimed loudly when she saw her favorite cheeseburger, fries, and three small bottles of Coke. She pried the cap off the bottle with an opener and watched it fizzle and foam as she poured it into a glass of crushed ice. "I am going to live like this forever. No more being hungry and poor ever again for Sabre."

She heard the bungalow door opening as she dumped an entire container of Heinz ketchup on the burger and fries.

"Hey, Sherwin, I'm in the bedroom eating lunch."

Sherwin Katz, head of VMG Music, walked into the bedroom and collapsed on the bed. "Hey, beautiful. What do you have there?"

"Just a cheeseburger and fries." Sabre grinned and carefully plucked a fry from her plate. "Here, Poppi, open." Sherwin obeyed her command like an excited little puppy, and she pressed the potato between his thin lips.

"That was delicious, sweetie, but you know I have to watch my cholesterol."

"I know. We can't let anything happen to my Big Poppi." Sabre grinned and he kissed her.

"Did you have time to go house hunting yet?" Sherwin talked while he undressed. He was in great shape and still very attractive for his fifty-one years. His muscles were firm and toned, and he didn't have a hint of a belly. He played golf and tennis weekly so his skin was very tanned. Sabre had only two problems with him: he was old and white, but his money was green and he was a very powerful man in the music business, and that made him irresistible.

"No, Poppi, something came up."

"I'm going to have a Realtor pick out some things for you or else you'll never get a house."

"Okay," Sabre agreed. "Maybe you'd better get me a Realtor. I want something on the beach."

"Okay, sweetie. You got it." Sherwin turned back the

covers on the king-sized bed. "And Mimi, the new publicist I hired for you? Are things working out with her?"

"Mimi's great." Sabre climbed on top of Sherwin and began massaging his chest. He reached up and grabbed her boobs and flipped her over on her back.

"Hey, these are great. We should have gotten them sooner." Sabre moved underneath his body and tried to get excited. The more Sherwin touched her, the heavier she panted and the louder she screamed.

"Oh, Poppi." She yelled at regular intervals, making sure she increased the intensity of each scream. In a matter of minutes, the ordeal was over and he rolled off her and slept heavily. Sabre sighed as she curled up into a little ball. Sherwin Katz was the nicest man she had ever known.

They would have several more sessions throughout the afternoon, then Sherwin would get on the phone and run his labels. Sabre went into the bathroom, scrubbed her face clean of makeup, and transformed herself back into the girl who had arrived at the hotel earlier.

"Bye, sweetie. I'll call you later." Sherwin kissed Sabre, and she picked up her things and left. When she stepped out of the main entrance of the hotel, her driver took her bag and assisted her into the car.

"Anywhere else today, Ms. Sabre?" Xavier looked at her in his rearview mirror.

Sabre took off the baseball cap and shook out her hair and polished her lips with a tube of pink lip gloss. "I have an appointment at Cedars." She brushed on mascara and sprayed on perfume as the limo stopped on Third Street in front of the towers. "I shouldn't be long," she told Xavier as he helped her out of the car.

Sabre signed in with the receptionist in Dr. Gradney's office and took a seat in the waiting room, where she noticed all of the artwork was by African American painters. It was the first time she had ever been to a doctor's office with paintings by black people on the walls. She saw Germain whisk by and couldn't help thinking again that he was the finest man she had ever seen. She picked up a *Black Enterprise* and read until she heard her name. A pretty young nurse with chocolate skin and braids named Denise led her into an examination room.

I wonder if he fools around. Sabre took off her sexy new Victoria's Secret Angels bra—it was so much fun wearing one now that she had something to put in it—and put on a Kente cloth dressing gown. Several minutes later, Dr. Gradney entered the room.

"Miss Sabre Cruz. How are you?" Germain gave her a smile that could melt butter, and suddenly she felt awkward and shy.

"I'm fine, Dr. Gradney." Sabre felt herself at a loss for words. No man had ever affected her that way.

Germain made notes in a chart. "Did everything heal nicely? Not having any sort of pain, are you?" He focused his hazel eyes on Sabre.

"No."

"Excellent." He instructed her to lie on the examining table and she complied, closing her eyes, anticipating the sensation of his hands on her breasts.

Sabre lay there until she heard female laughter. *What the fuck?* Her eyes popped open to see Germain coming back into her room with his nurse.

"Denise is going to keep us company while I examine you, Sabre," Germain explained. The moment he touched her she wanted to scream out . . . not from pain, but pleasure. She had always hated being touched by everyone until Germain. She found herself relaxing even with Denise in the room. He had the softest touch, and gentle but strong hands. She felt herself drifting somewhere she'd never been.

"You're good to go, Sabre." Germain smiled and wrote more notes in her chart. "Everything's healed up wonderfully. We'll see you back for another follow-up in a couple of months." He smiled again and was gone.

Sabre dressed slowly and tried to conceal her disappointment. *Why did he have to bring that damn nurse in the room?* A zillion thoughts flashed through her mind while the receptionist wrote out her next appointment on a card.

"Shopping at the Beverly Center today, Miss Sabre?" Xavier looked in the mirror trying to catch her eye. That was the usual routine after a day at the Beverly Hills Hotel.

"No thanks, X. You can just take me home." She stared out of the limo window at nothing in particular. *That bitch Topaz not only gave her baby away, but she cheated on that fine ass Germain. How could she? Spoiled-ass, stuck-up bitch. She doesn't deserve him or Niki. Why do people like her always end up with everything? Somebody needs to put her sorry ass in her place.*

The limo stopped in front of the Embassy Suites on Franklin just a little west of La Brea. Sherwin had the label find her new, temporary housing. She was only walking distance from the place she used to share with Victor. The corporate studio apartment seemed drab after the old-world glamour of the Beverly Hills Hotel, but it was clean and it was hers. Sherwin would find her a place in Malibu, hire a decorator, and she would tell them she wanted it to look like the rooms at the Pink Palace.

Sabre tossed the lingerie she had worn with Sherwin into the trash can and jumped into the shower. She liked the way the rose oil made her skin feel, but she just couldn't stand the smell of it, or Sherwin, although she'd put up with anything to ensure she was never hungry or homeless again.

She saw Bear sitting on her bed and thought about Niki and Teddy. *That was really nice of Nina and Kyle to raise her as their own. I'm glad Niki didn't get put in foster care like I did so she'll never go through none of the shit that I had to put up with.*

Sabre was just about to get into bed when she saw her mail lying on the floor. The concierge must have stuck it under the door while she was in the shower. He was sweet on her and constantly sought opportunities to have conversations with her. She picked it up and sifted through the magazines and catalogs, surprised when a handwritten envelope with a Brooklyn, New York, postmark slid out. She turned the letter over, but there was no return address.

"What the fuck is this?" she said out loud as she ripped it open.

Dear Sabre,
    I know I should have written sooner but I just wanted you to know that I think about my beautiful little girl every day. I've seen your videos and I have your CD, only no one believes you're my daughter. I'm in rehab again and as soon as I finish my treatment and get a job, maybe I can come see you. I'm really going to stay clean this time so

I can finally be the mother I should have always been. I know I have never been there the way you needed and I pray that you will find it in your heart to forgive me. I've included my address and phone number so we can keep in touch. All of your aunts, uncles, and cousins—on both sides of the family—look forward to seeing you whenever you come to Brooklyn.

I love you,
Mommy

"Family? What motherfuckin' family?" Sabre screamed. "Yo asses didn't want me, remember? Yo asses couldn't be found so I had to go in fuckin' foster care. And now yo asses want to claim me cuz I have a fuckin' record on the fuckin' charts?"

Tears streamed out of Sabre's eyes as she ripped the letter into tiny pieces and threw them into the trash can.

"You didn't want me back then and I don't want yo asses now."

She turned on her Barbie nightlight, grabbed Bear, climbed into bed, and cried herself to sleep.

Chapter 17

Production trucks lined the driveway of The Diamond as an unseasonable summer deluge pelted Los Angeles and its surrounding areas that Thursday morning.

"It Never Rains in Southern California" is the title of a popular seventies song, but the words are so untrue. Cars driving down Palawan Way actually splashed water on the sidewalk while the production crew donned bright yellow slickers, attempting to stay dry as the men ran cables from the truck into the club.

"Can you believe all of this rain on the day of 'A Topaz Night at The Diamond'?" Keisha stood in the doorway frowning at the rain. "I've never seen anything like it during the seven years we've lived in this city."

"It is pretty bad." Jade cracked the shell on a pistachio nut and thoughtfully chewed on the meat as she looked out at the dismal sky. "You know how Californians turn into the absolute worst drivers the minute one drop of rain falls." Suddenly there was the distinct sound of tires screeching as a driver stomped on the brakes, and Jade chuckled. "See what I mean?"

"I wonder if this some kind of a sign." Keisha sighed.

"A sign of what?" Jade looked at Keisha like she was crazy.

"A sign that things won't go well tonight."

"Key, you know you are tripping when you let something like that come out of your mouth." Jade cracked open another pistachio. "I'm surprised that you would even say something like that."

Keisha let out a long sigh. "You're right. It's just that I've worked on this night for months and now it rains? People hate to go anywhere here when it rains."

"Come on, girlfriend, we need to pray, because the show must go on." Jade led Keisha back into their office where the ladies grabbed hands and prayed about everything they could think of.

"I needed that." Keisha picked up a poster of Topaz with her golden locks twisted into curls. Her golden eyes and smile were magnetic.

"That is such a pretty picture of her." Jade tossed shells into the trash. "I wonder what it feels like to be the most beautiful girl in the world. It never rains on her parade even when it rains."

"Do you think Topaz doesn't have any problems? Because she does . . . lots of them."

"I know."

"Did you hear the story about the crosses?"

"I'm not sure." Jade removed a stack of posters from her chair and sat down. "What is it?"

"There was a woman who didn't like the cross she was given, so the Lord told her to pick out another one. So she goes into this room with all of these crosses.

Some were very beautiful, others were not so beautiful. Some were big, small, thorny. The woman picks out a cross encrusted with diamonds and pearls. It was blin-gin'. But she had the hardest time carrying it, so the Lord lets her choose another. She goes through this process until she finds this small plain cross that she was able to carry. And guess what?"

"What?"

"She ended up picking out her own cross again."

"Great story." Jade smiled and her eyes turned into slits. "I wouldn't want to trade my life with anyone. It's like my mom always said, the grass is always greener in someone else's yard."

It thundered and both ladies jumped. "Now it's storming," Keisha exclaimed as all of the lights in the building went out.

"The show must go on," Jade added. A member from the kitchen staff appeared in the doorway several minutes later when the lights failed to come back on. "What is it, Jorge?"

"The electricity is out."

Jade and Keisha looked at each other.

"What about the generator?" Keisha went into the kitchen and Jade followed.

"It's not working either."

"What are we going to use for power? We can't do the concert tonight without power." Keisha was trying to stay calm.

"It has to be repaired by then. You called someone to come out and fix it, right, Jorge?" Jade questioned.

"Yes, but the refrigerator isn't working. All of the fresh seafood for tonight is in there. I don't want it to spoil."

"And the Cristal and all those dozens of fresh-cut,

golden, Ecuadorian roses we searched high and low for.
We don't want them to wilt," Keisha added, still doing
her best to remain cool.

"Nothing's going to spoil or wilt. We're going to
Costco and buy up every last bag of ice in the store and
a bunch of those huge ice chests." Jade snatched up her
purse and Keisha followed her.

Outside in the parking lot, they ran into several guys
from the crew. "We don't have any electricity . . ."
Keisha began.

"That's why we bring the truck. We've got enough
juice in there to light up several blocks," one of the
techs explained. Keisha and Jade sighed with relief.

"The show must go on," Keisha declared enthusias-
tically.

Topaz sat in a chair in her dressing room while her
stylist added a few extensions to her hair. A magnum
of Cristal sat between them.

"April, I am so nervous about tonight." Topaz
nursed a fresh glass of champagne. "I haven't performed in years, and it rained. Can you believe that? I
wonder if it's an omen."

"You are going to look fabulous tonight." April gave
Topaz a hand mirror, and she inspected her freshly
coiffed tresses from several views.

"It's not too glamorous, is it?" Topaz looked up at
April in the vanity mirror.

"It looks just like the poster. Don't confuse beauty
with glamour, but in your case the two are interchange-
able. You can never hide your beauty, T."

"Thanks, April." Topaz took one last look in the mirror. "I sure hope I can pull this off."

"Pull what off?" Germain walked into her dressing room. "Is it safe for me to come in?"

"Sure, baby. I was just talking about tonight's performance." Topaz jumped out of the professional salon chair that had been installed in the bathroom of her dressing room. It also contained a shampoo sink and hooded hair dryer. She pressed herself into her husband's arms. "Oh, baby, I'm so glad you're here."

"I told you I'd be here for you," Germain said as he wrapped his arms around her.

"I know, but sometimes he gets in that office and doesn't even come up for air," Topaz explained to April.

"This is special, so I took off early."

"I can't believe it. You even beat the kids home from school." Topaz laughed as she walked April downstairs to the front door. "Thanks for hooking a sista up. At least I'll look good doing whatever it is I'm going to do."

She ran back upstairs where Germain was undressing. "What are you doing?"

"I'm going to take a nap. Would you care to join me?"

"Sure, honey, but I probably won't sleep. I'm too nervous." Topaz climbed into bed and scooted right up next to Germain so she could inhale his scent. His presence always gave her strength.

I don't know why I'm even doing this. I don't really want to be out there singing. I belong here with my husband and children. She wiped the tears from her eyes and tried not to sniff. She didn't want Germain to hear her crying. *It's just for one night.* She reminded herself as she drifted off to sleep.

* * *

The rain had diminished to a mist when Jade, Keisha, and Jorge returned to The Diamond with the restaurant's van loaded with ice.

"The electricity is still out, ladies." A member of the crew greeted them with the news before they were even out of the truck.

"I guess we're going to have to cancel." Jade looked at Keisha. "I can't believe this."

"We sold out of tickets the first day we put them on sale and Germain put out all this money for a production crew to tape so they can put out a DVD, and we have no electricity." Keisha felt like crying. She thought about all the months of planning. The rain was ruining everything. "T is gonna be so upset."

Jorge and another kitchen worker returned with a dolly and a flatbed cart and began unloading the ice.

"All of the seafood is still fresh. The stove and the grill are gas, so the chefs can begin cooking," Jorge announced.

Keisha sighed. "Thank God for small favors."

Greggo met them at the door. "The phones have been ringing off the hook; people are still trying to buy tickets. It's too bad we can't add another show."

"No way," Keisha replied.

"If we can get this one done. Now I know how Nina felt the day of Sky's showcase," said Jade.

"I've got everything under control here. I called the Party Rental. They're bringing over a huge white tent and a couple of generators. We can move the press out there. The head of the production crew said he could give us sound, so the only thing we're missing is air conditioning and lights. The china, linens, stemware, and flatware are also here, as well as the menus and place cards for the VIP tables." He made a few notes on his clipboard and looked up at the girls. "I suggest you guys go downtown and buy some pretty gold candles."

"Praise the Lord. I just fell in love with you, Greggo." Keisha smiled and wiped away a tear.

"The show will go on. Come on, Key. I'm feeling really creative. We've got shopping to do." Jade had Jorge drive them downtown to the Flower Mart where they purchased gold candles, cans of metallic gold spray paint, glitter, and yards of gold shimmering fabrics.

"What are you going to do with all of this stuff?" Keisha asked as Jade picked out dozens of golden Japanese fans.

"Make this a Topaz night to remember."

By the time they returned to the restaurant, it was almost five. "Thank God this thing doesn't start until nine. I am so glad we decided to do only one show."

Jade carefully cut the fabric into squares to overlay on the gold tablecloths. While the tables were being set, Jade took the roses, candles, and spray paint into her office and created the centerpieces. She proudly placed them on the tables with the gold-trimmed crystal and plates.

"Those big, expensive party planners ain't got nothing on me." Jade glanced up at the ceiling, which had been covered with gold fabric the night before, and smiled happily as the room began to shimmer. "Just wait until the candles are lit. It's going to be so pretty."

"I know you ladies probably haven't eaten a thing, so I thought you might like to sample these." Greggo set a plate of grilled citrus shrimp on Keisha's desk, and they immediately dug in.

*   *   *

Kyle walked in the office he shared with Nina, who was sitting behind the computer in her pajamas. "I take it you're not going to T's show tonight."

"I'm not ready to see anyone yet." Nina didn't even look at Kyle when she answered. "It's been raining. I can't believe you're even going to try to go into the city tonight."

"You know Niki's been talking about this for days. All of the kids are excited to see T sing."

"You guys have fun." Nina gave him a lifeless wave.

"I can't believe you're not coming," Kyle said as he disappeared out of her sight. "You've got to face her one of these days."

Germain helped Topaz and Baby Doll into the limousine while their driver placed her clothing and acoustic guitar in the trunk.

"Still nervous, pretty girl?" Germain placed a hand on top of hers.

"I'll be all right." She smiled into Germain's eyes.

Jade and Keisha returned to the restaurant with Sean and Eric. The candles were lit and the entire room sparkled.

"Wow!" Eric looked around the club. "Are you sure this is our old juke joint?"

"Juke joint?" Jade looked at Eric like he was crazy. "The Diamond is hardly a juke joint."

Keisha laughed. "Juke joint. Eric, you are so silly."

Topaz and Germain arrived with the kids, and the ladies escorted Topaz to her dressing room.

"Everything looks so beautiful, y'all. Thank you so

much for everything." Topaz looked as if she wanted to cry. "I wouldn't be doing any of this if it wasn't for you."

"Girlfriend, you are long overdue," Keisha said. "We sold every ticket the first day we put them on sale. The VIP tickets are gone too, and those were a thousand dollars."

"A thousand dollars?" Topaz's golden eyes grew wide with surprise. "You mean people actually paid a thousand dollars to see me?"

"Yes. And a large portion of the proceeds from those tickets goes to the foundation," Jade explained. "We just wanted to cover our costs."

"That is so cool." Topaz put a hand to her head. "Oh, the pressure. Now I'm even more nervous. Thousand-dollar tickets. I sure hope people think they got their money's worth when it's all over."

Everyone filed out of the dressing room except Germain until it was finally time to begin. Topaz walked on stage to a standing ovation, which was totally unexpected, and it gave her an adrenaline rush. She was exquisite in a simple pair of gold stretch denim jeans with a pair of topaz Manolo's and a white halter top. Her makeup was natural and flawless, and her hair was twisted in soft spiral curls with the white diamonds Jade had purchased for herself in Topaz's ears. The candlelight made the natural highlights in her hair sparkle and glow. Her guitar was sitting in a stand on the floor next to a director's chair that had her name written as a signature across the back in gold. The stage was set up to appear as if Topaz were performing in her living room for her guests.

She smiled briefly, picked up her guitar, and began to play. Her accompaniment was a grand piano, light percussion, and a trio of background singers. The melodies were alluring and hypnotic, as she sang about the thing that mattered most in her life—love and its unfortunate consequence, pain.

As she sang, the audience was transformed. People forgot everything and allowed themselves to be entertained. They forgot about the rain, and no one seemed to mind that the air conditioning didn't work as a gentle ocean breeze cooled the room.

"I'd like to dedicate this last song to my husband. Germain, you're my superstar, baby," Topaz said as she blew him a kiss. "I love you."

It was so quiet you could hear a pin drop when she began a capella. "Long ago, and oh so faraway, I fell in love with you."

As the instruments joined in, tears pressed their way out of Nina's eyes and rolled down her cheeks. Her cousin's voice was hauntingly beautiful—even longing and mournful. Nina managed to sneak in without anyone seeing her right before the show began, and she prayed that she would be able to keep it together and not come unglued in the middle of Topaz's performance.

"Loneliness is such a sad affair, and I can hardly wait to be with you again," Topaz continued as she wept real tears.

Eric looked into Keisha's eyes and kissed her softly on the lips. Kyle took a sip of champagne and swallowed hard, trying to force the lump out of his throat. "I must be trying to get a sore throat or something from all this rain," he said to himself. Niki, totally mesmerized, sat on Kyle's lap with her head resting on her father's chest. "Aunty sings so pretty," she whispered softly.

"Don't you remember? You told me you loved me, baby." Topaz's sultry vocals had the audience gripped in a vise as her voice tugged on their heartstrings and refused to let go.

Sean stood behind Jade, holding her as they both swayed gently to the beat. Chris was too proud of his mother. He was grinning ear to ear as he watched her. Baby Doll had a funny little smile on her face. There were tears in Germain's eyes when he blew her a kiss.

"I love you. I really do." Topaz sang the last words as she continued to sing runs and improvise.

The room thundered with applause. People stamped, cheered, and tossed the roses from the centerpieces onto the stage as they secretly wiped tears from their eyes.

"Encore!" everyone yelled. "Encore!"

Topaz smiled through her tears. She hadn't even thought about an encore when she put the show together. She looked at her pianist, Greg Phillinganes, who was also her musical director. He played the vamp to "Superstar" again, and everyone immediately quieted down, because they all had to hear it again.

The next day, every popular morning radio show in Los Angeles was talking about her performance, and they couldn't stop talking—it was the topic of conversation the entire day. Somehow, Stevie Wonder's KJLH mysteriously received a copy, as did Big Boy at Power 106, Steve Harvey, and *The Michael Baisden Show*. There were even a few copies overnighted to stations in New York City and other major markets.

Because Jamil had produced her first two CDs, Revelation Music was inundated with calls. The phone lines were jammed. Topaz.com, her Web site, was literally shut down because it couldn't handle all the hits coming in at once. Viacom was already on the phone with Topaz's lawyers arranging to televise the concert on VH1.

There was a review on the front page of the *Hollywood Reporter.*

A Topaz Night at The Diamond. Forget the ambience . . . the room glittering with gold, complete with golden Ecuadorian roses, the delicious fare, or the Cristal that flowed endlessly. It was definitely the night of glitz and glamour that I expected. Record labels are known for bringing the bling, especially when they want to compensate for a lack of talent. But that definitely wasn't the case here.

What we didn't expect was Topaz delivering a riveting collection of vocals and music that couldn't be described as anything but hauntingly beautiful love songs. Backed solely by a piano and light percussion, Topaz's performance was nothing less than stellar.

Topaz, well at the top of her game, executed expertly delivered punches from the first note. And just when we thought we couldn't take another hit, the gorgeous diva served up an amazing Luther influenced rendition of "Superstar" that was a bona fide TKO. There wasn't a dry eye in the house, myself included. Kudos to The Diamond for a five-star evening and for bringing a true Superstar back to her adoring public. I can't wait to get my copy of the CD.

Chapter 18

It was terribly hot and humid that morning, the after-math of the late summer rain. Temperatures soared close to the one hundred degree mark. It was September, one of the hottest months of the year in southern California.

Topaz drifted in and out of a stressful sleep, dreaming. In the dream, Chris, Baby Doll, and Niki were at the beach playing in the surf as the tide rushed in and out. Topaz was relaxing on a chaise in a cabana while she watched the children. Suddenly the waves were huge, much too large for even an adult to play in. Chris and Baby Doll ran out of the water and into the cabana, but Niki disappeared. Topaz jumped out of her chair and ran into the water to look for her. She spotted the little girl inside of a wave trying to scream for help.

"Niki, baby, no, no," Topaz screamed. She was just about to grab Niki's hand when the wave swept the child completely out of her reach. "No, baby, no." Topaz's screams were bloodcurdling.

Germain, who was in the bathroom shaving, ran out with gel on his face.

"What's wrong, baby? What is it?" His wife's screams frightened him. His heart raced with fear.

"Germain, you have to help Niki. She's going to drown if you don't get her out of there."

"T, baby, wake up. You're dreaming." Germain shook her gently.

"Noooooo." Topaz thrashed around in the bed all tangled in the sheets.

"Honey, wake up. You're dreaming again," Germain said a little louder.

"Huh?" Topaz opened her eyes, surprised to see her husband standing over her, then realized she had been dreaming and wondered what she had said.

"That was some dream you were having. It was probably the worst one yet." Germain went back into the bathroom to finish shaving. Topaz scooted past him so she could relieve herself.

She tried to stall as long as she could, thinking of some way to change the subject. "It's really hot, huh? I wonder if it's going to rain again." Topaz washed her hands and went to look out the window. The walls in the master bath were completely made of glass, offering a view of the ocean.

"Don't try to change the subject, T." Germain knew her too well. "You were dreaming about Niki."

"I was?" Maybe she could play dumb.

"Yes. You wanted me to go help her. She wasn't getting sick again, was she?"

"No."

"What was going on?"

"I don't remember, sweetie." Topaz squeezed Crest onto her toothbrush.

Germain put his hands around Topaz's forehead and massaged her temples. "Sometimes I wish I could get inside your pretty little head so I could know what you're really thinking. You're not keeping anything from me, are you?"

"No, honey." Topaz turned on the water in the shower.

"Are you sure? You know you can always tell me anything."

"I'm sure." Topaz knew he was watching her so she dropped her robe on the floor and stepped inside the steamy shower. He got in with her and didn't say another word . . . about Niki, anyway.

Topaz dropped the kids at school and drove to Beverly Hills later that afternoon, where she met Germain so they could meet with her attorneys. The law firm had received several offers that they couldn't wait to discuss with them.

The couple held hands as they walked into the law offices located on Wilshire Boulevard directly across from Neiman Marcus. Topaz and Germain were both anxious to know what sort of offer had been received that the attorney would not discuss on the telephone.

"I'll just get straight to the point." Miller Davis was an extremely intelligent and charismatic brother. While the majority of the entertainment industry was run by Jewish and Italian men, it was wonderful to have African American representation that was equally powerful and connected. Germain had met Miller on the golf course and asked him to handle Topaz. She liked the idea of her man having a say in her business. She refused to make any decisions without Germain, because what she did affected the entire family.

"VMG is offering you a one hundred million dollar deal for five CDs," Miller declared with a dazzling smile.

Topaz's mouth dropped open in surprise. She looked at Germain, who was also shocked.

One hundred million dollars. The words echoed over and over in her head. It was enough money for her family to live very comfortably for the rest of their lives. She took a sip from her bottle of water.

Germain spoke first. "A hundred million dollars. That's a lot of money, Miller."

"It most certainly is, and Topaz is worth every penny. She should have had a deal like this when she first came into the business. There are only a few singers who have ever been given this kind of money. Michael Jackson didn't even have a deal like this."

"He didn't?" Topaz was at a loss for words.

"No. I also have a list of managers who have expressed interest in Topaz's career." Miller pushed a sheet of paper across the table, and Topaz and Germain perused it quickly.

"Benny Medina?" Topaz had to drink more water. Everything Benny Medina touched turned into millions.

"Topaz, why are you so surprised by all of this? You should have always had a top-notch team managing your career."

"I know. It's just that I put my career on hold for a few years to focus on my family. We have a son who's twelve and a daughter who's eight."

"And . . ." Miller smiled.

"And I just never really thought about what it takes to get back out there. I take my kids to school and I pick them up. I run my household, supervise the staff, and when I have time, I write a few songs. I love my husband and I love my life. I'm not sure if I even want to be out there."

She saw a little smile work its way back into her husband's eyes. He was looking pretty intense for a moment.

"What about the concert at The Diamond? What was that all about?"

Topaz laughed. "My girlfriends own the restaurant. They asked me to perform. So I did it to help them out."

"And I decided to have it filmed for DVD. I read the entertainment section. I've seen the sales figures," Germain added.

"It was a very wise decision, because she was fantastic," Miller told them. "That concert by itself is worth millions."

Germain smiled and squeezed Topaz's hand.

"Thank you. I had so much fun. I didn't realize how much I missed performing. I do love being on stage."

"And the stage loves you." Miller was silent as Topaz looked at the list again. She never imagined how much one concert in a restaurant in the Marina would impact her life.

"Well, you two certainly have a lot to think about. I'll put out some feelers for a distribution deal for Topaz's DVD. You might just want to include that in whatever deal we make with a record label, if you decide to make one."

Miller shook hands with Germain, kissed Topaz, and the meeting was over.

"How about I take my handsome husband to lunch so we can discuss all of this?" Topaz looked up into Germain's eyes.

"As much as I would love to do that, I can't." He pulled her into his arms and held her. "I've got to get back to the office. I'll call you from the car."

They got into their cars and drove in separate directions.

"So honey, what did you think about that one-hundred-million-dollar offer? We could live extremely well forever. We can finally build a new house." Topaz was excited.

"We can do all of that now. We've never had a shortage of money."

"That's true."

"I'm not really feeling this, baby. If you took that deal it would really change our lives. You'd be gone all the time. You wouldn't be around for the children or me."

Topaz was silent momentarily. "So what are you saying, Germain?"

"I thought I already said it. You don't need to take this deal."

"You want me to pass up a hundred million dollars?"

"Yes."

"I don't think I can do that."

"You're going to do what you want anyway, so why are you even asking me?"

"Because you're my husband and your opinion really matters to me."

"Well, I gave you my opinion."

"Germain, you're not being fair." Topaz was already pouting.

"I don't like it. Final answer." Germain pulled into his reserved parking spot. "I'm at the office now."

"Germain, don't hang up."

"I've got to go."

Topaz called him again, but he didn't answer. "Ughhh." Frustrated, she tossed the phone into the passenger seat.

It rang and she answered, not bothering to check the caller ID. "Germain . . ."

"Topaz, it's your sister-in-law, Rosalyn Lawrence."

"How the hell did you get this number?"

"That's not important. You just need to listen to what I have to say."

Topaz hung up and tossed the phone back into the seat. She allowed it to ring and go to voice mail several times before she finally picked it up and checked her messages.

Rosalyn had left one that said, "You really need to talk to me about your daughter Nicole and my niece, Turquoise."

"My daughter Nicole? What the hell is this psycho bitch talking about now?" Topaz said out loud. She called the number that was in her phone. "What do you want now, Rosalyn?"

"My father's been sick. He's been asking about Turquoise. I think it would really be good for him if he could see her."

"No way," Topaz replied firmly.

"Nicole isn't Nina and Kyle's daughter. It would be biologically impossible for Nicole to be their daughter."

"What?" Topaz paused to collect her thoughts. "Even if that were true, what has that got to do with me?"

"Were you aware that you have the trait?"

"What the hell are you talking about now?" Topaz demanded.

"You have the trait for sickle cell disease."

"I never knew that."

"Most people don't know they have the trait. That's what makes it so dangerous. Two people with the trait could hook up, start a family, and end up with a child who may have serious health challenges."

"I still don't see what any of this has to do with me."

"Were you aware that your husband has the trait too?"

"Of course I know my husband has the trait," Topaz lied as she felt herself tensing up, not really sure where this line of questioning was going.

"Hmmm. That's the only part of this that makes no sense. I think Nicole is your daughter, only I can't figure out why you gave her away."

"You are one crazy bitch," Topaz replied coolly. She hoped her voice wasn't trembling the way her hands were.

"But I will figure it out, and when I do, I'm sure there are lots of newspapers and magazines that would pay royally for this kind of information. Inquiring minds do want to know."

"You're not only a crazy bitch, but a sick one too. Nicole is not my daughter. I would never give one of my children away. If that were true, I would have given up Turquoise so I wouldn't have to be bothered with her crazy-ass family. But I can't blame my daughter because I made a mistake. I thank God every day that she looks like me."

"So why did you give her away? Nicole's daddy didn't have money like my brother?"

"Money, is that all you ever think about? It always seems to be the motive behind everything you ever do or say."

"I'll admit, I do think about money a lot. We could use it for our research in finding a cure for sickle cell disease. But I also think about how to get back at your gold-digging ass for what you did to my brother."

"I didn't do anything to your brother but try to love him, but I guess your family needs someone to blame since Gunther didn't want to have anything to do with any of you."

"That's because your stuck-up ass didn't want to be married to a brother from South Central, so you turned him against us."

"What? That is not true."

"That's what Gunther told my father."

"Well, Gunther lied."

"No, he didn't, but I will get you back for what you did to him."

Topaz couldn't believe what she was hearing. Rosalyn wasn't making any sense.

"And don't you ever call Gunther a liar because you're the real liar, you lyin' ass, gold-diggin' skank ass ho." Rosalyn's voice was filled with disdain.

"You know you really need help because you are one scary, crazy-ass, psychotic bitch," Topaz screamed into the phone.

"Whatever, just be afraid, Topaz. Be very . . ."

Topaz hung up before Rosalyn could say anything further.

"Why did I even call her crazy ass back? I must be the one who's crazy." Topaz was talking to herself again.

She drove home, pulled into her driveway, cut off the motor, and sat in her Range Rover holding her head in her hands. "What am I going to do now? What the hell am I going to do?" she asked herself and broke into tears.

Chapter 19

It seemed like the parking lot at the Cross Creek Plaza in Malibu was always congested no matter the time or the day of the week. Nina looked at her watch and let out a loud groan. As usual, there was nowhere to park and she would be running late. She was just about to pull off when she spotted back-up lights on a vehicle in front of the Marmalade Café.

"Yes!" Nina whipped the car into the space, grabbed her things, and dashed into the café. She stood there looking around until she spotted her at a table reading the paper. Nina took a deep breath and made her approach.

"Hey." Nina pulled out a chair and collapsed into it.

"Hey." Topaz looked up and smiled. "Long time no see."

"Too long, girl." Nina looked at the menu still on the table. "Did you already order?"

"I got a little something. I wasn't very hungry." Topaz smiled.

"You, not hungry? Is the world coming to an end?" Nina gave her a half smile.

"Sometimes it feels like it." Topaz moved her newspaper to another chair and the waitress set a plate of scones and a bowl of fresh berries in front of her. "Thank you." She spoke to the server as she poured hot water into her cup and added a dab of honey.

"That's quite the bourgeois breakfast you're having." Nina looked up at the waitress. "I'll have a short stack of blueberry pancakes, bacon, and orange juice."

"What kind of breakfast is that? Wannabe girl from da hood?" Topaz had promised herself she would not get angry because she had been getting upset with just about everyone lately. "I'm tired of your shit, Nina. You've been tripping with me ever since you became Ms. CEO of Revelation Music."

Nina looked away as she sipped a glass of ice water.

"I still can't believe you didn't even come to my concert." Topaz crossed her legs and folded her arms as she zoomed in on her cousin.

"I was there," Nina replied quietly.

"Nobody saw you there. I asked Kyle where you were and he said you were at home. Something about you just got back from Hawaii. What were you doing over there? Signing another artist?"

"I went there to chill out."

"Without your man?"

"Yes."

"I wouldn't do that very often if I were you."

"Whatever. And why weren't you at Sky's showcase?"

"That's different." Topaz was wearing her hair straightened, and she slung it out of her face with much attitude. "That wasn't you up there performing."

"But that was my artist . . . my showcase. You never care about anything that isn't about you. Ever since you came to California, everything has always been about you." Nina's voice cracked and there were tears in her eyes as she became extremely emotional. "I just wanted to do something for me, for once, that had nothing to do with you. And you couldn't even support me."

"I never knew you felt that way."

"Well, I do." Nina continued wiping tears from her eyes as Topaz thought about all the things she said.

"Well," Topaz began, carefully searching for the correct words, "I'm glad you finally decided to share all of this with me. It was never my intention to make everything about me, and you're right, I should have supported you and I didn't. But I felt like you didn't want me around. You were always putting me down. You didn't like my music. You couldn't see me singing and playing the guitar . . ."

"I loved your music. I was wrong about everything. I didn't know you could be as good as you were. T, you were fantastic. I still can't believe how wonderful you were. I was crying all over the place when you sang 'Superstar'."

"You cried?"

"Like a baby. I was so wrong. I should have signed you, but I was tripping. Kyle was pissed with me because I didn't include him. I screwed everything up with VMG . . ."

"VMG? I forgot VMG is Revelation Music's parent label."

"What's up with VMG?" Nina took a bite off a slice of bacon.

"VMG offered me one hundred million dollars to sign with them."

"Get the fuck out of here."

"Nina, I hope you aren't using that kind of language n front of Niki and Kyle," Topaz admonished.

"My bad." Nina covered her mouth with her hand. `VMG offered you that much money? You go, girl."

"Germain doesn't want me to take it."

"I can understand that."

"You can? Why?"

"You've been home playing Suzy homemaker and he good little wifey. That's what Germain's always vanted. He loves being the breadwinner and taking care of you. He can afford to give you anything you ever wanted. You taking all that money means you don't need him, not to mention you'll be busy working and have no time for him."

"I'll always need Germain," Topaz added softly.

"I know that and you know that, but he doesn't."

"But I told him all that."

"I'm sure you did, but he's a man, girl."

"Just when I think I understand men, I realize I don't know anything at all."

"Welcome to the club, girl. I thought Kyle would be more understanding, but he started tripping when I went to work." Nina finished off the last of her pancakes.

"Yeah, but Kyle was supposed to be running Revelation with you. You didn't include him in anything."

"There might be a bit of truth to that." Nina grinned sheepishly.

"Nina!"

"I told you I fucked up. He was so pissed with me because I didn't tell him that you brought me music and I passed. Germain must have said something to him."

"He did. I was really hurt."

"I'm sorry, girl."

"I'm sorry, too. And if you ever feel like I'm making things be all about me, please say something."

"Okay," Nina agreed. "I missed you."

"I missed you more." Topaz reached for Nina. "Hug."

The ladies embraced and Topaz kissed Nina on the cheek.

"It felt so weird not talking to you. You're my best friend and closer to me than my sister."

"It was too strange. I started to pick up the phone and call you so many times, especially when I was working on the concert. It was the first time I did anything like that without you around. You've been with me since the very beginning."

"You were so good, girl." Nina shook her head in disbelief. "I still can't believe it."

"Thanks, Nina. Keisha, Germain, and Jade stepped in and did a fabulous job."

"You should make 'Superstar' the first single from your album. I would even call the album *Superstar*, too."

"That's good. I like that. Hey . . . I just got a wonderful idea."

"What?" Nina handed some cash to the waitress.

"Why don't you sign me to Revelation Music?"

"Huh?"

"Why don't you sign me to Revelation for say twenty million dollars for one CD?"

"Revelation doesn't have that kind of money, T."

"But VMG does." Topaz grinned.

Nina was silent as she allowed Topaz's words to register.

"I think we can work this out so everyone will be happy. You tell VMG that you can sign me to Revelation for one project . . . that way Germain won't be tripping over a hundred million and five CDs. Germain had the concert taped. Maybe we can even include that in the deal. Our lawyers can figure all of that stuff out. You can redeem yourself with Kyle and allow him to be your partner for real this time. VMG gets a little bit of what they want, you come out looking good, and everybody's happy." Topaz felt like the weight of the world had been lifted from her shoulders as she smiled at Nina.

"That's an excellent idea, girl. That just might work," Nina agreed. "I've been holding off a meeting with Sherwin Katz because I know he wants to replace me."

"There's no way he'll be able to do that now."

Nina smiled happily. "Anita called me a couple of days after your showcase and said the lines at Revelation were jammed with calls from people wanting to get your CD."

"Girl, there were so many hits on my Web site, it crashed." Topaz laughed. "We still don't know who sent 'Superstar' to the radio stations."

"It was probably your husband. The man is connected. You never know who comes through his office."

"Yeah, like Sabre."

"What?"

"Miss Thing was in his office. I would never have known if I hadn't stopped by with the girls on the way to the Jack and Jill tea."

"Everybody in Hollywood wants Germain to do their procedures. He's almost as famous as you."

"I know. But I don't trust that sneaky little ho. She never looks me in the eye."

Nina laughed. "She's probably still afraid that you might kick her ass."

The ladies laughed until they cried.

"If your fans only knew . . . Topaz will kick a bitch's ass. Brenda Richie ain't got nothing on you."

"Forget Brenda Richie. You just better handle your business with Kyle and Revelation before I kick your ass."

"A'ight, boss lady." Nina paused to look at her cousin. "I really do need you. I sure was fucking shit up when you weren't around."

"Nina, if you say one more curse word, I'm kicking your ass."

The ladies walked outside to their cars.

"How'd you find this spot?" Topaz asked. "I thought you would have chosen something in the Colony Plaza."

"This is one of Kyle and Niki's breakfast spots. Those two have become extremely close since I went to work."

"She's a very special little girl. You can't help loving her. She stole Germain's heart that night we had to take her to the hospital. He was trying really hard not to cry."

Nina was smiling like a proud mother while Topaz spoke.

"That reminds me. I brought you some pictures from the tea." Topaz reached in her bag and pulled out several photos of the girls and the family.

"Oooooh," Nina exclaimed as she examined them. "These are great. Thanks, T."

"After I took the girls to the tea, the guys met us at Mr. Chow's for dinner. I guess that was too much activity for one day."

"I don't think that was it. The doctor said she could have been feeling the stress of what was going on between me and Kyle, and my being at work all the time. Kyle brought her to the studio one evening and she started crying when she had to go home."

"Awwww, poor little thing."

"I am so sorry I didn't call when you guys took her to the hospital. By the time I got your message, it was almost a week later. After Kyle didn't call me again I just assumed everything was okay."

Topaz disengaged the alarm on her Range Rover. "Well, just know the Gradney family is always happy to have Niki."

"I know." Nina gave Topaz a hug. "Thanks for everything, girl."

It was still early so Nina drove to Pacific Palisades to pick up a few things from Gelson's to make a special dinner for her family. Sky was in New York for a few weeks, so they had the house to themselves.

She pushed her cart through the aisles picking up their favorite foods. She chose a nice thick steak for Kyle. No matter how hard she tried to get him off of red meat, he always loved a good steak. Fresh jumbo shrimp and lobster, turkey franks for Niki, and other items for a picnic dinner. She loaded everything in the car and made it back to Malibu before Pacific Coast Highway became congested.

"Hey, honey." She got Kyle on his cell phone. "Are you and Niki on your way home? I'm making dinner."

"That sounds nice. Yes, I am on my way. We're coming through Malibu Canyon right now."

"Good." Nina sighed with relief. She was glad he didn't spoil her plans by saying he was in the city having dinner with his brother and Jade. "Can you stop by Blockbuster and pick up a few movies?"

"I sure can. Anything special you want to see?"

"I don't know. You keep up with the movies more than me."

"I'll call you from Blockbuster and you can tell me then."

"Okay, baby." Nina was happy he was being so nice. Things had been extremely rocky for the couple. They both needed to get off the emotional roller coaster.

"Hi, Mommy." Tears came into Nina's eyes when she heard Niki's sweet little voice. "How are you?"

"I'm wonderful, sweetheart. How are you?" Nina didn't know why she was crying.

"I'm fine. Mommy, are you at home?"

"I sure am, baby." Nina put ears of corn into a pot. "I'm making dinner for you, Daddy, and me."

"Yaaay."

Kyle was back on the phone. "See you soon."

Nina had everything ready by the time she heard the automatic garage door open. She went out to the car to meet them.

"What did you make for dinner, Mommy?" Nina picked up Niki and kissed her as they all walked in the house together.

"What's your most favorite thing to eat in the entire world?"

"Steak and lobster?"

Nina looked at Kyle because those were his favorite foods. "Since when?"

Kyle laughed and shrugged his shoulders. "That's my baby girl."

"I got a steak for you. I also just happened to pick up some lobster. You'd better put that on the grill too."

When the steak was ready, they all sat down to a candlelight dinner in the dining room.

"This is nice, baby. Thanks. Everything looks delicious." Kyle put a small portion of steak and lobster on his daughter's plate.

"I saw Topaz today," Nina began after Niki said the blessing.

"Did you two finally make up?"

"Yes, we did. She had a wonderful proposal." Nina told Kyle everything they discussed at lunch. "So what do you think?" Nina was wearing a dress with the back cut out. With her hair swept up, she looked sexy and sophisticated.

"I think you are wearing that dress."

Niki giggled as she watched her parents kiss.

"Thank you, sweetie."

"And I think T's proposal sounds great. See what the two of you can accomplish when you work together?"

"Yes, boss." Nina smiled into his eyes. She didn't realize how much she had missed being with her family. "We can all remind each other not to get caught up in this crazy music business and that family always comes first."

"You got that right." Kyle led them upstairs to their bedroom where they all got into the bed.

Nina handed Kyle a magnum of Cristal. "We had a case left over from Sky's showcase. It was in the back of the truck."

He poured champagne into their flutes. "Here's to Jamaica, sexy girl. I picked up the tickets on the way home."

"For real?" Nina's eyes sparkled with excitement.

"Yes, Niki and I didn't get a chance to go on vacation."

"I didn't either. I had a terrible time without you guys. I was so bored."

"I still can't believe you went without me."

"I can't believe I went without you either. I'll never do that again."

"Don't worry, because as the real head of Revelation Music, I won't let you."

"Good. Sometimes I think I need someone to tell me what to do." Nina cuddled up under her husband.

"Babe."

"Huh?" Nina snuggled even closer.

"Did you tell Topaz about your conversation with Dr. Lawrence?"

"No." Nina was silent for a moment. "I thought about it, but I just couldn't bring it up. I know my cousin. If I told her something like that, she would lose it. Besides, what Rosalyn said doesn't change a thing. Niki's our daughter. We're family."

Niki was lying on the other side of Kyle, sleeping soundly. Nina kissed her and smoothed her hair.

"Exactly." Kyle started the DVD. "Rosalyn will never be able to prove anything, so just let sleeping dogs lie."

Chapter 20

Sabre took one last look in the closet of her Embassy Suites apartment just to be sure she hadn't forgotten anything. It was time to go, and like The Jeffersons, she was finally movin' on up . . . to a tri-level beachfront townhouse in Malibu. Sherwin came through for a sista big time.

It was amazing how many things she had acquired since relocating to Cali several years ago. Although she owned no furniture or household items, she did possess several boxes of books, countless pairs of shoes, suitcases filled with lingerie and sportswear. The entire back seat of her Mercedes was filled with clothing on hangers.

She put on a pair of Gucci sunglasses, turned on the radio, and headed west on Franklin to the Hollywood Freeway. It was a gorgeous autumn day. The sky was vividly blue, and the sun was intensely bright and hot. It was one of those days that made you really appreciate living in southern California; an absolutely perfect day for the beach.

Sabre was listening to Power 106 the first time she

heard it. Everyone had been talking about Topaz's new song. She turned up the radio so she could really listen to it.

"It's a remake." Sabre laughed out loud after listening a few seconds. "Oh, pa-leezee. She is no competition. I can't believe people are going crazy over that." She changed to one of her other favorite stations, and within minutes Topaz's song was on again.

"All right, this is getting a little ridiculous. Don't you have any other songs to play, like mine?" Sabre yelled at the radio. Angrily, she flipped to another hip-hop station.

"That Topaz has got to be the finest woman on the planet," the deejay said.

"Yeah, fucking animal planet," Sabre mumbled.

"And to top it off, she can sang. Not like some of these other artists who got lucky and got next to some label head when they're really nothing but background singers."

"Or a video ho," someone else cut in. All the men were laughing.

"Punk-ass motherfuckers. They're not talking about me, cause my ass can sing," Sabre responded out loud to the deejays' comments.

"Man, I was lucky enough to get a ticket to Topaz's show. It was off da hook. Man, when she walked out on that stage, I was in heaven."

"That woman is like an expensive bottle of wine. The older she gets, the better she looks."

"Yeah, yeah, yeah. Give me a fucking break." Sabre cut off the radio as soon as she heard the first strains of "Superstar."

She pulled off the freeway into a service station at the exit to Malibu.

"Damn, it's hotter than hell," Sabre exclaimed the moment she stepped out of the air-conditioned car. She strutted inside the convenience mart and purchased a pack of Newports and a huge container of Coke with ice. "Mmmh. This ought to get me to the new house." She lit a cigarette and inhaled deeply. "Caffeine and nicotine, my favorite things."

Sabre sped off with screeching tires. She had purchased a bedroom set and a big-screen TV for the condo and she needed to arrive before the delivery. She was flying down the road doing ninety when she entered the canyon where the highway narrowed and curved upwards through the mountain. "Oh my God. I can't drive through there." She slowed down until she practically stopped. A line of honking cars trailed behind her.

"Go the fuck around." Sabre yelled as if the drivers could hear her. A truck pulled out from behind her, moved in front, then stopped so suddenly she almost ran into the back of it.

Sabre broke out in a sweat. "I will never ever come this way to Malibu again in my life." Eventually, she reached Pacific Coast Highway and drove at a normal speed to Beach Club Way and collapsed when she stopped in front of the house.

When she initially visited the property, it was with an agent in a limousine. Sherwin was supposed to drive her to the condo but couldn't because he had to take a last-minute meeting. She was still shaking when she phoned him.

"Sherwin, I was scared as shit driving out to Malibu."

"Sabre, how are you? You'll never believe who I'm having lunch with."

Sabre could tell he was really excited. Sherwin was a pretty low-key, even-tempered guy, so she was surprised to hear him this pumped. She could have cared less who he was having lunch with, since it wasn't her. She was completely traumatized during her drive to Malibu and she needed to be consoled.

"Who are you having lunch with, Sherwin?" Sabre asked as nicely as she could.

"I am sitting here with the beautiful Topaz, her husband, Germain, and Nina and Kyle Ross, co-CEOs of Revelation Music. Topaz is going to be part of the VMG family. She just signed a deal with Revelation Music. We were tossing around a few ideas. We're thinking about putting you on the road as an opener for Topaz."

"What the fuck?" For a moment Sabre forgot who she was talking to. She glanced in her rearview mirror as a Best Buy truck pulled up behind her. "Sherwin, I gotta go. They just got here with my big-screen TV." She hung up before he could say another word.

Sabre lit another cigarette and got out of the car. Sherwin had asked her to stop smoking. She hadn't had a cigarette in months. Now she was so glad she had picked up that pack earlier.

She was wearing a cropped tee and a pair of Daisy Dukes with heels. She could feel the deliverymen's eyes on her as she switched up to the front door, unlocked it, and punched in a code for the alarm.

The Pacific was visible as soon as she entered the house. Blonde hardwood floors ran throughout with white sandstone and vanilla granite in the kitchen. All of the walls were painted a pale shade of pink. Sabre loved it because the townhouse felt light and airy.

"You can put the television there." Sabre pointed to a

pot in the living room near a wood-burning fireplace.
The deliverymen went to work unpacking her big
screen. She stood there smoking a cigarette until they
were done.

"You guys are so big and strong. I've got a few
boxes in the car. Could you help me carry them inside?" Sabre gave the men one of her best smiles.

"We've got a schedule," one of them began.

"I'll help you," the other blurted out.

Sabre swung her narrow hips as wide as she could
as she led them to the car. Within minutes, the men carried all of her boxes inside.

"Hey, aren't you that singer named Sabre?" asked
the man who had initially agreed to assist her.

"Un-huh." She tried to be nonchalant, but she couldn't
have been more pleased that the young man recognized
her.

"Do you know Topaz?" the other man wanted to
know.

Sabre sipped on her Coke until she sucked up the
last of the liquid in the container. "No, I don't," she
replied rudely.

"Man, I would love to deliver a television to her
house," he told his partner. "I'd buy a TV and take it to
her house if I could meet her."

"I heard that," the other man agreed. He looked at
Sabre who, by now, was mad enough to spit nails.
"Bye, Sabre. Nice meeting you."

She followed them to the door and slammed it behind them. "Stupid-ass motherfuckers."

It was cooler outside when she went to the car. She
grabbed some clothes and carried them up to her master suite. The room was big with a huge walk-in closet
and high ceilings. Sherwin was going to have the closet

expanded and remodeled Kimora Lee Simmons styl
He was also the cosigner on the loan for the two and
half-million-dollar townhouse.

From the third-floor balcony, she could hear t
waves rushing directly below her and see lights twi
kling along the horizon. It was so chilly, she needed
jacket, but the cold night air was invigorating. It wa
quiet, but with no one to talk to, no TV, and no mus
she felt lonely as hell. She stood out on the balcor
until she was completely chilled and her teeth we
chattering.

"Some moving day," she grumbled to herself as sl
went downstairs and opened the refrigerator. It wa
empty and sparkling clean. "No fucking food." It nev
entered her mind to go to the store and buy some gr
ceries. She sat on the floor in front of the TV. "No fucl
ing furniture." She put in *X-Men* just to have som
noise and company, called information, and ordered
pizza.

"Sherwin's ass never called me back," she sudden
realized. She called him, but the phone rang until
went to voice mail. She checked her cell phone for th
time. It was almost ten, so she knew he was probably
home with his wife.

"That must have been some motherfuckin' meeting
I wonder what else they came up with for me to d
carry her fuckin' suitcases." She tossed a half-eate
slice of pizza across the room; stared at it lying on th
floor, and came to the realization there was no on
around but her to pick it up. She tossed the pizza in th
trash, then dug inside her boxes until she found Bea
and her night light. Using the stuffed animal as a pil
low, she went to sleep.

* * *

"Hey, Victor." Sabre was on the phone early the next morning, her tone as sweet as sugar. "I just moved into my new townhouse in Malibu and I wanted to invite you over. I've missed you so much. Why don't you come out and spend the day with me?"

Victor was really smart about so many things. She was lonely and he'd be the perfect person to help her get the house together. Sabre almost always had an ulterior motive for everything she did.

Victor must have missed her too, because he was there within the hour. They went shopping, purchasing everything from linens and furniture to dishes and a set of pots and pans. Now that the townhouse felt more like a home, Sabre decided to plan a small housewarming party.

Victor sat on the balcony putting together a barbecue grill. "Sabre, the townhouse looks so good now."

"I know, huh." Sabre looked around admiring the comfortable vanilla sofas and glass tables. "You know I couldn't have done this without you." She watched him dump charcoal into the grill, and in a few minutes there was a roaring blaze.

"Victor, put that out before you burn my fucking house down."

"Aw, woman. Be quiet. I got this all under control." He let it burn for a while, then put on some burgers and chicken.

"Okay, Poppi." Sabre smiled warmly, so happy to have him there. "Victor . . ."

"Yeah, sexy." He came inside the house and took her in his arms.

She started to pull away but thought better of it. "We're having a party." Sabre sang like a happy child.

*   *   *

"Ooh child, this is too fabulous." The next day, Eduardo brought her an original Greg Breda. "This painting will go wonderfully here." He pointed out a spot over the sofa with sweeping gestures. "You know Angela Bassett has three of these in her house."

"Sabre, Ed forgot to tell you that the painting is a gift from your entire glam squad. Don't let him make you think that's it's just from him." Dawn smiled.

"Hey everybody." Victor came out of the kitchen carrying a platter of meat for the grill.

"Everybody, that's Victor." Sabre was enjoying herself playing hostess.

"It's gettin' hot in here and I'm gonna take my clothes off," Eduardo sang as he scrutinized Victor's every move. "Girlfriend, is that you?"

"Eduardo, we can't take you anywhere." Dawn pushed him out the door. "Let's go take a walk on the beach so you can cool your hot ass off."

Sabre looked at Victor and laughed. "Eddie's feelin' you, Poppi."

"Well, I ain't feelin' him," Victor snapped as Sabre continued laughing.

Sky arrived next, and Mimi was right behind her. Sabre bounced around making more introductions while Victor got everyone drinks.

"Sabre, this townhouse is gorgeous. Mind if I take a tour?" Sky asked.

"I'll be more than happy to show her around." Victor gave Sky a kiss.

"Sabre, you know Nina and Kyle's house isn't far from here," Sky informed Sabre as Victor took her upstairs. Sabre was silent as she watched the two of them chatting like long lost best friends.

Mimi brought several friends. She got up from the sofa where they were talking and watching *Crash*. "Sabre, sweetie, let's go in the kitchen."

"What's up, Mimi?" She hadn't seen her publicist friend for a while.

"Sherwin called last night. He was so excited. Revelation Music just signed Topaz and he wants me to handle her release party. They're calling her CD *Superstar*, and they're spending money."

"Are you still going to be my publicist?"

"Of course, sweetie."

"So, what does that have to do with me?" Sabre asked quietly.

"We're talking about doing a tour and you'd be the perfect opening act."

"Sherwin already told me. I don't want to open for her."

"Are you crazy? Do you know what performing in front of her audience would do for your career?"

Sabre tried hard to fight back the tears. Topaz was quickly invading her territory, spreading through the ranks like cancer. Victor and Dawn came back in the house.

"What's going on, you guys?" Dawn asked.

"Food." Eduardo helped himself to seafood kabobs, corn on the cob, and salad. "Mmmm, somebody put their foot in this."

Mimi stood there watching everyone with a little plastic smile on her face. "Topaz is going to be a VMG artist and one of my clients."

"Revelation Music artist," Sabre quietly interjected, but no one was paying her any attention. They were more interested in what Mimi had to say.

Sky and Victor returned from their tour and joined the session in the kitchen.

"Girl, stop. I've been waitin' on Miss Thang to come out with a new CD. I know y'all heard *Superstar*. That is the jam." Eduardo was smacking and eating. "I was there for her concert at The Diamond. Girlfriend tore it up."

"She performed at The Diamond?" Sky looked in the newly well-stocked refrigerator and took out a bottle of water.

"Yes, child." Eduardo was monopolizing the conversation as usual. "You should have seen all of the celebrities there. Girlfriend's husband is that fine-ass plastic surgeon. He took her a bouquet of flowers when she was finished. He wanted everybody to know that was his damn woman."

I wish somebody wanted everyone to know that I was his woman. Everybody was eating and laughing except Sabre.

"Her kids came on stage, too. Her son looks just like his daddy, and her daughter looks just like her." Eduardo was still dishing the gossip.

I bet she didn't have Niki up there. She is such a damn liar. Sabre got a Coke and went outside, but the others were so busy talking about Topaz they didn't even notice when Sabre left.

She just signed a fucking deal and she has Sherwin and Mimi, next thing she'll have Eduardo doing her hair and Dawn styling her clothes. Everybody talking about her is ruining my fucking party. Why is it that no matter what I do, no matter where I go, this fucking bitch always shows up? Well good, I'm glad she's going to be part of the VMG family. We'll see who's hot and who's not. That fucking Superstar *will never outsell my CD.*

I'm going to blow her old ass right off the charts. Then they'll be asking her ass to open up for me.

Victor came outside on the patio a few minutes later. "Topaz ain't all that, Sabre. She's just an established singer with a track record for selling CDs. I like your music much better."

"For real, Victor?" There were tears in her eyes. He had never seen her so vulnerable.

"For real, Sabre." She allowed him to pull her into his arms. Victor held her so tightly she could feel his heart beating, and for the first time in her life, she didn't want to pull away. She stood there in the dark, listening to the sound of the ocean and enjoyed the feeling of someone feeling her.

"Just remember two things," Victor continued. "You're my superstar, sexy, and no one stays on top forever, not even Topaz."

Chapter 21

Mimi traipsed around The Diamond in skinny jeans and a pair of ruby Jimmy Choo satin sling backs, the matching handbag swaying on her arm. Nina and Topaz both raised an eyebrow of interest the moment she entered the restaurant.

"So you're Jade Kimura Ross." Mimi gave Jade one of her best plastic smiles. "I've heard so much about you and I've seen your work. And Topaz, it's so wonderful to see you again."

"This is my best friend, Keisha," Topaz interjected, but Mimi acted as though she didn't hear her, politely dismissing Keisha as being someone unimportant, the way most people in Hollywood did once they realized a person was of no real value to them.

"I still don't understand why we have to do the party here. I was thinking White Lotus, the Roosevelt Hotel, or even the Sunset Room would be so much better." Mimi practically turned up her nose. "No one wants to travel this far south for anything."

"We're having the party here because my friends own this restaurant," Topaz replied firmly.

"Yes," Nina cut in. "T's concert was here and it was fabulous. Standing room only and there were lots of celebrities. Anyone invited will come because it's for Topaz."

"Oh, I totally agree, but there is no way we're having the party here if her concert was here. You can never use the same venue twice," Mimi decreed victoriously.

"That makes a lot of sense to me," Keisha replied softly. "Maybe you should choose one of the other restaurants like Mimi suggested, T."

"I'm hiring a celebrity party planner, so there really wouldn't be anything for you ladies to do. Topaz is a fabulous A-list artist, so she must have a fabulous room," Mimi added, obviously relieved that she would not be forced into using The Diamond.

"White Lotus might be nice." Nina sighed, trying her hardest to be on her best behavior when she was so tempted to tell Mimi to kiss off.

"You like White Lotus, Nini?" Topaz smiled at her cousin warmly, using one of Nina's pet names.

"White Lotus is so overdone," Jade cut in.

"What?" Mimi began. "White Lotus is . . ."

"Totally overdone," Jade repeated without a hint of a smile.

Everyone focused on Jade with surprised looks.

"What would you suggest, Jade?" Mimi fixed her big baby blues on Jade while Keisha tried not to laugh.

"Why not do something totally creative like having the party at Harry Winston on Rodeo? Topaz is a jewel. So have a party for her at Harry Winston where she can be a topaz amongst the diamonds," Jade coolly explained. "I get so sick and tired of everyone using the same places over and over in this city. That's why we opened The Diamond, which is celebrity owned. My husband and Eric Johnson are two of the biggest ball players in this city."

"Harry Winston. That is so fresh. I love it, Jade!" Topaz grabbed Jade and kissed her.

"Me too." Mimi smiled and seemed to relax for the first time since she had entered the restaurant. "It's totally fabulous."

"Girlfriend, you are a creative genius," Nina added.

"Thank you," Jade replied coolly. *Don't ever try to put my restaurant down.*

"Okay, let's have some lunch and drinks and finish our discussion. You will be joining us, won't you, Mimi?" Keisha's smile was genuine despite Mimi's earlier brush-off.

"That sounds totally fab, Keisha," Mimi replied.

Topaz and Keisha exchanged glances. It was always so interesting the way someone who didn't know your name earlier suddenly remembered it.

In the middle of a mouth-watering Diamond spread, Mimi exclaimed, "Let's have a reception for Topaz here, afterward. Harry Winston won't hold everyone, so we'll just have press and A-list celebs there, then we can have Part Two here at The Diamond. It totally fits. Harry Winston and The Diamond." Mimi flashed a brilliant, luminous smile.

"I love it." Topaz smiled at her girls.

"Me too," Nina agreed. "It'll be the talk of the town."

"Not to mention, it's great business for the restaurant. But most important, I get to give my girl a Superstar party." Keisha put an arm around Topaz and gave her a big hug.

"It's a win–win situation for everyone." Mimi stood

up from the table and picked up her bag. "Harry Winston. Sherwin is going to love it. Ciao, ladies." Mimi gave everyone a Miss America wave and strutted out the door.

"I saw those Jimmy Choos at the boutique on Rodeo Drive. They didn't have my size," Nina declared as she stared off into space.

"It's a good thing Mimi doesn't wear the same size as you or that chick would be short one pair of red stilettos with matching bag." Topaz laughed and pulled her cousin's hair. "Because we all know how much Nini loves her some red shoes."

Harry Winston was more than happy to lend the store as the site of Topaz's release party for her long-awaited third CD. After all, they were responsible for so many of the jewels that actresses wore to the Oscars; why not host a party for Topaz? They even designed a wonderful topaz and diamond necklace and earrings for her that made the pieces her late husband Gunther had given her seem like mere trinkets.

On the night of the party, Rodeo Drive was roped off and huge screens were set up outside so her fans could participate in the festivities. Searchlights danced across the sky heralding the launch of her *Superstar* CD. Footage from her live performance of "Superstar" had been made into a video. The song, officially released to radio as a single, quickly climbed to the top of the music charts and stayed there.

For the very first time, Nina and Kyle stood together as co-CEOs of Revelation Music, while Sherwin Katz observed everything like the proud papa. Flutes of champagne and an assortment of appetizers were of-

fered to the press and other VIP guests who were allowed to enter the store.

Sabre sipped on champagne as she pretended to be
absorbed in the exquisite jewels on display in the
cases. Mimi and Sherwin insisted she attend the party,
despite the fact that "Superstar" had knocked Sabre's
song out of the number one spot, making her yesterday's news. She watched as the "Black Friends" talked
among themselves. They were the only people she really knew at the party. Sky and Victor were attending
the reception at The Diamond. She closed her eyes,
took a deep breath, and forced herself to walk over to
the group.

"Hello, everyone." Sabre opened her eyes and found
that she was standing in front of Nina.

"Hey, Sabre." Nina greeted her with a kiss. "You
look wonderful."

Sabre was wearing Versace and she did, indeed, look
wonderful. Her glam squad had hooked a sista up.
"Thanks, Nina. You look wonderful, too. So when is
Topaz arriving?"

"She should be here any minute." Nina smiled at
Kyle, who was too fine in an Armani tuxedo.

"I love the way she sang 'Superstar,'" Sabre offered.

"We all do," Nina smiled.

"Mimi mentioned the tour to me. I'd love to be a part
of Topaz's tour," Sabre continued. "Do you have any
dates in mind yet?"

"We're thinking about the first of next year."

"Sounds perfect." Sabre smiled sweetly. "Hey,
Keisha and Jade." She kissed them both on the cheek.
"How's the restaurant doing?"

"Extremely well." Jade smiled. "You have to come by
for dinner some night. Bring your friends."

"I'll do that," Sabre replied happily. It felt so nice to belong.

Sabre was in the middle of a conversation with Keisha when motorcycles escorted a limo to the front of the store.

"She's here, you guys," Nina declared excitedly.

A driver opened the door and Topaz stepped out of a classic Bentley in a sweeping gold Cavalli gown. She looked like Cinderella arriving at the palace except Prince Charming arrived with her. When Germain stepped out of the limo in his designer tux, Sabre felt her heart skip a beat. Lights from cameras flashed as he ushered Topaz up the red carpet, the epitome of Hollywood royalty.

Nina and Kyle were in the center of the store waiting for Topaz and Germain. "I knew you were coming fashionably late, but please, Miss Thing," Nina teased.

"But, am I not fabulous?" Topaz was glowing.

"Totally," Nina agreed as Mimi walked up and they both laughed.

Mimi began arranging photos for the press. She called Sabre over to pose with Topaz.

"Hi, Topaz, this is a wonderful party." Sabre smiled warmly and brushed her cheek lightly against Topaz's. "Congratulations on the release of *Superstar*."

"Thank you, Sabre," Topaz replied happily.

They posed for several photos together before Sabre rejoined the Black Friends. After the photo opportunity, Mimi allowed the press a brief question-and-answer period.

"Topaz, this last CD was so passionate. What was your inspiration?" a woman shouted.

"My wonderful husband." Topaz kissed Germain on the lips. There was applause, and more cameras flashed.

"Topaz," a man yelled for her attention. "I understand you were made a substantial offer from VMG. Why sign with the fledgling Suicide Records? Does this have anything to do with the fact that the CEO is your cousin?"

Mimi started to answer for her, but Topaz responded to the question herself. "I signed with the fledgling Suicide, I think you called it, for several reasons. First, it's the label of my first producer, Jamil Winters, who signed me to my first deal. I'd do anything to help Jamil. Second, because of Jamil's great music. You'll find a couple of his songs on my new CD. And third, I did want to work with my cousin, Nina, who is the co-CEO along with her husband, Kyle. Nina has been a part of my career from the very beginning. I chose less money because money isn't everything, but family is, and my family is very important to me." She took Germain by the hand. "And when I get ready to put out my next CD, I'll discuss it with my family and we will decide what's best for us. Right now, Revelation Music is what's best for this family."

Everyone cheered as Topaz and Germain kissed again.

"Girl, you told him," Nina whispered in her ear. "That was amazing."

"Topaz, I applaud you on your view of family values," another press person began. "But answer this for me. If you're so big on family, why are you allowing your cousin Nina and her husband, Kyle, to raise your daughter Nicole as their own?"

The room was so quiet you could have heard a rat piss on cotton as everyone waited for Topaz's response. Germain was also silent as the color faded from his face. Nina felt herself shaking, and the wind was knocked out of Kyle. Topaz was as poised and collected as ever when she replied.

"I have no idea what you're talking about."

"Topaz, isn't it true that this is your daughter?" A woman produced a photograph of Topaz and Germain with Chris, Baby Doll, and Niki that had been taken at the Chocolate Affair.

"Turquoise, who we call Baby Doll, is my daughter. Niki is Nina's daughter." Topaz was amazingly cool.

"But Nicole has sickle cell disease, and according to the facts, that makes it biologically impossible for her to be your cousin's daughter." The reporter was relentless.

"Then shouldn't you be talking to my cousin?" Topaz fired back.

"There will be no further questions." Mimi directed security to remove Topaz, Germain, Nina, and Kyle from the jewelry store. "If there are any further questions about Topaz's music, direct them to me."

The room buzzed with conversation as Topaz and her entourage were led out of the store.

Chapter 22

"What the hell was all that about?" Germain asked the moment they were back inside the limo. Kyle and Nina couldn't look at each other as they sat across from Germain and Topaz.

"Absolute madness." Topaz laughed nervously. "Nina and Kyle, you guys throw a hell of a party." Topaz fished around in the cooler and found a bottle of Cristal. "Kyle, would you do me the honor of popping the cork on this baby and pouring us all a glass? I sure need one after all that craziness."

By the time Kyle handed everyone flutes of champagne, Topaz's glass was empty. She handed her glass to Kyle for him to refill. "So are we off to The Diamond for Part Two of this soiree?"

Nina looked at Topaz like she was crazy. "You want to go to The Diamond?"

"Yes! Keisha and Jade planned a fabulous party. People are waiting for us. What would it look like if we didn't show up because of some outrageous lie and an obvious attempt to sabotage the release of my new CD?" Topaz was on her third glass of champagne.

"She does have a point." Kyle was finally able to look at his wife.

Germain was still dazed. "Baby, who would want to do something like this to you?"

"Dr. Roslyn Lawrence," Topaz replied firmly.

"Who is Dr. Rosalyn Lawrence?" Germain demanded.

Nina poured herself another glass of champagne. She couldn't wait to hear how Topaz was going to explain this one.

"My former sister-in-law."

"Your former sister-in-law?" Germain looked puzzled.

"Gunther's little sister." Topaz placed a hand on her forehead, then she broke into tears. "How long must I pay for that mistake of a marriage?"

Germain pulled her into his arms where she cried for several minutes. He took out a handkerchief and dabbed at his wife's tears.

Topaz sniffed and continued. "Before you and I remarried, I tried to let Baby Doll have a relationship with his family even though Gunther hated them. I thought it was the right thing to do."

Nina interlocked her fingers with Kyle's as they rode in silence.

"It was, sweetheart." Germain was too good to be true.

"He left a will and he didn't leave his family a cent. Gunther had a son almost the same age as Baby Doll who I knew nothing about until Rosalyn decided to sue me for a portion of the estate. It got real nasty. We were in and out of court, and things were being written in the tabloids."

"I remember that now. Kids were saying things to Chris in school," Germain added.

"I couldn't go anywhere. It was crazy. So Keisha told me to settle. She told me to give the tramp that had Gunther's baby and his family some money. My lawyers drew up an agreement that had one stipulation. His family would not be allowed any further contact with Baby Doll. Rosalyn called me a few weeks ago and said her dad was sick and he wanted to see Baby Doll, and I told her no. Then she told me I'd be sorry. I guess with all the publicity for *Superstar* she obviously decided this would be a good time to ruin my life." Topaz's voice cracked and there were tears in her eyes again.

"But where would she get an idea to make up something as crazy as Niki being your daughter? It's not true, is it?"

Nina didn't realize she was squeezing the life out of Kyle's fingers.

Topaz sat up and looked Germain in the eyes. "Baby, why on earth would I give away my child? Tell me, when did I even have a baby? You've been with me these last six years."

Germain looked thoughtful. "That is true."

Nina relaxed somewhat.

The limo pulled up at The Diamond. "Shall we go inside and continue this party? We're not going to let that psychotic bitch ruin the biggest night in our careers, are we?" Topaz smiled at Nina and Kyle.

"No way," Nina agreed. "Let's do this."

They all ignored the paparazzi as they got out of the car and walked into The Diamond as couples. Big-screen monitors were mounted throughout the club where the party was at a high. Mimi's event planner had redecorated the club, bringing in special furniture, statues, and fabrics . . . it looked like an Egyptian palace. Sean met his brother and led them over to a special VIP section to a reserved table.

"How's everyone doing?" Sean spoke softly.

"We're all good, man." Kyle gave his brother a hug. "The ladies are ready to party so here we are."

Jade brought out a magnum of champagne and joined them at the table. "Can I get you guys anything?"

"Babe, just send over a waitress. I know my brother's gonna want something from the bar," Sean whispered in his wife's ear.

Eric and Keisha appeared. Keisha took a seat by Topaz. She looked Topaz directly in her eyes and Topaz looked away. Keisha always seemed to be able to read her innermost thoughts and she couldn't handle it.

"What's up, girlfriend?"

"I'm good." Topaz locked her fingers with Germain's.

"Can y'all believe what they did to my juke joint now?" Eric was always good for a laugh.

"Honey, how many times have I asked you not to call the restaurant a juke joint? People might get the wrong idea." Keisha looked at Eric and shook her head. "I'm kinda feeling this décor though."

Topaz's beautiful face continually lit up the screen on the monitors. She had recorded a great dance track, and people were on the dance floor. "Come on, baby. Let's go dance." Topaz popped out of her chair and pulled Germain behind her.

Nina watched them as they danced. They really seemed to be having a good time. Keisha was also watching them. She picked at the food on her plate and had very little to say to anyone. Topaz and Germain returned to the table laughing.

"What's up, cuz?" Topaz smiled at Nina as she took a seat next to her. It was obvious that she had consumed a great deal of champagne.

"Can we get out of here for a minute?" Nina's eyes were intense.

"Sure, I need to go to the powder room anyway." Topaz spoke briefly to Germain before she followed Nina out of the club.

"Let's use the bathroom in here." Nina led Topaz to the office Jade shared with Keisha, opened the door, and then quickly closed and locked it behind them. "You deserve an Oscar for your performance." She spoke so only Topaz could hear.

Topaz made no comment but went into the restroom and returned several minutes later. "I'm ready."

Nina looked at her like she was crazy. "Ready for what?"

"Ready to go back to my party with my husband."

There was a knock at the door and Keisha walked in. "How are we doing?"

Topaz rolled her eyes. "Not now, Keisha. I'm on my way back out to the party."

"I'm sure you won't be missed for a minute. Sean and Eric took the guys up to their new billiard room. Germain will survive without you for a few minutes." Keisha opened her refrigerator and took out a Coke. "You guys really need to come out with the truth about everything before things really get out of hand."

"Topaz, what did you tell her?" Nina exploded.

"I didn't tell her anything, but you and your big-ass mouth just did." Topaz's eyes were stormy.

"Don't fall apart now, you two. No one told me anything. I figured it out after you returned from Europe with Niki," Keisha calmly explained.

"What?" Topaz and Nina chorused.

Keisha simply nodded.

"Why didn't you say anything?" Nina demanded.

Keisha took a long swig of her Coke. "For several reasons. First, I prayed and hoped to God I was wrong. I didn't want to be right. For you guys to go to that length to keep a secret, I'm sure you thought you had a very good reason."

Neither Topaz nor Nina said a word. They just sat there looking very tired and very defeated.

"How did you know?" Topaz managed to whisper.

"Despite the obvious things?"

Nina looked like she was going to be sick. "What obvious things?"

Keisha drank the last of her soft drink. "Niki's beautiful golden eyes . . . I've never seen anyone with those eyes but you, Topaz. Even though your mom and Nina's mom are sisters, those eyes did not come from your mother's side of the family, they're from your father. When we were little girls I remember you telling me I got my golden eyes from my daddy."

Topaz looked like a wilted flower. "Go on," she mumbled.

"Niki can sing like you. She looks nothing like Nina or Kyle. Nina, you never looked the least bit pregnant. I've heard of people not showing, but girlfriend, I was never convinced," Keisha finished.

No one made eye contact as the ladies all sat there in an uncomfortable silence.

"Kyle's in on this too, isn't he?" Keisha broke their awkward silence with yet another probing question.

"Yes," Nina whispered.

"Damn." Keisha hit the desk with her fist. Topaz and Nina practically jumped out of their chairs. "Why do you always do this to Germain? He's a good man. He doesn't deserve all of your lies and deceit."

A huge tear pressed itself out of Topaz's eye and rolled down her cheek. "No matter what you or anyone else thinks, I love my husband very, very much."

"Then tell him the truth!" Keisha shouted.

"We kept everything a secret to protect Jade." Nina's voice trembled as she spoke.

"Jade?" Keisha repeated. "What does she have to do with this?"

Nina looked at Topaz, who was dabbing at the corner of an eye with her finger. "Sean is Niki's father."

"Are you sure?" Keisha was whispering now.

"Yes, I'm sure. I ought to know who I slept with," Topaz yelled.

"Girl, would you be quiet?" Nina looked at Topaz like she was crazy. "You remember when Jade and Sean were having problems?" Nina said to Keisha. "We didn't want to see them get a divorce over one night that was a huge mistake."

"You guys are so considerate," Keisha replied sarcastically.

"Look, whatever was wrong in Jade's marriage was wrong before Sean and I slept together," Topaz said defensively.

Keisha made no comment. She simply shook her head. "Y'all are too messy. This is a mess . . . a huge mess."

"If Jade knew Topaz had a baby by Sean, she would have him in divorce court so quick he would still be trying to figure out what happened," Nina offered.

"And if she finds out she still might divorce his ass," Topaz added.

The office door opened and Jade appeared in the doorway. "What's going on in here, you guys?"

Everyone was so shocked by her abrupt entrance, no one said anything.

"Are you guys keeping secrets from me?" Jade giggled.

Topaz stood up and smiled. "No, sweetie, we're not keeping anything from you. I just got a headache and came in here to get away from all the noise. I'm feeling better now, so I'm going to find Germain." Topaz made a quick exit as Jade took her seat.

"I guess she would have a headache after all that drama at the press party. Can you believe that reporter actually accused Topaz of having a baby and giving it away? She's better than me, because I would have cursed her out."

"That's why she's a superstar. The girl is a professional," Keisha smiled. "Are the guys still upstairs, Jade?"

"Yes, they were talking about playing poker and ordering hot wings." Jade laughed.

"Is anyone still at the party?" Keisha questioned.

"Oh yes," Jade laughed. "As long as there's free food and drink, no one's going home."

Keisha went back into the club where things were still in full swing. Topaz was dancing with Usher. When the song was over, Keisha went and dragged her off the floor. "You need to get Germain and get out of here."

"He's playing poker with the guys, Keisha." Topaz was irritated.

"So get him out of that card game and take him home so you guys can talk."

"We talked in the limo on the way over here."

"Did you guys tell him Niki really is your daughter?"

"No."

"Why not?"

"Because he's fine with things the way they are. I told him all about Rosalyn."

"As in my father's top researcher Dr. Rosalyn Lawrence?"

"Yes."

"What does *she* have to do with this?" Keisha demanded.

"She called me and told me if I didn't allow Baby Doll to spend time with her father, I would be sorry."

"She threatened you?"

"She's a psychotic hatin' bitch."

"So you didn't let her see Baby Doll?"

"You were with me at my attorney's office when I set up the stipulations of the agreement that her family signed."

The ladies were seated back in VIP at Topaz's abandoned table.

"Oh, this is too crazy. What made her think Niki was your daughter?"

"She said something about me and Germain both having the trait, and Nina and Kyle not having the trait, so Niki couldn't be their daughter."

"Oh my God . . . T . . . the blood drive for the Chocolate Affair. She knows all of our blood types."

"She sure does." Topaz paused to speak to Shemar Moore, who had stopped by her table.

"Topaz, Germain has the trait?" Keisha's eyes were about to pop out of her head.

"She said he did."

"Oh my God . . . that means Niki could be Germain's . . ."

Topaz put her hand over Keisha's mouth before the rest of her words could escape. "She's not, so don't even think it. We weren't together then." Topaz couldn't handle hearing the question that had stayed on her mind ever since Rosalyn's crazy-ass phone call.

"Wait . . . now I remember. The first time Niki had a crisis Jade came up to the hospital and she mentioned that Sean had the trait because she saw it in some paperwork she had to fill out for their insurance policies."

"Niki is Sean's baby."

"I don't think Niki looks like Sean either."

"Keisha, leave it alone, okay?" Topaz let out a long sigh.

Germain came back into the club and joined them at the table. "Those Negroes already took all my money."

Topaz and Keisha laughed because Germain was practically pouting and he looked just like Chris.

A smile brightened Germain's fallen countenance. "What are you guys laughing at?"

Topaz kissed him on the cheek. "You, baby, because you are too cute when you pout."

"I wasn't pouting."

"I know, baby. Come on. Let's go home now so Mama can take good care of Daddy." Topaz smiled at him and Keisha.

"Sounds like a plan to me. I do have surgery in the morning." Germain stood up and extended a hand to his wife. "Shall we?"

Topaz took his hand and stood up. "We shall."

"All right, you two, good night." Keisha kissed and hugged Germain and then Topaz.

"I don't have a good feeling about this, girl. Tell him the truth. All of it. Tonight," Keisha whispered in Topaz's ear.

The rest of the friends returned, and the guys were teasing Germain about losing all of his money.

"Let sleeping dogs lie, Key," Topaz whispered back. "Isn't that how that old saying goes?"

"Yeah, that's how it goes, only your dogs aren't asleep. They're awake and starting to bark all over the place."

Chapter 23

As the sun crept into an eastern sky, it gently warmed the Pacific, casting a soft glow over the Malibu coastline. It was morning and the tide was out, extending the beach on the oceanfront property. Nina lay in Kyle's arms as she had all night, neither of them sleeping or talking.

"Babe, you awake?" Nina shifted her position and rested her head on her husband's chest.

"Yeah, you?"

"Of course I am, silly." A smile found its way onto Nina's face.

Kyle rubbed her hair and gently eased himself out of the bed. "Gotta take a leak." She watched him walk on his toes as he headed into the bathroom and watched him as he came back out. He was pigeon-toed and she felt it added character to his handsome physique. He climbed back into bed and they resumed their positions.

Nina ran her fingers gently across the hair that was beginning to grow again on his chest. Kyle was a metrosexual who took great pride in his grooming. He would have made a great underwear model. "Babe, you love me?"

"No."

"Kyle."

"Ask a silly question, get a silly answer."

"I was just thinking about Topaz and Germain."

"I haven't been able to think about anything else."

Nina let out a long sigh. "I still can't believe how she told him all those lies."

"They weren't all lies. Actually, she told him the truth according to the conversation you told me you had with Dr. Lawrence when you were in Hawaii."

"She told him everything except that she is Niki's biological mother."

They lay in silence as the hard truth of Nina's words sank in.

"Now that part of the truth came out, I can't keep lying to Germain. When we agreed to adopt Niki I didn't know Germain. Now he's family. He's the brother I never had." Nina wiped a tear from her eye before it could land on her husband's chest.

"I feel exactly the same way. He's my best friend now. We're boys."

They were both quiet until Nina's BlackBerry became an absolute pest. "Guess we better get to the office." She got out of bed and Kyle watched her as she walked into the bathroom. He was immediately aroused and joined her in the bathroom, where Nina was turning on the shower. She dropped her robe and stepped into the warm pulsating water as it massaged her well-toned body. There wasn't an ounce of fat anywhere. Would she lose her figure and get cellulite if she had a baby? She looked at Kyle as he stepped inside the shower.

"I knew you'd bring your bighead in here. You know you got to be where I be."

"Get over here, woman." He pulled her toward him and kissed her until she was burning with desire. "You don't need to be so sassy. You're not off punishment yet."

"Punishment?" She smiled and kissed him again before she began to scrub her body with a pink puff.

"What's up, girl?" Kyle's eyes were pleading.

"We've got meetings. We don't have time to go there right now."

"We are the bosses."

"That's true, but we don't want to be too late. I'll give you a quickie."

Forty-five minutes later they were in Kyle's Escalade heading through the canyon to Burbank. They both returned phone calls during the drive into the city.

Mimi was waiting for them in the conference room when they arrived. "Good morning, you two."

"Hey, girl." Nina kissed her on the cheek.

"Good morning, Ms. Bluest Eye." Kyle gave Mimi a Denzel Washington smile.

"I may not be able to keep the tabloids off the Topaz baby story."

"Oh no." The smile on Nina's face disappeared.

"Publicity like this definitely won't hurt. It'll blow over eventually. Meanwhile we book shows and sell millions of CDs."

"It's all about the Benjamins. My kind of woman." Kyle was such a flirt.

Nina smiled at her husband. With Kyle around she could get through anything.

Mimi smiled at Kyle, too. "Speaking of shows, I've

got Topaz booked for a performance on the Grammys. She received five nominations for *Superstar*, too."

"Praise the Lord! This is wonderful." Nina was ecstatic.

"Isn't it? I'm so excited," Mimi said.

"Me too," Nina replied. "It is such a blessing to be a part of this. I passed on her project, and God gave it back to me."

"What do you mean God gave it back to you?" Mimi fixed her baby blues on Nina.

"Topaz brought me her music and I passed. I was tripping, and God brought this wonderful project back to me."

"That's because you were chosen by the Almighty, darlin'. You too, blue eyes." Kyle smiled at Mimi, who beamed every time Kyle spoke to her.

"That's a very interesting perspective," Mimi said. "But you are definitely some kind of lucky."

Nina simply smiled.

"The press can't write enough good things about the CD. People love her singing with that guitar. That was ingenious," Mimi said.

"That was all Topaz," Kyle added.

"She was amazing," Nina added.

"Wasn't she? And the concert at The Diamond . . . oh my God. I actually cried," Mimi confessed.

"She was phenomenal," Kyle commented.

"I cried too," Nina said quietly.

"Sherwin is doing something wonderful for her as a signing bonus. It's a secret, so don't bother asking," Mimi declared.

"Dish, girlfriend," Nina demanded.

"Yeah," Kyle agreed. "We're good at keeping secrets."

"No, I promised." Mimi smiled.

"Awwww. We won't tell," Nina prompted.

"No. You'll know when it happens. It's something totally awesome," Mimi said.

Nina flipped through a small stack of tear sheets from the covers of major magazines—*Vibe, Allure, InStyle, Essence . . . Glamour.* Many had made last-minute changes and run Topaz's feature article instead of previously selected cover stories. The girl was on fire, and people couldn't get enough of her.

Ne-Yo was waiting for Nina with a bunch of new tracks for Sky. Nina had released her CD despite the catastrophic showcase, and one of the singles had caught on really big in Europe and Africa. There was talk of sending her over to do a promotional tour.

"These are some great tracks, playa. I think we need to get Sky back in the studio as soon as possible. Her fans will want new music. We have to be ready with the next CD." Kyle made a few notes on his pad. "I can work a great tie-in with American Express."

"Cool," Nina replied quickly. "Let's get a video crew on the road. We can do a Diary-type show and run it as a six-week reality show on one of the music channels."

"I'll get video to do a treatment and run a budget." Kyle made more notes on his pad.

Nina walked Ne-Yo to the door. "Get the studio time booked and get back to me. I've got to get as much done with you while you're still available, because I know everyone's knocking at your door." Nina smiled at the talented young songwriter and producer.

"Nina, you can get me in the studio anytime." The young man flirted with Nina easily, not even caring that Kyle was there.

Kyle looked Ne-Yo up and down. *He's trying to mack my wife.*

"A'ight, baby. Call me with that schedule." Nina extended a hand. Ne-Yo kissed it and strolled out the door. Nina turned around to face Kyle. "This is so cool. I love working with you, Kyle Ross. We make a great team."

"We do, don't we? Now that you decided to give a brother a chance."

"My bad. I was seriously tripping."

"Yes, you were." Kyle looked up at Nina. "You and your thugs."

"Are you a thug?" Nina smiled at Kyle.

"Hell, yeah. I'm straight up gangsta."

"Bourgeois style." Nina laughed.

"Valley girl."

Kyle was silent again as they made the drive back into Malibu. Even though it was after seven, traffic on the Ventura Freeway was still very heavy.

"We should think about getting a place closer to the office so we don't have to deal with all this traffic every day." Nina sighed as red brake lights lit up for miles in every lane on the freeway in the stop-and-go traffic. "This is ridiculous."

Kyle made no indication of whether he had heard her or not. His mind raced with ideas.

Nina took out her BlackBerry that was surprisingly quiet and pressed a button. "What are you doing?"

"Just finishing up dinner with Germain and the kids."

"You received five Grammy nominations."

Topaz screamed. "Oh my God."

"They love you, girl."

"They love me?"

"They love the woman and her guitar, Superstar."

Topaz screamed again and Nina laughed. "Have you spoken to Mimi lately?"

"No. I've just been here with my man waiting for everything to blow over."

"The music press is all about the music, but the tabloids are having a field day with this baby story."

"I could kill Rosalyn Lawrence."

"As long as everything's cool with you and Germain, don't worry about it."

"We're great." Topaz sighed. "He's all excited about his birthday. You know I have to do something."

"Give him a party at The Diamond, and then you two should take some away time. Go to Fiji or something."

"I'll have to talk to you about this later."

"Is he in the room?"

"Sorta kinda like."

"A'ight. Later." Nina clicked off the phone.

"I was thinking," Kyle began, "why don't you, me, and Niki have some away time? I know I got those tickets for Jamaica, but we need something in the interim."

"I'd like that. What did you have in mind?" Nina focused on her husband.

"A three-day Disney cruise to the Bahamas."

"Kyle, Niki would love that and so would I."

"I was thinking about my little princess and my queen when I came up with the idea." Kyle grinned.

"When do we go?"

"Next weekend over Veterans Day. We'll take the red-eye to Miami Friday night, hit the ship over the weekend, and fly back to LA on another red-eye Monday."

* * *

"Look, Mommy. Isn't it pretty?" Niki looked up into Nina's eyes with soft topaz eyes. They were much prettier than Topaz's because Niki's were flecked with blue. When you looked into her eyes, you had to take a second look. Her eyes were pure and clear like glass.

The airplane ascended over the glittering Los Angeles skyline. Niki looked out of a window seat in first class with Mama Nina leaning over her shoulder. Kyle took out the *New York Times* and began reading.

"We're going to have fun." Niki sang a little melody and Nina smiled.

"We sure are. Now everybody go to sleep because we're getting on the boat first thing in the morning." Nina covered Niki and Teddy with her favorite Cheetah Girls comforter and pillow. Then she covered herself and Kyle with a cheetah-print throw, leaned on his shoulder, and went to sleep. Kyle looked up from his paper and cast the women in his life an appreciative glance, then folded the paper and slept.

The plane arrived in Miami late. There was a stretch limo waiting to take the family to the harbor. Traffic was so congested they almost missed the ship. Once onboard, it was only a matter of minutes before the anchor lifted and the ship slowly glided out to sea.

"Yay." Niki was so excited she was ready to explode. She was on a cruise with Mickey Mouse. Kyle booked an oceanside state room suite with a verandah. It was two rooms . . . a bedroom with a king-sized bed for Nina and Kyle and a pullout bed for Niki in the living room.

"What do you guys want to do first?" Kyle looked at Nina and Niki.

"Let's go up on deck and chill. It's very warm out-side," Nina suggested.

Outfitted in summer gear, the family stretched out with books and magazines on chaises by the Mickey Mouse pool. Water and sky were brilliantly blue. They read books until one by one, they drifted off to sleep.

When Nina opened her eyes, Niki was wearing her swimsuit. "Mommy, can I go in the pool now? I've been waiting for you and Daddy to wake up."

"Sure, baby. Just make sure you come out if you begin to feel chilly." She watched Niki slide into the pool, found the camera, and snapped away.

"Look, Kyle." Nina beamed with motherly pride. "Isn't our baby girl the cutest little thing?"

After dinner, they attended a concert.

"This reminds me of when you had me come to New York for the weekend. We had so much fun, and you were the perfect gentleman."

"You were cute," Kyle recalled.

"I fell in love with you that weekend." Nina posi-tioned herself in her husband's arms.

"I know."

"Kyle . . ."

"That was the plan, woman. I had to get you to fall for me. I fell in love with you the day you came up to Sean's ranch for Kobe's christening party."

"You did? Baby, that is so sweet." Nina had warm fuzzy feelings when she finally fell asleep.

When the ship docked, they took a tour of Nassau, where Nina and Niki had their hair braided on the beach. They purchased identical pairs of gold bangles and a gold watch for Kyle in a jewelry stall near Straw Market. After a Bahamian dinner, they went back to the ship where they watched movies in the stateroom. On the final day of the cruise, they enjoyed massages in the spa. The turnaround was much too soon before they were back in the airport waiting for the return flight to Los Angeles.

"Thank you for bringing us, baby. We really needed that little vacation." Nina smiled at Kyle.

"We'll take a longer cruise next time and bring Chris and Baby Doll for Niki."

"Niki would love that, but I think she really enjoyed hanging out with Mommy and Daddy." Nina pushed the braids out of her daughter's face.

"That's my little princess road dog." Kyle grinned as he carried the sleeping child onto the airplane.

Chapter 24

Sabre cranked the volume on Gnarls Barkley's "Crazy" in her new 500 Mercedes coup.

"I love this song. I'll have to put it in my MP3 player," she said to herself.

It was a gorgeous Saturday in November in the City of the Angels. She glanced at the two lanes of bumper-to-bumper traffic on Santa Monica Freeway headed west to the beaches.

I'm glad I have a house right on the ocean so I don't have to go to the beach.

She thought about the days in foster care, living in homes where she wasn't wanted until she went to live with her grandmother. With Grandma Marisol, Sabre finally had a real mother. That was after Tina slashed up Mr. Rufus with a butcher knife for molesting Sabre and Tina was sent to prison. Sabre could still see the bloodied sheets. Mr. Rufus didn't die until several weeks later. That old demon held on as long as it could.

Sabre's cell phone rang and MIMI flashed in the caller ID. "Hi, Mimi," Sabre spoke into her headset.

"Hi, sweetie. I'm not going to be able to make lunch today."

"Awwww." Sabre always loved hanging out with Mimi. They were going to have lunch at The Diamond, then Sabre was going shopping.

"I'm at The Ivy waiting on Topaz. She's running late."

"What are you guys meeting about?" Sabre demanded.

"Lots of stuff. She just received five Grammy nominations for starters."

Sabre was still pissed because she only received three: Best New Artist, Best Video, Best Female R & B Artist.

"There's a bunch of shit in the tabloids about Topaz. That baby story has her on the front page of every last one."

"Poor thing. Is she still with her husband?"

"No one's going to leave a spouse over some stupid article in a tabloid. I see her coming now. I gotta go, sweetie. Bye-bye."

"*Even when the article is true?*" Sabre wanted to ask.

Sabre drove north on Fairfax Avenue to the Miracle Mile to Sky's apartment. She could hear music before Sky opened the door.

"Whassup?" they yelled at each other, imitating the old Budweiser commercial, and laughed.

Sabre met Sky in school at a neighborhood Catholic church. Sabre had always hated the first day of school because she never knew anyone. By the time she did make friends, it was time to move again, but this time Sabre knew it was going to be different.

Sky's neatly braided hair was always tied with ribbons that matched the blue in their school uniforms. Their desks sat next to each other, and the girls were in the same reading group. They lived on the same street and became best friends

"You're not supposed to be here now." Sky lowered the music.

"Mimi stood me up for Topaz."

"She is a superstar."

"I'm starvin'. Let's go to Pink's before we go to the Beverly Center. I want one of those cheeseburgers with a Coke."

"You and your cheeseburgers and Cokes." Sky laughed.

There was a line in front of Pink's as usual. Sabre and Sky stood in it wearing super-dark shades.

"You know everyone is staring at me." Sabre brushed on fresh lip gloss.

"They're staring at us." Sky smiled at a very handsome brother who was throwing her mad attention.

"Victor and I have been hanging out again," Sabre commented.

Some teenagers stood in line and immediately recognized Sky and Sabre. "Y'all gotta stand in line?" one of the young men asked.

"Yeah," Sabre smiled. "That's really fucked up, but I love their cheeseburgers."

"I come up here for the chili dogs," the young man told them. "What do you like?" he asked Sky.

"I like the chili dogs, too." Sky smiled and whispered to Sabre. "What's he gonna do, buy us lunch?"

The young man disappeared, then returned and ushered them to the front of the line where they added fries, onion rings, and drinks to their order, which he brought to them on the patio.

"What's your name?" Sky asked as Sabre bit into her burger.

"Ronnie." He grinned

"Ricky, Ronnie, Bobby and Mike." Sabre sang a line from an old New Edition song. Normally, Sky would have joined in but she didn't, and that bothered Sabre.

"Thanks for lunch, Ronnie." Sky dipped an onion ring in ketchup. "I'd invite you to join us, but we're just staying long enough to finish our food."

Sabre let out a loud, disgusting burp. She felt their eyes on her, so she looked up. "I always do that when I drink Coke."

"And you're always disgusting." Sky smiled at Ronnie, who handed her his number, written on a piece of paper.

"Whatever. Let's go." Sabre reached for the paper with Ronnie's number. Sky handed it to her, and Sabre ripped it into pieces.

"Why did you do that?" Sky demanded.

"Oh please. You weren't going to hang out with that busta." Sabre laughed.

"That was my number. Why do you always trip when you're not the center of attention?"

"I don't do that."

"You should see yourself. Whenever everything's not about you, you start tripping."

They got back into the car, and within minutes they were at the Beverly Center. They hooked up with Dawn, Lolita, and Victor at the MAC store.

"My peeps!" Sabre grinned.

After everyone hugged and kissed Sabre, she introduced Lolita. Victor gave her a hug, and Dawn recalled meeting Sky at Sabre's housewarming party.

"I loved So Fine. I still play your CD," Dawn said to Sky. "When are you guys going to record again?"

Sky was beginning to get a little uncomfortable because the attention had shifted to her and she didn't want Sabre to get an attitude. "We might do another CD sometime in the future. We're all extremely busy with our individual careers now." Sky was very diplomatic.

"What are you doing now?" Sabre asked her friend. She knew Sky hadn't done much of anything since the showcase.

"I'm getting ready to go back in the studio and record some songs for my new CD before I do some promotional dates in Europe and Africa," Sky replied coolly.

"That is so cool, Sky Sky." Victor gave Sky a big hug that lasted a little too long for Sabre's liking. Victor was always hugging on Sky every chance he got, and Sabre wondered if he had feelings for her.

"It sure is," Dawn and Lolita agreed.

"When you come back, you'll be a big star," Victor said.

"That's what Nina and Kyle said too." Sky smiled. "Can we go in here? I could use some new makeup."

"I'll help you pick some out," Lolita offered. "Did you know I'm Sabre's makeup artist?"

"Really? This is so perfect. A pro is in the house." Sky glanced at Sabre. "You don't mind if Lolita helps me, do you?" Sky knew Sabre did mind, but she was doing a pretty good job of pretending she didn't.

Within an hour, they were on their way to Dolce & Gabbana to pick out things for Sabre.

"I love this store." Sky's entire countenance changed the moment they stepped inside. "Jade and I were in here the day of my showcase buying something for me to perform in because I got my period and I couldn't wear what my stylist had picked out for me."

"Oh, you poor thing." Lolita gave Sky a little hug. "What a terrible thing to happen."

"You went shopping with Jade?" Sabre paused to look at Sky. She was immediately angry with Sky and didn't know why.

"Ladies and gentleman." A handsome African American sales associate greeted them warmly. "What can I assist you with?"

"I'm Sabre, and my Glam Squad and I are here to buy some clothes." Sabre was enjoying being the center of attention.

"You're So Fine." The associate's eyes rested on Sky and then back on Sabre.

Dawn led Sabre to an area in the store where they sifted through various articles of clothing on hangers.

Sky began perusing through items in the front of the store as Victor stood with her.

"Gotta let the Queen Bee be." Victor put his hands in his pockets.

"I know." Sky took a dress off the rack to give it a closer look. "I don't know why she's always been so insecure. Always the prettiest girl in school and she never believed it."

"That's very noble of you," Victor said.

"Why?" Sky hung the dress back on the rack and looked at Victor. "It's true."

"I would have thought you were the prettiest girl in the school."

Sky was surprised. "Thanks, Victor."

Dawn took a pink and silver skirt and jacket suit off the rack and looked at it. It was gorgeous and any woman wearing it would look like a million dollars.

"Ughh." Sabre looked at it and turned up her nose. "I hate it."

"Tell me something I don't know." Dawn laughed. "I didn't pick this out for you."

Sabre looked puzzled. "Who's it for?"

"This would look fabulous on Sky."

"Oh yes," Lolita agreed quickly.

Sabre gave the outfit another long look.

"Sabre, why don't you get started with these things so we can see what's what."

"Okay." Sabre was excited. "I'll be in the dressing room."

Dawn walked over to Sky and held the suit up in front of her. "This would look fabulous on you."

"It sure would." Lolita handed her some accessories. "Go try it on."

"Thank you, guys." Sky skipped off to the dressing room as Queen Bee stepped out in a to-die-for black dress. Sabre was sexy but classy.

"Girl, you are wearin' that dress," Sky called out as she disappeared inside a changing room.

Sabre agreed with Sky's declaration as she did model-like moves in the mirror. Sabre looked fine in that dress and she knew it.

Sky came out of the dressing room looking very high couture in the suit. Lolita put a necklace around Sky's neck that set off the suit perfectly. She struck a pose in the mirror. "I love it." Sky twisted and turned so she could get a glimpse at every angle.

"Now that's what you wear to your big fund-raising tea when you're chairman of the board because it's your foundation." Dawn straightened the collar on the jacket.

"Okay." Everyone laughed at their private little joke about the extremely wealthy and the famous.

Sabre walked out in a very nice suit, but the jacket

was too long. She looked at herself in the mirror and felt dumb, then focused on Sky, who was as regal as Jackie Kennedy Onassis in the suit.

"She looks wonderful, doesn't she?" Lolita smiled at Sabre.

"She looks a'ight. I don't really like pink." Sabre went to take the suit off that did absolutely nothing for her petite figure. "It's getting late, you guys, and I have an appointment."

Sabre and Sky changed back into their jeans and heels.

"You have to get that suit, Sky," Dawn informed her.

"I wish I could. That thing is five thousand dollars," she said so only Dawn could hear.

"I know what you mean," Dawn replied.

Sabre saw Dawn return the suit to the rack. "Sky's not buying that?"

"She can't afford it right now," Dawn explained.

Sabre looked the suit up and down. She really wanted it for herself after she saw how good it looked on Sky, but way down inside Sabre knew it would never look like that on her. "I'll buy it for her." Sabre was surprised when she heard herself say it. She had never done too much of anything for anyone but herself. *Not even Grandma.*

"Sabre," Sky squealed with delight. "Thank you." Sky knew better than to hug her. She knew how much Sabre hated being touched. Sabre had issues, but Sky had always loved her anyway.

"That suit looked real good on you. And like you always say, I was hatin' so I need to redeem myself," Sabre explained and smiled. She felt good buying the suit for Sky.

Sky looked her childhood friend up and down. This was another Sabre.

Sabre paid the bill and everyone went to Dolce, where they were led to a great table in the heart of the restaurant.

"This is so cool." Sky had never been to the restaurant. Sabre had come several times by herself, but never with a group of friends.

Sabre ordered martinis for everyone. "This is on me, y'all. So get whatever you want." She checked her Sidekick. It was time for her to go. "Look, y'all, I have an appointment."

"Where are you going?" Victor demanded, asking the question they all wanted to know.

"I have a personal appointment. But I'll be back. I'm hanging out here all night."

"Then we'll be here when you get back," Victor replied.

Sabre drove the short distance to the tower at Cedars-Sinai. She checked her purse. *Yep, it was there.*

"Hello." The receptionist greeted her. "Dr. Gradney will be right with you."

"Sabre Cruz." Germain had a way of making you relax as soon as he spoke to you.

"Hey, Dr. G." Sabre turned her wattage up a notch. "How's everything going?"

"Couldn't be better." Germain took a quick glance at her chart.

"You're not bothered by all those tabloid stories?"

"The price of fame."

The nurse walked in, and Germain examined her breasts. Sabre felt waves of passion rolling over her.

"You've healed *very* nicely." Sabre's eye caught Germain's and he looked away.

He's attracted to me too, Sabre concluded.

"Dr. G, have you ever wondered if that baby story on your wife is true?"

Germain finally looked at Sabre. "No."

"Not even once?"

Germain hesitated, and Sabre gave him a diabolical laugh.

"I think you should know it is true," Sabre said with a straight face.

"What? What would you know about it?" Germain's features were dark with anger.

"I know this." Sabre took Nina's journal out of her purse and handed it to Germain.

He took the pink book and opened it. The first page had Nina Beaubien next to dates and the year, all written in Nina's beautiful cursive writing.

"Turn to the page where the ribbon is. What you need to read is on that page."

Germain sat on the edge of the desk and began reading Nina's detailed account of Topaz having a baby in Europe. He looked at the date. *I kept Baby Doll for her while she was over there having some other man's baby.*

"Where did you get this?" Germain demanded.

"From a bookcase in Nina and Kyle's house."

Kyle . . . my best friend is in on this too? "Why should I believe you? You could have made all of this up." Germain handed the journal back to Sabre.

"You know I didn't make it up." Sabre wrote her cell phone number on the back of her appointment card. "Here."

Germain looked at Sabre, but he didn't take the card. "What's that?"

"My cell phone number so you can call me if you need to talk," Sabre replied coolly. "And I know you're gonna want to talk after you read that journal."

She left the book and the card with her phone number on the examination table.

Chapter 25

Jade hummed softly as she headed to The Diamond's kitchen to make sure everything she ordered for Sean's birthday weekend was included in the boxes of supplies traveling to Santa Barbara. All of the Black Friends, as Sabre called them, would be attending the party that included a day of sailing on the Rosses' new yacht christened *The Jade* by Sean. A ninety footer, it was very light, airy, and high-tech with blond hardwood and jade and black marble running throughout.

Her favorite chef was coming along to prepare all the food. They had worked on the menu together and planned some delicious meals for the weekend. She spotted a couple of cases of Cristal that had been purchased for the yacht.

Topaz. Jade smiled as she thought about her crazy girlfriend, who had exposed her to some of the finer things of life.

"Looks like everything is here, fellas. See you in Santa Barbara." Jade went by the high-rise condo in the Marina where Sean was waiting for her.

"Hey, birthday boy." Jade paused to look at Sean,

who was staring out of the window. She could tell his mind was someplace else. "Ready to go?"

"E is on the way."

Jade kissed him. "Good. We're going to have so much fun." The house phone rang and she picked it up. It was the concierge informing them that the Johnsons were waiting downstairs.

"Howdy do, black people. I do believe I've been given the privilege of driving the mister and the mizzus up to Santa Barbara this here afternoon." Eric had gotten a chauffeur's cap from somewhere, and he tipped it to Keisha. "How you doin' on this here fine afternoon, pretty lady?"

Everyone laughed at Eric's impersonation of Morgan Freeman in *Driving Miss Daisy*.

"You don't have the good sense the Lord gave you, do you?" Keisha shook her head and laughed.

"He just got hit in the head with one too many basketballs," Sean explained as Eric headed for the San Diego Freeway.

"Hi, Uncle Sean. Hi, Aunty Jade." Eric and Keisha's ten-year-old daughter, Kendra, popped up in the rear of Eric's Suburban. "I wanted to surprise you, but it was getting really hot under that blanket."

"You surprised us." All of a sudden, Jade had an attitude.

"Kendra's plans for the weekend fell through at the last minute, so we had no choice but to bring her along," Keisha explained quickly.

"That's fine with me." Sean turned to smile at Kendra. "We'll just put her to work in the galley or else she walks the plank." Sean gave her his best pirate imitation, and Kendra giggled.

"Daddy, do you hear Uncle Sean trying to put me to

work in the kitchen?" Kendra flipped through the pages of one of her teen fashion magazines. Kendra inherited her father's height and her mother's curves. She was tall without being awkward, so there was a lot of talk about Kendra pursuing a career in modeling.

Jade looked out the window at the landscape and tried to convince herself that Kendra's presence would not make a difference one way or the other on Sean's party, but no matter how much she tried to convince herself, she couldn't. She focused on Sean, who had said very little to her since they left the Marina. Jade wondered if he shared her concern over Kendra's presence, but she knew something other than Kendra was occupying her husband's mind and had been since the night of Topaz's party.

Kyle was silent as he carried their bags out to the Escalade. Moments later, Nina fastened Niki in her car seat and Kyle headed out of Malibu.

"I really don't want to go," Kyle said, breaking the silence. "I'm not up for a party."

"I'm not either, but we can't miss your brother's birthday. Jade put a lot of work into this. You'll feel better once you get around the fellas."

"I hope so," Kyle agreed, but his face showed he wasn't convinced.

Topaz paced back and forth in the living room, trying her best to remain calm. Germain should have been home hours ago. Now they were going to be extremely late for Sean's birthday party. She tried Germain's cell phone again, but there was still no answer, and he had not returned any of her previous calls; she couldn't help worrying. It was so unlike him not to return her calls or for them to go without speaking the entire day. Somehow, they weathered the storm of publicity from her release party only to arrive here . . . Germain's behavior was totally out of character and Topaz had no idea why. She was trying to think of someone else to call who could tell her of his whereabouts when his black 911 Porsche zipped into the driveway.

"Germain, where have you been?" Topaz was practically in tears. "I was worried sick."

"Working." He avoided her hug and gave her a lifeless peck on the cheek.

"Your office has been closed for hours and you didn't answer your cell phone."

"Look, I'm here now so don't get all dramatic on me because we're a little late for *your friend,* Sean's, birthday bash."

Topaz followed Germain upstairs to their bedroom. Chris and Baby Doll were away at sleepovers, and she had given the staff the weekend off since they were going to be away. "My *friend* Sean? I thought he was our friend."

Germain, who was busy changing his clothes, didn't acknowledge her comment.

"I know the invitation stressed we be on time, but I don't care about that. I was just concerned about you, baby."

Germain was on his way down the stairs when he stopped to turn around and look at his wife. "You were concerned about me? Now that's a novel concept."

"Germain, you know how much I love you," Topaz wailed.

"So you've said. You just have the funniest ways of showing it." Germain got into the limo first with no regard for Topaz, who slid in after him. He always held the door open for her and allowed her to enter first, but she pushed the incident out of her mind. She watched him toss ice cubes in a glass, pour in Tanqueray with tonic, drink it down, and quickly prepare another. They were both silent as the limo headed toward Santa Barbara in the congested Friday evening traffic. Something was definitely bothering Germain, but she was too afraid to ask what.

Up at the ranch, all of the other Black Friends had arrived on time. Nina noticed that the group was unusually quiet while Kyle became overly friendly with a bottle of flavored rum. Now that the truth about Niki was somewhat out, his mind was plagued with thoughts that he had previously not allowed himself to think.

What if someone tries to take Niki from me and Nina? What if Topaz tells Germain the truth and he wants to raise her since Niki is Topaz's biological daughter? And what about Sean? He's Niki's biological father. What would he think? Kyle looked at Sean and went for another drink. *Well, I don't care what anyone thinks. No one's taking my little girl away from me.*

Meanwhile, Jade was growing angrier by the minute. "We should all be on the yacht right now having dinner under the stars."

"We'll get there, sweetie." Keisha looked up from the movie she was watching with Kendra and Niki and smiled.

"Why is it that every other event that I've planned for my friends has gone beautifully, but when I try to do something for my husband nobody cares?" Jade ranted.

Nina pulled herself away from watching Kyle toss down shots of Bacardi and stood by her sister-in-law. "What are you over here fussing about now, girlfriend?" Nina smiled, trying to lighten things up.

"Topaz always has to be late so she can make some big, grand entrance. Tonight isn't about her, it's a birthday party for my husband. Now it's ruined because she's late. Can't she be on time for something just once?" Jade was so angry she could spit knives. "The invitation stressed the importance of being on time because we were having dinner on the yacht, but she doesn't care. I'm paying for a crew with nothing to do as long as we're sitting in this damn house. We should have just left her ass, but no, Sean wanted to wait. Topaz doesn't care about anyone but herself."

"Maybe something happened. I hope there wasn't an accident or anything. It is Friday night. You know how bad traffic can be on a Friday night." Nina looked concerned.

"I know what happened. Her divaness is running late as usual. Does she think we're her lowly subjects and all we have to do is sit around and wait for her to show up and say, 'I'm here. Now the party can start.'" Jade mimicked Topaz perfectly.

Nina tried not to laugh, but Keisha snickered, and the two of them were practically on the floor laughing.

"That is so Topaz." Keisha laughed.

"Yeah, Jade," Nina agreed. "You did that perfectly."

"I'm glad you two think this is funny because I sure don't." Jade looked at Sean, who was abnormally quiet for the guest of honor. "And you should be happy. It's your birthday. All this damn work I did." Sean had tried to talk his wife out of giving him a party, but she refused. She thought a weekend on the yacht would do all of the friends some good.

Sean walked outside onto the deck overlooking the water. Lights flickered in the dark against the horizon. It was unusually warm for November. It would have been a perfect night for sailing, but Sean still didn't care. He had done his best to forget that one night of passion with Topaz, but ever since the release party, he couldn't get that night off his mind. He was an NBA legend so he was quite familiar with tabloids. He knew firsthand that where there was that much smoke, there was always fire. He stared into the black mass of water replaying thoughts that had clouded his mind for days. *Did Topaz get pregnant that night? Is Niki my child? Why would Topaz keep everything a secret from me? What will Jade do if it's true? And my marriage? Jade will definitely try to kill me, but if Niki is my daughter, I do have a right to know.*

It was just about midnight when Topaz and Germain finally arrived at the ranch. They had ridden in silence the entire way, both of them drinking on empty stomachs, and now they were drunk.

"Hey, everybody. I'm here. Now the party can start." Topaz managed to give them a dazzling smile. "Sorry we're late."

"Sure you are." Jade didn't return Topaz's smile as she emptied the last of a bottle of champagne into her glass.

"We really are sorry, but something came up," Topaz explained, although Germain never gave her an explanation of his whereabouts.

"It seems like things are always coming up with you, Topaz," Jade fired back. "You never think of anyone but yourself."

Keisha looked at Jade, and Jade looked away. "Don't look at me like that, Keisha. Topaz is *your* best friend. She could piss and call it ginger ale and you'd believe her."

"Baby, it's okay. I'm sure Topaz and Germain have a

good reason for being late." Sean tried to soothe his wife. "Don't say things you'll regret later, baby, because you're angry. We'll take the yacht out first thing in the morning."

"What are you now, Secretary of Defense? You haven't said one damn thing to me all day, but as soon as Topaz walks in the door you jump to her defense. She doesn't need you to rescue her, Sean. She has her own husband for that." Jade was definitely not interested in calming down. She was even angrier now that Topaz, who looked absolutely gorgeous in skinny jeans and a halter, had arrived.

Nina eyed Topaz carefully. She knew the moment the Gradneys entered the room that something was definitely wrong between them. She got up from her seat and walked over to Topaz, who totally ignored Jade and her rude outburst.

"Hey, cuz. I'm really glad you guys made it. It definitely wouldn't have been a party without you." Nina tried to hug Germain, but he pulled away from her and went to the bar where Keisha was preparing plates of food. The chef had assembled a wonderful dinner despite the change of plans.

"Here, sweetie, have a little something to eat." Keisha handed Germain a plate, but the alcohol in his system caused him to accidentally knock it out of her hands. It crashed to the floor and shattered into pieces.

Jade sucked her teeth, went into the kitchen, and returned with a small broom and dustpan and angrily swept up the food and fragments of the broken dish. "I know, you're sorry. You already ruined my party. Now you can just finish things off by breaking up all of my damn dishes."

Topaz stepped in front of Jade. "I already apologized for us being late. You should have gone without us if it meant so much to you to be out on that damn yacht. But if you talk to my man like that again, I will kick your ass all over this house."

Nina closed her eyes and silently prayed. She was hoping they could avoid an altercation between Topaz and Jade, who insisted on being a bitch.

"We would have gone without you, but your friend Sean wanted you at the party so we had to wait for the superstar." Jade was livid.

"That figures." Germain finally spoke for the first time since they left Pacific Palisades. "After all, he is her baby's daddy." They were all silent, stunned by his words. "What? Y'all didn't know?"

After several moments, Sean jumped to his feet. "What the hell are you talking about, man?"

"Yeah." Jade folded her arms and focused on Germain as he stood in front of Sean.

"I'm talking about how you had sex with my wife before we remarried. I wasn't back with Topaz then, so I can't say anything about who she was dating, but Sean was married to you at the time, Jade."

"That's not true." Topaz was trying to remain controlled and together.

"You had sex with Topaz?" Jade asked Sean. She did her best to get in his face, despite the fact that he was over six feet and towered over her.

"It's not what you think," Sean replied.

"Did you have sex with *her?*" Jade pointed a finger at Topaz. "Just answer the damn question, man. It requires a yes or no answer."

The tension in the room was so thick you could have reached out and smacked it. After what seemed like forever, Sean finally replied. "Yes."

Germain lit into him like a crazy man, and Eric and Kyle pulled them apart.

How did Germain find everything out? Fear raced through Topaz's body as she watched Sean and Germain fighting over her. Everything seemed so surreal.

"I remember now." Jade's voice trembled as she spoke. "We were having marital problems. It was after Kobe was born." Jade spoke to no one in particular, but everyone heard. "I always knew you cheated with someone, but never once did I think it was my girlfriend. One of my so-called best friends. Mama always told me to be careful with my man around women."

"Mama always knows best, darling," Germain cut in.

Jade focused on Keisha. "I'm going to ask a real dumb question, but I have to give you the benefit of the doubt. Were you in on this too?"

Germain looked at Keisha, one of his dearest and closest friends, waiting to hear what she had to say.

"Yes and no," Keisha began as she watched a look of surprise fill Eric's honey-colored eyes.

"Of course you were a part of this. You're Topaz's best friend. What was I thinking?" Jade shook her head. "That night in the club, the night of the *Superstar* party. All of you were sitting in my office talking until I walked in. I even asked if you were keeping secrets from me. You said no, but you were talking about this." Jade grew more hysterical by the moment. "I am such a fool. I was a fool to think any of you ever were my friends."

"Everybody plays the fool sometime. There's no exception to the rule," Germain sang, slurring words and still drinking.

"That's not true, Jade. We are your friends. We were

trying to protect you," Nina explained, ignoring Germain.

"That's right. No one was trying to hurt you sweetie." Keisha tried to reach for Jade, who pulled away from her like she was poison.

"Liars," Jade screamed. "Backstabbing, two-faced liars. All of you."

"Welcome to the club, darlin'." Germain lifted his glass to Jade in a toast. "Get yourself a glass, so we can give a toast to the fools . . . us."

"Germain . . ." Topaz sighed. It was killing her, seeing him this way.

"I was engaged to Topaz when she, Nina, and Jami went to London to work on her CD while she gave birth. And you know what else, man?" Germain looked at Sean. "Topaz was ready to leave your child in another country."

"Niki *is* my daughter?" Sean couldn't believe what he was hearing.

"No, she's my daughter." Kyle jumped to his feet, unable to take any more.

"What do you mean your daughter?" Sean looked at Kyle like he was crazy.

"My name's on her birth certificate." Kyle's fists were clenched. "That's how I mean my daughter."

"Not for long, if she's my biological daughter," Sean replied angrily.

"We'll see about that," Kyle said.

"Yeah, we'll see," Sean yelled.

"You always get what you want, but not this time, man," Kyle told his brother. "Not this time."

Germain looked at Kyle. "You were in on this too? You're supposed to be my boy." Then he focused on Jade and gave her a lopsided grin. "I told you, we got played. You and me got a lot in common, darlin'. You know, we really need to hook up, Jade."

"We really need to go home now, Germain," Topaz declared firmly.

"What? Too hot in the kitchen for you, darlin'?" Germain stared at Topaz out of eyes glazed with alcohol and pain. "Go home by yourself, because I'm not going anywhere with you." He finished the last of his drink. "Jade, let's you and me go out on the yacht. I'm sure Sean won't mind. He owes me that much."

"You're disgusting." Jade sneered at Germain.

"Germain, let's go home now." Topaz reached for his hand, and he yelled at her.

"I told you to go home or wherever it is you want to go by yourself. You don't need me. I'm hanging out here with my girl, Jade."

"Come on, doc. Let's get you out of here." Kyle's emotions were mixed. He hated seeing his best friend in so much pain. "You ride with me and Niki. Nina, you go with Topaz."

"Are you sure you're able to drive?" Nina asked Kyle. "You were hitting that rum pretty hard."

"I can drive," Kyle reassured her.

"Why don't you let Niki ride in the limo with Nina?" Sean suggested.

"I don't believe you, Sean," Jade screamed.

"What?" Sean looked surprised.

"Who the hell are you, head of transportation?" Jade shouted.

"Is it wrong for me to want my family to get home safely, Jade?" Sean asked.

"You are not Niki's father, so just stay out of this," Kyle yelled at his brother.

"Can we please go home?" Topaz was falling apart.

Her marriage was going down the tubes in front of everyone, and she had never seen Germain that drunk nor had he ever been this angry with her.

"Don't you get any ideas about taking my daughter away from me either, Topaz," Kyle said. "You didn't want her, remember? You wanted to leave her in London."

Nina was glad Kyle had spoken up about Niki's being his daughter. She had been afraid to admit, even to herself, that losing Niki had become a huge unspoken fear.

But Niki was the last thing on Topaz's mind as her eyes brimmed with tears. She had fought them back as long as she could. Now they were determined to flow, but she was not going to break down in front of everyone. Not here and not now, so she quickly brushed the tears from her eyes.

Jade walked up to Topaz and slapped her as hard as she could. "You skanky-ass ho."

Topaz stood there frozen and obviously in shock. Her mind raced in so many directions with so many emotions. "You better get your woman before I hurt her, Sean," Topaz managed to say. Normally, Topaz would have fought Jade, but right now she was more concerned with Germain than she was with Jade slapping her. *Where the hell did he get all of that information?*

Jade slowly turned around and faced her husband. "Happy birthday, Sean. Happy birthday to you," she sang and broke into tears.

Kendra tiptoed back upstairs to the bedroom where Niki was sound asleep and climbed into bed. Unbeknownst to anyone, she heard and saw everything.

Chapter 26

It was just about two in the morning when Topaz and Nina were driven away from the ranch. Topaz began crying as soon as her driver closed her door. It was amazing . . . in less than two hours, the world she knew was ripped apart. Somehow, deep down in her heart, Topaz knew things would never be the same. Nina felt helpless as she watched her cousin sobbing all over the backseat of her limousine.

"Everything's gonna be fine, T. You'll see," Nina finally said, trying to convince herself as well.

"No, it's not," Topaz screamed. "Nothing's ever going to be the same."

"No, things won't ever be the same, but Germain will forgive you. He loves you."

"No, he doesn't, Nina. Did you see how he treated me? He's never treated me like that before."

"Germain had a lot to drink. You hurt him, Topaz. You hurt him really bad."

Topaz cried a fresh batch of tears. "He hates me, Nina. Did you hear him asking Jade to have sex with him right in front of me?" Topaz's amber eyes were huge and wet with tears.

"Oh please. He's not interested in sleeping with Jade. He was just hurt and angry because you slept with Sean."

"But he said we weren't together then." Topaz sniffed.

"You weren't together, but you had a baby, and you kept it a secret from him. He feels used. Why didn't you just tell him the truth that night when the reporter dropped that bomb at the release party?"

"I was afraid that he would leave me. I'll die if Germain leaves me." Topaz broke into tears again. "He's gonna divorce me, Nina. I just know it."

Nina's BlackBerry rang. She checked the caller ID thinking it might be Kyle and saw that it was Keisha. "Hey, girl." Nina was tired. It had been a very long day and even a longer night.

"How's T?" Keisha sounded equally tired.

Nina held the phone over Topaz for a moment so Keisha could hear her. She was still sobbing, and Nina put the phone back to her ear.

"Let me try to talk to her," Keisha said.

"Good luck." Nina moved closer to her cousin and gently shook her. "Keisha's on the phone, Topaz."

"I don't want to talk to anybody but Germain," Topaz wailed.

"Did you hear her?" Nina asked wearily.

"Yeah, I hear her. Poor thing. I told her to tell Germain before this thing blew up in her face."

"I wish she had listened to you. I haven't had a decent night of sleep since the release party."

"Me neither."

"I feel so guilty, especially about keeping everything from Germain. I didn't know him back then. Now he's my brother and a great friend."

"It's a mess . . . a huge mess."

"How's Jade?" Nina inquired, changing the subject before she began to cry too.

"She locked Sean out of their bedroom."

"Why is Jade tripping?"

"She's hurting and she feels betrayed."

"Rightfully so."

"Just like Germain." Keisha was doing her best to hold back the tears as well.

Nina quickly wiped away a tear while Topaz cried from the depths of her soul. She knew how much her cousin loved Germain, but what seemed like a brilliant idea at the time—concealing Niki's true parentage—had turned into a nightmare. It was amazing how one decision had touched and affected every last one of the friends' lives.

"Nina." Keisha broke the silence.

"Huh?" Keisha's voice jolted Nina out of her thoughts. Nina had even forgotten she was on the phone.

"Are you guys sure this is Sean's baby?"

"Who else's could she be?" Nina sat up straight in her seat.

"Germain's."

"Germain's? How?" All of a sudden a conversation Nina had with Topaz resurfaced in her mind. They were sitting by the pool at the house in Bel Air where Topaz first told Nina she was pregnant and unsure of who the baby's father was.

"You are so ghetto, not knowing who your baby's daddy is." Nina had laughed at the time, until Topaz told her she had been intimate with Sean and Germain.

But, after the baby was born with dark skin and hair, they both knew Niki had to be Sean's child.

"Did you guys ever have a paternity test done to find out who is really Niki's father?"

Nina's mind was racing as she pondered Keisha's words. Niki changed so much that first year. Her skin and hair had lightened, and now that she thought about it, Niki looked nothing like Sean. Nina hadn't given it much thought because it never really mattered to her. Because in her heart and mind . . . Niki was her daughter.

"Nina, did you guys have a paternity test done?"

Nina's throat closed up and she was unable to speak.

"Nina, are you still there?"

"No." Nina's voice cracked as she whispered her response.

"You never had a paternity test?" Keisha repeated.

Nina shook her head, unable to speak. Tears flowed from her eyes as she tried not to think the unimaginable. *Niki was Germain's daughter?*

When Keisha heard Nina's sniffles, she closed her eyes and shook her head. "Oh my God. I can't believe you guys made a decision like that and never bothered to find out the truth. I'll talk to Sean and Germain and get their permission for my dad to do a paternity test. I'll be home on Sunday. Tell T to call me." Keisha hung up, and Nina looked at Topaz, who had cried during the entire drive from Santa Barbara to Pacific Palisades.

The limousine pulled into the driveway and stopped. Marko opened the door and greeted them cheerfully at four that morning. "We're home, ladies."

Topaz dragged herself from the backseat and stumbled up the walkway into the house. Nina followed, opting to remain in the kitchen while Topaz mounted

he stairs to her bedroom with the weight of the world on
ner shoulders. Nina speed dialed her husband's cell.

"Hey," Kyle answered softly.

Nina tried to speak, but she couldn't, so she sat there
crying in the dark.

"What's wrong, baby?"

Nina continued crying.

"Are you okay?"

"No."

"What is it?"

"Germain is Niki's biological father," Nina managed
o say.

"Germain?"

"Yes."

"Says who? Topaz?"

"No."

"Then why would you say something like that?"

"Keisha . . ."

"What does Keisha have to do with this?"

"She asked if we had ever done a paternity test."

"Why would you need to do that unless . . ."

"Topaz thought the baby was Germain's until she
was born and turned out so dark."

"You're telling me that she wasn't a hundred percent
sure that the baby was my brother's?"

"We thought she was, Kyle."

"Damn . . . I gotta go." Kyle glanced over at Germain, who appeared to be sleeping. *Niki isn't your biological daughter, is she? She can't be.* He sighed long
and hard as he slowly drove onto the Gradneys' property and parked. Things were becoming more complicated by the minute.

"Yo, man. We're at your crib."

Germain opened his eyes and looked around at familiar surroundings before he opened the car door. "Thanks, man."

"No problem, man." Kyle watched Germain as he got out of the Escalade and disappeared inside the house.

Moments later, Nina ran out and jumped inside the SUV. She took one look at Kyle and broke into tears while Germain went downstairs to the family room and collapsed on the sofa.

Topaz's children returned home Sunday evening. She hadn't seen Germain since she left Santa Barbara and the phone was unusually quiet.

"Where's Daddy?" Baby Doll demanded the minute she entered the house. "His car is missing."

"He had to run an errand," Topaz lied.

"Did he go to the Blockbuster?" Chris asked. "Sunday evening is movie night."

Topaz picked at a salad and broiled sea bass. "Why don't you call your daddy and make sure he's bringing home the right movies." Topaz managed a smile for her son.

"I'll call him." Baby Doll ran to the telephone and quickly punched in the numbers.

"Is everything okay, Mom?" Chris sat down beside his mother.

Topaz's dazzling smile lit up her face, but the sparkle was missing from her eyes. "Everything's wonderful, baby. Why?"

"You just seem a little sad." Chris looked into his mother's eyes.

Topaz pulled her son into her arms and kissed him as he snuggled up next to her. Even though he was almost a teenager, he still enjoyed being held in his mother's arms. "I'm not sad, Chris. I just have a lot of things on my mind." She rested her chin on his head.

"What kind of things?" His legs were as long as Topaz's. He had also inherited his daddy's six-foot frame.

"Grown folks things. You know you're getting too big to sit in my lap." Topaz was an expert at changing the subject when questions became uncomfortable for her. "What would your friends think if they saw you sitting here like this?"

"They'd be jealous because my friends are always saying 'Your mom is so hot.'" Chris laughed.

"Boy, get away from me." Topaz laughed happily as Baby Doll hung up the telephone and ran over to her mother and brother. Baby Doll tried to sit on Topaz's lap next to her brother.

"Daddy's coming with movies." Baby Doll tussled with her brother for space on Topaz's lap. "He's bringing pineapple and pepperoni pizza, too."

"Cool." Chris jumped up and allowed Baby Doll to sit on their mother all by herself, but once Chris moved away, she quickly lost interest in the game. She watched her brother as he searched the fridge for Cokes. "Baby Doll, call Daddy and tell him we need Cokes."

"I thought you guys weren't hungry." Topaz looked at the children.

"We're always hungry for pizza, Mommy," Baby Doll explained.

Baby Doll had just put popcorn and oil in the antique popper when Germain burst into the room with two large pizzas and a case of Coke.

"Daddy." Germain could barely put down the pizza

and soda before Baby Doll was in his arms. "I missed you."

"I missed you too, baby girl." Germain gave Baby Doll a bear hug, and Topaz knew he had been drinking again.

"Hey, Dad." Chris gave his father a hug. "Where are the movies?"

"Ooops. I must have left them in the car, son." He served Baby Doll a slice of pizza and took a huge bite out of another slice.

"I'll go get them." Chris raced out of the family room while Germain and Baby Doll ate pizza.

Topaz nervously tapped her foot. Germain hadn't spoken to her or even attempted eye contact. Chris returned with the DVDs and a box of Red Vines and some other candy.

"Here, Mom." Chris gave her the box of licorice. "Dad bought your favorite candy."

Topaz felt a lump forming in her throat, *I can't cry now, not here in front of the children.*

"Thanks, honey." Topaz turned to smile at her husband.

"You're welcome, darlin'," Germain replied with absolutely no eye contact.

Darlin'? That was so generic. Germain called every woman he met darling. It was part of his southern charm. But he had never called Topaz darlin'. A single tear pressed itself out of Topaz's eye, and she quickly wiped it away. There would be no battle between Topaz and tears tonight . . . not in front of the children.

"Dad, did you have a good time on Uncle Sean's yacht?" Chris asked.

"I sure did, son. Baby Doll, cut those lights off, baby.

It's showtime." Germain was becoming almost as good at performing as his wife.

Topaz was glad Germain told Baby Doll to turn off the lights. Germain grabbed her and sat on the sofa next to Chris.

When the movie was over Baby Doll was asleep. Chris got up and turned on the lights while Germain carried Baby Doll upstairs and put her in bed. Topaz stood up and stretched.

"I'm going up to my room and do some reading, Mom." Chris was so much like Germain, it was scary sometimes. Not only did he look like his father, but he also had his ways.

"Did you finish your homework, baby?" Topaz smiled.

"Yes, Mom."

"Good night, my sweet." Topaz hugged and kissed her son.

"Are you sure you're okay, Mom?" Chris fixed an identical set of golden eyes on his mother again. "You were awfully quiet during the movie. We didn't have to tell you to be quiet one time because you were talking to the characters."

"Yes, baby. I'm sure." Topaz feigned a yawn. "I fell asleep during the movie. Now stop worrying about me. I'm the mother and it's my job to worry about you."

"Okay, Mom. I'll see you in the morning. Love you."

"I love you, too, baby." Topaz blew kisses at Chris as he disappeared up the stairs. As soon as he was out of sight, she collapsed on the sofa like a rag doll.

Topaz was hoping Germain would come back downstairs so they could talk, but he never did. She finally went up to their suite, where she was surprised to find him in bed, reading.

"Don't get any ideas. I'm only lying here until the kids are asleep and then I'm going back downstairs."

"Can't we talk about this?"

"There's nothing to talk about as far as I'm concerned."

"Are you ever going to talk to me again?" Topaz was on the verge of tears.

"I haven't made up my mind yet."

"Do you want a divorce, Germain?" Topaz had finally voiced her greatest fear.

"I said I haven't made up my mind yet."

"Does that mean you're considering a divorce?"

"I just told you I don't know what I want. Damn, woman. Would you leave me the hell alone?" Germain jumped out of bed and grabbed his robe and book. "The kids should be asleep by now." He left the room without another word, and Topaz cried until her pillow was soaked with tears. Exhausted, she finally fell asleep.

The next morning Germain was gone before she was out of bed. He had breakfast with the children and left just as she was going into the bathroom. Topaz heard his Porsche as he drove away. All she really wanted to do was stay in bed and feel sorry for herself, but she had to be Mommy and drive the kids to school. She took a quick shower and chose a pretty blue lace top to wear with a short skirt and boots. She was really feeling much better about things when she walked into the kitchen.

"You look beautiful, Mommy." Baby Doll was never big on compliments, but she loved to receive them.

Topaz smiled at her daughter. "Thank you, sweetie. I feel beautiful. Now let's go before you're late for school."

Topaz dropped them off just in time. She was just about to pull off when she thought she heard someone calling her name. She looked around and saw Keisha frantically waving.

"Hey, girl. What are you doing here?" Topaz asked.

Although Kendra also attended Buckley, Keisha rarely, if ever, drove her to school because Kendra was picked up in front of her house by the school's van.

"You never returned my call. I didn't know if you were avoiding me, so I decided to catch up with you here," Keisha explained.

"What call? I didn't get any phone call from you. I thought you had kicked me to the curb, too." Topaz smiled.

"I called to check on you after y'all left the ranch the other night. Didn't Nina tell you?"

"Nina didn't tell me anything. I haven't seen or spoken to anyone except my children and Germain."

"Germain? So things are okay with you two? I know you didn't get your sexy on for nothing. Those boots are kickin', girl."

"Germain's not talking to me. I got my sexy on for me."

"I'm sorry, girl."

"Whatever." The smile slowly faded from Topaz's face. "So you want to go to Starbucks or something?"

"We need to go somewhere so we can talk privately."

"We can get coffee and sit in the car so we don't have to worry about someone snooping."

Keisha followed Topaz to Encino where they ordered coffee, tea, and scones and sat in Keisha's car.

"So what's up?" Topaz sipped on a cup of green tea.

"I can't believe how well you're handling everything."

"I have to keep it together for the children. Chris was all over me last night. He even asked me if everything was okay."

"Chris is a very sensitive and intuitive child. What did you tell him?"

"I can't remember what I told him, but he's watching every little move I make."

Keisha smiled. "Eric is too upset with me."

Topaz was shocked. "What for?"

"Because I didn't tell him what I thought I knew."

"You guys do tell each other everything." Topaz took a tiny bite of a scone.

"I guess I never said anything because I wanted so badly to be wrong, but every time I looked into Niki's eyes I knew I wasn't."

The ladies sat in silence for several minutes.

"So Nina never told you I called," Keisha began. "That's interesting."

"What's so interesting about it?" Topaz focused on Keisha.

"I had a very enlightening conversation with her."

"About what?" Topaz finished the scone and stuffed everything into a bag.

Keisha took a deep breath. "Nina told me you guys never did a paternity test for Niki."

"So."

"So?" Keisha's eyes widened with surprise. "How do you know if Sean is really her father?"

"Because he just is, he has to be." Topaz was obviously shaken by the thought.

"She doesn't look anything like Sean."

"So."

"You were seeing Germain before your little trip to England. She could be his daughter."

"No, Keisha, no. She can't be. She just can't." Topaz crumpled like a balloon losing air.

"Why not?"

Topaz faced Keisha with a tear-streaked face. "Because that would mean . . ." Topaz turned and looked out the window, unable to complete her thought.

"That would mean what, T?"

Topaz was crying and dabbing at her eyes with a fresh tissue. She had already amassed a small pile of them. "That would mean I gave me and Germain's baby to Nina." Topaz finished in a whisper.

Keisha took some papers out of her bag, and Topaz watched as she slowly unfolded them.

"What's that?"

"Consent forms."

"Consent forms for what?" Topaz looked at the papers in Keisha's lap and then at Keisha.

"I got permission from Sean and Germain for my dad to do a paternity test."

"What?"

"A paternity test. It has to be done. Everyone deserves to know the truth."

Topaz said nothing as she sat with her eyes glued on the forms in Keisha's lap.

"There aren't any other contenders, are there?"

"No." Topaz was still whispering.

"Kyle gave me his permission. I faxed everything to my father this morning. Daddy already has everyone's information in his lab and he's going to run the test himself and fax me the results."

"Oh my God, Keisha." Topaz was horrified. "What if Niki is Germain's daughter?"

"We'll cross that bridge when we get to it."

"When is he going to call?" Topaz demanded.

"As soon as he gets the results."

"How long does it take to run a paternity test?"

"Topaz!" Keisha yelled a little too loudly. She was just as anxious as her friend to get the results of the test. "Chill, girlfriend. Daddy fired Rosalyn after I told him about all the drama she caused. She was a great researcher, but she had issues."

Topaz opened a bottle of water and took several sips, making a valiant effort to calm herself.

"Want to do a little Christmas shopping while we wait?" Keisha suggested, knowing very well that neither of them would purchase anything.

They were driving down Ventura Boulevard toward one of Topaz's favorite boutiques when Keisha's cell phone began to ring.

"I guess I'd better answer that, huh?" Keisha looked at Topaz, who slowly nodded her agreement. Keisha pulled over out of traffic. It was Greggo calling from the restaurant. Topaz sighed, relieved for the moment as she gazed out the window.

"Okay," Keisha said. She handed Topaz the phone. "It's for you. It's my dad."

"I thought you were talking to Greggo," Topaz whispered.

"I was. Daddy called while I was on the line. He wants to speak to you."

Topaz swallowed hard as she took the phone from Keisha. She knew the information she was about to hear would change her life forever.

"Hello."

"Hello there, Miss Topaz." Dr. Nichols had referred to her as Miss since they were little girls.

"Hello, Papa Nichols."

"I've got some information here I'm sure you'll be very glad to hear."

"What is it?" Topaz broke out in a cold sweat, and her entire body shook with fear.

"Germain is Niki's father."

"Okay." She handed Keisha the phone and suddenly everything faded to black as Topaz drifted off into peaceful oblivion.

Chapter 27

Nina and Kyle sat in bumper-to-bumper rush-hour traffic on the freeway, making the ninety-minute plus journey from Burbank to Malibu. Nina had suggested a driver so they both could relax on the way home, but Kyle wasn't ready to succumb to such pampering. He had even muttered something about his manhood when Nina tried to bring up the subject again.

She completed a phone call and tucked her Black-Berry into her briefcase and focused on her husband, who had been unusually quiet and into himself all day.

"This traffic is mad crazy," Nina declared, glad that she wasn't the one driving. "I called the Realtor today. They're faxing over houses for us to look at in Toluca Lake and Sherman Oaks."

Kyle made no comment, so Nina continued talking. "Sherman Oaks could work out very well. We'll be right by Niki's school and no more than thirty minutes tops from the office, even in the craziest traffic. We wouldn't even have to take the freeway. There are a couple of routes to take on the surface streets."

"Sounds good, baby." Kyle smiled at Nina and ran his hand over her head. Nina stretched across her seat and rested her head against his arm.

"I wish you'd let me hire that driver so we could snuggle up together in the back of the car."

"I'll drive my woman."

Nina smiled and made a face in the dark. Kyle could be so stubborn and such a man sometimes.

"Baby."

"Huh?" Nina was still resting her head on Kyle's arm even though she was totally uncomfortable leaning on his hard shoulder.

"There's something I need to tell you."

"What?" Nina sat up and looked at her husband.

"I gave Keisha permission to do a paternity test on Niki."

"You did what?"

"I gave Keisha permission to do a paternity test."

"I don't believe you." Nina shook her head. "Why would you do something like that without talking to me first?"

"Because we need to know the truth. I thought you knew for sure that Niki was my brother's daughter. That's the only reason I agreed to go along with your crazy scheme."

"I never asked you to go along with anything. I told you I didn't want you in the middle of it, but oh no. You said God told you I needed you and you came to London to take care of me." Nina was practically yelling.

"God did tell me to come to London and take care of you. But you didn't tell me everything I needed to know."

"What are you trying to say, Kyle? You regret marrying me?"

"Nina, don't put words in my mouth."

"Then what the hell are you saying?"

"Watch your tone, Nina."

"You watch your tone, Kyle."

"What the hell were you and Topaz thinking? Don't you know anything? Babies change. You should have never made a decision to put Niki up for adoption without getting a paternity test."

"I didn't make the decision. Topaz did. I wanted to bring Niki home because I couldn't stand the thought of leaving her in some foreign country."

"Did you know there was a possibility of someone else besides my brother being the father?"

Nina stared out of the window wishing for the impossible . . . that she could turn back the hands of time.

"Did you?" Kyle demanded.

"Yes, Kyle. I knew."

"Then why didn't you tell her to get a paternity test?"

"I don't know. You know how brown Niki used to be. It never crossed my mind that Sean might not be the father."

"What a ho." Kyle smirked. "I don't know why the doc would get himself involved with someone like her. The sex must be some kind of great."

"Kyle!"

"What, Nina?"

"Don't talk about my cousin like that."

"I just call 'em as I see 'em."

"So why didn't you suggest we get a paternity test when we came back to California, Mr. Know-it-All?"

"I was going on *your* information. But don't worry, I'll double-check everything you do, now that I see you aren't capable of making intelligent decisions."

"Are you trying to call me stupid?"

"No, but you certainly do some stupid things, like passing on Topaz's music, signing Sky, and not getting a damn paternity test," Kyle yelled.

"I thought we were past the music thing and you weren't going to bring it up anymore."

"I just can't believe you and Topaz would do something so stupid. Do you realize how many lives are affected by this? What the hell were you thinking?".

"According to you, I wasn't thinking at all. So sue me."

"I bet Jade would love to sue you two and then some."

"Well, too bad I wasn't born perfect like you, then we wouldn't be having this conversation."

"I never said I was perfect."

"No . . . you just expect me to be perfect." Tears streamed out of Nina's eyes.

Kyle focused on the traffic as they drove in an uncomfortable silence.

Nina looked at Kyle out of teary eyes. She was trying to think of something to say that would hurt him just as badly as, if not more than, he had hurt her.

"I have a question."

"What's that?" Kyle asked, hoping they would call a truce and apologize.

"I was wondering why you ever got involved with someone like me, since I'm not perfect."

Kyle sighed long and hard. He was tired of the traffic and tired of arguing with Nina, tired of problems, tired of the pain. He just wanted everything to magically work itself out and just go away. In a perfect world it would, but he knew the world was far from perfect.

"You know, Nina. I've been wondering the same thing. Why are you still taking birth control pills? You know how much I've wanted us to have our own baby."

"I thought Niki was our baby."

"You know what I mean."

"Let me think. I'm on the pill because I don't want your baby?" She finally had the ammunition she needed.

"Why not?"

"I'm young. I have a career and a beautiful body. I'm not trying to lose any of that."

"Then why did you even marry me?"

"That's a good question. But it wasn't so I could have your baby. I already have a daughter, remember?"

They were in the garage now. Nina jumped out of the SUV and ran ahead into the house. In the kitchen, Niki was having dinner with her nanny. The little girl's face lit up the moment she laid eyes on Nina.

"Mommy, you're home."

"Yes, baby, I'm home." Nina picked her up and hugged her as tightly as she could.

"I can't breathe, Mommy," she heard Niki say.

"I'm sorry, baby." Nina laughed as she released her grip on the child.

Kyle came into the kitchen with the weight of the world on his shoulders. Nina saw the sadness in his eyes and was immediately sorry for all the unkind things she had said. They were both under an incredible amount of pressure in their personal and professional lives. He was her best friend, and unfortunately, she had succeeded in hurting him.

"Daddy . . ." Niki ran to greet him and Kyle swooped her up in his arms, trying to squeeze the love out of her that his soul so desperately needed.

"How's my princess?"

"I'm fine, Daddy. How are you?"

"I'm a little tired, but I feel much better since I got that hug from you."

"Here, Daddy, have another one then." Niki hugged Kyle again, and Nina smiled as she watched them interacting. Kyle was a good man and he was a great father.

Why haven't I gotten pregnant?

She really didn't know why. Kyle had mentioned that he wanted them to have a baby, but he had never pressed the issue. Niki was such a joy and she didn't have to go through nine months of pregnancy or the burden of labor to have her. She had been Nina's from the moment she entered the world.

Nina still remembered Jade's pregnancy with Kobe. She had put on a lot of weight and her labor had been long and painful, yet babies seemed to just pop out of Topaz effortlessly. But didn't things always come too easily for Topaz?

I'm almost thirty. Maybe it is time for me to give a baby some serious consideration.

Nina went upstairs to their bedroom to change her clothes. In the bathroom, she studied the container of birth control pills, then tossed them back into the drawer. She heard a sound in the bedroom and found Kyle hanging up his clothes. Nina just stood there silently watching him. The next thing they were in each other's arms.

"I'm sorry, baby, you're right. I should have gotten a paternity test," Nina managed to say in between kisses.

"I messed up. I should have suggested the paternity test. I was so excited that you were going to marry me, I wasn't thinking either," Kyle replied.

"Ah, that's sweet."

They brushed lips briefly.

"Baby, I'm so scared." Nina was crying again.

"I know." Kyle held her like he had never held her before. "I only agreed to the test so we can know the truth. No one's taking our little girl away from us."

Nina had never felt so safe or protected as Kyle gently kissed away her tears. "Baby, I didn't mean any of those things I said."

"I know." Kyle picked her up and carried her across the room to their bed. "And you are perfect."

"No."

"You're perfect for me."

"Kyle, I want to have your baby more than anything."

"Really?"

"Yes."

The best thing about fighting was it was so much fun making up. They kissed for what seemed like forever. A trail of clothing marked a path to the bed. After they had spent what seemed like seconds pleasuring themselves, the doorbell rang.

"Did you hear the doorbell ring?" Nina whispered.

"Who would be ringing our doorbell at midnight?"

"It's only nine o'clock, baby."

Kyle sat up and looked at the digital clock when the doorbell rang again.

"Who the hell is that?" Nina looked at her husband.

"I have no idea," Kyle replied as he went into the bathroom.

Nina followed him. "Do you think we should answer it?"

Meanwhile, the doorbell continued to ring repeatedly.

"Who would just show up without calling?" Kyle

watched the security monitor waiting for it to give them a view of the front door.

"It's Topaz and Keisha."

"Why would they drive all the way out here now?" Kyle wondered out loud.

"I don't want to find out. Don't answer it. They'll think we're not home and leave."

"As you wish."

But they didn't go away. Topaz took out her cell phone and soon the house phone began to ring.

"I'm not going to be a prisoner in my own house." Kyle sprinted down the stairs, dashed into the living room, and opened the front door.

"Hey, you guys," Keisha smiled. For some reason she was extremely nervous. "I'm sorry we just showed up . . ."

"I told you they were here," Topaz cut in as she pushed her way into the house. She handed Nina a sheet of paper. "These are the results of the paternity test. It proves that Niki is Germain's daughter, and I've come to take her home."

Kyle yanked the paperwork out of Nina's hand and quickly read it over.

"Niki is Germain's daughter?" Nina could barely get the words out.

"According to this piece of paper she is." Kyle folded the paper and handed it back to Topaz.

Nina stood frozen, obviously in shock.

"Where's Niki?" Topaz demanded.

"In her bed, sleeping, where she's supposed to be," Kyle replied.

"Go and get her so we can go home. It's getting late," Topaz commanded.

"T, honey." Keisha began searching for her words. "You agreed we were going to discuss this."

"There's nothing to discuss except Niki is my daughter and I came to take her home."

"Niki is not your daughter." Nina finally joined the conversation. "She belongs to me and Kyle. You didn't want her, remember?"

"That was before I knew Germain was her father. There's no way I'm going to let you raise our little girl."

"She's not your daughter," Nina screamed.

Topaz looked at Keisha. "I told you she was going to trip."

"What did you expect, Topaz? Niki's not a pair of shoes or a dress that you've come to pick up. It's going to take time to work this out. You've got to think about Niki, because Nina is her mother. You're just Aunty."

"I still want to see my daughter," Topaz demanded.

"And I want you to get the hell out of my house before I call the police." Kyle opened the front door.

"Call them because I'm not going anywhere." Topaz folded her arms.

"Come on, Topaz. We should go now." Keisha kissed Kyle and Nina. "I'm sorry, you guys. I thought she would be a little more reasonable."

"Topaz reasonable? Huh! It's always her way or the highway." Nina rolled her eyes.

"You should listen to your girlfriend and go home now, Topaz." Kyle was trying to be patient.

Nina stepped in front of Topaz. "I thought you had changed, but Jade was right. You never think of anyone or anything but yourself. You get the results of your damn paternity test and run out here and tell me I'm supposed to give you my daughter because Germain is her biological father? You must be crazy."

"I'm not crazy, you are if you think you're going to keep my daughter," Topaz yelled.

They stood there face to face. Neither of them moved an inch.

"You'd better get out of my face, Nina, and go get my daughter."

"You'd better get out of my face before I kick your ass. I'm not afraid of you, Topaz."

Keisha closed her eyes and sighed.

"Would you two stop yelling before you wake Niki." Kyle glared at them both, but they weren't listening.

"I want her to wake up so I can tell her I'm her mother and we can go home."

"Are you stuck on stupid? You'd better get this straight because I'm tired of repeating myself. I'm Niki's mother and Kyle is her father and you and Germain are just going to have to deal with it. If we hadn't adopted her, she'd be in Europe only God knows where and we wouldn't even be having this conversation."

Kyle took out his cell phone and dialed 911. "I didn't press Send yet."

"Topaz . . . let's go." Keisha was outside shivering.

"Fine." Topaz stepped out of the house, and Nina slammed the door as hard as she could behind her.

"This isn't over!" Topaz yelled through the window. "I'll see you two in court."

Chapter 28

Beverly Hills was always beautifully decorated for the holidays from the storefronts of Barneys and Neiman Marcus featuring glamorous holiday wear to the numerous designer boutiques and shops on Rodeo Drive. Christmas lights twinkled and ornaments sparkled, casting a luminous glow around the famous hotels and stores on Wilshire Boulevard.

Sabre's beloved Pink Palace was no exception. Snow-flocked Christmas trees greeted her as she practically skipped into the hotel lobby. Tables sprinkled with ornate boxes wrapped in shades of gold reminded Sabre exactly why the Beverly Hills Hotel was one of her favorite places.

"Deck the halls with boughs of holly," Sabre sang happily as she made her way through the paths to the bungalow, swinging a shiny pink Victoria's Secret shopping bag in her hand. "'Tis the season to be jolly." She laughed as she pulled a red satin baby doll lingerie set with a red and black thong out of her Louis Vuitton bag and carefully laid them out on the bed. "I know somebody's about to get decked all up in here."

Victor had made a CD of old-school slow jams, and Sabre put that on to set the mood. She went into the bathroom and turned on the water in the marble tub. *There won't be any of that nasty-ass rose shit from Neiman's in this bath, but my favorite almond cookie oil sold by a sista in Brooklyn.* It filled the room with a warm, sweet, nutty aroma as it burned in the dozens of candles she had placed all over the suite.

"Where is my alcohol?" Sabre asked out loud. Moments later, there was a knock at the door, and she quickly unlocked it before she scooted into the bathroom. She was so caught up in her preparations she had almost forgotten the need for discretion.

She heard the bellboy bring in her usual cheeseburger luncheon and several bottles of Cristal and Coke and depart quickly. Sabre poured a glass of champagne and took a few bites of the burger, but she was much too nervous and too excited to eat now. Instead, she took the bottle of Cristal and a jar of sea salt scrub back into the bathroom where she covered her body with the sweet concoction that smelled good enough to eat before she stepped into the water for a long soak.

I can't wait to see him. Sabre took a quick shower in icy cold water to keep her skin firm and tight, patted herself dry with a huge fluffy towel, then covered her body with almond cookie soufflé. She stood in the mirror admiring her nude body and the sensation of her fingers as she ran them across her soft supple skin. In the bedroom, she slipped on a pair of Manolo Blahniks and paraded around the room in the buff.

"I should meet him at the door like this." Sabre laughed out loud as she stood in front of a full-length mirror drinking a glass of champagne, still admiring her body. Her cell phone rang, interrupting her narcissism. She checked the caller ID and smiled as she slipped on the thong and red satin nightie. In a matter of seconds, there was a brief knock at the door, and Sabre pulled it open.

"I'm so glad you could make it." She smiled at Germain and purposely stood in the center of the doorway, causing her body to brush against his as he came inside the bungalow. She sucked in her breath, aroused, the moment they touched.

"Hey." Germain very casually looked Sabre over. She was a beautiful young woman.

Sabre, overcome with joy, had never wanted a man the way she wanted Germain, and she was giddy. "Want some champagne?" She held up a bottle of Cristal.

Germain looked and saw it was Cristal—Topaz's favorite drink. He had been the first one to expose her to it when she was eighteen. "No." He shook his head. "I want a real drink."

"I can order whatever you want." Sabre picked up the phone.

"Tanqueray on the rocks."

Sabre dialed room service and hung up. *What am I thinking? This is Sherwin's bungalow, and if he found out I was here with Germain, he'd kill me. Germain ain't offering to pay my rent, but he will be after today.*

Sabre hung up the phone. "I don't think I should call room service. I don't want anyone to know you're here."

"Good looking out, darlin'. So how did you get the champagne?"

"It's a standing order for the room," Sabre explained and dug in her bag. "I have a couple of twenties. I could have a bottle delivered from the liquor store."

"That sounds like a good idea, darlin'."

Sabre smiled as she made the order and placed some cash in an envelope outside the entrance to the bungalow. She found a blunt that Victor had rolled and looked at Germain, who was sitting on the bed still dressed in his suit and tie. When he phoned he had said he wanted to talk. For privacy, Sabre had suggested they meet at the hotel.

"Here." Sabre pulled him to his feet. "Let me help you out of that jacket, Dr. G."

He allowed her to take his jacket and watched her as she hung it in the closet. She was a sexy little thing and she smelled wonderful.

"And this tie . . ."

When Sabre loosened his tie, it took every ounce of strength he had to keep off of her. He wanted some . . . real bad.

"And these shoes . . ." Sabre made sure she rubbed her bare ass all over him as she slipped the Gucci loafers from his feet and stashed them under the bed, wondering if Topaz had picked them out. *I will not think about that bitch today.* She smiled sexily at Germain. "There, that's better, huh?"

Sabre thought she heard a knock at the door. She opened it and found the liquor in a brown paper bag, dropped cubes of ice in a glass, and poured in the Tanqueray. "Here you go."

Germain drank it in a series of gulps, and she refilled the glass. "Thanks, darlin'."

Sabre sat down on the side of the bed and crossed her legs and looked into Germain's eyes. "So what did you want to talk about?"

Germain closed his eyes and leaned back on the bed pillows. The candles, music, and alcohol were intoxi-

cating and very relaxing. He was all talked out on th
subject of Topaz and Niki. *There's nothing more to sa
What's done is done. Topaz divorced me, married Gu
ther, slept with Sean and only God knows who else befor
she married me again. And me? I've never been with ar
other woman since I laid eyes on her because no othe
woman ever measured up.* He looked at Sabre and wor
dered why he was really there.

"I don't want to talk," Germain answered withou
opening his eyes.

"You didn't really come here to talk, did you
Dr. G?"

Germain was beginning to feel stupid. He knev
Sabre had the hots for him.

"We don't have to talk."

*I can't believe he's going to come up in here with m
looking as good as I do and not give me some. Oh hel
naw. Dr. G just needs a little push. Now where are m
jumper cables?*

Sabre was used to running the show with the men i
her life. She tried not to laugh as she pulled the blun
and a lighter out of her bag. *I'm gonna rock his world*
She slid over on the bed next to Germain, swung he
legs over his so she was facing him, sat in his lap, an
took a hit off the blunt. "Do you smoke?"

"Not since college." Germain had forgotten how h
used to get high and study or take an exam, and h
graduated *summa cum laude.*

He took the blunt and inhaled several times before
he gave it back to Sabre. A feeling of euphoria tool
over his mind and body as all the pain and heartbreak
Topaz had caused slowly began to dissipate.

Sabre took the blunt and blew smoke out of it into hi
mouth. When their lips touched, both of them explodec

like dynamite. She ripped the remaining clothing from his body with animal-like passion, and Germain threw her down in the center of the bed. She ran her fingers over the smooth taut muscles of his chest and sculpted abs. She had never wanted any man the way she wanted him, and there were tears in her eyes as her lips found his.

To Germain, she was wickedly delicious, like forbidden fruit. He was mindless as he kissed her everywhere . . . from her eyelids to the arches of her feet. Her skin was soft and smooth as he kissed his way down her thighs and he lingered over her until she screamed his name over and over. She held onto him as waves of pleasure flooded her body and realized she had never known love like this before.

The room was practically dark when Sabre awakened except for a few flickering candles. She panicked as she sat up in bed, wondering if Germain had left, but she was unable to contain the smile taking over her face when she realized he was still there, lying in bed next to her. She never intended to fall asleep, but he put a sista out.

I am so in love. She wanted to dance and shout, but she lay right next to him. He reached for her and gently caressed her arm in his sleep. She sighed happily as she watched Germain sleeping.

So this is what it's like to be in love. She kissed him softly on the lips and he opened his eyes, surprised because he thought he was at home in bed with Topaz until he looked into Sabre's black piercing eyes. Waves of guilt immediately flooded his mind and heart.

I was dreaming, Germain realized.

"Want something to eat, sweetness?" Sabre ran a finger down the bridge of his nose. He was almost too pretty for a man.

"Okay."

I am going to have so much fun being his wife. She rolled back on the bed and sighed contentedly. *So this is what it will feel like being Mrs. Germain Gradney.*

"What would you like?" Sabre asked sweetly

"You." Germain forgot his guilt as carnal desire took over. He and Topaz always had a lot of sex, and right now his tank was still a little low. He hadn't made love to his wife since he read that stupid journal. He rolled on top of Sabre and began kissing her again.

"You make me feel so good, I feel like crying," Sabre whispered in Germain's ear as he rocked her ever so gently.

When they finished there were tears in Sabre's eyes. "I love you, Germain." She spoke softly, right into his ear. She had never told a man she loved him and had never really felt it, until Germain. Deep down in her heart, she knew she loved this man with every fiber of her being. She didn't care who knew when she phoned room service and ordered a late dinner. She was surprised when Germain went into the bathroom when the food arrived.

Sabre felt like a queen when she handed the hotel attendant several crisp hundred-dollar bills. Germain had given her the money for the tab. It wasn't her usual cheeseburger, so she inspected the order to ensure that everything was included.

Germain had a healthy appetite that evening. He hadn't been able to eat for days, and after only a few hours with Sabre, he was ravenous when he tore into the steak and lobster.

Sabre, however, wasn't hungry . . . at least not for food. She barely touched her lobster. She took a small piece, dipped it in butter, and popped it into her mouth.

Butter dribbled from the corner of her mouth, and Germain kissed it off her bottom lip.

She picked up the chocolate sundae she ordered with nuts, chocolate, and caramel sauce on the side. "Ready for dessert, baby? Sabre's got something real sweet for you." She took the container of caramel sauce and poured it all over her body and lay across his lap.

Germain licked off a little of the sauce. He had tried to pour honey on Topaz once, but she got up and showered as soon as a drop of it got into her hair. That was years ago. He wondered how she would react if he did it now.

"That looks good, darlin', but I think I'm going to have some ice cream and whipped topping to go along with this caramel sauce."

He laughed when Sabre squealed because of the coldness of the ice cream and she didn't care when some of the caramel got into her hair. She had him feeling just like a teenager, and then he remembered Sabre was just nineteen.

"You are such a bad . . ." Sabre was unable to complete a thought once he touched her.

With the softest touch, he removed every bit of the sundae from her body with his tongue. Sabre burned with passion and desire for the first time in her life. She trembled with anticipation as she drizzled chocolate across his tight abs.

"How come every time you come around my London bridge goes down?" Sabre sang Fergie style.

Germain laughed. "My little girl is always singing that song. Somehow, it will never be the same now that you sang it."

"That's right, because I'm Sabre-licious." She go up and went into the bathroom and ran water into the tub. "Come with me." She took his hand and led him to the sunken tub of scented water, but he flipped the script and pulled her into the shower where he did all sorts of wonderful things to her.

I'll be his love slave. I wanna get freaky with you, Sabre hummed as she dried him off and massaged almond cookie oil into his bronzed skin. *Now whenever he smells this, he's going to always think about me.*

"That smells good, darlin', but I'm going to have to wash it off before I go."

"Go? Where are you going?" Sabre demanded.

"Right here beside you until I leave." He made love to her again, and then they lay in bed and cuddled for what seemed like only a few minutes to Sabre, but it was actually several hours. She was surprised when Germain got up, went into the bathroom, and turned on the shower.

"What are you doin'?"

"I'm taking a shower, darlin'."

"You're not going to leave now, are you?"

"Yes."

"But it's after midnight. I thought you were going to be here with me all night."

"Sorry, darlin', but I gotta go home."

"Where?" She was trembling as she asked.

"Home."

She looked at him like he was speaking a foreign language. "Where's home?"

"Pacific Palisades."

Sabre was about to get into the shower with him and persuade him to stay when he placed a hand out in front of him to stop her. "I gotta do this by myself, darling, or I'll never get out of here." He kissed her, then hopped inside the shower.

Sabre stood there thinking as he showered. *Topaz lives in Pacific Palisades. He's going home to her,* Sabre suddenly realized.

"Are you still living with *her?*"

Germain stepped out of the shower with a towel around his waist, surprised to find her still standing in the bathroom. "You still here, darlin'?"

She shivered every time he called her darling. "I just wanted to help my man dry off."

"I don't need any help drying off." He walked into the bedroom and began dressing.

Sabre folded her arms. "You never answered my question."

"What was the question?"

"I want to know if you're going home to Topaz."

Germain went back into the bathroom. "She is my wife."

"Your wife? After she cheated and lied?"

Germain made no response.

She couldn't stand the thought of Germain going home to Topaz. "I thought you and me were going to be an item."

"An item?" Germain looked puzzled.

Sabre put her arms around his neck and hoisted her petite body up his six foot frame and kissed him. "I gotta be with you all the time. No man has ever made me feel the way you have. I'm in love with you, Germain."

"Love me?" Germain pulled her off him. "You don't even know me."

"I know I love you, and I want to spend the rest of my life with you."

"Okay, what do you want? Money?" Germain took out his wallet. He had never been in a situation like this and he wasn't sure how to handle it.

"Money?" Sabre screamed. "I don't want or need your money. I want you."

Germain swallowed hard as he started to wonder if he had gotten himself involved with a fatal attraction. He put on his tie and sports jacket, trying to think of something to say while Sabre watched him. When he picked up his keys off the floor, she knew he was really leaving, so she threw herself in front of the bungalow door.

"No!" she screamed. "You can't go. I won't let you go."

"Sabre, I have to go now. I already missed saying good night to my children, so I'm definitely going to be there to say good morning."

"Why don't you just say you want to go home and fuck her now that you're done fucking me?"

"You're crazy." Germain stepped over her and put his hand on the doorknob.

"No!" Sabre grabbed his leg. "Please don't go!" Germain tried to walk, but she was hindering him by holding onto his leg.

"Sabre, let go of me."

"I'll be a good girl . . . just stay with me a little while longer," she begged as if her life depended on it.

"Sabre, I told you I have to go."

Sabre began crying. "Everyone I love always leaves me. Now you want to leave me too."

"But I don't love you, Sabre."

"Don't say that. You do love me. You just don't realize it yet."

"No, Sabre. I don't."

"But the way you made love to me. No man has ever been so kind and gentle and sweet."

"I'm sorry, Sabre."

Sabre sniffed and wiped her eyes. "But you could love me, couldn't you?"

"No," Germain replied firmly.

"Why not?"

"Because I love my wife." Germain knew he still loved Topaz, but his anger had gotten the best of him. Now he just wanted to be at home with his children sleeping down the hall and in bed next to Topaz more than anything. *I have to get away from this crazy woman.* Sleeping with Sabre was a huge mistake.

"Go then, you punk-ass motherfucker. You're a sorry son of a bitch for lettin' that fuckin' bitch punk yo stupid ass." Sabre let go of his leg but remained seated on the floor in the opposite direction so she couldn't see his face.

Germain practically ran out of the room as soon as she released her grip on his leg, and she slammed the door closed behind him. Sabre crawled across the floor to the bed, crying and feeling sorry for herself, until she spotted Germain's cell phone lying on the floor. A smile lit up her tear-streaked face.

"I bet wifey would love to know what you've been doing."

She opened his cell phone and scrolled through it until she found the number and pressed Send. It rang and went to voice mail. She was delighted when she heard Topaz's voice and called again. "Her man's not home . . . she's gonna answer the damn phone."

Sabre called the number again. It rang until it went to voice mail. "Answer the phone, bitch." She dialed it again, and this time it was answered.

"Hi, baby." Topaz sounded like she had probably been asleep. "Why are you calling on my cell phone?"

"My man accidentally left his phone with me," Sabre said boldly.

"Your man? Who is this?" Topaz demanded.

"Your husband just left. I just fucked his brains out, so I sent him home to you."

"Who is this?" Topaz was obviously irritated, and Sabre loved pulling her strings.

"Look, just tell my man he left his cell phone at my place, and I'll drop it by his office tomorrow." Sabre hung up the phone and laughed. "I got you good, you old stupid-ass bitch." She climbed into bed and stretched out between the sheets enjoying the lingering fragrance of Germain's scent.

"I don't care what you say, you're my man now, Germain, because once you go Sabre, you never go back."

Chapter 29

The ocean never sounded louder to Topaz that night. She tossed and turned until she finally got up to look out at the water. A full moon was fixed in the royal blue heavens, casting an eerie glow over the rushing water and white-capped waves. Normally, she would have thought it was the perfect romantic setting; tonight it only reminded her that she was lonely and alone.

She strained her ears for the sound of Germain's Porsche, but there was nothing. "Who was that on the phone?" Topaz wondered out loud. *Is Germain having an affair?* She had finally allowed herself to think the unthinkable. Fear licked through her body like venom at the thought of her beloved Germain in the arms of another woman.

She pulled on a robe and went to check on the children. Baby Doll had kicked the covers off as usual, and had fallen asleep wearing her iPod headphones. Topaz removed them, turned off the device, and kissed the little girl on the cheek as she pulled the comforter over her daughter. She took one last look at Baby Doll, who looked sweet and peaceful, and closed the door. Chris, as usual, fell asleep while reading. He was so much like his father. She took the book, carefully marked the page, and put it on the nightstand beside his bed. She kissed him, turned off the light, and closed the door quietly behind her.

She went back to bed where she continued to toss and turn, unable to fall back asleep. She hadn't slept well in months with all the dreams about Niki. Now, her insomnia was even worse, with things so messed up between her and Germain. They had never spent one night apart since they remarried.

He has to be just as miserable without me as I am without him. But maybe he's not, if he's out with some other woman. Angrily, she threw off the covers and got back out of bed. It was just about three in the morning when she went downstairs to the kitchen for something to drink.

Topaz took a sip of water and decided to go to the family room to watch television. She was surprised when she saw Germain asleep on the sofa and stopped dead in her tracks. Unsure of what to do or say, she stood there watching him sleep, resisting the urge to slide underneath the blanket beside him. Sensing her presence, Germain's eyes popped open.

"Hey."

"Hey," Topaz replied softly. She sat down in a chair across from the sofa. "I didn't mean to wake you."

"I wasn't asleep. Just resting my eyes. What are you doing up?"

Answering what I thought was a call from you that turned out to be some woman who has your cell phone, Topaz wanted to say, but she didn't know how she wanted to deal with the phone call. He could have acci-

Identally left his phone somewhere, or someone could have stolen it. She also knew women loved to play games, especially with another woman's man.

"I couldn't sleep. So I got up to check on the kids and came downstairs to watch television. I didn't know you were here."

Topaz wanted to know so badly where he had been. She wasn't sure when he came home, but she knew he hadn't been there very long. She tried to get up and go back up to bed, but she couldn't will herself to move.

Germain closed his eyes and sighed. "I can't sleep either."

He doesn't seem to be angry, Topaz noticed. It was the first civilized conversation they'd had in weeks, but Topaz was afraid to hope for more.

"I've been thinking . . ." Germain began. After his revenge sex with Sabre, Germain's anger was fading and he was no longer as upset with his wife. They'd overcome many obstacles, together they could overcome this as well.

"What were you thinking, baby?" Topaz couldn't help being anxious to hear what her husband had to say.

"You didn't sleep with Sean after we got back together, did you?"

"Oh no, baby. From the first phone call when you invited me out on the date to Disneyland, I haven't been with anyone but you. I haven't thought about being with anyone but you. You're the only man I've ever loved."

"But Sean?" Germain looked at his wife. "What did you like about him?"

"It only happened one time. I hadn't been with anyone since Gunther died."

And Pete, a voice in her head reminded. Pete was her late husband Gunther's extremely handsome and extremely wealthy best friend from high school. She'd had a brief fling with Pete, a gorgeous blond investment banker with blue eyes. He had asked Topaz to marry him, but she turned Pete down because she wasn't in love with him. There was no reason to tell Germain about him now. A girl did have needs.

"Keisha was trying to get us back together, and you kept telling her no. I had given up hope. Keisha told me to write you a letter, so I did, then we prayed."

"I remember all of that," Germain quietly interjected.

"I did what Keisha said, but I didn't think it would work. I didn't know God would answer my prayer, but He did, because you called and asked me for a date."

"So how did you end up with Sean?"

"It was after the letter. I went to a Lakers game with Keisha and Nina. Afterward, we all went out to dinner. Sean came with Eric. I rode with Keisha. Nina left for some MTV interview, and somehow Sean ended up taking me home. He came in to see the house. We were talking. He was having problems with Jade and I gave him some advice. Sean was really old-fashioned. He didn't put it in words, but he thought that a wife belongs in two rooms, the kitchen and the bedroom."

"I could see that."

"He asked me about you and I started crying. He knew how badly I wanted to be with you and Chris again. But you didn't want me. He was comforting me and one thing led to another. I never meant for it to happen. And I never meant to hurt anyone, especially you," Topaz explained as she wiped a tear from her eye.

There was a long silence. For a minute, Topaz

thought he had fallen asleep, but then she remembered he was processing everything she had just told him.

"Will you ever forgive me, Germain?" Topaz finally asked.

"There's a lot more to this situation than Sean."

"I know, baby, but I don't ever want you to think this was about another man, especially Sean."

"We need to take time and sort things out."

"That sounds wonderful, baby." Topaz jumped up to give him a hug, and Germain did his best to keep her at a distance. Sabre was an appetizer, giving him an even greater desire to be with his wife. There was no way he was going to make love to Topaz after just leaving Sabre's bed. It was difficult enough dealing with the guilt of being unfaithful to her.

"I'll call you tomorrow from work and let you know what I want to do," Germain said.

Topaz left him in the family room and went up to their bedroom. She didn't fall asleep but lay in bed thinking about what could be a possible reconciliation while doing her best to keep thoughts of the anonymous phone call out of her head. Somehow, she finally fell asleep, if only for a minute.

The next morning a beautiful bouquet of roses arrived at the house with a gift card. *"Meet me for dinner at seven. Love, Germain."*

Topaz didn't know where the limo was headed that afternoon, but their driver did. She couldn't help wondering where they would be dining when the driver turned off Sunset onto a winding wooded residential road. Moments later, the limo stopped in front of Hotel Bel-Air, probably the most romantic hideaway on the planet for the A-list crowd. Anybody who was anybody had stayed at the hotel, and Oprah even had a slumber party for her fortieth birthday here.

"Oh, Germain." Topaz clasped a hand over her mouth as her eyes filled with tears. The grounds were breathtakingly gorgeous. Flowering gardens and a blue pond with white swans were straight out of a fairy tale, but it wasn't the hotel's beauty that brought Topaz to tears; this was the spot Germain had chosen as the site for their first date when the couple reconciled over six years ago.

He made the reservation in her maiden name, Topaz Black, and it drove her crazy wondering why. *Did he bring me here to break up with me? That would be too cruel, not that I don't deserve it, but I don't want to break up with Germain.* Her mind raced with a barrage of thoughts. She was crying again as the bellboy led her inside a room with a view of the swans swimming in the pond—the same room they had stayed in on their first date. *This has to be where we made Niki,* Topaz realized as she dried her tears and quickly pushed thoughts of the little girl out of her head. *I've got to get my man back first . . . I'll deal with getting Niki later.*

She started to call Keisha for a pep talk, but she knew Keisha would pray and tell her everything would be fine, so Topaz got on her knees in front of the bed.

"Lord, I know I don't do a lot of things right, so I really need your help with this. I love Germain more than I love anyone, even myself. But I get so afraid sometimes and I do dumb things that hurt people and I don't want to hurt anybody anymore. I need to trust Germain and know that he loves me and won't leave me. I need to trust you more. So could you help me out tonight? Let this night be perfect for both of us."

She stayed on her knees for several more minutes

before she continued speaking. "And God, could you please give us back Niki and bless Nina and Kyle. I know they love her, but she's our little girl. Maybe Nina could get pregnant." Topaz stood up, then quickly knelt again. "And God, please don't let Jade and Sean get a divorce. And bless Keisha and Eric. Amen."

Topaz felt so much better that she had the limo take her to Neiman's where she chose something black, short, and sexy to wear to dinner. A pair of Stuart Weitzmans was screaming her name as she dashed out of the store and made it back to the hotel in time for a massage and body scrub, before her stylist came to do her hair. She would have done it herself, but she wanted everything to be extra special on this night.

She checked her makeup one last time before she left the room. Germain had phoned to say he would meet her on the terrace. Topaz pulled the black shawl around her shoulders as she slowly walked to the main part of the hotel. She was a bit chilly and nervous but opted to wait in the bar by the fireplace where a pianist provided the perfect musical backdrop for a setting straight out of a romance novel. A waiter brought her champagne as the music calmed her nerves. Germain had selected the most perfect place as usual.

"Mind if I join you?"

"Huh?" Topaz was so absorbed by the music and atmosphere she wasn't aware that he had arrived. She looked up into Germain's smiling eyes and thought she would melt. "I'm waiting on my husband, but you can sit with me until he arrives." She returned his smile, then wondered if she had said the wrong thing. She didn't want Germain thinking she was always talking to strange men whenever she was out alone in public.

"What time were you expecting him?" Germain asked, continuing the charade as he was seated.

"He should be here any minute now." Topaz looked around the bar.

"I hope so because he'd be a fool to leave a beautiful woman like you alone for just one minute."

Topaz felt the lump forming in her throat as tears spilled down her cheeks.

"I'm sorry. I didn't mean to make you cry."

Topaz shook her head as Germain gave her his handkerchief. "You always know what to say."

They were both silent now as they focused on the pianist.

"He's good, isn't he?" Topaz finally remarked.

"Yes." Germain was also drinking champagne. The waiter had brought them a bottle, and Topaz was relieved to see he wasn't drinking Tanqueray and tonic. She had never seen him drink like that until all the drama.

Another waiter came and escorted them onto the terrace, where their table provided an excellent view of the elegant swans swimming in the moonlight. The tiles in the floor were heated, and she was very comfortable.

"Germain, you always pick the best places." Topaz smiled as she shook off her shawl and exposed bare sexy shoulders. Her hair, blown silky straight, gently framed her face.

"You look absolutely beautiful tonight. But then you always were the most beautiful woman in the world to me. Sometimes I get caught up in my work and I guess I forget just how much you need to hear that. After all, I am married to a superstar."

"Germain, you know none of that superstar stuff matters to me and you're always telling me how beautiful I am."

Germain looked down into his menu, and Topaz reached for his hand.

"I love you with all my heart. I love you more every day," she said just loudly enough for him to hear.

He bit on his bottom lip and looked back into the menu.

"Don't you believe me, baby?"

"I really want to, Topaz."

She sighed and looked out at a swan gliding across the water. Things were not proceeding as she had hoped.

"Ready to order some dinner?"

Topaz sighed as she flipped open the menu. "I'm not really hungry. Why don't you order for me?"

They didn't talk all through dinner, and the silence between them was killing Topaz. She picked at the grilled veal chops Germain ordered for them.

"Want some dessert?" Germain asked, breaking the silence.

"No, thanks, baby." Topaz managed a faint smile.

Germain passed on dessert, too, and paid for dinner. "I'll walk you to your room."

"You're not going to stay?"

"No, I don't think I should."

"Then why did you order the room?"

"I'm not sure." They were walking very slowly. "It was probably a bad idea."

"A bad idea?"

"I was hoping things might go better."

"What do you mean better?"

"I was thinking maybe we could resolve some things. The last thing we need to do is jump in bed together."

"I was thinking that was the first thing we need to do." They were standing in front of her room. "I miss you and I can't sleep without you."

"We've never had a problem communicating in the bedroom. It's outside the bedroom where we could use a lot of help."

"Okay, so we'll go see a marriage counselor. I'll do whatever you want me to, only don't go. Please, don't go."

It pained him to hear her begging him to stay, but he stood his ground. "You know, I've been wondering if our marriage is based on sex."

"Sex?" Topaz thought about what Germain just said. "It is that, but so much more. It's the love we have for one another, it's our beautiful babies. We have a wonderful family and you're my best friend. I know I've made mistakes, but somehow we've always gotten through them and we'll get through this."

Germain was silent, and Topaz was quiet, allowing him to think. It was very chilly in the December night air. She found the room key and opened the door.

"Come inside with me, baby. I don't want you to catch a cold."

"I never catch cold except from the children."

"Germain." Topaz was beginning to get frustrated with him, which usually led to a fight.

He looked at her with the most vulnerable eyes. "I'm scared, Topaz."

There were tears in her eyes. "I'm scared too." Without thinking she pulled him into her arms and kissed him. They were breathless when they finally pulled apart.

Germain pushed her into the bungalow and closed the door. He grabbed her and, holding her close, looked at her with eyes full of intensity. "Promise you won't keep secrets from me anymore?"

"I promise," Topaz managed while they kissed.

They fell into the bedroom as they undressed each other, knocking paintings out of place on the walls and leaving a trail of clothing all the way to the bed.

Topaz smiled as Germain held her in his arms. "Baby, you know you've got whip appeal."

"What?" Germain was surprised because she had never told him anything like that before.

"You are an incredibly sensitive lover. Why do you think I lose my mind when you're not with me?"

"Because you're a spoiled brat."

"Germain." Topaz played with his hand, putting it next to hers, stroking his long smooth fingers and twisting the platinum band on his ring finger. "You know you're da bomb."

His mind drifted to the countless messages Sabre had left on his cell phone. She had it returned by messenger service. She also apologized profusely for her misconduct and promised it would never happen again, and she couldn't wait to see him. There was something very desperate about her, and Germain couldn't help wondering if she was okay. What he didn't understand was that only Topaz could handle him physically and emotionally, because she was his wife and the marriage covenant sanctified their tumultuous and passionate union. Any other woman would fall prey and become a victim of his tender lovemaking, like Sabre, who thought she was in love.

"I haven't done any shopping and Christmas is only days away," Topaz said later.

"Me neither, and Baby Doll gave me a long list."
Germain laughed.

"You let me see that list before you buy one thing.
You're such a softie when it comes to her."

"What do you want for Christmas?"

Topaz leaned her head against his chest. "Just you . . .
and all my beautiful babies."

"You already have that."

"Then I want more of you than I already have."

Germain sang softly. "I'll give all that I have."

"If you give all that I need," Topaz finished.

"I want to groove with you," they sang together.

"I love that song."

"I know, baby." Topaz hopped out of bed, rambled
through her bags, and pushed a CD in the player. Momentarily, the song was playing. She pulled Germain
out of bed. "Come on, baby. Let's dance."

"Dance? Girl, are you crazy?"

"Only for you."

"How did you manage to bring that CD?"

"It's magic, baby," Topaz whispered as they danced
in the nude to his favorite Isleys tune. "I'm the only one
who always has exactly what you need."

The song ended and Topaz reflected on the words.
"Germain, what do you need?"

The truth. He heard from deep within, but that was
already settled and there was no reason to rehash their
conversation. It would take time to learn to trust again,
and she was more than willing to work on their issues.

"All I need is you, baby. All I need is you."

Chapter 30

It was warm enough to go swimming in Santa Barbara. The sky was a perfect blue and the sun was bright and warm. But looks can be deceiving; the Pacific was too cold for swimming, but the sparkling heated pool at the Ross ponderosa was a tepid eighty.

The freshly cut, long needle pine in the middle of the foyer had been professionally decorated with red opaque glass bulbs and gold bows that Jade had constructed out of metallic ribbons. Fragrance from the fifteen-foot tree filled the entire house.

Guests invited to the ranch for the annual Christmas party were asked to buy or even make an ornament for the family's Christmas tree. Jade sifted through a box of ornaments, pausing to reflect and savor the memories from Christmases past. She picked out a photo of Nina, Kyle, and Niki that had been expertly placed inside a ball of blown glass; an engraved Santa Claus from Keisha, Eric, and the kids; and a snow globe from Topaz, Germain, and the kids. The miscellaneous ornaments hung by their donors gave the tree more character. There were more decorations, but Jade didn't want to see them. She closed the box of memorabilia and took crystal ornaments out of another container and carefully began to hang them on the tree. There wouldn't be a tree-trimming party this year since all of the drama escalated between the friends.

Jade's six-year-old son, Kobe, ran into the room and turned on the television.

"Want to help Mommy with the Christmas tree?" Jade yelled over the noise of his video games on the television.

"Okay, Mom."

Jade smiled and handed him a collection of wooden ornaments. She watched as he carefully placed them all around the tree. She was pleased to see that her son had inherited her artistic eye.

"That looks wonderful, baby. You're a great helper."

Kobe was a perfect blend of his parents. He had Jade's Asian eyes and full lips and Sean's athletic physique. When he was born, Sean had said he wanted four more sons so he could have a basketball team, but there had been no further additions to the Ross roster or even a discussion about having more kids. Jade knew her husband wanted a daughter, which was probably why he had been so obsessed with Niki.

Sean came into the room. "The tree is looking really good, you guys. What can I do to help?"

Jade pointed to the upper half of the tree. "You could finish putting the lights on, then we could use your help with the ornaments."

Sean laughed. "I did ask, didn't I?"

Jade smiled and continued hanging ornaments on the lower half of the tree. The couple worked in silence as they decorated. Things had been rocky between them ever since Sean's birthday party. But Jade had no intention of divorcing Sean because of his infidelity; she just had to get over the fact that the other woman had been Topaz.

Of all the women in the world, why did Sean have to sleep with her? Every time Jade thought about the gorgeous singer being intimate with her husband, she became extremely angry. *Thank God Niki isn't his daughter.*

"Did you hear me, Jade?" Sean moved the stepladder away from the tree.

"What? Did you say something, Sean?"

"I said if we're going to make it to the Valley in time for the Christmas play, we need to be out of here in the next half hour."

"I was thinking about letting him miss the play. It's not like he's the star or anything." Jade stepped away from the tree to scrutinize her work.

"That's true, but what kind of message will we be giving our son? If he's not the star, it's not important? Kobe went to all the rehearsals and I want him to learn that whatever he does is important, and no matter how big or small, he'll always have our support."

Jade made adjustments to several ornaments. "You're right, Sean." She let out a loud sigh that sounded almost like a moan. "I just wish we had left him in the other school."

"Why? The curriculum is much better at Buckley and he loves going to school with his cousin and friends."

"Niki is *not* his cousin," Jade lashed out.

"You know, you're right, Jade. Technically she's not, but as far as Kobe's concerned, she is his cousin, and don't ever let my brother or Nina hear you say that. They'd be terribly hurt."

"Are you sad that Niki isn't your daughter?" Jade asked nastily.

"No, Jade, I'm not. Actually, I'm glad she's not my daughter. Things are already complicated enough," Sean said as politely as he could.

Nina turned off the blow-dryer and sighed with the satisfaction that comes with the completion of an arduous task. "Wow. I'm glad that's done. You've got a lot of hair, baby, and it's thick and long. From now on, you're going to get your hair done with me."

Niki, oblivious to all of her mother's hard work, sat on the stool and hummed. "I want a pretty hairstyle today, Mommy."

Nina laughed. "A pretty hairstyle? And what's a pretty hairstyle, baby?"

"Curls."

"Curls?"

"Baby Doll always wears curls."

"Baby Doll goes to the hairdresser." Nina knew Topaz couldn't manage Baby Doll's coarse thick hair, so she allowed her stylist, who had a standing appointment at the house, to put a mild perm in Baby Doll's hair. Now her hair was silky and down her back. Niki's hair was naturally curly and thick like Topaz's. Nina looked at the clock. Time was quickly running out.

"How about this?" Nina brushed Niki's hair into a bun and pinned it to stay in place on top of her head and handed the child a mirror.

Nina hopped off the stool and carefully watched her daughter inspect her hair. *What a little diva.* She watched Niki primp in the mirror and tried not to smile. *Between me and Topaz, she had to be a little anal over her hair.*

"I like it, Mommy." Niki smiled, exposing two missing front teeth. She was so adorable.

Nina smiled. "I am so glad you approve, Miss Nicole Ross."

Kyle appeared in the bathroom door. "Here are my glamour girls. Are you guys ready to go?"

"We will be as soon as I finish getting dressed."

"Well, hurry up," Kyle said with twinkling eyes. "I can't keep my daughter's public waiting."

"Okay, Sean. Thanks for calling, sweetie." Keisha hung up the phone and looked at Eric with sad eyes.

"What's wrong, baby?"

"That was Sean."

"And?" Eric asked with baited breath.

"I called to see if they would be interested in getting together for dinner after the Christmas play, and he said no."

"What did you expect, girl?"

"I expected our friends to be mature and put this thing behind them."

"Keisha, you are the kindest, sweetest, and the most forgiving person I know. But you can't expect everybody to be like you."

"I can hope, can't I?"

"Yes, you can, but when things don't go like you want, I have to be around to see your beautiful eyes looking so sad."

"I'm sorry, baby." Keisha tried to smile.

"You don't have to apologize to me."

"Sean said Jade didn't even want to come to the play. What is wrong with that girl?"

"She's hurt, baby. People have to heal in their own way and time."

"It's the holidays. I'm just disappointed that we're not spending them with our friends. Jade cancelled the tree-trimming party. Nina said they're going to Philly to spend some time with Kyle's parents. And I don't know what Topaz is doing. I haven't heard from her in days."

"Maybe no news is good news, you think?"

"She'll be at the play. Chris and Baby Doll are in it too. But this is going to be so strange with all of us together and no one talking."

"It's going to take time, Key. Things like this always have a way of working themselves out."

"I miss my friends. They've been our family ever since we moved out here. Maybe we should think about spending Christmas in Atlanta with my family. My parents would love it and your grandmother could come down from Jersey," Keisha suggested.

"Sounds like a plan, baby. Now let's get our prima ballerina out to the Valley."

"Isn't it funny that Rick is the only kid out of our group not in the play?" Keisha finally smiled.

"He's a jock like his old man. He ain't got time for foo-foo stuff." Eric laughed, and Keshia did too.

Keisha was surprised to see Topaz standing front and center when they walked into the school's auditorium. Topaz was already smiling, but she lit up like a neon sign when she spotted Keisha and Eric and waved them down front.

"Girl, you look fabulous," Keisha remarked as the two childhood friends embraced. Topaz did look beautiful in a classic red pantsuit with her hair in an elegant updo.

"Why haven't you returned any of my phone calls? What have you been up to?"

"Handling my business." She was unable to contain her smile. Germain appeared from nowhere and slid into the seat next to Topaz.

"What's up, Keisha girl?" He planted a kiss on her cheek and exchanged pounds with Eric.

"Now I see why I couldn't find you. You two made up and you're both glowing."

Topaz shook out a sable fur coat the same color as her hair and carefully folded it before she sat down.

"Details," Keisha demanded.

"There's not much to tell. He came home one night, we talked. Then we went out on the most wonderful date. The ambience was wonderful, but we almost didn't connect. We talked a little more, I promised no more secrets, and we're going to counseling to work on our issues."

"Oh, T. That's the best news I've had in weeks." There were tears in Keisha's eyes as she hugged Topaz.

"Thanks, Key."

"I was about to make plans to go home for Christmas."

"No way. We're having Christmas at our house, especially since my cousin and I aren't talking." Topaz had a serious look on her face, and Keisha looked around just in time to see Nina and Kyle finding seats on the opposite side of the auditorium.

Keisha sighed unhappily. "You two will be friends again."

"Humph." Topaz rolled her eyes. "Not anytime soon."

Topaz watched Nina wave Jade and Sean to seats by

her. Jade looked like she was mad at the world as she zipped by like a quiet storm, and Sean, who saw them, waved as he passed by.

"Their husbands *are* brothers," Keisha remarked.

"Whatever," Topaz whispered as one of the teachers walked out on stage and the audience applauded.

"We're very pleased to welcome you to 'Christmas Our Way,'" she announced, and left the stage.

"This is supposed to be really good," Keisha whispered.

"I know it's good," Topaz whispered back. "My babies are in it."

Keisha smiled as the lights went down, and she saw Germain take Topaz's hand. Their son Chris walked out on stage dressed in a Victorian costume. A makeup artist had applied thick, bushy eyebrows, a beard, and mustache. Those who knew him couldn't help laughing. He read from a very tall book and walked offstage as a small troupe of ballerinas garbed in pink tutus, white tights, and pink satin toe shoes graced the stage to music from Tchaikovsky's "Dance of the Sugar Plum Fairy."

"There's my girl." Eric sat up in his seat and grinned as Kendra danced and twirled across the stage.

"Look at her," Keisha whispered to Topaz. "She's getting so tall and she's so pretty."

Topaz whispered back, "Did you see my baby boy? Pretty soon he'll be taller than me."

When the ballerinas were finished, Chris returned to the stage dressed as an older man in a flashy suit. He did an excellent impersonation of Steve Harvey. Germain doubled over with laughter.

"He is so good." Keisha wiped a tear from her eye.

"But he came about it honestly between you and Germain. The king and queen of drama."

Topaz laughed. "Didn't he?"

Mariah Carey's "All I Want for Christmas Is You" came on, and girls and boys dressed in the cutest Santa outfits complete with Santa caps pushed a sleigh filled with beautifully wrapped gifts onto the stage, where they executed a tightly choreographed hip-hop routine. Baby Doll, front and center, was clearly the best dancer.

"She is so good," Keisha whispered as the audience cheered and clapped.

"I'm so proud of her," Topaz smiled.

The Santas left the stage to thunderous applause. Chris made several other introductions including Hanukkah and Kwanza and then the final production number, the nativity.

Chris appeared as a shepherd and read from a scroll as the curtain opened on a small group of students portraying Jesus, Mary, wise men, angels, and shepherds.

"Look at Kobe and Niki." Keisha pointed them out. "Aren't they the cutest little angels?"

Kyle focused his camcorder on Niki.

"Kobe looks so cute," Nina whispered to Jade.

"All he does is stand there," Jade whispered back.

When the lines to the scene were done, Niki began to sing.

"O holy night, the stars are brightly shining. It is the night of dear Savior's birth."

You could hear the audience gasp, astonished by her rich clear voice.

"She is fantastic." Keisha gripped Topaz's arm tightly.

Topaz couldn't speak as she held her breath. Tears

rolled out of her eyes as she continued to listen to the little girl sing.

"Fall on your knees, O hear the angels' voices. O night divine. O night when Christ was born."

The other children were singing the chorus, but the audience was already clapping.

Nina wiped tears from her eyes and so did Jade.

"I didn't know she could sing like that," Jade whispered to Nina.

Nina sniffed and dabbed at her eyes with a tissue. "I didn't know she could either."

"Sing it, baby girl," Kyle yelled, not caring what anyone thought. "That's my daughter."

Topaz tugged on Germain's sleeve. "Baby, there's something I need to tell you."

Germain was caught up in a trance with the rest of the audience. "Do you have to tell me now?"

"Yes," Topaz whispered.

"Wait a minute, baby." He took out his BlackBerry and read a text message. "I need to make a quick call. Be right back." He popped out of his seat and quickly left the auditorium.

"Your kids turned it out," Keisha was whispering again. "Did you hear that child hit those notes? And she sang with such passion."

"I was never that good when I was her age," Topaz confessed.

All of the children were onstage taking bows as the audience gave them a standing ovation. When Niki stepped forward everyone stamped and cheered.

Proud parents and family members began to leave the auditorium while others stood around conversing. Kyle had Niki in his arms. He and Nina were definitely the proud parents as everyone made their way over to

ongratulate them on Niki's performance. Topaz couldn't
help being envious as she watched everyone make a
fuss over her and Germain's daughter.

Germain finished his phone call to the hospital. One
of his patients had been hospitalized and the nurses
needed to check the dosage of her medication. While
trying to make his way back into the auditorium, Germain ran smack into Sean, who was on his way to the
restroom.

"Hey, man, congratulations. I know you must be
proud of your daughter."

Germain, not one to hold a grudge, smiled easily.
"Thanks, man. Baby Doll danced her little behind off."

"Yeah, she did," Sean agreed. "But I was talking
about Niki."

Germain's countenance clouded. "Man, what are
you talking about?"

"Keisha and Topaz did a paternity test. Niki is your
daughter, man."

"What?"

"Didn't you know?"

"This is the first I've heard about it." A myriad of
emotions raced through Germain's body.

"My bad," Sean began, but Germain was already
forcing his way through the crowd back to Topaz, who
was laughing and talking to Keisha and Eric.

Germain grabbed her tightly by the arm and whispered in her ear, "Niki is my daughter?"

Topaz looked into Germain's eyes and immediately
knew she had made a huge mistake by not telling him
sooner. Who had told her husband? Words escaped her
as she slowly agreed.

"When were you going to tell me?" he whispered
through gritted teeth.

"I can explain."

"You promised no more secrets."

"I was trying to tell you."

"When? Next year? It seems like everyone knew bu me."

"Give me a chance to explain."

He gripped her arm even more tightly. "You ha your chances. I'll never forgive you for this," he whis pered, and left the auditorium.

"Germain!" Topaz wailed.

Keisha looked in her face. "What is it, girl?"

"Take the kids home with you." Topaz gave Keisha quick peck on the cheek. "I'll explain everything later.

Chapter 31

Topaz ran outside to the parking lot where a light misty rain had begun to fall. Normally, she would have pitched a fit about the rain ruining her hairstyle, but tonight she couldn't have cared less. She ran to the spot where they had parked the car, but she didn't see it anywhere. She scanned the line of bumper-to-bumper cars just in time to see Germain attempting to exit the campus. It was much too congested for him to go anywhere with everyone leaving at the same time.

She ran up to the car and tried to open the door, but it was locked. "Germain! Open the door." For a moment, he looked her way then inched ahead in the traffic.

"Germain!" The misty rain was steadily coming down, saturating her clothes and hair. She ran out of the building so quickly she never had a chance to put on the fur coat that was slung over her arm, and she was chilled to the bone.

"Germain! Open the door, please. It's cold out here."

He stopped and switched open the lock, and Topaz climbed into the car with chattering teeth. "Were you actually going to leave me?"

"I was trying my best." He focused on the traffic a he drove away from the school.

Topaz found a tissue in her purse and wiped awa the moisture that had collected on her face. "Turn o the heat, Germain." Her teeth were still chattering an she could barely speak. Finally, she turned it on herse and Germain turned it back off.

"Germain, I'm freezing!" she wailed.

"I'm not." His tone was mean and cold, but he di turn the heater back on.

Topaz looked at him sideways. She knew he wa hurting. "I sent the kids home with Keisha and Eric s we can talk."

"I have nothing to say to you, Topaz. You're a lia and everything you say is a lie."

"No, Germain. That's not true."

"Is Niki my daughter?" He finally made eye contac for the first time since she had gotten into the car.

"Yes."

"You never told me. Why does Sean know the truth and I don't?"

"I was going to tell you, but it was never the righ time. I went to Nina's house and told her to give Nik back to me the day I found out, but Nina refused. I'n taking them to court."

Germain looked at her like she was crazy. "I swea your elevator doesn't go all the way to the top. Is ther an ounce of gray matter in your head?"

Topaz was shocked by Germain's words. He had never taken that tone with her.

"Nina's taken care of Niki since she was born, and rightfully she is her mother and Kyle is her father. They're the only parents Niki's ever known. You can'

natch Niki out of her home and away from her parents. What were you thinking? Oh, I forgot you don't
think . . . at least not about anyone but yourself."

"I was thinking she needs to come home to her real
mommy and daddy with her brother and sister so we
can all be a family."

"We're already a family. All of us." Germain shook
his head. "As usual, you're dancing around the real
issue. Do you have rocks in your head? What does all
that have to do with you not telling me Niki is mine?
You have denied me something I can never regain . . .
the right and privilege of hearing my flesh and blood
call me Daddy. The right to see her take her first steps,
hear her say Dada, watch her teeth come in, read her a
bedtime story, hear her say her prayers."

"I missed all of those things too."

"You had a choice. You knew she was your daughter
when you gave her away. You were going to leave her in
London, and Nina wouldn't let you do it so Nina
brought her home. That precious little girl. What kind
of a monster are you?" There were tears in his eyes,
and Topaz hated seeing him in such pain.

"I didn't know she was yours."

"But you knew she was yours. You should have
stayed here and had the baby. We would have worked
things out, even if she was Sean's. But you had to
sneak off to Europe . . . not willing to trust the fact that
I loved you more than anything and would be by your
side to go through anything with you. We took vows,
baby, remember, for better or worse?"

"I was afraid I'd lose you again. Won't you even try
and see things my way?"

Tears streamed out of Topaz's eyes and down her

face as he sped into the driveway with screeching tire and shut off the engine. He jumped out of the car an stormed into the house.

Topaz sat in the cold car for almost an hour collectin her thoughts. She was really hoping that Germai would come see what was keeping her.

Germain doesn't care about me. Wearily, she opene the car door, climbed out, and headed for the house She could hear the big-screen TV down in the famil room and knew Germain was probably camped out i front of it with that awful Tanqueray and tonic he use to drown his sorrows.

"You're not the only one in pain, Germain Grad ney." Topaz climbed the stairs to their bedroom.

She went into her dressing room and hung up he fur, took off the pants suit, and strolled into their bed room wearing nothing but a red satin thong. Germai was rummaging through the drawer of his nightstand He looked up at her, then looked away.

"Put on some clothes." He continued searching throug the drawer.

"Why?" Topaz strutted her voluptuous curves. "You know you want me no matter how angry you get, s just come on and get some of this, baby."

"Not tonight, darlin'." He pulled Nina's journal out of the drawer. "In case you were wondering how I found out about your little rendezvous with Sean, it was all in here. Sean also put me up on game tonight. Thank God somebody told me because that definitely was not your intention."

"That son of a bitch." Topaz was immediately angry. "He had no right to tell you anything."

"Don't blame your old boyfriend for telling me what you should have told me the minute you found out."

"Sean was never my boyfriend. I hate his simple, stupid ass."

"Really?" Germain seemed amused, and that angered her even more. "He still has a thing for you."

"No, he doesn't. He loves Jade. He's just a nice guy."

"You must have really freaked the church boy out." Germain tossed Nina's journal on the bed as he left the bedroom. "Take a look at that in your spare time."

"What is that?" Topaz demanded, but he had already left the room. She picked up the pink book and was surprised to see Nina's name inscribed on the front page. "What the hell?" She couldn't believe the details of her life spelled out on the pages. She read passages for over an hour before she angrily stormed into the family room where Germain was asleep on the couch. She threw the book across the room, and it smacked him on the side of his head.

"Woman, are you crazy?" Germain sat up and looked at her.

"Who's keeping secrets now? Why didn't you tell me you had this?"

Germain was still trying to wake up.

"No, you just get drunk and go to Sean's birthday party and spill your guts. I would never embarrass you like that."

"You already did. If you had to fuck somebody why did it have to be Sean? Now every time I see that stupid motherfucker, I'll know he's thinking that I slept with your woman."

Topaz's mouth dropped open in surprise. Germain had never used such foul language.

"When did you get that journal from Nina?"

"I didn't get it from Nina."

"Then where did you get it?"

Germain pretended he didn't hear her. She slappe him on the side of his head, and he gripped her hand so tightly they turned red. "Go back upstairs, Topaz and leave me alone." He gave her a dirty look an pushed her away.

"I want to know where you got the damn journal if i wasn't from Nina."

He changed the channel on the television and sai nothing.

"Who gave you the fucking journal, Germain? Topaz screamed, aggravated and angry.

"Sabre."

"Sabre? What the hell has she got to do with this?"

"She thought I should know."

"Thought you should know what?"

"The truth."

"And you believed her?"

"That was Nina's handwriting."

"Nina is such a little bitch. I'm gonna kick her ass.' Suddenly a crazed look came into her eyes. "It was Sabre. You fucked Sabre."

"I don't know what you're talking about." Germain, not the greatest liar, was doing his best to play it off.

"Some woman called the house real late one night. Of course, I thought it was you because the caller ID was your cell phone. But some female said she was done fucking you so she was sending you home to me. That was Sabre, wasn't it?" Topaz screamed like a mad woman.

"Now you know how it feels," Germain said quietly.

Topaz screamed all the way upstairs and into the kitchen as she searched through drawers for the biggest knife she could find. She snatched it and ran back downstairs, still screaming loudly. "I'm going to kill

ou, Germain. And then I'm going to kill that bitch,
Sabre."

Germain had never seen her so upset. The circumstances had brought out the absolute worst in both of
them.

"Just calm down," Germain said softly, knowing
within himself things had gone too far.

"Don't tell me to calm down," Topaz screamed.
"You fucked that bitch. You know how much I hated
her. Why?" Topaz broke into tears.

"I wanted to hurt you as badly as you hurt me," he
yelled back. "And Jade. It doesn't feel good, does it?"

"I'll never forgive you, Germain Gradney."

"I'll never forgive you, either."

"Fine. Don't forgive me. At least I never cheated on
you while we were married."

"I gotta get out of here." Germain ran up the stairs
and she ran behind him.

"Why? Are you going to see Sabre, that little tramp-
ass ho?"

"Why would you care if you're never going to forgive me?"

Germain was out of the house and in his new
Porsche 911 Carrera Cabriolet. It was a beautiful piece
of machinery, cocoa with terra-cotta interior—an early
Christmas, late birthday gift from Topaz. He drove off
the property going nowhere in particular, just out of the
house to give them both some much needed space. He
opened the window. The chilly night air felt good and it
helped clear his head.

Topaz went upstairs to take a shower. *How had
things gotten so out of hand?*

She broke into tears at the thought of Germain with
Sabre. She had accused him of cheating while they

were married when suddenly she remembered her ow
indiscretion during her climb to the top of the mus
industry.

I slept with Jamil when we were still married. Oh
God. She slid down into the shower and cried her ey
out.

Germain turned onto the infamous Mulholla
Drive. The Porsche could go from zero to sixty mil
per hour in a matter of seconds. He sped down th
road, enjoying the feel of the car as it hugged the pav
ment.

Why couldn't I keep my big mouth shut? I love m
wife, and no matter what, I will always love her. I vowe
to be with her for better or for worse. She's a part of m
We've seen better, but things could always be worse. Ni
is mine. Germain wiped a tear from his eye and smile
That little sweet thing is mine. Like Mom always used
say, into each life a little rain must fall.

He carefully turned the car around and headed f
home. *Makeup sex is a great thing. She is so dramat*
and tender, like fire and rain.

He was driving over a hundred miles an hour whe
he took out his voice-activated cell phone and calle
Topaz. He spoke after the beep. "I'll always love yo
baby, no matter what." He was about to say more whe
he glanced at the lights twinkling in the Valley. It was
spectacular view. He hit a large patch of water on th
road. It splashed everywhere and the car swerved o
of control. It spun around, crashed, and flipped over th
barricade. Time stood still as the Porsche sailed int
oblivion, tumbled down the hillside, and crashed on th
rocks below.

Topaz got out of the shower and phoned Germain. I
rang and went to voice mail, so she decided to leave

essage. "Hi, baby. I just wanted you to know I'm
orry and I do forgive you. I'll always forgive you be-
ause I love you. See you later, sweetie." She smiled as
he hung up the phone and went to look through her
ngerie drawers for her sexiest nightgown.

Topaz had been asleep for hours when she thought
he heard the doorbell ring. She opened her eyes and
as immediately sad because Germain wasn't lying in
ed beside her. She found her slippers and robe while
he bell continued to chime. Security would take care
f it, but it was unusual for callers invited or uninvited
o arrive at their home so late.

Her intentions were to see if Germain was asleep in
he family room, but she was surprised when she saw
ecurity in the foyer with a California Highway Patrol-
an.

"Are you Mrs. Gradney?" the officer inquired.

"Yes."

"Your husband is Dr. Germain Gradney?"

"Yes." Uneasiness crept through her body, and she
new something was terribly wrong.

"I'm afraid there's been a terrible accident."

She clasped a hand to her mouth, and tears filled her
yes. There was a lump in her throat and she couldn't
reathe. "Not Germain."

"We found his car on the hillside below Mulholland
Drive."

"He's okay, right?"

"No one could have survived that fall. It looks like
he lost control and crashed through a barricade on
Mulholland. I'm sure he was killed on impact."

Germain . . . killed? "Oh my God." Topaz screamed
and fell to the floor like a crumpled leaf. "Not Germain, not my sweet baby."

"Ma'am. I'm sorry, but we're gonna need you to g
to the hospital and identify the body."

"Nooooo." She screamed from the depths of h
soul. She lay on the floor sobbing, then she jumped u
with a straight face. "I don't believe it. Germain is n
dead."

"Ma'am, we still need you to go to Cedars and mak
the identification. I hope it's not your husband. Goc
night."

The security guards escorted the patrolman out c
the house while Topaz stood there wondering what sh
should do.

"I'll drive you to the hospital," one of the guards o
fered.

"That won't be necessary," Topaz replied cooll
"Germain wasn't in an accident."

The men looked at one another as Topaz climbed th
stairs in a daze.

Before she realized it, she dialed Keisha's number.

"What's up, girl?" The Johnsons had been expectin
her call for hours, so when the phone rang at two-thirt
that morning, they weren't surprised at all. Eric looke
at the caller ID and handed the phone to Keisha.

"Girl, you know the strangest thing just happened."

"What's up, T?" Keisha yawned.

"A highway patrol came to the house and told m
Germain had a car accident and that he was dead."

"Topaz, no," Keisha screamed. "No."

"What is it?" Eric sat up straight.

"Please don't let it be true." Tears rolled out o
Keisha's eyes.

"That's what I said. They want me to come t
Cedars to identify the body, but I'm not going becaus
I know Germain isn't dead."

"What's wrong, Key?" Eric couldn't understand why his wife was crying.

"You don't go anywhere. Just get dressed and we'll come and take you to the hospital," Keisha ordered.

"Girl, you don't have to come all the way out here tonight. Germain will be home by the time you get here." Topaz laughed hysterically.

"Good, then we'll eat some ice cream and have a party." Keisha hung up. Eric was already getting dressed.

"What's up with queen of drama now?" Eric smiled as he pulled on a Lakers warm-up jacket.

"CHIPs came to the house and told Topaz that Germain was killed in a car accident, but she doesn't believe it."

It was close to four and every light in the house was on when Keisha and Eric finally arrived in Pacific Palisades. It was so windy that night. It howled like a banshee. Topaz, still in her nightgown, was drinking Germain's Tanqueray and tonic.

"Girl, get dressed." Keisha took the glass from her and pulled her up the stairs to her bedroom.

"He slept with Sabre, Key. Can you believe Germain slept with that bitch?"

"No." She dragged Topaz downstairs and out of the house. "I think she's in shock," Keisha whispered to Eric.

Eric drove as quickly as he could to Cedars while Topaz rambled on about their fight and things they had said to each other. They left the car in front of the emergency room and were eventually escorted into a room where they saw Germain's badly bruised and mangled body lying on a steel table.

Keisha screamed and fell out on Eric at the sight of

her Atlanta homeboy and beloved friend. "It's him!" she yelled. "It's Germain!"

Topaz just stood there looking at Germain's lifeless body. "That's not him," she whispered.

"It is too!" Keisha screamed. "Girl, what's wrong with you? He's wearing a wedding ring just like yours." She took Topaz's hand and held it next to Germain's slender surgeon fingers, and Topaz snatched it back.

"That's not my man. Germain's at home waiting for me," Topaz said with a spaced-out look on her face. "Now come on, Key, let's go. You know Germain wouldn't want you crying like this for nothing."

Eric stood there watching his wife sob uncontrollably. Topaz looked like a zombie. He looked at the body on the table and knew immediately it was Germain. His spirit and soul had clearly vacated the premises, but what was left definitely had belonged to Germain. He looked at Topaz, who was very much alive and knew she had left the planet, too. Then he prayed for the strength to be the man he needed to be to get them all through this.

The drive back was silent except for Keisha's occasional sobs and sniffles. Eric knew he had to get Topaz out of the house before the paparazzi got wind of the story and set up camp in front of her home.

Upstairs in the bedroom, Keisha began packing Topaz's things. She was opening the nightstand drawer when she saw a red light blinking on Topaz's answering machine.

"T, you have a message, honey."

Topaz pressed a button and Germain's voice came

through the speaker loud and clear. "I'll always love you, baby, no matter what."

Keisha looked at Topaz, who was shaking like a leaf.

"Germain killed himself. He killed himself and he did it because of me." She tried to breathe and things went dark as she passed out cold on the bedroom floor.

Chapter 32

A limousine was waiting for Nina, Kyle, and Niki when they arrived at Philadelphia International early that morning. They had caught the red-eye out of LAX right after Niki's stellar performance in the school Christmas play. It was cold and snowing. Christmas lights and decorations were everywhere.

"Now this is what I call Christmas." Kyle laughed as he scooped up a bit of snow with his hands, formed it into a ball, and threw it at Nina. "None of those pink Christmas trees in eighty-degree weather in Cali this year."

"I like that eighty-degree weather." Nina laughed. "I kinda like those pink Christmas trees, too."

"I love the weather, but not at Christmastime. It's supposed to be cold."

Nina could only laugh. "Whatever, baby."

"I haven't seen you smile for a long time. I miss your smile."

"It's great to have something to smile about. No more grown-up problems." Nina was serious again.

"I know, baby. That's why I brought my girls here, so

can make them smile." He kissed both of them. "I've got to have a cheesesteak sammich at my spot on South Street. I know my dad will go with me. He's always down for a sammich." Kyle was really excited to be home.

"It's sandwich, Daddy, not sammich." Niki, who was sitting in Kyle's lap looking out of the window, turned around to laugh.

"You tell him, baby girl." Nina smiled at her daughter and then she poked Kyle. "Like you came from the hood and grew up eating sammiches."

"I did."

"Oh please." Nina laughed. "You're as bourgeois as they come. Got my baby ordering sushi. Take her with you so she can eat her first cheesesteak."

"Like you can talk, Miss I-was-raised-in-Sherman-Oaks. You ain't nothing but a Valley Girl." Kyle tugged gently on Nina's hair.

"And proud of it."

"I'm a Valley Girl too." Niki looked at Kyle. "Right, Daddy?"

"Nope, you're a Malibu beach bunny. My little heartbreaker who's gonna be out there breaking all those young boys' hearts."

Kyle winked. Nina only smiled and looked out the window.

The limo hit the suburbs, drove down several blocks, and pulled into the driveway of a comfortable three-story house. An ominous-looking huge oak tree stood in the front yard covered with light snow. Christmas decorations were on the lawn and strung around the outside of the green and white house. No matter how great a fortune the Ross brothers amassed, their parents refused to move out of their childhood home,

although they had allowed them to redecorate th
house and purchase a few trinkets. Mama Ross owne
a brand new Mercedes ML truck with seat warmers
Papa Ross got a silver gray Rolls Royce Phantom.

"Hey, is anybody awake in this joint?" Kyle yelle
as he burst in the front door.

"Now you know I'm going to be awake to see my
boy who came all the way here from California."
Mama Ross came out of the kitchen and gave them al
a hug.

"Daddy's not a boy," Niki whispered to Nina.

"No, he isn't, but that's his momma, so to her he wil
always be her boy, just like no matter how big and
beautiful you get, you will always be my beautiful baby
girl," Nina explained.

"Okay." Niki smiled as Mama Ross scooped her up.

"And how is my beautiful granddaughter?"

Niki just giggled. This was the first time she had
been to Philadelphia to see her grandparents, but
Kyle's parents traveled to California several times a
year to see Kyle and Sean and the grandchildren.

"Who is that giggling?" Papa Ross was just an
older, wiser version of his handsome sons.

"It's me, Grandpa." Niki kissed him on the cheek
when he hugged her. "You look like Daddy, Grandpa."

"Daddy looks like Grandpa."

"That's what I just said."

Everyone laughed. "Don't be too smart, little girl,"
Nina warned.

Papa Ross carried Niki into the kitchen, where his
wife had prepared a huge breakfast. Fried chicken,
waffles, biscuits, grits and gravy, sausage, bacon,
scrambled eggs, and fresh-squeezed orange juice were
all begging to be consumed.

"Dang!" Nina was almost drooling. "Denny's ain't got nothing on you." Nina, who always loved to eat, pulled out a chair at the table.

"Look at you." Kyle laughed and pulled out a chair. "You just forgot all about your baby."

"Leave that girl alone, Kyle, and let her eat. She's already a little too thin." Mama Ross smiled at her daughter-in-law, who was already making her plate. "I've been cooking fried chicken with waffles ever since you and Sean took me to Roscoe's when we were in LA."

"Roscoe's ain't got nothing on you, Mama." Kyle began making his plate too, while Mama Ross helped Niki pick out her favorite breakfast foods.

Papa Ross smiled at his wife and offspring and blessed the food so they all could eat.

"Your brother should be here by now," Mama Ross said. Kyle's identical twin brother, Kirk, lived across the bridge in New Jersey. Out of the three brothers, it was Kirk who decided to follow in his father's footsteps by accepting the call of God on his life. He and his wife, Karla, were also pastors at his father's church. It was as if Kirk heard his name called. Kirk, Karla, and their fifteen-year-old daughter, Kyrie, walked into the kitchen.

"Hey, now some real Hollywood swingers are in the house." Kirk, the elder of the twins grinned at Kyle.

Kyle stood up to give Kirk a hug. "Look at you. You look good for an old man."

"Old man?" Kirk looked insulted.

Kyle laughed. "You're older than me."

"Only by a few minutes," Kirk replied. "Just make sure you don't eat too much because we're going to Jimmy's for cheesesteaks for lunch," Kyle said.

There were more hugs and kisses between the in-laws and cousins as the rest of the family sat down to Mama Ross's delicious breakfast.

"It's too bad Sean, Jade, and Kobe weren't able to come. It would have been real nice having the entire family for Christmas." Mama Ross looked sad for just a moment at the thought of her youngest missing in action.

"Well, I brought the next best thing." Kyle got up from the table and went for his briefcase and produced a DVD. "All of the kids were in the school play, and our Miss Niki stole the show," Kyle declared proudly.

"Oh, I want to see it now, Kyle. Let's go in the TV room and watch it there," Mama Ross suggested.

The TV room was actually a small theater with a dozen or so red suede rocking and reclining chairs and a myriad of framed classic movie posters on the walls. An antique popcorn popper and an old-fashioned Coke machine completed the décor.

"I like this room, Mommy," Niki declared as she rocked back and forth in her chair.

"I bet you do." Nina pinched her nose and Niki laughed. "We'll get Daddy to put one in our new house in Sherman Oaks."

"I want one in Malibu, too. Okay, Mommy?"

"Anything for you, baby girl," Nina replied.

They were silent as the DVD began. Kyle's cell phone rang, but he ignored it. He took it out of his pocket and turned it off without looking at the caller ID. "I'm on vacation. What could anyone possibly want the day before Christmas Eve?" he said softly to Nina.

A light flashed on and off in the theater, signaling that the house phone was ringing.

"I'll get it." Papa Ross got up and went for the phone. Moments later, he came over to Kyle and spoke softly in his ear. "Sean's on the phone."

"Tell him I'll call him right back, Dad."

"I told him we were watching the kids' Christmas play, but he said it was important," Papa Ross explained.

Kyle got up and went for the phone in the back of the theater. "What's so important that I had to interrupt the viewing of my daughter's command performance?"

"Sorry, man, but I've got some real bad news. Germain was killed in a car accident earlier this morning. His Porsche flipped over a barricade on Mulholland," Sean informed him.

Kyle said nothing as his brother's words registered in his brain. Then he managed, "The doc is dead?"

"Yeah, man. Everybody's taking it real hard."

There were tears in Kyle's eyes as he tried to accept that his best friend was dead. "Okay, man. Thanks for calling. We'll be back in LA as soon as we can." Kyle hung up and tried to compose himself as he returned to his seat next to Nina.

"What did Sean want?" Nina whispered.

He sniffed and coughed before he could reply. "I'll tell you later."

Nina looked at her husband rubbing his eyes. "Have you been crying?"

"No, I'm cool."

"You are not cool. What did Sean say on the phone? Is Jade okay?" Nina wanted answers, so Kyle motioned for her to follow him out of the screening room. In the light, she could see Kyle had definitely been crying. She took her husband in her arms and tried to comfort him. "What is it, baby? What's wrong?"

"It's Germain. He was in a car accident and he's d . . ." He couldn't make himself say the word.

"Germain is dead?"

Kyle nodded his head to say yes.

"No . . . not Germain. Tell me that's not true," Nina cried.

"I wish I could."

"I saw him last night at the play and we didn't even speak. Now I'll never have a chance to speak to him again." Nina shook her head in disbelief. "Poor Topaz . . . she must be losing her mind."

Nina and Kyle cried together. "We have to go home right away," Nina said, and sniffed.

"Yeah." Kyle was finally able to speak again. "We'd better go back to the airport now. I hope we can get a flight."

"I have to call Topaz." Tears poured out of Nina's eyes. "What do we tell Niki? Germain was her biological father."

"I don't know," Kyle said. "She's just a little girl. She won't understand all of this. Maybe we should leave her here with my parents."

"No." Nina shook her head firmly. "She needs to be with us. But I do think it may be time to tell her she's adopted. We wouldn't want her to overhear anything that could be damaging."

"We need to tell my parents and Kirk the truth about Niki first."

"Okay," Nina agreed.

In the screening room, the family was watching Niki sing her solo.

"That's my grandbaby," Mama Ross declared proudly.

Nina had to smile because she sounded so much like Kyle the night of the Christmas play.

It was hard for Nina to relax now that she had learned the horrific news. She couldn't sit still. She wanted to see her cousin because she knew Topaz's heart was forever broken.

"You've got yourself a serious little vocalist," Papa Ross declared. "But where did she get those pipes from? It certainly wasn't from our side of the family."

"Dad, there's something Nina and I need to tell you," Kyle began.

"Does this have anything to do with Sean's phone call?" Papa Ross inquired.

"Yes, sir. We need to have a family meeting. Kyrie, stay with Niki and watch movies. Grown folk gotta talk, sweetie. I'm sure you're a Cheetah Girl too."

"Sure, Uncle Kyle." Kyrie smiled at him. She loved Uncle Kyle. Kyrie, a pretty girl with cocoa skin, dark eyes, and dark curly hair, would be a real beauty one day.

Kyle led the rest of the family upstairs to his father's study. When everyone was seated, he began. "I just learned that my best friend was killed in a terrible car accident. You remember Germain? He's married to Topaz?"

There was a series of reactions as the family offered their condolences.

"There's something else you guys need to know. Niki is not my biological daughter. She's Germain and Topaz's little girl."

"How did you end up with Topaz's daughter?" Kirk demanded. He was never a fan of the golden-eyed singer, and he let it be known the time Sean expressed interest in her.

"We've got to catch the first flight out of here back to LA, so I need to make this quick. Sean slept with

Topaz once after he married Jade. She also slept with Germain, who she was divorced from around the same time, and got pregnant. No one knew about it except Topaz and Nina. Germain decided to remarry her. Since she didn't know who the baby's father was, Nina, Topaz, and her producer went to Europe to work on an album until Topaz gave birth." Kyle could see his brother shaking his head in disbelief, but he continued the disclosure. "Around the same time, I met Nina and we started dating, and I knew I wanted to marry her from the beginning. While she was in Europe, and I'm really serious about this, I heard a voice clearly tell me to go to Nina because she needed me."

Kirk pretended to play a violin.

"Man, this is serious." Kyle frowned at Kirk. "So Topaz had the baby and thought it was Sean's. Without getting a paternity test, she decided she didn't want the baby because she thought it was Sean's."

"Oh no." Mama Ross looked like she was going to be sick.

Kyle continued, "Nina wouldn't let Topaz abandon the baby in Europe, so she decided to raise the baby as her own. When I arrived, she told me the entire story. We were married and our names were listed on Niki's birth certificate as the birth parents. We had Niki tested just a week ago and found out Germain is her biological father and not Sean. There's been nothing but drama since the truth came out. We've got to get to the airport now so we can go home," Kyle finished.

"That sounds like something straight out of a soap opera," Kirk declared.

"Don't go there, man. Not today and definitely not now," Kyle fired back.

"Kirk, you always did have too much mouth," Mama Ross scolded. "That is quite a story, Kyle. But what about the baby? Are you going to give her back to Topaz now? That poor child must be going out of her mind. What a tragic loss."

"She's our little girl, Mom. We've raised her since she came into the world."

"That's true, son. And God used you and Nina to do a good thing. You kept her child, and now that she's lost her husband she's gonna need that little girl more than ever. You and Nina are young and healthy. You'll have more children of your own." Mama Ross smiled warmly.

"What if Niki doesn't want to go with Topaz?" Nina questioned.

"God will help you make the right decision," Mama Ross said.

It was the vacation that ended much too soon. Kirk and Karla drove them back into the city to the airport, but not without making a pit stop on South Street for some of Jimmy's famous cheesesteak sandwiches. The ladies waited in the car while the brothers went inside.

"I don't really feel like cheesesteak now," Kyle told Kirk.

"I'm real sorry about your friend," Kirk said.

"Thanks, man."

"You don't know how long you'll have to wait in the airport before your flight. You will get hungry and the first thing you'll think about is one of these babies."

They both watched as a woman assembled the sandwiches.

Kyle managed to smile at his brother. "You're right, man. Thanks."

Kirk dropped them in front of the terminal. "We'll

be praying for you. If you need me, we'll be out on the next thing smoking."

"Thanks, Kirk. Merry Christmas." Kyle hugged his twin and Karla one last time.

"Good-bye, Uncle Kirk. Good-bye, Aunty Karla." Niki gave them both a hug.

Mother and daughter were silent while Kyle worked on getting them a flight.

"Mommy, why are we going back to California so soon?"

Nina thought for a moment, trying to find the best answer. There were too many things to explain to the child at once. *What do I say? How do I start?* Nina pulled Niki into her lap. "We have to go home because Uncle G had an accident and now he's in heaven. Aunty T, Chris, and Baby Doll are all very sad now so we have to go home and cheer them up. Aunty will be very glad to see us, especially you."

"She will?" Niki looked puzzled.

"Yes."

"Will we see Uncle G?"

"Yes, but not for a long time. Until we do, Uncle G will always be with us in our memories and in our hearts."

"Okay, but why are you crying?"

"Because I love Uncle G and I'm gonna miss him very much. I never had a chance to say good-bye." Nina found a handkerchief and dried her tears as Kyle finally joined them.

"We're on a two o'clock flight. We should be back in Cali and on our way home by six."

Nina nodded her approval.

"Mommy's sad because Uncle G went to heaven and we won't see him anymore," Niki explained to her dad.

"I'm sad too, baby girl." Kyle picked up Niki and the family proceeded through the security line to the departure terminal. They settled into a private waiting room to relax before the flight.

"Mommy, where's my iPod video?" Niki searched her backpack.

"I have it, baby. I'll give it to you when we get on the plane."

"Okay, then I'll read." Niki reached in her backpack again.

"No, baby girl." Kyle sat her in his lap. "We need to have a family talk first."

"Did I do something wrong?"

"No." Kyle smiled at her. "You know you're always a good girl."

"What's up?" Niki made a little face, and everyone laughed. Nina couldn't help thinking how much the child's expression reminded her of Topaz.

"Remember when we talked about where babies come from? Out of the mother's stomach?"

"Yes."

"Even though you didn't come out of my stomach, you're still my and Daddy's baby girl."

"That's right," Kyle added. "And we love you very much."

Niki thought about what her parents had said. "I didn't come out of your stomach?"

Nina shook her head. "No, baby."

"Then whose stomach did I come out of?"

Nina and Kyle looked at each other. "Aunty T," Nina finally said.

"I did?"

"Yes."

"Okay." Niki looked as though it was perfectly acceptable to her.

"Is there anything you want to ask us?" Kyle inquired.

"No."

"Any comment?" Nina asked.

Niki looked thoughtful. "Well, there is something."

"What's that, baby girl?" Kyle fingered her cheek and hair.

"I always wondered why I had eyes like Aunty T, Chris, and Baby Doll, but not you," Niki replied.

Nina and Kyle exchanged glances again.

"Everybody always thinks Baby Doll is my sister and Chris is my brother. I can sing like Aunty T. Baby Doll can't, so does that mean Aunty T isn't her mother?"

"No, baby girl. Aunty T is Baby Doll's mother. When children are born they inherit or receive certain traits or gifts from their mothers and fathers. You have a lot of Aunty T in you because she's your mother."

"Okay." Niki didn't seem to have a care in the world. "Can I have some of your steak sammich, Daddy?" There was a definite twinkle in her golden eyes.

"I'm hungry, too. Why don't you help me eat Daddy's sammich."

Nina watched as Kyle spread a napkin in her lap and sliced off a portion of his sandwich. She turned away as tears poured out of her eyes and she desperately tried to brush them away. She couldn't imagine life without Niki, and just the thought of it was heart-wrenching pain . . . deep down in her soul.

She's our little girl. Nina wanted to scream. *Why even go home?* They were in the airport. They could take Niki and just disappear. Nina and Kyle's names were on the birth certificate and every other legal document that pertained to Niki. *We could get on a plane and go anywhere.*

Then Nina thought about what Topaz must be going through and cried even harder, but giving Niki to Topaz now wouldn't bring Germain back. Topaz had never mentioned wanting her until she knew Germain was Niki's father. But Niki was Germain and Topaz's love child, which made her very special. Topaz's brief connection with Sean had been purely physical, and it was definitely not about love.

What should I do? What should I do? Nina anguished over her decision. *What is best for Niki? I have to do what's best for Niki.*

Nina sighed and closed her eyes.

Chapter 33

"He was the Godfather of Soul. He wrote, played, and performed the funkiest music on the planet. The hardest working man in show business died Christmas Day at the age of seventy-three. The world will miss James Brown, but he will continue to live on through his music."

Eric groaned and switched to ESPN. He didn't want to hear about anyone else dying. First Germain, then James Brown's death put even more of a damper on a picture-perfect Christmas Day. President Gerald Ford also died. It seemed like famous people really did go in threes.

Topaz and Germain's family and friends had gathered at Keisha's house in Ladera where they were going through the motions of celebrating Christmas Day. Guests included Germain's mom and dad, Kathleen and George; Topaz's mother, Lisa; her sister, Lena, who was Nina's mom; and her husband, John, Nina's dad. Germain's grandmother, Inez, and Keisha's parents, Melvyn and Michele, were also there. Still in shock, no one knew what to do or say, so everyone walked on eggshells with polite smiles plastered on their faces.

Sean and Jade had cried separately, then together when they learned of Germain's death.

"Life is too short to waste your life being mad at anyone, but especially someone you love," Keisha had said.

It was a wake-up call for Jade. She and Sean put their differences aside and agreed to disagree. They kissed, made up, and now they were whispering to each other, not wanting to disturb the uncomfortable silence in the house.

Topaz, still in another world, looked beautiful as usual. She stood alone staring out a kitchen window with a dazed expression. She had just chewed out her mother, who only suggested she eat something, and now Lisa was on the verge of tears. No one else wanted to upset her, so they left Topaz alone.

Keisha and Eric prepared Christmas dinner themselves. It was a wonderful spread: turkey, ham, greens and yams, string bean casserole, macaroni and cheese, and gumbo. There was a beautiful Christmas tree and presents, but it was hard to have a good time because Germain's upcoming funeral cast a dark cloud over their heads. Keisha and Germain's mother, Kathleen, made all the arrangements,

Keisha told the kids to entertain themselves. Chris definitely needed cheering up. He understood all too well that his dad had been killed. He still couldn't believe he wouldn't see his father again.

"I don't know how you guys can sing and dance." Chris, unable to contain his grief, snapped at the girls who were watching music videos in Kendra's bedroom. He made a trip up to her bedroom to tell them to shut up, and the girls immediately quieted down.

"Especially you, Baby Doll. Don't you care about Dad?"

"Yes." Baby Doll giggled and whispered in Kendra's ear.

Chris shook his head, unable to understand why his little sister wasn't displaying mournful behavior.

Baby Doll simply laughed and called him a sour face.

It was a breath of fresh air when Nina, Kyle, and Niki walked into the house. Their plane had a stop in Denver and they wound up stuck in the airport for hours, but they finally made it into LA during the wee hours of Christmas morning.

"Niki," they all said, and the plastic smiles melted into the real deal, if only for a minute.

The first person Niki went to was Topaz, who scooped her up and hugged her. Somehow the little girl sensed that her mother needed her.

"Merry Christmas, Aunty."

"Merry Christmas to you too, baby." Topaz squeezed the little girl as tightly as she could, and Nina looked away.

Nina hugged Topaz next. Everyone's eyes were glued on the ladies as they waited to see what would happen, but Topaz carried Niki around the room in her arms.

"This is my mother, Grandma Lisa. There's Nana and Pop." That was Nina's mom and dad. "This is Great-Grandma Inez and Grandma Kathleen and Grandpa George." Topaz continued making introductions, and Niki checked them all out.

Now that everyone knew Germain was her biological father, they were busy checking Niki out. It was amazing how much she looked like Germain. She had all of his expressions; she also inherited his kind ways and good heart. Niki was darker than Chris and Baby Doll; that skin color and those golden eyes made her exotic.

Tears rolled out of Kathleen's eyes as she watched her newly found granddaughter. Topaz and Nina took her around until she had spoken to everyone. Afterward, all of their spirits lifted and their faces brightened.

Nina took Topaz, who refused to let Niki out of her sight, into another room.

"It's about time you got here with my baby," Topaz declared with a little too much attitude.

"Niki, you go play with the other kids now." Nina looked like she meant business, and Topaz lowered the child to the floor and released her.

"Thanks, Mommy." Niki ran off, too happy because she was able to play with her siblings and cousins.

"I'm really sorry about Germain, T." Nina was finally able to say his name without tearing up.

"How dare you give Sabre your journal to read! That was my business, no one else's." Topaz lit into Nina with a vengeance.

"My journal? How do you know whatever Sabre read came from my journal?" Nina demanded.

"It had your name on it."

"My name? Are you sure?"

Topaz led Nina upstairs and into the bedroom that was temporarily hers and took the journal out of her bag. "Germain gave me this the night of the accident. He said Sabre gave it to him."

Nina took the journal and carefully scrutinized the book. It looked like one of hers. She opened it and she saw her name and handwriting. "This is mine, but I never gave it to Sabre or anyone else. I would never do something like that."

"Somebody gave it to Sabre, and she gave it to Germain. You should have never written all that stuff about my life."

Nina was offended. "Your life? Those things were about my life that was too much a part of your life."

Topaz let out a long sigh. "How in the hell did she get this journal?"

"I have no idea. I wish I knew. She obviously took it while she was in my house, only I can't remember her being there except one time when the group auditioned and a second night when she came over to tell us she had seen India's ring in Char's jewelry box, and she never went upstairs."

"That bitch had sex with Germain. Just wait until I see her skanky ass."

Nina covered her mouth in shock. "No, she didn't. How did you find out?"

"Some woman called the house one night and said some crazy things. I put it all together after Germain showed me this journal."

"Germain said he slept with Sabre?" Nina repeated herself just to be sure she heard Topaz correctly.

"He said it was only one time. He wanted to hurt me as badly as I had hurt him when he found out I had sex with Sean."

"When did all of this take place?"

"After the school play." Topaz began to cry again.

Nina sat there trying to figure out how and when Sabre had been in her house. "It had to be Sky. She

tayed at the house while I was in Hawaii. Maybe
Sabre came over then."

"Whatever. You were the one who brought those
wood rats out here. This is your fault, and I will never
forgive you. Germain died because of you."

"Whatever, Topaz. You need to take responsibility
for your own actions. You will never know how sorry I
am about Germain. He was like a brother to me. But
you're right, it is your business, and you should have
told Germain a long time ago."

"Like when I was having those stupid dreams,"
Topaz mumbled.

"I want Niki to stay here with me," Topaz said to
Nina, who was on her way out.

"If Niki wants to stay, she can," Nina said, and she
was gone.

Topaz went back downstairs and found Niki. "Want
to spend the night with Aunty?"

"No, thank you." Niki immediately went to Nina
where she carefully eyed Topaz until Nina and Kyle
took her home.

The next morning everyone was at Keisha and Eric's
dressed in black. It was truly an ebony fashion affair.
Topaz came downstairs in black Versace with a pair of
Jimmy Choos dangling in her hand, looking like the
star she was.

A huge black and white diamond sparkled on her
hand. It was her Christmas present from Germain. He
and Chris had shopped for it at Harry Winston. He had
purchased the diamond and the gift card the morning
of the kids' play. Chris handed her the package on
Christmas morning. Topaz stared at the package for an

hour before she opened it. She simply put on the ring and continued to gaze out the window.

Topaz's stylist did Niki's hair, and it looked like silk. It was so shiny and beautiful. She had on a black velvet dress with a white lace collar. She was too cute in her black opaque stockings and shiny patent leather slip ons. Topaz smiled at her for a second and continued looking out the window. Lisa dressed Baby Doll in a black taffeta dress. It was a miracle that Topaz managed to dress herself.

Topaz whimpered softly when the cars arrived to take the family to Forest Lawn where the service would be held. *I can't go through with this.*

She wanted to run upstairs and get back in bed. This was a little too real for her. She was still expecting Germain to come walking through the door any minute but he didn't and he wouldn't. It was time to go to the funeral and say good-bye.

She took her place at the front door and was relieved when Keisha and Eric took her by the hand. No real thinking there. She could continue to be mindless and just follow them. Chris, Baby Doll, and Kendra were behind them. Nina fell in the ranks with Niki.

"Mommy, I want to go with Baby Doll and Chris."

Nina looked at Chris. "Watch out for your sisters."

"Okay." He took both girls by a hand. But Chris had always watched after them like a good brother. The job just had an official title now. His little face looked so unhappy. Germain had always been there for him. He had survived without his mother but never without his dad.

An attendant ushered them outside to the cars. With each passing moment, it became more difficult for Topaz to breathe. She took lots of small, shallow breaths, but nothing deep. She couldn't because she had made up her mind that she was also going to die. No one was talking. Even the children were quiet as Topaz examined the Bentley. It was a gift from Sherwin on behalf of VMG. *Superstar* was still selling like crazy, and the car was their way of saying thank you. The customized vehicle was a bit too flashy even for her, so Topaz seldom if ever drove it. She had purchased Germain's Porsche to match the Bentley.

They were driven south to Slauson and west to the 405. Topaz closed her eyes; she felt like she was suffocating. She put a few cubes of ice in a tumbler and poured out of the bottle of alcohol closest to her. She drank the liquor quickly. It tasted terrible and it felt like fire as it ran down her throat. Moments later, she was already feeling the effects. She poured another and drank it down.

Finally, the cars drove onto the manicured grounds of Forest Lawn in Burbank. People from all walks of life were waiting to say good-bye to Germain, too. As they were ushered into the chapel and past the casket, Topaz's knees grew weak when she saw Germain's body. She paused for a second to look at his remains. She couldn't stand to see him with all the makeup that was used to cover the bruises on his face. It didn't look like Germain at all. The family was just about finished viewing the body when Sabre arrived.

 She entered from the back with their publicist, Mimi, who tiptoed to seats Sherwin had saved for them. Sabre ran up to the casket as it was being closed and screamed.

"Germain." She sank onto the floor and cried.

Everyone looked at her like she was crazy.

"Mother, who is that woman?" Chris demanded.

Sabre was wearing a fine black straw hat. It covered half of her face, but Topaz still knew it was Sabre.

"Sabre," Topaz whispered sharply to Chris. She couldn't believe how the girl was carrying on at her husband's funeral. *That bitch better sit down before I kick her ass all over this chapel.*

"That was a performance," Kyle whispered into Nina's ear.

"Topaz told me Germain slept with her."

Kyle's expression registered his shock. "I don't believe it."

"Straight from T. She and Germain got into a fight about it," Nina informed him. "Look at her."

Sabre was on her knees sobbing at the foot of the casket. Topaz crossed her legs and looked pissed as hell. Nobody knew what to do, so no one did anything. Others coughed and whispered because they were embarrassed for Sabre, but she didn't care. She sat on the floor crying until Mimi coaxed her back to her seat on the pew. You could still hear her crying when the service finally started.

Kyle continued whispering, "Dramatical."

Nina had to smile. Flavor Flav invented a new word on his reality TV show that described Sabre's little scene perfectly. Dramatical.

People had nothing but good things to say about Germain. His family, staff, and even a few patients shared humorous anecdotes that warmed the heart.

"Germain was a great man, a wonderful husband and father, and the perfect son-in-law," said Topaz's mother, Lisa. You knew what Topaz would look like in eighteen years when you saw Lisa.

Nina was not surprised when Kyle went up. He stood there smiling at everyone and looking just like

Papa Ross. "The doc . . . that's what I always called
him. He was a hell of a man, and I am honored to say
he was my best friend."

Topaz found a smile for Kyle, who gently squeezed
her hand as he was seated.

During the last part of the service, Topaz was scheduled to sing. Nina couldn't believe it when she saw
Topaz's name in the program. But then, Topaz would
attempt to sing since it was for Germain. The minister
announced her and she went up, sat in the chair, and
picked up her guitar that was sitting in a stand by the
microphone. She strummed the opening chords to
"Tears in Heaven." When she tried to sing nothing
came out. She stopped playing and took a sip of water
from a Baccarat tumbler.

"Excuse me." Topaz looked out at the audience and
then at the guitar sitting on her thigh. There was no
way she could sing. Her throat had closed up and she
could barely breathe. *I can't do this.* She wanted to
scream and have a big pity for herself until she saw
Chris's worried face and realized she had to keep it together. She didn't want Chris worrying about her.

Topaz played the opening notes again, but when she
tried to sing, a few screechy, breathless words came
out.

"Would . . . you know my name?" She was filled
with too much pain and grief so she sobbed, "I can't do
it."

She ran outside where the day was gray and the
lawns a bright forest green and yelled, "Germain is not
dead!" She just couldn't accept it. She was about to
jump in her car and run away when Keisha walked out
of the chapel and held her tightly.

"How ya doin', girlfriend?"

Topaz couldn't speak.

"You're being so strong for the children."

Nina came outside next and finally Jade. No one talked, but they all stood out there, in a little group feeling badly for Topaz. Each of them saying in their own way, no matter what they would always be friends. They stayed until everyone inside came out, following the casket and sprays of flowers out of the chapel.

As soon as Topaz saw it, the lump was back in her throat and she could barely breathe. She watched as they loaded the casket into the hearse. The girls fell in line, got into the cars, and drove farther out to the entombment. Topaz was numb as they walked away from the grave back to the cars. It was over.

Next, they were driven to The Diamond for dinner. Keisha led Topaz over to her usual table where the other Black Friends and some family members joined them. It was their first gathering since the weekend of Sean's birthday party. The group was unusually quiet, but as they ate and drank, the conversations began.

"Topaz is handling this so well," Keisha commented to Nina.

"Too well," Nina added.

"Hello, everyone." It was Mimi. But no one really heard anything Mimi said because they were all focused on Sabre.

"I'm sorry for your loss." Sabre put a hand on her hip and stood in front of Topaz. She was really trying to be sincere.

"Sabre, how did you get my journal?" Nina demanded as calmly as she could.

"It was at your house in a bookcase. I was bored and it was kind of interesting."

"How dare you steal something from my home. I'm going to press charges."

"You bitch, I swear I'll kick your ass." Topaz grabbed Sabre and threw her onto the table. Before Topaz knew it, her hands were around the girl's throat and she was choking her. "How dare you come here, bitch," Topaz screamed.

"He was too good for yo ass, you good-for-nothin' ho!" Sabre screamed back.

Nina and Keisha managed to pull Topaz off Sabre, and the two women carefully eyed each other until security came to remove Sabre.

"What? Why do I have to go? I'm a star too." Sabre was furious. No matter what she did, Topaz always won.

"It's my party," Topaz reminded her.

"You're just like my damn mother. She gave me away so her ass could run behind some man. Just like you gave Niki away. Thank goodness for Nina so Niki didn't end up in foster care with a bunch of issues like me."

"Get her out of here," Topaz commanded. "Now."

Sabre and Mimi left the restaurant, but Topaz couldn't get Sabre's words out of her head.

Run behind some man? Just like her mother? Issues?

"Nina, get me some tequila shots," Topaz demanded.

Tequila shots? Nina had never seen Topaz drink a shot of tequila in her life, and they had done some partying. "That's a strange request."

"It's a strange day. Now get me some liquor, chile." She forced a believable smile while she thought, *I'm never going to see Germain again.* She drank the shot of tequila in a swallow, frowned, and then disposed of a second.

"Slow down, T." Nina gave Topaz a look of concern.

"I have got to get out of here." Topaz gave the children a quick kiss good-bye. "Bye, babies." She kissed Baby Doll and Chris and then Niki, who all looked at her with happy golden eyes. She threw on her fur coat and gave a Diana Ross wave and ran out of the restaurant before anyone tried to stop her.

"Where is she going?" Keisha asked Nina.

"That's a good question," Nina replied. "Where *is* she going?"

Topaz swiped a bottle of tequila from the bar as she left the restaurant. "Merry Christmas." She flashed the bartender her million-dollar smile and she was gone. Once inside the Bentley, she headed for her house in Pacific Palisades.

Keisha frowned. "We didn't even think to ask where she was going."

"And she didn't tell us," Nina finished.

"I'm a terrible mother. I gave my child away and I lost Germain. How am I going to live without you, Germain?" She cried from the depths of her soul and smacked the steering wheel. "I can't, baby. I can't. I can't live without you," Topaz screamed. "When am I going to wake up and find out this is all a terrible nightmare?"

Nina dialed Topaz's cell phone, but it rang and went to voice mail. "She's knows I'm calling her. Why won't she answer?"

Topaz, now sufficiently liquored up, drove onto the property and went to the security room where her guards watched the estate.

"Mrs. Gradney. We're so sorry to hear about the boss's accident. We love the doc."

"I know, boys. Thanks a lot." She gave them a dazzling smile and they swooned. "Can I have one of your guns, please?"

"A gun?" one of them repeated, puzzled.

"A gun. In case I need to shoot something. Just a little extra something for me to have while I'm out driving. I just need to be by myself for a while and I might need some protection," Topaz explained.

The guys looked at one another, unsure of how to handle her request.

"I won't tell anyone, and I'll give it back first thing in the morning." Topaz smiled.

"I don't know," the youngest began.

"Oh, give it to her." The other man handed her a gun.

"Thanks, boys, I'll be right back with it." Topaz got back into the car and drove east on Sunset Boulevard. The Hollywood sign grew bigger and brighter as Topaz drove into Hollywood and traveled north to Mulholland.

"Answer the damn phone," Nina yelled at the device and looked at Keisha. "Where is she?"

"I know where she is," Kyle said to Nina.

"Let's go." Nina ran behind Kyle as he walked swiftly toward the car.

Topaz rolled down the window. She was beginning to get dizzy. The alcohol on an empty, nervous stomach was taking its toll.

"I'm coming, baby. I'm on my way." She punched the gas and the automobile glided down the curvy mountain road. "Superstar" came on the radio, and she almost lost control of the car trying to turn it off.

"Where are you going?" Nina asked Kyle.

"Where T is. I know she's there; I've been wantin
to see myself," Kyle explained.

"See what?" Nina demanded.

"Just sit back and see." Kyle smiled.

"You looked like Papa Ross today." Nina laughed.

"I am Papa Ross." Kyle grinned and Nina giggled.

"Where is it?" Topaz slowed down almost to a cree
and then pulled off the side of the road. She saw th
dented barricade and felt like someone stabbed he
with a knife. This was the spot where Germain'
Porsche flipped off the road.

Highway patrol came to the house with a report
Germain was driving over ninety miles per hour whe
the car skidded and flipped over the metal railing
Topaz cried a fresh batch of tears. Germain had die
somewhere between where she was parked and th
rocks below. It tore her heart to pieces every time sh
thought about it. Now she was finally here.

She sniffed and glanced over the steering wheel a
the lights in the basin below. It was a spectacular view
Did Germain drive up here to think about me?

Forensics had also placed the time of death righ
after the last call from his cell phone, which was to her

Topaz spoke out loud to herself. "You were trying to
call me, baby. You said I love you. But you didn't drive
off this place trying to get away from me, did you?"
She had finally said it. She was still crying when she
took out the bag of powder cocaine and snorted it unti
she was medicated sufficiently.

Kyle and Nina drove by on the other side of Mulholland and spotted her Bentley.

"Is this the place?" Nina looked into Kyle's eyes as

e agreed with a nod of the head. "Why would she ome here now?" Nina began to cry.

Topaz tried to open the car door with the gun in her and, but her strength was gone. She looked up and aw Nina and Kyle coming toward her. She tried to run, ut she tripped and fell and skinned her knees. She could feel them smarting, but she crawled as quickly as he could through the dirt and rocks trying to reach the edge of the cliff.

"Topaz! No!" Nina screamed. "Kyle, get her!"

But Topaz was determined. When she saw she couldn't make it to the cliff without their stopping her, she closed her eyes and put the gun to her head. She pulled the trigger, but there was only a click. Her eyes popped open. The gun had no bullets. Security had given her an empty gun.

Topaz tossed the gun on the ground and collapsed on her back in the dirt and rocks. "I can't do anything right. I couldn't even kill myself."

When Kyle and Nina reached her, she was laughing hysterically, and they both thought she had lost her mind.

"I tried to kill myself and I couldn't do it," Topaz mumbled and fell out cold.

Postlude

It was the Friday before MLK Day, and another long weekend was already underway. At Revelation Music things were extremely busy with the Grammys quickly approaching and a party during the NBA All Star weekend. Amid the busyness, Nina and Kyle were also finalizing projects for the second half of the year. It felt good to be back at work because it gave them an escape from what had become a new reality . . . life without Germain.

Nina watched Kyle playing with a 20Q that she had picked up for him in an airport. She couldn't even remember which one now, because so much had happened since the trip to Philadelphia. Her cell phone rang and she was thankful for the distraction.

"Five bedrooms in Sherman Oaks, north of Ventura, and it has a pool?" Nina sounded excited, and Kyle looked up to see to whom she was talking.

"But it has only three baths?" Nina paused to think. "That's worth looking at. I'll be right there."

She quickly jotted down the address on a notepad and clicked off her phone.

"Are you going to see a house?" Kyle seemed extremely interested.

"Want to come with?"

Minutes later, they were on the Ventura Freeway. Kyle made an exit at Van Nuys Boulevard and pulled up in front of the house.

"Wow. It's nice and the street is nice too. Is this blingy enough for you?" Kyle looked at Nina.

"I have to see inside before I can make a decision. It's just going to be our weekday house. We have bling in Malibu."

The real estate agent took them on a tour of the house, but Nina was sold as soon as she saw the kitchen. It looked like a kitchen where kids would bake cookies, talk about what happened at school, and eat grilled cheese sandwiches. There were cherry hardwood floors everywhere, plenty of sunlight, and a nice view of the pool from the family room.

Kyle watched her dash up the stairs and he followed her. She was checking out each bedroom with a little smile on her face.

"What are you thinking?" Kyle finally had to smile.

"This house is perfect for Kyle, Nina, Niki, Baby Doll, and Chris. There are two rooms that share a bathroom. We can put Niki and Baby Doll in those. Chris can have the one at the end of the hall, and we'll take this one with the Jacuzzi tub."

"What Jacuzzi tub?"

"The one that will be there when I finish decorating. You like?" Nina gave him one of Niki's favorite expressions and he laughed.

"What about the extra bedroom? Is that for Mama T? Where will we put her when she comes to visit?" Kyle asked.

"We'll put her on the sofa so she'll go home. If not the diva will try to take over the house." Nina laughed.

"It's going to take time for everyone to heal and merge into one family." Kyle sighed. "But it's the best solution."

"Letting all the kids live together in both of our homes is really going to help. I've been around Miss Baby Doll since she was born. Chris is really going to need you, Kyle. He's becoming quite a young man. And we can still be with Niki, and Topaz can too."

"What about when the baby comes?"

"What baby?" Nina smiled.

"The one that fifth bedroom is for." Kyle smiled back.

"Ya think?" Nina teased.

"Definitely."

The real estate agent found them in the master bedroom. "What do you folks think?"

"We think we like it." Nina smiled.

Topaz waited in her Range Rover for the kids to come out of school. Baby Doll skipped out first and waved good-bye to all of her little girlfriends. She hopped in the SUV and immediately changed the station on the radio.

"Hi, Mom." She took out a notebook and began drawing.

"Hi, sweetie." She kissed Baby Doll and smoothed her hair. "Where are your brother and sister?"

"I don't know. Is Niki really my sister?"

"Yes, sweetie."

"Then why isn't her name Gradney like me and Chris?"

"It will be one day, baby." She had already discussed changing Niki's last name, but they had decided to wait until Niki was older and let her make the decision when she would have a better understanding of the situation.

"I miss Daddy, Mom." Baby Doll looked up from her sketch at her mom.

"I do too, baby. I do too." There wasn't a day that went by when thoughts and memories of Germain didn't overtake her.

"There they are." Baby Doll pointed to Chris carefully leading Niki by the hand to the car. He helped her inside then got in himself.

Just like his father. Topaz managed a smile.

"We got out late and Niki was waiting on me." Chris smiled and Topaz did too. It had been a long time since she had seen him smile, and she knew Niki's small act of kindness had touched his heart.

"I need you guys to help me with a very big project." Topaz began as she drove away from the school. "I have to sing at the Grammys tomorrow night and you guys have to help me, or else I won't be able to do it."

"We get to be on stage?" Baby Doll gave her mother her undivided attention.

"Yes. You just have to sit with me while I sing. We're on our way to the Staples Center now so we can rehearse."

"We have to rehearse sitting down?" Baby Doll questioned.

"Everything has to be rehearsed for the Grammys," Topaz explained.

* * *

The Black Friends were in the audience sitting together. Topaz called and personally invited everyone. Nina was backstage as she prepared to go on. Topaz was stunning in all white. The children were wearing white, too.

"Do I look okay, Nina?" Topaz turned and twisted in the mirror.

Nina smiled. "Gorgeous as usual."

"What about me, Mommy?" Niki tried to sit in Nina's lap. She'd been with Topaz all day.

"You are the prettiest one in this whole big building," Nina whispered in her ear.

Nina was seated next to Kyle just as the show began. When the lights came up, Topaz was holding a golden guitar sitting on a cloud in what appeared to be heaven. The stage was lit to an ethereal white. A spotlight held on Topaz as she began to strum her guitar; the chords were strong, certain, and clear when she began to sing.

"Would you know my name if I saw you in heaven? Will it be the same if I saw you in heaven?"

Keisha held her breath and prayed she'd make it through the entire song. All of the friends knew she was singing to Germain—the song she couldn't sing at his memorial service. She had recorded it, and "Tears in Heaven" would be included on the re-release of *Superstar.*

There was a second guitarist on stage. Eric Clapton joined her on the second verse.

"Would you hold my hand if I saw you in heaven? Would you help me stand if I saw you in heaven?"

Nina had promised herself she wouldn't cry. She thought she had wiped away a tear on the down low when Keisha handed her a tissue.

"Beyond the door, there's peace I'm sure, and I know there'll be no more tears in heaven."

The camera locked on the children sitting at her feet.

"Look at my baby," Kyle whispered loudly enough for everyone around them to hear.

"I must be strong and carry on cause I know I don't belong here in heaven."

Topaz let out a small sigh of relief when she completed the song. The entire room thundered with applause as everyone rose to their feet and gave her a standing ovation. Topaz bowed humbly as the children gathered around her to exit the stage.

The fifty-story bronze edifice has a mighty presence at the north end of Las Vegas Boulevard. "Wynn" was written in lowercase letters; Steve Wynn's latest hotel extravaganza is five-star luxury and the location for Sabre's Bash, an annual fundraising event to raise money in memory of Marisol Cruz, Sabre's grandmother. The NBA All Star game was also in Las Vegas, making Sabre's joint at Tryst the hottest party that night during All Star weekend.

Sabre and Sky made several purchases from various designer shops inside the hotels, but Diamond Life was their favorite boutique. The ladies were shopping alone, and although they both had the perfect stylist-selected outfits in their rooms, they wanted to get something new to wear to the party, like they did back in high school.

"We are going to have so much fun. I can't wait to see who's coming tonight." Sky was excited.

"Omarion, Chris Brown, Meagan Good. Girl, all kinds of people," Sabre rattled off.

"We need some fun around here after you got all weird on me over Dr. Germain. You were in bed for a week, then you just took off for Japan."

"I was in love with Dr. Germain. He was so sweet." Sabre smiled. "Did I tell you we had an affair?"

"No way." Sabre had Sky's full attention as they headed toward the spa.

"Sure, we did." Sabre had a faraway look in her eyes.

"You actually had sex with Dr. Germain?"

"Sure did."

"Where? At your place in Malibu?" Sky demanded with an I-want-details expression.

"It was at the Beverly Hills Hotel," Sabre whispered.

Sky didn't know what to think. Sabre could be such a liar at times.

"Girl, he rocked me ever so gently when we made love." Sabre was definitely in another world.

Sky had never seen her look that way. "You're serious, aren't you?"

"Yes, I was in love with him and he was in love with me," Sabre declared smugly.

"Girl, please. Everybody in the industry is talking about how much Dr. Germain loved Topaz. Stop trippin'. She even sang for him at the Grammys with her kids around her. It was so sweet." Sky relaxed on the massage table; hot almond oil deep-tissue massages followed by brown sugar body scrubs were on the agenda next.

"I was there."

"Topaz won like seven Grammys?" Sky asked.

"She only won 'em because everybody felt sorry for her," Sabre commented.

"Whatever, girl. So was Dr. Germain going to leave ole girl and be your man?" Sky asked.

"He would have . . . eventually," Sabre confessed.

"See, I knew you were lying."

"No, really, he did make love to me." Sabre smiled until the happiness eased out of her face as she recalled hanging onto his leg, begging him to stay. She knew he was going home to Topaz after Germain admitted to Sabre he would always be in love with his wife.

"I wonder if I'll ever meet someone like him again."

"Sabre, please . . . kill the dramatics."

"No, really. He was the first man I ever loved that I had sex with."

"He was the first man you ever liked that you had sex with," Sky corrected.

"That's an interesting thought."

"Maybe you thought you loved him because of the way he made you feel."

"Maybe that is why I loved him." Sabre looked thoughtful.

"Girl, you don't know what the hell you're talking about." Sky was laughing.

Sabre smiled and laughed too.

Whatever Sabre had felt that one night, it was definitely over. She thought about Germain's memorial service, and it brought tears to her eyes. It made her remember what she never forgot . . . her grandmother's funeral. She felt like her heart was ripped out, and now she knew Topaz had to feel that way too. Sabre exhaled a long sigh as she realized a new truth.

Death and life are hard no matter who you are.
For now, Sabre shook the memory from her head.
"Come on, Sky. Let's rock this damn party."
"Meet me at the club." Sky laughed as she and Sabre danced and sang together.

Don't miss
Saved and Single
by Sheila Copeland

On sale now from Dafina Books

Turn the page for an excerpt from
Saved and Single . . .

I
Tiffany

"Tiffany! We have a situation!"

"A situation? What is it now?" I practically moaned into my headset.

Myles Adams, Living Word Church's most eligible bachelor, was finally getting married. He had to be the finest man on the planet. He was gorgeous— chocolaty velvet skin with an after-five shadow trimmed to perfection, full lips just made for kissing, and an infectious smile that could melt butter. That smile, that smile. It could bring sunshine out on a rainy day.

Lord knew I wished it were me he was marrying instead of that tired ole Melody, but she was an actress, and she was beautiful. Men like Myles always seemed to go for that type. It was Myles who'd hired me to be his wedding planner after he'd seen the wedding I'd done for Charity, the daughter of one of our choir members. Talk about cheap and wanting everything for free. But it had gotten me the job with Myles, and that made it all worthwhile.

"Tiffany! Where are you?"

"I'm coming!"

I'd been putting out fires all morning. This was the biggest wedding of my career, and everything had to be absolutely perfect. The drama level had been pretty normal, considering the fact that every wedding had its share of chaos. Compared to most of my others, this wedding was a piece of cake. Myles and Melody weren't trying to make last-minute substitutions to cut the price by bringing in Boobob to deejay—with sound equipment that didn't work—or purchase their own alcohol from Junebug—who we all knew would steal everything—or get Aunty Mae, who was a designer, to make these botched and torn-up-looking bridesmaid dresses. Myles and Melody were a dream. They paid for everything on a timely basis and used every vendor I suggested.

However, things had gotten scary when Roxanne, the florist, who'd needed a thousand ecru lilies to execute her vision of heaven—complete with clouds and angels—had gotten into a fight with Carson, my designer, who had told Roxanne she was using way too many flowers. Roxanne always spoke with this New Jersey–meets–Valley Girl accent, but when Carson—a nice, quiet, nerdy-looking white boy I had met online—had had the audacity, as Roxanne said, "to interfere with her sh—," her accent had gone straight out the window. Roxanne, who was always Miss Sophisticated, had gone straight South Central and threatened to kick Carson's butt all over Bel Air and Beverly Hills if he didn't get his skinny white ass out of her face.

In my humble opinion, Carson had only been telling her the truth. He'd said she would destroy the simple elegance of the sanctuary with all those damn flowers, and if she weren't so ignorant and ghetto, she would have known that. I'd used Roxanne before, but this wedding was totally out of her league.

I had thought they were really going to fight, but after a bunch of name calling, they had finally worked everything out. The excess lilies would be sprinkled down the aisles by the flower girls, and the church decor was absolutely breathtaking. Needless to say, I wouldn't be using Roxanne again. Now, Carson— that's my boy. With our creativity combined, I knew the world would see a Tiffany Wedding on the Style Network real soon.

"Tiffany!" My assistant, Destiny, sounded a little frantic.

"What?" I hadn't meant to snap, but she needed to handle her business. She knew how I liked to fine-tune a wedding site.

"We need you in the bride's room ASAP!"

"What is it?"

"Just come in here now! Please!"

It had to be Melody, the bride-to-be who was a diva, a major drama queen, and a royal pain in the butt. She had probably broken a nail or wanted more Perrier for her entourage and was insisting that I handle it personally. Melody, a famous actress, was also a wannabe singer and was very beautiful. She didn't even attend Living Word, where Myles played keyboards for the music ministry. Our church had the best band in the city because of him. What he saw in her I'd never understand. I wasn't the kind of girl who was into hating, but Melody didn't even go to church. She'd told me she didn't care if Myles was into Jesus, but that was his thing, not hers. Why would a God-fearing brother like Myles date a sistah who couldn't even pray for him?

My little sister, Shay, had said when it was all said and done, all men really wanted is a sistah who looked classy but was a freak in bed. I guessed Melody must have really put something down on Myles. She'd made the man forget all about his religion.

Myles had toured with Levert before Myles was saved. They had all grown up together in Cleveland, but Myles had relocated to Los Angeles. He had also played for Mary J. Blige, Boyz II Men, and Destiny's Child. His latest gig was playing in the band for *Don't Forget the Lyrics,* one of those TV shows in which contestants won money for singing the correct lyrics to all types of songs. Most of our wedding meetings were held at the studio where the show was taped.

Myles could really be a trip. Sometimes I had to listen while he called Melody, who was at another studio filming a movie, and listen to him say, "I love you, baby," for most of the conversation when he was supposed to be asking her opinion on some aspect of their pending nuptials. Afterward I'd go see Melody on her set where she had a really nice trailer all to herself. During her break she'd curl up on a leopard-print chaise like the Queen of Sheba for the duration of our meeting while she sipped Perrier out of a martini glass. She always made me explain everything twice and asked so many dumb questions I knew she had to be sipping something stronger than Perrier.

That was Ms. Melody. I had to smile as I paused to take one last look around the sanctuary before I went to see what was up with the pampered princess.

Outside, the sun resembled a rose-colored ball of fire against the fading blue sky as dusk settled upon the City of Angels. Inside, candles lit up the aisles like airport runways, and a harpist played softly as praise

lancers, adorned in white, glided down the aisles to the
front of the church. It was so romantic. Talk about a plat-
num wedding. I should have submitted this wedding
for television; Myles and Melody would have been the
perfect fairy-tale couple for one of those shows.

I sighed sadly as the harpist began another selection.
It seemed I was always planning the wedding I wanted
for someone else. This was the location I had chosen
for my wedding, if I ever had a wedding; I was thirty-
two, and I wasn't even in a serious relationship. All I
wanted was a man who really loved the Lord and
wanted to live his life by God's Word—a man who
loved me the way I needed to be loved, someone with
whom I had things in common, someone with whom I
could laugh and have fun. He didn't have to be rich or
the finest man in the world—just someone for me. I
didn't know what was so hard about that—it seemed
impossible. But the God I served loved doing the impossible. I had written it all down in a list, and I prayed
about him constantly, so I knew he'd find me eventually. Meanwhile I kept planning weddings, which I
loved to do.

Even though this church was my special place, I had
suggested it to Myles anyway because he was still special, even if he was marrying Melody.

My feet were killing me after walking around all day
in high heels, which were something I never wore, but
my sister had made me wear them. I had to admit I was
too cute in my new dress, a Marc Jacobs I had found
marked way down at Bloomingdale's. But sometimes I
wondered what the point was. I never seemed to meet
anyone nice, but I had faith. I believed God would
come through for me, too, in my season.

Walking out of the santuary, I saw a really nice-

looking brother checking me out, but I didn't mak
eye contact. I couldn't have any unnecessary distrac
tions. It was crunch time, and the wedding of the cen
tury was just about ready to begin.

As I entered the hallway leading to the bride's room
I heard desperation in Destiny's voice as she called out
"Tiffany, where are you?" I wondered why she wa
tripping so hard.

"I'm right here," I replied as I entered the room.

"Finally." Destiny looked like a deflated balloon
"You need to talk to her," Destiny whispered, and
looked at Melody.

"What's wrong?"

"Just talk to her," Destiny whispered back.

Melody was sitting in a chair in front of a makeup
table; she was wearing only a white satin bra and
panties and was crying her eyes out. Her face was we
with tears, and her nose was all red. There was a pile of
crumpled-up tissues lying on the floor by her chair. It
was more than obvious that she had been crying for a
while.

"What's up, Melody?" I asked.

"I can't go through with it," she managed between
heaving sobs.

"Why can't you?" I handed Melody another tissue and
pulled out a chair to sit beside her. The last time I had
been in there, the entourage had been eating, drinking,
and laughing. Now everyone was silent and looking
very worried.

"I'm not ready to be anyone's wife," Melody
sobbed.

"Everyone gets cold feet. It's only natural. Your life
is about to change forever." I had talked numerous

rides and grooms down the aisle, and I was proud to
say they were all still happily married. "Now let's get
you in this beautiful dress so you can strut down that
aisle. I know Myles is going to love you in this."

Melody smiled for a moment at the thought and then
cried a fresh batch of tears. Her stylist had combed her
hair into one of the most beautiful updos I had ever
seen. A tiara with Swarovski crystals completed the
style. Even with no makeup, Melody was still a very
pretty girl. She had delicate features and big doe eyes
like Bambi. She looked just like a princess. She pulled
the tiara out of her hair and tossed it on the makeup
table.

"No. I can't do it."

"Melody! Why?" I was horrified. No one had ever
gone to this extreme; this was pretty over the top, even
for Melody.

"I just can't go through with it," she continued as
she pulled the pins out of her hair and shook her head
until all her hair fell down her back.

I heard her stylist gasping for air. Melody's hair was
the real deal. I had watched earlier while her stylist had
done his thing with a blow-dryer and a flatiron.

No one said a word. We only watched in shock as she
pulled on a pair of faded, ripped jeans and a simple
white tank.

I couldn't let this happen. I finally found my voice.
"Melody, you don't want to do this. Myles loves you so
much, and I know you love him. He's going to be so
hurt."

"I don't want to hurt Myles, but I just can't go
through with it. I'm not in love with Myles, and I don't
want to be married."

"You do love Myles. You're just frightened," I reminded her. I thought about all the meetings in which Myles could barely function without calling Melody and telling her how much he loved her. I didn't remember her ever calling him. Maybe she really didn't love him.

Myles had always been more excited about their wedding than Melody. He'd made all the arrangements—not Melody. In my experience, the bride always had the vision for the wedding, not the groom, because it was her day. I'd had a few grooms who were really into the details of the wedding, but for the most part, the men were usually unconcerned. It was up to the bride.

Melody hadn't chosen anything, not even one flower. Myles and I had planned the entire affair. All Melody had done was write a check for the reception.

I watched as she picked up her oversize Louis Vuitton bag. I had seen that bag at the boutique in Century City and had gone downtown to try to find a knockoff. *I bet things always come easily for her, probably too easily.* This girl had everything, even the love of a wonderful man like Myles Adams, and she was throwing it all away.

Melody pulled off the five-carat diamond engagement ring and pressed it into my hand. "Give that back to Myles for me, please."

"Melody! You mean you're not going to tell him yourself?" I couldn't believe the nerve of this heifer. She was truly a piece of work, and Myles would definitely be better off without her.

"No. He'll just talk me into getting married. I always have a hard time telling him no. It's better this way. A nice, clean break."

Nice? I wonder what you would consider cold, I almost said out loud.

"What about your reception at the Beverly Hills Hotel?" I thought about the tens of thousands of dollars that had been spent on everything. It was such a waste. She should have told Myles she didn't want to marry him when he'd first asked.

"Have a fabulous party on me." Melody smiled. "And tell Myles to be happy. This is so much better and less painful than a nasty, expensive divorce."

"Melody, why are you doing this?" I had to know. I just couldn't fathom a sister running out on a man like Myles.

"I never wanted to be married. Myles was the one who wanted marriage. He started to trip about the sex. He said he had to do the right thing and make me an honest woman. Granted, the sex was great, but I don't have any issues with not being married. If Myles hadn't insisted on getting married, we'd still be together. This is really all his fault, so he'll just have to deal with the consequences. He should have just let things be the way they were. We were so good together." She looked at her maid of honor, who had taken off her dress, too, and was also in jeans and ready to leave.

"She's a cold piece," I heard Destiny whisper in my ear.

"Let's do this." Melody smiled at her friend and then at me. "Oh, Tiffany—tell Myles that Wendy and I will be taking the Jamaica honeymoon. I'm definitely in need of a vacation after all this drama."

And then she was gone. Someone had brought her convertible Mercedes up to the church, and I heard her zip away. Nobody moved, and no one said a word. We were all too shocked.

I stood there, shaking my head. I just couldn't b‹
lieve it. Melody had just gotten up and left. Po‹
Myles. He had definitely missed it when he'd chos‹
her as a wife. This definitely wasn't God's plan for h‹
life. The Word said not to be unequally yoked togeth‹
with unbelievers. Melody had made it quite plain th‹
she was not a believer, but Myles had gone ahead wi‹
his plans anyway.

I looked at Melody's Vera Wang gown that she ha‹
tossed carelessly aside just like she had tossed Myles.
didn't know what else to do, so I hung it up. Despi‹
everything, Myles would be better off without he‹
God opened one door and closed another.

I wondered if Myles would take Melody back if sh‹
returned. I shook my head at the thought as anoth‹
quietly enveloped my mind. I'd had a major crush o‹
Myles since our first meeting. He was single and avai‹
able now. Maybe this was God finally sending me m‹
husband. I got butterflies at the thought and tried not t‹
smile. Me and Myles?

I looked at Destiny, who was speechless. "I gues‹
we'd better let everyone know Myles won't be gettin‹
married. At least not today," I said softly as I freshene‹
up my makeup before I made my visit to the groom‹
Now I was glad I had listened to Shay and worn thos‹
heels and bought a new dress. Everything happened fo‹
a reason.

I dabbed at my eyelashes with mascara and touche‹
up my cerise lipstick with a dab of clear gloss. I smile‹
at my reflection as I smoothed a patch of highlighte‹
hair in my new sassy, short haircut. It was colored per‹
fectly for my cocoa skin. Once I was alone out in th‹
hallway, I couldn't resist trying on Melody's engagemen‹

g. It fit perfectly. The diamond overpowered my
nall finger, but it was so pretty. *All things are possible
ith God.* Jennifer Lopez had gotten her guy in *The
Wedding Planner.* Maybe I would, too.